# I HAVE
# THEM

The cone of light revealed the intruder dead at his feet, lying in a spreading pool of blood. He resembled an adult male elf except for the startling fur.

Lofotan cursed again and stepped back out of the gore. Remembering that he was in the presence of a Haven girl, he apologized, saying, "Forgive me. It was stronger than I expected."

The old soldier edged into the light. He was wounded. A long, bleeding gash ran from his left ear down across his throat. The front of his white tunic was soaked with blood. A patchwork of scratches covered his face.

"What happened here?" she asked

A new voice said, "It came to kill me."

The servant and the girl looked down the stairs and saw Balif, bearing an oil lamp in one hand and a naked sword in the other. Lofotan instinctively straightened. Ignoring his hurts, he raised his bloody blade in salute.

"The other one got away," Balif said, approaching. Mathi stared at the pair of unsheathed blades handled with such casual skill.

"My lord, shall I fetch the city guard?" Treskan asked. Death by sword was uncommon in Silvanost.

"This is no one's affair but my own. Remember that. Whatever happens in this house is my affair and mine alone."

TRACY HICKMAN
*Presents*
THE ANVIL OF TIME

*The Sellsword*
Cam Banks

*The Survivors*
Dan Willis

*Renegade Wizards*
Lucien Soulban

*The Forest King*
Paul B. Thompson

TRACY HICKMAN

*Presents*

THE ANVIL OF TIME • VOLUME FOUR

# The Forest King

PAUL B. THOMPSON

# THE FOREST KING



Published by Wizards of the Coast LLC.



Printed in the U.S.A.

Cover art by Daniel Dos Santos
First Printing: June 2009

9 8 7 6 5 4 3 2 1

ISBN: 978-0-7869-5123-9
620-24023740-001-EN



U.S., CANADA,
ASIA, PACIFIC, & LATIN AMERICA
Wizards of the Coast LLC
P.O. Box 707
Renton, WA 98057-0707
+1-800-324-6496

EUROPEAN HEADQUARTERS
Hasbro UK Ltd
Caswell Way
Newport, Gwent NP9 0YH
GREAT BRITAIN
Save this address for your records.

Visit our web site at www.wizards.com

*for Glenn*

# Chapter 1

## *Stars*

Darkness, true darkness, is usually found deep underground, where layers of soil and stone block every ray of the sun. Night is only half dark. The darkest night in the world cannot compare to subterranean darkness. Absolute dark clings to the eyes and heightens the senses, for no living creature is immune to the imagined perils of the unseen.

Strange, then, that the darkest place in the world was not deep underground, but high atop a shining tower in the city of Silvanost. In that place the clear light that was music and life to the elf race was shut out by all the skill and craft of their ancient wisdom. Dark deeds are best judged in dark places, and that was the darkest spot elf artifice could create.

It was called the Night Chamber. Built at the order of the Speaker of the Stars, Silvanos Goldeneye, its exact location was hidden from the outside world. By clever use of light and shadow, the penthouse containing the Night Chamber could not be seen from outside. The tower it capped was just like so many others in the city, constructed of thousands of deeply fluted bars of rock crystal. Some of the exterior surfaces were polished like mirrors, while others were etched with acid until they resembled pure milk. It was an ordinary facade in an extraordinary city, but the veiled dome at its peak was one of the most closely guarded secrets of Silvanost. On cloudless nights the invisible penthouse could just be seen as it eclipsed stars passing behind it. In heavy rain or fog, a vague outline was discernible, though it looked more like an errant cloud than solid architecture.

The Night Chamber had a single entrance. When in use—and to date it had been used only once before—the great lords whose duty brought them there entered one by one, in order of absolute precedence. First was the Speaker of the Stars. Bearing his own luminar, a lamp lit by a cold fluorescence, Silvanos ascended to the highest seat in the domed room. Once there, the rest would follow. Lords of the houses, senior sages of the magical fraternity, and the commander of the royal army all entered alone and silently took the seats protocol assigned to them. Each bore a faint lantern, just bright enough to prevent undignified stumbling in the black hall.

Those high persons were the judges. Their task was to hear the evidence of a great crime and render an absolute verdict. From their decision there was no appeal.

Next to enter were witnesses summoned under dire oaths of secrecy. They were given no lamps, but were directed to seats by the chamber's bailiff. Each was isolated from the other. No one was allowed to speak until bidden to do so. Last of all, the accused entered. There was no seat for him. The accused stood on the last step of the rising spiral stair. Once there, the passage they had ascended was closed.

The second trial ever in the Night Chamber began in the fifty-fifth year of the reign of Silvanos. It was high noon on the median day of summer, the longest, hottest, sunniest day of the year. The recorder of the secret transactions noted the irony in his shorthand record. Inside the Night Chamber, weather and climate were meaningless.

Preceded by bailiffs, the accused climbed the winding stairs. From below, only a black half circle revealed where they were going. With each step, the prisoner dragged his heavy shackles over the polished marble treads. The guards walked behind with drawn swords. If the accused faltered or tried to resist in any way, the warriors' orders were to run him through.

But the chains were heavy, and though the prisoner was not trying to stall, he could not climb with any grace. Shuffle, shuffle, *clank*—that was his cadence. Above, the entrance of the Night Chamber looked like a pool of black water fixed impossibly to the ceiling. The prisoner reached the last step before entering the dome. His feet rested side by side for a moment.

Two lengths of glittering bronze blade lay lightly on his shoulders. The bailiffs did not speak, but their message was clear. With a heave, the accused mounted the last step.

When the guard gained the top step, he raised his sword hilt to his face, saluting the Speaker of the Stars. He could not see him, seated well up on the curved wall of the dome, but the highest lamp in the hall was his. To that pallid light the bailiff paid honor then departed down the steps. Weapons were not permitted within the chamber. As the plume on his helmet descended below the level of the floor, the passage silently flowed shut.

When the well of light from below was cut off, a brilliant beam lanced down from the dome's peak, impaling the prisoner in its blinding glare. He threw up a manacled hand to ward off the light.

"Is that necessary?" he called loudly. There was no reply from the ranks of dim, blue lamps. "At least let me shield my eyes. Or is it your desire I be blinded?"

There was a soft chime, and the restraints on the accused's wrists and ankles fell away. He gave them a vindictive kick, sending them skittering into the outer darkness.

"The prisoner will show proper respect during the proceedings, or his bonds will be restored," intoned a deep, distant voice. Transfixed in the shaft of light, the accused raised the flimsy hood of his prison garb to shade his face.

"All give attention! Silence before the throne of the stars!"

The prisoner did not know which way to face, but he stood up straight.

"The Night Chamber is now in order. Sitting in judgment is His Gracious Serenity, Silvanos, called the Golden-Eyed, first Speaker of the Stars, supreme ruler of Silvanost and all those of our ancient race wherever found. Pray, give thanks for his wisdom and understanding!"

Some words came to the prisoner's lips. Wisely he stifled them.

"I am the Advocate of the Speaker. It is my duty to conduct the case against the prisoner," said the booming voice.

"Who are you?" asked the accused. "Where are you? I want to see your face!"

"Your requests are irrelevant. Do not speak again unless so ordered. Is that clear?"

Fuming, the prisoner folded his arms. The sight of his hands, bristling with hair, provoked a stir in the void beyond the light.

"My lords, Great Speaker, you all know the accused. You have seen the specification of his crimes. Because of the blasphemous nature of his deeds, I will not degrade our Great Speaker by speaking aloud his odious actions."

"Are you so afraid of me, you won't even speak my name?" called out the prisoner.

At once the cone of light around him shrank by half. The accused felt a tremendous pressure bearing on his chest, limbs, and head. Gasping, he fought for air. The light was not simply theatrical. It was a magical barrier, restraining him as thoroughly as his bronze shackles had. Speaking out of turn earned him his punishment. His available space was violently reduced by half. If he continued to defy his judges, things could become very tight for him indeed.

"Your deeds are known. What do you say to them, prisoner? Are you guilty or not?"

"How can I answer when I don't know what I am accused of?" he replied, eyeing the cone of light. It did not shrink again.

"Guilty or not?"

"I cannot answer—"

"Guilty or not?"

Arms tight against his chest, the accused lowered his hooded head and said nothing.

"Let the record state the prisoner stands mute. We shall proceed."

His eyes had adjusted to the glare as much as they could. Around his dazzling cell were various elves, waiting to be questioned by the tribunal. The advocate called out the name Wenthus. At the mention of his name, a second beam of light shone down, picking out a lean, rangy elf clad in green leather. Over his head he wore a black velvet hood.

"You are Wenthus, son of Garathan?" said the advocate.

"I am, your lordship." His voice was not muffled, despite the cloth.

"You are a forester and hunter, are you not?"

"I am, your lordship. My family has ranged the South Sward for five hundred years—"

"In what capacity do you know the prisoner?"

The woodland elf shifted on his feet. "I don't know him, your lordship." The accused suppressed an urge to laugh.

"Did he not hire you to supply him with a certain number of animals, which you would trap in the wildwood?"

"No, your lordship. I was hired by another. A high lord."

"What lord?" the advocate prompted.

"The one we in the green lands call *Camaxilas*." Camaxilas was forest dialect and meant Sword-Lord.

"What did this Camaxilas require you to do?"

"He sent me to catch animals, as you said, your lordship. He wanted small predators like foxes, martens, and ferrets. I thought he wanted them for their fur, but he would only pay for them if they were alive," Wenthus said.

"How many animals did you supply this Camaxilas with?"

The hunter counted on his fingers. "Thirty-six live animals, your lordship. Fourteen dead ones he wouldn't buy."

Three more foresters were called. All had their faces concealed. Each told a similar tale. A great lord called Camaxilas hired them to trap wild animals, small carnivores all. The creatures had to be alive and in good health, or the Silvanesti lord would not pay for them. In total he purchased just greater than one hundred live animals from the rustic elves. The prisoner listened to their testimony indifferently. When the advocate was done with them, the woodland hunters were dismissed.

"Is the one known in the woodlands as Camaxilas present in the Night Chamber?" the advocate boomed.

Footsteps rang on the polished floor. Striding into the outer aura of the prisoner's wall of light came a male elf in the prime of life. By the standards of his race, he was tall, with dark blond hair cut short, in a warrior style. Most Silvanesti males affected long hair, drawn back in a braid.

His posture was military too, though he was dressed in a simple kilt and white tabard. Even in the unnatural dimness of the chamber, his eyes were arresting, large and very blue, like beads of lapis lazuli. The prisoner gave the new witness a quick sidelong glance then averted his eyes altogether.

"My lord," said the advocate with clear deference, "will you state your name for the chronicle?"

"I am Balif Thraxenath, Chosen Chief of House Protector, First Warrior of the Great Speaker. I am the son of Arnasmir Thraxenath, of the Greenrunners clan. The people know me as Balif, loyal subject of the Great Speaker." He bowed in the direction of the highest lamp, knowing Silvanos sat behind it.

The unseen advocate apologized for summoning Lord Balif to the Night Chamber but added, "Are you called by the name Camaxilas?"

"Yes, my lord. In the southern and western woods, I am sometimes called that. It's more a title than a name."

A moment passed. The advocate said, "Did you commission several foresters to catch animals?" Balif admitted he had. "Why? For what purpose?"

"My counselor requested it."

"And who is your counselor, my lord?"

Balif extended his left arm, pointing straight at the prisoner. "That is him."

"Speak his name for the chronicle."

"Uristathan Cavolox, called Vedvedsica."

That was a name as well known as Balif's, if not so respected. Vedvedsica—the name in rural patois meant wise, wise fellow—was a magician of great erudition. He was known for his vast knowledge of the magical art and for his refusal to join any established temple or guild. Whispered rumors clung closely to his gaunt frame. Not only was he a master of the art of high magic, but it was said that he soiled his hands by dabbling in low arts such as alchemy and divination. No real crimes had ever been laid at his feet, but a vague air of ruthlessness and personal corruption rendered his company unworthy and his name suspect to most Silvanesti.

Hearing his name spoken at last, the accused raised his head. His hood dropped away, revealing a nearly bald pate. The light shone down harshly, rendering Vedvedsica's lean face in high relief.

"Thank you, my lord. You may go."

Balif turned but the captive cried out, "Am I not allowed to question those who speak against me?"

The cone of confinement contracted again, crushing Vedvedsica's arms against his chest. He had so little room, he could hardly draw breath.

Seeing his predicament, Balif said, "My lords, if it pleases you, relent. Let the prisoner speak."

"We have no desire to hear his blasphemies!"

Balif walked in a circle around the gasping wizard. "He will guard his tongue. Won't you?" Vedvedsica could only blink in agreement. "Relent, my lords. Let him pose his questions."

The beam of light expanded, releasing the wizard. He reeled around, greedily sucking in fresh air. When at last his discomfort subsided, he said, "Thank you, my lord."

"It is nothing," said Balif.

"The prisoner will address the Chamber only!"

Vedvedsica bowed mockingly. "My lords. I would like to ask Lord Balif how long we have known each other." The advocate agreed; the elf lord could answer.

"A century and a half, I think."

Through the clumsy process of voicing his questions through the Night Chamber advocate, the wizard went on to ask what services he had performed for Balif over so many years.

"Healer, soothsayer, counselor, and adviser," Balif replied. Vedvedsica had been his retainer a long time. Everyone knew that.

"In all that time, in all those capacities, did I ever fail you, my lord?"

"Never."

"How is it I find myself on trial now for my life?"

"I delivered you into the hands of the highest authority in Silvanesti," said Balif tersely.

"And we are grateful for your diligence," the advocate put in.

"So grateful," snarled the wizard.

At the time of the conjunction of the three moons three years past, Vedvedsica had come to his master with a modest but unusual request. He was trying out a new magical operation. He needed some live animals. Not the usual sacrificial beasts such as goats, sheep, or doves. Vedvedsica wanted wild animals. Carnivores and scavengers only, no rabbits, squirrels, or boars. After a hundred and fifty years of service, Balif did not question his counselor's intention. He contacted some woodland hunters he knew and arranged for them to trap the animals the wizard wanted.

"That's the last I heard about the affair until six months ago," Balif concluded. That's when he discovered the outcome of Vedvedsica's experiments.

"Stop. Say no more," warned the advocate. "The Speaker's ears must not be soiled by hearing about these abominations."

Balif agreed. "I sent word to House Protector. Vedvedsica and some others were taken by the royal guard. Because of his long association with a high lord, the wizard was treated carefully, but his assistants were put to the question."

"Tortured, you mean," said Vedvedsica bitterly.

They revealed a secret complex of houses, far away in the western forest, where the results of the wizard's work were kept. A company of griffon riders swept down on the hidden site. There was resistance. Those who fought were put to the sword. Those who surrendered were in the worst dungeon in Silvanost, Thalasdown, located deep under the waters of the Thon-Thalas river.

"I have done nothing wrong," Vedvedsica proclaimed. "Nothing the gods themselves have not done!"

At that, the light collapsed so tightly that it barely encompassed the wizard from his skin inward. Unable to stand yet unable to fall, he drifted slowly in a circle with only the tips of his toes touching the floor. As he turned past Balif, the elf warrior saw the deep hatred in his eyes.

The captain of the guard who captured Vedvedsica testified, as did the commander of the griffon riders. Seeing the fate of the outraged wizard, the warriors wisely obeyed the advocate and did not speak too clearly about what they found, only about what they did.

The griffon riders' commander, a veteran soldier named Pirayus, dared to offer advice to the Night Chamber. "Destroy everything, my lords. Use fire until nothing remains of this horror but ashes!" He gave the prisoner a meaningful glance. "Destroy *everything,* my lords."

The warriors were dismissed. Balif took that as his cue to go too. When the stairs opened in the chamber floor, the other elves descended. Balif went down one step, paused, then went down one more step. He halted there.

"My lords, what will you do with the prisoner?"

"That decision has not been made."

He didn't believe that. Vedvedsica's fate had been decided before the Night Chamber's doors even opened.

"May I address the chamber?" The advocate gave Balif leave. He walked back to where the wizard twisted slowly on a spit of white light.

"My lords, I beg you to consider the intent of the prisoner in your judgment. He was not trying to loose evil on the world. His motives were creative, not destructive."

Silence in the dark dome was ominous. Rows of dim lamps burned like unblinking eyes.

"His acts are an offense against all that is decent and proper, I agree. But do not exterminate what has been created. As Astarin teaches, life is the highest force in nature. A living thing, no matter how wretched, owes its life to the gods and not to any lesser being. Do not kill, my lords. Punish, yes. Imprison, certainly. But do not stain your own souls with the death of innocents."

"Innocents?"

The word echoed throughout the hall. It was not the

advocate who spoke, but Silvanos himself. Balif faced the far-off voice.

"Yes, Great Speaker. No child chooses its parents. They are innocent of their creation."

"Are you a priest now?"

Balif spread his hands. "I am a failure as guide and master to my counselor. Perhaps I should become a cleric and learn to deal with my failings."

"You are too modest, my friend, and too gentle. There are lives that deserve to be expunged, just as there are crimes that must be punished."

No one had ever accused the greatest warrior of the elves of being too gentle. No one but the Speaker of the Stars would presume to make such a charge.

"The Great Speaker is the final arbiter of justice," Balif replied. "But take care, sire. Expunging lives can be habit-forming."

There were audible gasps from the unseen lords. Everyone understood Balif's meaning. Decades past, when the Silvanesti nation was still forming, Silvanos had ordered the destruction of the Brown Hoods, a sect of woodland wizards opposed to the Speaker's assuming absolute power. Only one Brown Hood out of dozens survived the purge: Vedvedsica. He cast his lot with the Speaker against his forest colleagues, but in so doing, Vedvedsica swore allegiance not to Silvanos, but to Balif, his captor. Because Balif owed fealty to the Speaker, Vedvedsica was spared.

For a long time, nothing was said. Apparently deliberation was carried out in some fashion Balif could not hear, for at length the advocate declared, "The Night Chamber has reached a verdict."

Who were they announcing it to? No one remained on the floor but Balif and the prisoner.

"It is the judgment of this tribunal that the prisoner shall be confined in the keep of Thonbec fortress for the balance of his life, however long that may be."

Life in prison for an elf was no act of mercy. Confinement was more vindictive than execution.

"His writings on all matters shall be gathered and burned. The ashes shall be ground between two millstones and scattered over the sea.

"His name shall be excised from all documents, chronicles, and monuments. No trace of the blasphemous one will be allowed to remain."

Balif bowed his head then lifted it slowly. "What of the fruit of his labors? What becomes of them?" he asked.

The advocate spoke carefully, as if listening to another voice the elf warrior could not hear. "All offenses against the gods shall be . . . removed."

"Removed? Speak plainly! Or do you mean to execute innocents by euphemism?".

"You forget yourself, my lord! It is not your place to question the decisions of this tribunal."

With an angry shake of his head, Balif said, "I do question! What will happen to them?"

The passage in the floor split wide, admitting an upward wedge of natural light. Four bronze-clad warriors marched up the steps and took up positions around the floating prisoner. In the bat of an eye, the confining light evaporated. Vedvedsica collapsed in a heap, wheezing. Fetters were snapped on his wrists and ankles. Two soldiers took him by the arms and dragged him to his feet. The other pair stood by with swords drawn.

The wizard's head snapped around. Most of the lamps had been extinguished, but the highest one still burned, dim in the intrusive light from outside.

"I am not done!" Vedvedsica vowed as loudly as he could. *"I am not done!"*

It was then Balif realized that, immobile as he was, his former counselor had heard everything—his pleas, the verdict, and the Night Chamber's judgment. Before he disappeared down the spiral stair, he had some words for his master.

"Weak reed! Pay the price of betrayal!" Vedvedsica cried. The guards hustled him out of sight.

The passage remained open. Balif looked from it to the place where the Speaker's lamp had been. All was black above. He was alone in the chamber. Turning to the open exit, he descended the steps with a slow, measured tread.

He was not the last to leave. From behind a sweeping buttress, a single figure stirred. He carried a thick rectangle of polished wood on which he scribbled briskly with a slim, metal stylus. Streaks of light appeared briefly on the wood surface then faded away. Padding forward on soft sandals, the last one to leave the Night Chamber waited until Balif was gone before he started down the spiral stairs.

He was surprised to discover many hours had passed, a far longer interval than had seemed to transpire. It was dusk. The day was over.

Outside in the street, he inhaled the clean air of Silvanost. Glancing up, the dome of the Night Chamber was impossible to see. No one passing by had any inkling of what had occurred a hundred feet above them. That's the way the Speaker of the Stars wanted it. The Night Chamber was his personal instrument.

Balif was walking away from the tower, head lowered in thought. Elves hailed the great warrior from left and right. Balif did not heed them. Ignoring his waiting coach, he walked home alone and on foot.

# Chapter 2

## *Words*

It was dusk when Balif reached home. The imposing pile of white marble, alabaster, and crystal had been built for the general at the Speaker's order as a gift from the grateful nation for the general's innumerable services. Done in the grand style of the city, the facade was all flutes and flying buttresses designed to make the house look as if it might take wing and fly at any moment. The villa was surrounded by a hedge of glass fronds made to look like the sea grasses of the Silvanesti coast. Forged in tempered glass by the best artisans in the city, the glass fronds bent and fluttered very realistically with every breeze. They were also a first-class defense. Anything trying to run through them would be cut to pieces by the delicate-looking but razor-sharp leaves.

A single torch burned outside the front door. The evening breeze tormented the flame, whipping it from one side to the other but never quite extinguishing it. Balif homed in on the torch like a moth.

The paved area before the ornate door was big enough to parade a company of infantry. A few stone benches dotted the expanse, finely carved out of the hardest purple porphyry, veined with red like blood vessels. The seats were splotched with lichen. Moss welled up between the seams of the pavement.

At the door Balif paused to look back over his shoulder. The plaza appeared empty, but the general surveyed it for a long time.

The great front door opened before Balif could grasp the brass knob. Waiting inside was Balif's majordomo, Lofotan Brodelamath, impeccably turned out in his servant's uniform. A soldier who had served more than half his long life with the general, Lofotan had followed Balif home when he retired. Balif did not ask him to come, nor did the old warrior request a position as the general's servant. He simply came. It was his job, so long as he lived, to serve Balif.

"Good evening, my lord."

"Hello."

He stood with his hands over a polished copper bowl while Lofotan poured warm water over his hands. It was the homecoming ritual enacted in every elf home in the city, every day. In that evening's case Balif called for a second rinse. His hands felt unusually soiled.

Lofotan did not ask about the day's events. It was not his place. He did say, "My lord, there are two persons waiting to see you."

Drying his hands on a snowy linen towel, Balif raised an arched brow. "Couriers or courtiers?"

"Neither, I should say. One has the look of a priestess. The other is a scribe."

"I've not summoned either." Discreetly checking the sash at his waist for the dirk concealed there, Balif crossed the dimly lit hall.

"In the morning hall, my lord." Balif went to the room indicated.

Within, a single bank of oil lamps burned. While many in Silvanost relied on magical luminars to light their homes, Balif was old-fashioned enough to prefer flame. Seated in the circle of light by the lamp stand were two elves unknown to him. Hearing the general enter, the strangers got to their feet. A stylus and a writing board clattered to the floor.

As Lofotan said, the young female was dressed as a priestess, though without any badges or talismans indicating her temple. Her hair was long, dark and plainly cut. She had slim arms and long fingers but a curiously round face, not at all like the high-cheeked elf women of the city.

The other stranger was middle-aged with the blue-tinged hair of a western woodlander. His clothes were plain homespun with the green stripe of House Servitor worked in with the black cuffs of the scribal guild. Seeing his writing equipment on the floor, the visitor went down on both knees to retrieve it.

Balif approached. He said, "You don't look like assassins."

"Sir?" said the clerically dressed female.

He surveyed them with folded arms. "You didn't come here to slay me, did you?"

The scribe stared blankly. Beside him the apparent priestess replied, "No, my lord! Why in the world would anyone want to harm you, my lord?"

At arm's length, Balif paused, sizing up the strangers. "No reason. I make a poor jest. What are you called?"

"Mathani Arborelinex, at your service!" She bowed from the waist. The middle-aged scribe stiffly imitated her gesture. His black metal stylus hit the floor again.

"That's a feast of a name," Balif observed. "Are you known as Mathi to those with less time for the full treatment?"

"Yes, my lord, or Math, if you prefer."

"Why are you here, Mathi?"

"The sisters of Quenesti Pah sent me from the Haven of the Lost, my lord."

Balif understood. He was patron to several worthy causes, one of which was an orphanage run by priestesses of Quenesti Pah in the far west of Silvanesti. The Haven of the Lost was a refuge for victims of the almost constant border warfare between the elves and marauding bands of human nomads on the frontier. Anyone, from infants to adults, could find shelter there. After a certain age, residents of the haven were expected to support themselves.

"You are a ward of the temple?" Mathi bowed her head yes. "You are welcome. We shall discuss your case at dinner tonight." Balif turned his penetrating eyes to the scribe. "Who are you?"

"Treskan of Woodbec, my lord."

"Why are you here?"

The scribe looked crestfallen. "I was told you required a scrivener—"

Balif turned away. "I can't imagine who told you that. I have less than no need for a scribe. Good evening."

He walked out, leaving the hall door ajar. Treskan was speechless, but Mathi followed Balif, saying, "My lord! Your servant says there is no one in the house but yourself, him, and a cook. Surely an important elf like yourself has need of a professional scribe?"

Balif laughed shortly. "Don't confuse being well known with being important." In the entry hall, Lofotan had been lurking by the door with a stout staff, gripped like a halberd. Seeing there was no trouble, he set it aside.

"My affairs these days are very simple. I do not need a scribe."

The girl said to the scribe, "I am sorry."

Treskan replied in a low tone, "Never mind. My hopes were not high. Now I shall have to relinquish my stylus to the guild." Treskan started for the door.

Balif watched him go, staring at him until he reached the door. "Why will you have to relinquish the tool of your profession?" he asked, suddenly curious.

"I have been without employment too long. With this rejection, I shall lose my membership in the guild."

"Try elsewhere in the city. Many households in Silvanost employ scribes."

With a last clumsy bow, Treskan of Woodbec departed. Balif bade Mathi follow. They strolled across the soaring hall, footsteps echoing on the bare, polished walls.

Balif said calmly, "How long were you among humans?"

Mathi halted as if clubbed. "How did you know that, my lord?"

"Where were you captured?"

She looked somber. "In the west. Beyond the forest."

Trailing behind, Lofotan said, "You were captured by the barbarians?" The girl nodded. "A slave?" She gave another nod.

Balif reached the far side of the monumental hall. "I would know more of this. You shall stay for now, as my guest. Lofotan, have an extra place set for dinner."

Mathi went down on one knee. "May the goddess bless you, my lord!" She tried to kiss the general's hand, but Balif was not having it. He ordered the girl to stand.

"Lofotan will find you quarters. Dinner will be at the eighth hour. Lofotan will fetch you then."

Shadows were building fast. The interior hall had no windows to the outside, and it rapidly darkened as the sun set. The general of the armies of the Speaker of the Stars lit a lamp from a side table and, after a polite farewell, took his leave. Mathi watched the globe of light recede down a long hallway, finally disappearing around a corner.

It was only the seventh hour. She said to Lofotan, "What should I do until dinner?"

"Remain in your room. I will show you there now."

Without another word, the old soldier lit a lamp of his own and gestured for the girl to follow. Lofotan started up a broad staircase in the center of the hall. When Mathi lagged behind, Lofotan sharply ordered her to keep up.

"This place is a maze, even in daylight. By night it's a labyrinth not easily navigated."

Mathi hopped up the steps. "Why is the house so dark and empty?" she said. She was whispering, but she wasn't sure why.

"My lord is a great elf, but his needs and tastes are simple. This stone pile was urged upon him by the Speaker, but it is not the sort of place Lord Balif would choose to occupy." At the top of the stairs, a yawning cavern of an upper hall opened before them. Lofotan's lamp made little impression on the gloom.

"Once, two hundred servants lived and worked here. There were body servants and maids, grooms for the general's horse and griffon, butlers and cooks and all their assistants. As the years passed, my lord found reasons to dismiss them one by one until only I and the cook remain."

He led her down the mammoth corridor, flanked on either side by statues of marble and bronze. Some were in the stiff, archaic style of the era before Silvanos. More modern images, with features that changed with the light, unnerved Mathi as she passed by. The robes on the statues seemed to flow and flip in unfelt breezes. One elegant female figure tossed her head, mouth parted in silent mirth.

"How can you stand to walk here?" Mathi said, quavering.

"Ignore them. They're only stone."

At what seemed like an arbitrary point, the majordomo stopped. He pointed to a door. "You will sleep here. There's a filling font in the antechamber. Whatever else you want, you must forgo or see to yourself."

He turned to leave. "One other thing: don't roam around after dark. As I said, this place is a maze, and you may find unpleasant company." Puzzled, Mathi asked him what he meant. "My lord sleeps in different parts of the house each night. If you disturb him, he may greet you with a blade in the ribs."

Leaving the astonished girl alone in the dark, Lofotan returned to the stairs. His lamp faded until Mathi was submerged in the enormously dark house. Somewhere out of sight, a door slammed. Mathi darted inside the indicated door and shut it quickly.

Sunset streamed in the high windows. She was in a suite fit for a lord. Furniture stood around the main room in orderly ranks like disciplined soldiers, draped in ghostly white dust cloths. Mathi tugged her belt pouch around and dug out a small luminar. She spoke the illuminating word, *simtha,* and the crystal glowed to life.

As Lofotan promised, there was a font in the antechamber. A great conch shell had been set up as a basin. Arching over it was a golden tap shaped like a leaping dolphin. When Mathi touched it, water poured forth. She washed her hands, splashed more on her face, and drank a few handfuls before allowing the font to shut off.

She felt lost in such an enormous space. Holding the luminar by its silver handle, she walked through the great suite. Only the main room was furnished. The adjoining salons and bedchambers were empty, just frescoed walls and stone floors. She went back to the main room and pulled the cover off an elegant couch. Sitting in silence for a long time, Mathi nibbled the last of the rations she had brought from the country.

The sleeve rode up on her arm, revealing red scars. She tugged the homespun back over them. It was too soon to look at them. Worse reminders of her time in the forest still stung on her legs, but at least the long hem of her acolyte's gown always covered them.

She set the luminar on the floor between her feet. It shone brightly, filling the space around her with hard, white light. Everything was going well, she kept reminding herself. She was exactly where she was supposed to be.

She dozed while sitting up on the couch. A loud click stirred but did not rouse her. It sounded again, and her sharp senses dragged her awake. She picked up the luminar, which had gone out. A vast tapestry of stars shone in the high windows. For a moment she heard nothing. A silhouette appeared, close to one of the glass panes. Whoever it was rapped gently for attention.

Slowly Mathi approached. At the last instant, she called the luminar to light. It blazed on, dazzling her and the mysterious figure outside. When her eyes adjusted to the light, she saw Treskan the scribe crouched by the window, one arm thrown over his eyes.

Mathi extinguished the light. She tried to open the floor-length window, but the catch refused to turn. Putting all her weight and strength on the handle only bent the brass.

Treskan had dropped his arm when the light went out. He tried to open the window from the outside but could not. By silent gestures he indicated to Mathi she must turn away. She did, afraid he meant to break a pane. There was a quick, small flash of light. The latch squeaked, and the scribe entered.

"Why are you here?" she whispered.

"I had to come back. I will lose my job if I fail to attach myself to Lord Balif."

Mathi slowly shut the window. Feeling the catch, she found there was no lock on it. So why did it resist opening, and how did Treskan get in?

"Will you speak to Lord Balif for me?" Treskan begged. "You're having dinner with him, are you not?"

"Yes, and soon." Mathi looked down at the shabby scribe. They had traveled most of the way from the west country together for mutual company and protection. He was an odd fellow, seemingly useless one moment and amazingly erudite the next. She wondered anew how he got the window open.

Loud footsteps heralded the arrival of Lofotan. Treskan ducked out of sight. Mathi hurried to the couch and sat down demurely. The majordomo came right in without knock or announcement.

"My lord dines. He asks that you attend him," Lofotan said. Before Mathi could reply, he turned his head from side to side, frowning. "You have had a window open?"

"Why, yes." How did he know?

"This suite has not been aired in many months. The fresh air is quite distinct."

Mathi went to the door. Lofotan remained, hands clasped behind his back. "How did you get a window open?"

"Oh, I tried one after another until one opened," Mathi replied. He demanded to know which one. Outwardly blithe, Mathi took him to the exact door Treskan used. It opened under the majordomo's hand.

"I see. Can you find your way downstairs by yourself?" He stepped through onto a broad balcony. It followed the bank of windows from one end to the other. When Mathi emerged behind Lofotan, she saw he had a short sword in his hand.

"Go back. Now."

She did, retrieving her luminar along the way. Downstairs she followed her nose to the dining room. It was not the grand feasting hall she imagined, but a more modest, shelf-lined room she guessed was meant to be a pantry. Balif sat at a round table. A candelabra of sixteen tapers illuminated the scene.

Balif stood. "Come, girl. Sit down."

There was only one other setting, so she sat there, at the general's right hand. He poured spring water into an amethyst goblet.

"How came you to the Haven of the Lost?" Balif asked without any opening palaver.

She told him the story she had long rehearsed on the journey to Silvanost. Her family were beekeepers living on the edge of the great western forest. The only settlement near them was Woodbec, a military post three leagues from

Mathi's home. In the early morning hours, a band of humans on horseback raided them, killing her father outright and taking her and her mother prisoner.

Somberly he said, "And when was this?"

"Six summers past, my lord."

"What happened next?"

Gazing at her empty plate, Mathi described how she and her mother were taken far to the north, on the open plain, and sold as slaves. Her mother could not bear her captive life and took the ultimate escape.

"How?"

"Fly agaric."

There was no antidote for the poisonous mushroom. It was a slow death but a sure one. In silent kindness, Balif said nothing for a while. When Mathi was ready, she continued her story.

After that, Mathi's human master, a warrior named Herndan, took her and his whole entourage east, to the Plains River. He got involved in a dispute with another human warrior, fought a duel, and was killed. All that was Herndan's became the property of the victor, but Mathi used the confusion of her master's defeat to escape.

"Tell me," Balif said remorselessly.

"I am a good swimmer," Mathi said. "I resolved to swim the river or die trying. The human males could not pursue me, weighted as they were with metal armor, so I was able to swim away with arrows flicking past my ears."

Balif opened a covered silver tray. With tongs, he picked up a delicately poached fish fillet and laid it on her plate. The second, smaller fillet he took himself.

"I regret the arrows," he said. "They are my fault."

"How so, my lord? You were not there."

He replaced the silver dome on the empty tray. "Humans have bows because I gave them to them. My apologies."

Mathi didn't understand. She pulled her fish apart with

her fingers and ate with them too until she noticed Balif using a tiny two-pronged metal spear to get the food to his mouth. As she was provided with an identical tool, Mathi tried to emulate her host.

"I wandered along the eastern shore of the river, going south. I fell in with a party of woodlanders, who delivered me to the Haven. I lived there a year until the sisters of Quenesti Pah decided I was fit enough to go out on my own. They sent me here to seek your guidance, my lord."

The general tore a loaf of flat bread in two, placing half on his guest's plate. For a great lord of Silvanost, he certainly kept an ascetic table.

"The scribe, Treskan; you met him on the journey here?"

"Yes, my lord. He hails from Woodbec, not far from my old home."

"What do you know about him?"

Mathi poked her cheek with the little spear points. Wincing, she replied, "Only what he told me, my lord. He has had much bad luck in his life. Three of his patrons died, one after the other, and he acquired the reputation in Woodbec of being bad luck. Hence no one would hire him."

"Hah! Bad luck doesn't frighten me. I'll hire him. You may tell him that," Balif said. Another cover lifted, revealed a bowl of fresh greens. Balif served Mathi. Oil and honey dressing was in the diamond cruet, he said.

Mouth open, Mathi did not know what to say.

"Food to your liking?" asked the general.

"How did you know—?"

"That the scribe is still about? My dear child, this house is protected by powerful conjurations. When someone breaks a door ward, the effect is noted immediately. Is he in the house right now?"

She nodded dumbly.

"Your suite?"

"Yes, my lord. Do forgive me! He's desperate and I only meant to do him a kindness—"

"I understand. It is because of your kindness, your belief, that I changed my mind."

Balif refilled her cup and his own. "This city, splendid as it is, is in many ways as cold and hard as the crystal towers soaring over us. Scarcely a week goes by that I'm not accosted by some worthy seeking favors, charity, or largesse. Lofotan has standing orders to throw such beggars out. Being from the Haven, you deserve every kindness, and by showing grace, you earn grace for your friend."

Mathi wasn't about to deny being Treskan's friend. She barely knew him, but she was delighted to have done him a service.

Lofotan appeared as if on signal with a very chastened scribe in tow.

"You know record-hand as well as script?" Balif said, raising his voice to fill the room in commanding fashion. Record-hand was an abbreviated form of writing used to keep records of events. Treskan swore he knew it perfectly.

"You are retained. Lofotan will find you quarters. You may eat in the kitchen."

The old soldier clapped a heavy hand on Treskan's shoulder to pull him away. The scribe said, "Thank you, my lord! May Astarin and Matheri bless you—but wait! What will my duties be?"

"You will handle all the writing that needs to be done in the household, of course. Good night!"

Lofotan steered Treskan away. Balif parted his last bit of fish with his fork and said loudly, "If you ever enter my house illicitly again, it will cost you your head. Understood?"

Treskan stammered, "Ah, perfectly, my lord. Thank you for this chance!"

"You will surrender the ward-breaker you used to Lofotan too."

"Already done, my lord," said the majordomo, holding up a small metal and crystal talisman.

Dinner ended with Mathi hardly less hungry than when she started. Balif did not escort her to her room. He merely asked her to return there if she was finished.

Mathi got up and bowed to her host. "Thank you, my lord. May I ask one question?" Sipping spring water, Balif nodded. "What shall become of me?"

"That is for the gods to decide, is it not?" He smiled not unkindly. "I shall inquire around the city for you. What skills do you have?"

"My best talent is beekeeping," she said.

The general asked if she had any special deficiencies.

Mathi lowered her head. "I do not get along well with domestic animals," she said. That was a problem she never realized in her sylvan home, but while a slave of the nomads, Mathi discovered that their domestic animals could not abide her. Cows, goats, sheep, even dogs were restless around her. Birds took wing, and cats fled in terror.

"To what do you attribute such a reaction?"

"I do not know, my lord. Perhaps my scent disturbed them. I cannot say."

"Very well, your warning is duly noted. Good night, Mathani. Remember to stay in your room tonight unless summoned by me or Lofotan."

She bowed and departed. Mathi's head was reeling with many conflicting thoughts. The mighty general was nothing like she expected. Kind but aloof, humble yet commanding, he seemed like an elf at war with himself. All his precautions—all his defenses—had to be in place to ward off a real threat. But from whom . . . or what?

*****

Far off in the silent, empty house, she heard a sudden loud clang. Mathi was awake at once. Rapid footfalls echoed in the long hall outside her door. She picked up her luminar but left it unlit. Tiptoeing to the door, she cracked it open a finger's width.

Something flashed by. She bit her tongue to keep from crying out. Mathi was sure what ran past was on all fours, such as a dog. There was a shout from the top of the stairs, a wordless cry of alarm. Mathi pushed the door shut, held her luminar up and spoke the word to make it shine. Then she flung the door wide and ran out.

Where the broad steps met the wide hall, two figures struggled in a deadly embrace. Both stood upright. Light glinted on a red metal blade. The taller one was Lofotan. He had a short sword in one hand as he grappled with a darkly clad opponent who seemed to be wearing fur robes. The old soldier's eyes caught the glare of the luminar.

"Put out that light!" he cried.

His enemy turned to see who Lofotan was shouting at. In that instant Mathi saw his face. It was elf-shaped but covered with brown fur. Enormous dark eyes, all pupils and no white, reflected the light, glowing red as hot coals.

Mathi stumbled back, dropping the light. The luminar hit the floor and went out.

She heard rather than saw what happened next. Someone landed several hard blows, each one followed by grunts of pain. There followed the unmistakable sound of flesh being cleaved. A sharp howl filled the hall. Lofotan uttered a soldier's oath. Then all was quiet, save for the elf's labored breathing.

"Come here, girl."

He had to call twice before Mathi gathered enough presence of mind to comply. "Bring your light," Lofotan added. He coughed dryly. Mathi brought the luminar but did not activate it.

"Shine it there."

The cone of light revealed the intruder dead at his feet,

lying in a spreading pool of blood. He resembled an adult male elf except for the startling fur. Elves were not hirsute. They regarded humans and dwarves as beastly simply because they had body hair and beards.

Lofotan cursed again and stepped back out of the gore. Remembering that he was in the presence of a Haven girl, he apologized, saying, "Forgive me. It was stronger than I expected."

The old soldier edged into the light. He was wounded. A long, bleeding gash ran from his left ear down across his throat. The front of his white tunic was soaked with blood. A patchwork of scratches covered his face.

"You're hurt!" she exclaimed.

"It's nothing." He prodded the corpse with the point of his sword.

"What happened here?"

A new voice said, "It came to kill me."

The servant and the girl looked down the stairs and saw Balif, bearing an oil lamp in one hand and a naked sword in the other. Lofotan instinctively straightened. Ignoring his hurts, he raised his bloody blade in salute.

"The other one got away," Balif said, approaching. Mathi stared at the pair of unsheathed blades handled with such casual skill.

"Can this one talk?"

It was beyond speech. After a hard cut to the shoulder, Lofotan had run the beast through. It could answer only the gods.

Padding down the hall came more footsteps. Balif and Lofotan squared off, swords ready, until they recognized the scribe, Treskan. Judging by his appearance, he had been sleeping in his clothes. He took in the scene with wide eyes.

"My lord, shall I fetch the city guard?" Treskan asked. Death by sword was uncommon in Silvanost.

"This is no one's affair but my own. Remember that.

Whatever happens in this house is my affair and mine alone." He sighed deeply. By the ruddy oil light, Balif looked aged and tired. "Let's get this cleaned up."

Lofotan held out an arm, blocking his general. "Don't dirty your hands, my lord. Let us take care of it."

"You're wounded, my friend. The scribe is in shock, and this girl is too tender in years for such a task."

Mathi held up her chin. "My lord, I was raised on a farm and lived many days as a captive. Blood is no stranger to me."

Lofotan also dismissed his lord's concern. "My wounds are nothing. Not like the Battle of the Burning Tree, eh, my lord? Come, scribbler. Lend a hand."

Grimacing, Treskan took hold of one pair of the dead creature's hands and feet. Lofotan took the other. Mathi went ahead with her luminar to light the way. They dragged the body to the top of the steps. Treskan suggested they roll it down the stairs, but Lofotan sharply squelched that idea.

"Do you want to mop every stone between here and the cellar? I don't. Pick him up. Your clothes will wash more easily than a mile of white marble!"

They hoisted the dead creature to their shoulders and followed Mathi down. Balif trailed, carrying his lamp. In the entry hall, Lofotan directed Mathi down a side passage to another, narrower set of steps. Down the inky steps they went. Mathi could see nothing but winding stone stairs. She kept her shoulder tight against the cold stone wall and uttered a prayer as they descended.

"What is that you're saying?" asked Lofotan.

"A prayer."

"For this unnatural creature?"

"No," said Mathi, struggling under the weight of the corpse. "I asked Quenesti Pah to guide my steps, so I don't fall!"

The air grew cooler and damper. Far below ground level,

the steps ended in a vaulted room crowded with barrels and draped shapes of uncertain purpose. They put the body down. Lofotan went alone to root around in the shadowed recesses of the cellar. Balif, standing on the last step, noticed the girl was trembling. Treskan the scribe scrubbed absently at the stain on his shoulder.

"Have you not seen death before?"

"Yes, my lord." In her life Mathi had witnessed battles, murders, and all kinds of mayhem. "But I still shake at the sight of blood."

Treskan remarked, "It was a heavy burden!"

"Burden." Balif pursed his thin lips. "Try bearing the weight of a hundred such creatures."

Mathi studied him. Was Balif boasting he had killed a hundred intruders like the one before them?

Lofotan returned, dragging an empty crate. They wrapped the body in a makeshift canvas shroud, put it in the crate, and nailed the lid on. Lofotan promised to have the crate removed later. The body would be taken out of the city unseen and buried secretly. Not even Balif or his majordomo would know where it would ultimately lie.

Mathi didn't understand why they were acting like accomplices to a crime. Surely Lofotan acted in self-defense against an attacker of plainly unnatural origin. Why hide the incident?

"Too many questions will be asked," Balif said calmly. "Guilt will be applied where none is needed."

The four of them climbed the stairs to the entry hall in silence. Mathi's mind was racing. If forces were arrayed to kill Balif, why didn't the Speaker of the Stars send troops and magicians to protect him?

"Your head is full of questions," Balif said sagely. "I understand. Some things cannot be explained in ordinary conversation. If you prove yourself worthy, the answers shall come."

Balif made a graceful if weary exit. He did not go back down the corridor where he had previously gone. Having been disturbed once, he was off to find a different location to sleep.

"What if I don't prove worthy?" Treskan asked.

"Then I shall personally cut your throat." There was no animosity in Lofotan's promise, just blunt honesty. Mathi believed him completely.

Wrung out, she returned to the couch in her vacant suite. Mathi was about to extinguish her luminar for the night when she spotted writing on the distant marble wall. It had not been there when she first came to the room. Someone had written it since—

The intruder. The intruder had been in the suite while she slept. Mathi walked slowly to the graffito. The runny red letters were not written with paint.

*Honor demands honesty,* it read. *Survival needs secrecy.*

# CHAPTER 3

## *Honors*

A voice called out to her. For a brief moment, she thought she was back in the forest, but Lofotan's gruff voice reminded her where she was.

"Up, girl. The sun may still sleep, but we who serve our lord must rise."

Mathi sat up, stiff in strange places. The cunning couch, designed to be wonderful to look at, was not so wonderful to sleep on.

"Good morning?"

"The day begins. Come," urged Lofotan.

"Is there water? I'm dry."

"In the font."

Lofotan was dressed in a spotless military tunic and kilt and heavy sandals. He wore an officer's woven silver band around his forehead. No trace of the previous night's blood remained, though the gash on his neck was still visible. Mathi padded behind him, pausing at the bowl for a hasty gulp of water.

"You have a light tread," the old soldier remarked. "Were you born in the wildwood?"

Mathi explained her quietness by saying she'd had to step quietly around her human captors. If she disturbed them or drew unwanted attention to herself, she was usually beaten for it.

"Savages."

He led her deeper into the house to Treskan's room. The scribe proved harder to rouse. Lofotan's battlefield bark hardly moved him, so the old warrior grasped Treskan by the shirt-front and shook him. The scribe awoke with limbs thrashing. Lofotan stepped back, out of reach. Treskan subsided after a brief struggle with himself.

"Arise, scribbler. My lord must be served." Eyes clenched and mouth agape in a mighty yawn, Treskan followed.

The house was still cloaked in darkness. Unlike the dead hour when the beastly invader was caught, the predawn tingled with change. There was newness in the air. Early-morning flowers were open, releasing their scent to the rising sun. Shadows buried by the profound black of night slowly took on form again as the faintest rays of daylight penetrated the gloomy villa.

On the ground floor at the extreme rear of Balif's grand residence was the domestic area. The kitchen, sized to accommodate the vast house, was lit by a few slender wax tapers. Pots banged and clattered. Holding forth in one corner of the enormous room was Balif's cook, the only other soul who dwelled in the house. His name, Lofotan said, was Mistravan Artyrith.

"*Lord* Artyrith," corrected the cook. He was younger than Lofotan, with fashionably long hair looped behind his prominent, pointed ears. The living embodiment of the Silvanost look, Artyrith had the angular features and pale hair and eyes considered handsome in the city.

Surprised by his claim to nobility, Mathi looked to the majordomo for confirmation.

"My lord's cook has delusions. Pay them no heed," said Lofotan dryly.

"Delusions? Who is heir to the ancestral estate of the

Artyriths? Whose grandsire was chamberlain to the Speaker of the Stars before he was Speaker?" demanded the cook.

"If you can find an estate to be heir to, why don't you go there?"

"It exists! My enemies have taken it over, my enemies—" At that point Lofotan made a gesture with his hand indicating he considered the cook insane.

It was plain the two often sparred over Artyrith's airs. Mathi said, "I am honored to meet you, my lord."

The cook smiled, showing impressive white teeth. He was quite striking in a rakish way, the sort of elf young females found charming but their parents found alarming.

"It's welcome to have another elf of good breeding around. Lately the halls have been too crowded by big heads and large mouths," he said. Lofotan gave him a warning look that set the cook grinning even more widely.

"Which of you is my new apprentice?"

"I am a scribe," Treskan said flatly and yawned again.

"What about you, dear child?" he said, favoring Mathi with an incandescent smile.

"I don't know, my lord. I could be. I am a ward of the Haven of the Lost—"

His smile vanished. To Lofotan he protested, "I was promised help! I've waited a long time!"

"You have longer to wait," the majordomo replied. "Is our lord's breakfast ready?"

Glaring, Artyrith filled a wheeled cart with white porcelain platters. On each platter he placed a single item—a perfectly peeled peach, pitted and quartered; a pyramid-shaped roll, still steaming from the oven; a puree of wild berries in a gossamer-thin silver shell. By each of those treasures, he placed a utensil. They were gold, blown in a molten state like glass until they were light as air and almost transparent. Mathi and Treskan had never seen such metalwork. The scribe picked up a spoon, marveling at its artistry.

Artyrith snatched it from him and replaced it on the cart with great precision.

Last the cook set a weighty urn of spring water on the lower shelf of the cart. That was Balif's morning meal, typical for a well-born Silvanesti. The fare was beautifully prepared and presented but extremely simple.

"Take it away," the cook said. "If my lord wishes more bread, I have it, but that is the only peach. I can get more from the market after sunrise."

Lofotan took hold of the cart rail. He ordered Mathi and the scribe to follow him. They found Balif in the east salon, sitting on a stone bench before a breathtaking bank of windows. The first rays of the sun were just hitting the panes. Mathi stopped at the doorway, staring. She'd never seen such a room. In plan the salon was serpentine, a great outward curve of the wall being balanced by a sweeping inward curve. The outer wall was glass from a low sill to the ceiling. Intended as an indoor garden, the salon was empty save for a few stone benches and what Mathi took to be pedestals where statues once stood.

Lofotan pushed past the gawking Treskan and Mathi. Balif was seated facing the windows, his eyes closed. At the sound of the cart's wheels, he turned his head and opened his eyes.

"Good morning." He glanced at the door where the newcomers were still marveling. "Still with us, I see. I half imagined you two would flee after our little adventure last night."

"Still here," Lofotan said. He arranged Balif's breakfast on the stone slab beside him. Mathi slowly approached, marveling at the architecture. She stumbled over a high stone tile on her way to the general.

"Though empty, this place has its hazards. Be careful," Balif said.

"I've never seen such a magnificent room!" said Treskan, trailing the girl.

"It was designed by the same architect who built the palace of the Speaker. He always claimed that it was better than anything else he ever built." Balif looked to the windows. "Like many masterpieces, this one exacts a price of its owner. This room is uninhabitable once the sun comes up. All the glass traps the heat, turning the room into a furnace. The exotic greenery planted here at the Speaker's order quickly withered. Tapestries and carpets faded then turned to powder under the glare. The only thing that endures in this room is stone."

It was already warm, and the sun was barely up. Mathi easily imagined the place was like a fiery crucible at midday. Treskan asked why the general didn't shade the windows? It would take acres of velvet to mask the enormous panes, but at least the room would livable.

"I prefer it this way." Little beads of sweat stood out on his high forehead. "Sit down, child. Break your fast."

Mathi was so startled by his invitation that she looked to Lofotan. The dour majordomo, standing behind his general, gave her a stern look whose meaning was inescapable.

"Thank you, no, my lord. It is more proper that I stand."

A flicker of amusement flashed over Balif's face. "Suit yourself."

He ate the peach with swift, silent efficiency. When it was dispatched, he asked Lofotan what his day's duties were.

"My lord has no demands on his time today," was the reply. Treskan, stylus and writing board under his arm, looked crestfallen. The second elf of the realm, and Balif had no duties to perform?

Balif shrugged. "Just as well. If I had to sit through another military parade or inspect troops or griffons, I think I would rebel."

The creeping sun hit the windows full-on. A blaze like fire flashed across row upon row of polished panes, mirrored and magnified. Balif's morning sojourn in the sunrise salon was over. The elves quit the room.

"Such is my life in total," he said as they strolled down the refreshingly cool, dark corridor outside. "A brief moment of glory in the sun then retreat into the shadows."

As the elves crossed the entry hall, loud chiming filled the air. The front doors were made of bell-quality bronze. Someone was knocking for admittance.

"See who it is, Mathi."

Puzzled to be doing Lofotan's job, Mathi bowed and went to the front door. Halfway there it occurred to her that if it was another attempt on the general's life, she was walking directly into harm's way. All of a sudden the floor seemed to cling to her feet. Slowly she reached out to the ornate door handle.

The doors clanged again, a pleasant but loud tone amplified by the great vacant hall behind them. Lofotan and Balif stood side by side, poised to fight or flee. Treskan, still rumpled from his uneasy night, peered between them.

Mathi struggled momentarily with the unfamiliar door handle then tugged the panel open. Though the metal-sheathed door easily weighed a ton, it swung easily inward. Mathi's pulse quickened when she saw a company of soldiers arrayed outside. An officer in brightly gilded armor raised a sheathed sword, pommel first, in salute.

"Greetings to the most excellent lord Balif, High General of the Realm, Protector of the Nation, and most loyal servant of our Great Speaker, Silvanos!"

"Hello," was all Mathi could think to say.

"I bear this message for your master." He presented the girl with a golden scroll case, exquisitely embossed with sun symbols and the glyphic monogram of Silvanos Goldeneye.

"I will convey this to the general," Mathi promised.

Under the glittering helmet brow, the officer's eyes were as cold and sharp as icicles. "I am to wait for a reply."

Mathi shut the door. When she turned around, she found Lofotan and Balif on either side of the closed door, swords in their hands. She was so rattled that she dropped the royal message case.

"Steady on," Lofotan chided, stooping to retrieve the tube. He and Balif returned their blades to their scabbards. "Assassins, as a rule, don't arrive bearing messages."

By some unseen hinge, the tube opened along its length. Within, a gold-colored sheet of parchment unrolled itself in Lofotan's hands. Balif asked what it said.

Peering over the old warrior's shoulder, Treskan scanned the message. "You are commanded to the royal residence at once," he said.

"Does it say 'residence'?"

Treskan looked again. "Why yes, my lord. Not the royal palace, but residence."

Lofotan said, "What does it mean, my lord?"

Balif unbuckled his sword belt and gave it to his old comrade-in-arms. "The Speaker grows more subtle every day. Maybe he has some empty new honor to bestow. Maybe I will be arrested. Who but the gods can say? If I do not return, take the treasure I have hidden—you know where it is, Lofotan—and leave Silvanost at once. Don't try to find me or help me."

"My lord, I—" Lofotan began. Balif silenced him with a stern glance. "Yes, my lord. I'll pay off Artyrith and go, as you say."

"Our association may be brief," he told Mathi, taking her hand gently. "Perhaps we will meet again."

Balif asked how many soldiers were waiting outside. Mathi, whose eyes were quick, knew exactly.

"Thirty-six, my lord."

"An honor company. How kind of the Speaker."

His hand on the door, Balif said to Treskan, "Come along, scribe. There may be work for you."

Lofotan protested. If anyone were to accompany the general, it ought to have been him. Balif firmly ordered him to stay at the house.

"No one else knows where everything is. Our late-night visitor must be disposed of too. Stay, Captain. Come, scribe."

Before the general opened the door, Lofotan said, "My lord, are you dressed to be received by the Speaker?"

Balif was wearing the same clothes he wore to the Night Chamber the previous day. "Whatever fate Silvanos has for me I can meet as I am." He smiled. Mathi observed the great general had an easy smile and used it often. "Guard the gates, Captain. I shall return soon or not at all."

He threw open the door and strode out. The honor guard, idling on the weedy terrace, snapped to attention. Watching through the open door, Mathi had never heard arms click into place so quickly. Thirty-six elves in the immaculate livery of the Speaker of the Stars stood in rigid order, two parallel lines facing each other. Their officer, no less attentive, faced Balif.

"My lord! Good morning!"

"It is a good morning." Balif's tone was relaxed, but every fiber of his being was alert. He stepped down from the doorway, tugging on pale doeskin gloves. "This is my personal scribe, Treskan. He will be accompanying me."

"My orders were to bring you alone, my lord," said the officer.

"And *my* orders are that Treskan shall come. Do you dispute them?"

The officer opened his mouth to speak then thought better of it. He raised his sword hilt to his face in acknowledgment, turned on one heel, and snapped orders to his waiting troops. As Balif crossed the terrace to the street, thirty-six blades thrust skyward. The hiss of so much bronze being bared made Mathi flinch.

"My lord!" she called, stepping through the door. Balif paused and looked back. "My lord, allow me to come!"

He made no reply, so Mathi ran to meet him and Treskan. The guards' commander protested anew. Enjoying the officious elf's predicament, Balif agreed to let Mathi accompany him.

"My lord, this is a serious breach of protocol!" said the officer.

"Yes," said Balif, not smiling.

Any other noble lord of Silvanost would have entered a fine carriage and ridden off to the Speaker's palace with the honor guard following on foot. Balif disdained such airs. He remarked to Mathi that he had at one time been provided with a silver-chased carriage of the finest make, drawn by four matched white horses. He rode in it once then gave the horses to deserving soldiers of his army. The carriage went into storage and had not seen the light of day since. Ever since, he had walked where he needed to go. If his destination were far, he would hire a common carter to carry him.

Five steps behind Balif, Treskan made careful note of what he heard. The day had just begun, and already he had much to write about in his chronicle.

The square on which Balif's grand house stood was fronted by three other imposing homes. When Balif reached the street, he chose to walk down the center of the lane, trailed by Mathi, Treskan, and the glittering honor guard. Gardeners and other servants working on the neighboring estates stopped their work and bowed as Balif passed. He walked serenely on, paying the honor no special heed.

At the end of the lane, he reached a busier thoroughfare, the Sunpath. That street led into one of the great byways of Silvanost, the circular street known as the Star Way. Everything in Silvanost was natural, Mathi noticed. As she walked behind General Balif, she got her first full view of the elf capital. Beneath her feet the paving stones were natural river stones, taken from the Thon-Thalas and fitted together with astonishing accuracy. Stones large and small nestled together with such unity that one could not be pried out without lifting a half dozen others surrounding it. Each stone was a different pastel color. Mixed together, the effect was very pleasing, like a well-made carpet of living rock.

On either side of the street were shade trees and flowering shrubs, guided by elf hands into living colonnades. Spread beneath them were hand-laid strands of white river sand. The people of Silvanost passed back and forth on their daily affairs. Beyond the shaded footpaths were the gardens of individual homes. From them rose phalanxes of fiery orange lilies, scarlet roses on thorny ropes of green, and golden daisies the size of warriors' shields. All the flowers were not outsized, though. That would be too garish. The Silvanesti also loved miniature blossoms. Hyacinths and cyclamens, shrunk to the size of jewels, made carpets of color on many lawns.

Farther back from the street were the houses of Silvanost. The residents of the Sunpath were mostly artisans who worked in trades supervised by House Artisan. There the skill of the elves in manipulating wood and stone was well displayed. Mathi saw houses formed from living tree trunks, conglomerations of native boulders, and even some woven from leafy vines. The effect was not as primitive as it might sound. The elves loved vertical forms, and each home thrust skyward with exuberance. A glance might mislead a visitor into thinking a house was made of cut marble, but no chisel ever touched a Silvanesti home. Through natural magic and secret art, the people of Silvanost had learned how to shape natural substances into any form they desired. Only careful study could reveal that a lovely green townhouse was actually made of live ivy. A tower that resembled cut glass from afar might, close up, turn out to be polished quartz, the crystals mined and assembled like logs.

Not long after entering the Sunpath, the crowds lining the route began to multiply. Gardeners went to fetch their masters and mistresses. Artisans left their tools. Elf children—who seemed scarce to Mathi, compared to the children of a nomad tribe—came running from under bowers and arbors. Everyone wanted to see the celebrated general.

For his part Balif kept his course resolutely ahead. At times he acknowledged a familiar face with the slightest of nods, but the acclaim of the growing crowd he ignored. Mathi looked back. Stretching behind them, the street was filled with curious, excited elves. They crowded the honor guard, jostling the rear ranks until the soldiers started elbowing them back. The proud residents of Silvanost did not take kindly to such treatment. They shoved back. Before the procession dissolved into a riot, Balif halted.

He walked back among the guards, who had likewise halted. Ignoring their captain, he parted their ranks until he reached the rear of the company. There some angry elves stood apart, loudly complaining about their treatment at the hands of the Speaker's soldiers.

"Friends, forgive me," Balif said to them. His simple plea silenced everyone. The soldiers had expected he would admonish the townsfolk. The Silvanesti thought he would do the same to the guards.

"I am the cause of this disturbance. My apologies," he said, facing the crowd. "Please do not trouble yourselves or the Speaker's troops. They are here to honor me, nothing more."

"Where do you go, general?" someone called.

"To hear the words of the Great Speaker."

A murmur swelled in the crowd. Balif assured them, "Our Great Speaker seeks my counsel on some matter; that's all."

"May you live forever, Lord General!"

That cry was repeated by many throats. Balif surveyed the onlookers.

"Do not let your affection for me lead you to say things you may regret," he said severely. "Save your hails for him who sits on the Throne of the Stars."

"Better that you sat there!"

From where she stood, Mathi saw two reactions: the captain of the guard glowered under his ornate helmet, and Balif went pale. Without another word, he strode back to the head of the procession.

"Forward," he said in a low voice to Treskan, busily writing. "And you, girl. Do not look around or say anything." Mathi nodded. "At a walk, then."

Down the Sunpath they went, trailed by the ever-growing crowd. Passing the grounds of the temple of Astarin, a troupe of pipers formed on the green came down. The musicians were young acolytes of the temple, dressed in green robes and bare headed, as befit their status as new servants of the god. They fell into place ahead of Balif, playing a light marching air. Mathi could not tell if the general was at all pleased. Wasn't it Balif's intention to draw notice? Why else take such a conspicuous route to the Tower of the Stars? Why walk down the center of a busy street?

It didn't take long for her to imagine a reason: If I thought I was going to be arrested or killed, I would want a large, friendly crowd at my back too!

By the time they reached the Star Way, more than a thousand elves filled the boulevard. The pipers struck up an ancient air, "Sun and Stars," and the crowd began to sing. Their voices made the hair on Mathi's neck prickle. She had never heard such harmonious singing before. That was the magic of Silvanost, the city that rural elves believed was inhabited by the gods.

Since the procession was hardly stealthy, word of Balif's progress reached the Tower of the Stars well in advance of the general. Everyone could see the bright white pinnacle ahead, the tallest tower in the city. What no one saw until they rounded the wide, circular lane was a phalanx of royal troops drawn up before the tower gate. Ranged behind them were two companies of cavalry. Overhead, griffon riders circled. Quite a few griffon riders, in fact.

The massed might, arrayed in perfect formation, caused the pipers leading the parade to falter. Their pipes fell raggedly silent when their lips dried. The divine chorus behind Mathi likewise sputtered and fell dumb. Everyone stopped and stared at the Speaker's power, so openly displayed. All, that was, but one.

Balif shouldered through the Astarin acolytes, politely excusing himself as he went. Mathi and Treskan were lost in the press until the general called out to them to follow. Feeling a bit like a rabbit racing by a dog pen, Mathi hurried to catch up.

At the head of the troops lined up before the Tower of the Stars was a familiar face. Balif hailed his old comrade Farolenu, commanding the tower guard.

"My lord!" said Farolenu, once a master metalsmith. "I was ordered to defend the tower against a riot. Instead I find you leading a festival parade!"

Balif said, "Just a few well-wishers, old friend."

Farolenu raised his sword in salute. "Face the honor!" he cried. The commander of all elf armies was present, and the warriors had to pay homage. Blades and spears rose skyward.

In response the crowd of Silvanesti chanted, "Balif, Balif," in two long syllables like "Bay leaf, Bay leaf," a pronunciation the general particularly disliked. Lofotan had advised Mathi that he preferred his name be pronounced "Bah-liff," with the emphasis on the second syllable.

The captain of the guard led his honor troop forward. They had to break ranks and filter through the crowd, a path they plainly resented. Mathi and the scribe came with them, filling in behind Balif like mismatched shadows.

"The Great Speaker awaits," Farolenu said, stepping aside. Balif mounted the shallow steps to the tower. The guard captain tried to restrain Treskan and Mathi from following.

Balif said, "Let them be."

"The scribe perhaps, but a common girl cannot be admitted to the presence of the Speaker of the Stars!"

"I am of common birth. The fact that everyone calls me 'my lord' doesn't change that. So either admit us both or deny us both. Do as you will, but do it in haste. The sun grows hot and my friends restive."

Thinking of the crowd at his back, the captain relented. "On your responsibility, my lord," he said grudgingly.

Balif went on. Very quietly he told Mathi and Treskan to stay three steps behind him and say nothing. Tingling with anticipation, the girl and the scribe readily agreed.

They climbed the steps between the enormous curled rails flanking the entrance. Made of white metal, they were brilliantly polished. Sunlight reflecting off them was almost painful. Treskan fell six steps behind when he strayed to get a closer look at the ornamentation. Without looking back, Balif urged him onward.

"Those are solid electrum," he said. An alloy of gold and silver, the metal was notoriously difficult to work. The entwined forms were curled as naturally as shoots of honeysuckle but made of hard metal six inches thick.

They passed out of the bright sun into a cool antechamber. Farolenu and the guard captain were close behind. When Balif disappeared into the tower, another shout rose from the crowd. Mathi was close enough to the general to see his enigmatic expression. He might have been smiling, but his brow was deeply furrowed. Balif walked ahead, hands clasped behind his back and head lowered. Corridors passed by on either side. Court officials and favor seekers, looking cool and vastly self-important, lingered in the side halls, awaiting their chance to gain the Speaker's ear. They stared at the elves who had the audacity—and influence—to walk directly into the monarch's presence. For the first time, Mathi felt truly worried. Could she really stand before the Speaker of the Stars?

The arched passage opened abruptly into a great open area, the hall of the Tower of the Stars. The scale of the place diminished everyone. Mathi looked up and saw that the awesome height of the tower was lined with a spiral row of windows reaching all the way to the domed roof. The tower walls were faced with black basalt. The only light came from an open skylight, the Moonlight Shaft, at the very peak of the dome. There were two rows of galleries above the hall, capacious enough to hold the assembled lords of the realm if need be.

Amazing as the tower was, the floor was positively breathtaking. The floor of the great hall was covered with the finest mosaic Mathi had ever seen. Thousands of pieces of polished black jet were laid out to mimic the sky. Stars rendered in gold or silver dotted the floor in exactly the positions occupied by their heavenly counterparts. Most astonishing of all, tracks allowed models of the three moons to travel around the floor. A hidden mechanism under the floor kept them moving in the same place as the moons in Krynn's sky. The floor of the Tower of the Stars was a giant orrery, an astronomical device by which the seasons could be tracked and the days of the year numbered. Such a complex mechanism was no less magical to Mathi than the invisible spells she knew protected the place.

Balif approached to where the orbit of Solinari crossed the floor. There he stopped. He went down on one knee, facing the throne.

"Great Speaker, I have come."

Mathi raised her eyes from the amazing instrument at her feet. Silvanos Goldeneye looked down at them from his throne atop a two-level dais. Lined up on the lower level were five solemn figures, richly dressed and wearing silver-star headbands. They were the Speaker's counselors, heads of the five noblest families in Silvanost. On the second level, at the Speaker's right, were the high priests of the major temples—Astarin, E'li, Matheri, Quenesti Pah, and the Blue Phoenix. Standing at Silvanos's left were two females. One was young and very beautiful. The other was older, quite handsome, but more modestly dressed than the other. Mathi assumed the elder female must be the Speaker's wife, and the younger, his daughter.

"Balif Thraxenath, Chosen Chief of House Protector, First Warrior of the Great Speaker, son of Arnasmir Thraxenath of the Greenrunners clan, and loyal servant of the Great Speaker of the Stars, I greet you," Silvanos said. His voice was deep and booming, though a lot of its power came from cunning acoustics in the hall.

Though the place was dim, the Moonlight Shaft cast its light on the Speaker's throne. Mathi got her first good look at the founder of Silvanesti. He was, as his epithet said, golden eyed. Silvanos's famous eyes were large and almost red in color. His hair was also red-gold and worn very long. He had a strong face but not a handsome one. Silvanos's nose was long and aquiline, his chin sharp. The height of his ears was truly dramatic. Long of limb, his hands appeared half again as big as Balif's, who was well built. Mathi got a good impression of the strength of will of the elf, who had forged the proud old line of the elves into a nation. Everything about Silvanos seemed typically elflike but taken to unexpected heights. Even his powerful voice befitted a monarch with an almost godlike command over his people.

"May I pay homage to your sister, the Votress of the Greenwood, and your royal wife?" said Balif. The younger woman smiled winningly. The elder one moved not a muscle.

Mathi felt a strong hand on her shoulder. Before she knew it, she was forced to her knees. Farolenu pushed her down along with Treskan then knelt between them.

"Avert your gaze," he whispered. Mathi stared at the black floor.

"I have summoned you to undertake a new task of great importance to the nation," Silvanos said.

"As the Great Speaker commands, so shall I do."

From her place Mathi was puzzled. How could anyone as wise as Balif agree to a task he hadn't heard about yet?

"Word has come that an invasion is under way in the eastern lands."

Silvanos was referring to the land east of the Thon-Tanjan river. A mix of wild woodland and open plains, it was bound on the north by desert and on the east and south by the sea. It had no native population. Silvanos claimed the land for Silvanesti when he first took the crown, but little had been done to enforce the claim. The elves' attention had been focused on the west, where nomadic humans constantly encroached on Silvanos's claims to the great central plains.

"Humans?" asked Balif. The east was a long way from the heaviest concentration of barbarians. It was unlikely humans could have migrated across the elves' northern territory without notice, nor could they cross the desert in any numbers.

"Not just humans," Silvanos said, leaning back. "Another race . . . of small stature. My governor says the land is thick with them."

"Send the army," Balif said flatly. His tone made the Speaker of the Stars' face harden like a marble statue.

"The army is engaged elsewhere," Silvanos snapped. Balif did not shrug, but he might as well have. "I want you to go. Take a small band with you and survey the situation. Having just concluded a twenty-year fight for the west, I do not propose to lose the east by negligence."

"Is that your order, Great Speaker?"

"It is. Go at once. Find out the truth of the situation, and bring your considered word back to me."

Balif bowed his head. "It shall be done, Great Speaker. May I draw on the royal stores for supplies?" Silvanos said Farolenu would provide whatever Balif needed for the journey.

"Leave tomorrow," Silvanos said. "I am anxious to have true knowledge of what's going on."

"Is tomorrow soon enough? I can leave tonight, if it please the Great Speaker. Better to meet the invaders as far from the royal city as can be done."

Silvanos snapped, "You presume a great deal on my affection, my lord general! Save your sharp tongue for others worthy of it. I am not spoken to thus!"

"Forgive me, royal master. I meant no disrespect."

Balif said the words, but Mathi did not believe him at all. He was mocking Silvanos's pretense of importance. The mission could be done by any of a thousand reliable warriors. Why send the first general of the realm?

She heard whispers from the throne dais. Peering in that direction, Mathi saw the elder of the two elf women conferring quietly with the Speaker.

Silvanos shifted forward, perching tensely on the edge of his golden chair. "My noble sister reminds me that your wit, like your sword, is in my service too," he said, trying to control his annoyance and only partially succeeding. "I trust you will use both as I command. Go with the sun, my lord general. May Astarin guard your steps."

"I thank you, Great Speaker, and the noble votress as well." Balif bowed low. "I shall return before long with what intelligence I can gather. Health and long life to you, Great Goldeneye."

"And to you, Balif Thraxenath."

There was something in the Speaker's tone that made Mathi's blood run cold. Anyone could hear the hostility between Balif and Silvanos sparking the very air in the Tower of the Stars. His farewell to the general dripped with irony. Mathi had been awed to enter the Tower of the Stars and look upon the face of the Speaker. After their exchange, what she wanted most of all was to get away, and the sooner the better.

Balif withdrew, shooing the girl, the scribe, and the captain of the guard ahead of him. By the time he'd backtracked to the entrance, Silvanos was deep in conversation with his counselors, ignoring the general's departure.

When Balif emerged from the tower, the crowd was still there. They roared when he reappeared. Smiling, he raised his hand in greeting.

"Is it wise to encourage such disloyalty here?" asked Farolenu in a low voice.

"These people saved my life," he replied. "This is gratitude, not disloyalty."

They descended the steps. The mob surged forward, crushing the royal guards back. Fearing his soldiers would be trampled, the captain ordered his guards to shoulder their arms and give way. Cheering, the elves poured through the sullen warriors like floodwater.

Raising his voice to be heard over the din, Balif said, "I will send over a list of the supplies I need!" Farolenu nodded.

A slim elf girl, dressed all in white, emerged from the tower and darted down the steps. She slipped through the crowd with easy grace and pressed a note into Balif's hand. Though she came from inside the tower, she continued on past Balif, melting into the throng. Balif cupped his hand around the missive and gave it a quick glance.

"Any answer, my lord?" Treskan asked, stylus poised.

"No. Go home, both of you. Tell Lofotan to prepare for a land voyage of three months' duration. Have him send his list of needed supplies to Farolenu at House Protector."

Treskan dutifully took down his commands. When he looked up to ask for more instructions, Balif was gone. The crowd didn't seem to notice. They cheered the elves remaining on the tower steps. When at last they noticed their hero was gone, the elves peacefully dispersed.

# Chapter 4

## *Dreams*

Mathi and Treskan returned to Balif's desolate mansion. It was not a comfortable journey. She had never been in Silvanost before, and though Treskan vowed he could backtrack on the route they had taken readily enough, they lost their way more than once. On the way to the Tower of the Stars, no one bothered to look at them because they were in the shadow of the great Balif. Going back, they felt like everyone they passed could tell they were strangers in the city. Because they were obviously not from the city, many elves shunned them, ignoring their painfully polite queries for directions. Treskan's awkward gait and rather coarse appearance caused an arched eyebrow or two, and Mathi's rustic clerical gown gained looks of aesthetic disapproval, but no one challenged them. No one helped either.

By guess and by luck, they found the villa. It was more empty than usual. Lofotan was nowhere to be found. The scribe retired to an empty room off the main hall to transcribe his notes on Balif's audience with the Speaker. Mathi roamed the vast halls, calling the majordomo without success. In the end she found her way to the kitchen. From far down the hall, she heard Artyrith laboring mightily, clattering cutlery and pans. He punctuated his struggle now and then with high-flown Elvish oaths. What elf obscenity lacked in earthy vigor it made up for with poetic ferocity. After hearing a few barrages from the cook, Mathi halted outside the kitchen, fascinated and horrified at the same time. What was that he said? Put the mixing spoons how deeply *where?*

The door shielding her from the cook flew open.

"The country girl! Why are you lurking in dark hallways?" Artyrith exclaimed.

"I am looking for Lofotan," she replied. "Have you seen him?"

"I've seen no one since you two came down to collect the general's breakfast." His belligerent tone softened. "Did he like it, by chance?"

Mathi honestly could not remember. She said, "He liked it very well."

"Strange, he usually eats like a songbird. Maybe feeling like a condemned convict improved his appetite."

Artyrith grabbed a broom from the corner outside the door. Mathi noticed that the broom, like most artifacts she'd seen in Silvanost, was impossibly elegant for such a homely tool. The handle was made from a long, white bone, a wing or leg bone of some unidentifiable creature. At the other end, the broom's head looked like a solid block of some kind of soft, gray material.

She followed Artyrith. The kitchen was well lit by assorted luminars—proof Balif never came down there. A transparent vase lay smashed on the floor. Saffron dust spilled out in drifts from the point of impact. Sighing, Artyrith started sweeping up the spill. He muttered something about how much gold per ounce the spilled powder cost.

"Why do you call the general a convict?" Mathi asked.

"Because death or exile hangs over his head like a sword. Have you not heard?"

"I've not been in Silvanost long, my lord."

Having his pretensions polished made Artyrith beam.

"Of course. You are a hopeless provincial." She must have frowned, for the handsome cook explained, "No offense, my dear. One is either from Silvanost or not."

So far the distinction did not seem much of an honor to Mathi. She saw Artyrith start to dump a pan full of broken glass and golden-red powder in a waste bin. Mathi objected. Why not sieve it, filtering out the bits of glass?

Artyrith was delighted. "Trust a practical peasant to know how to squeeze a coin!"

He placed a large copper bowl on the table and laid a slightly smaller sieve of the same metal on top of it. Dumping the spilled powder in the sieve, he noted with satisfaction that it passed through, leaving slivers of glass behind.

"Tell me about Lord Balif," Mathi said. "I know the songs they sing about his courage and generalship. Who is the real one I owe my rescue to?"

The cook tapped the sieve to speed the powder through. "Ah, the general. No one is so talked about in Silvanost as our lord! Time was Balif was the second most powerful person in the kingdom, and without doubt the most respected. But something happened to change all that. It was that rogue, Vedvedsica."

Artyrith's voice dropped when he said the name, as if he feared invoking the magician by speaking his name too loudly.

"I have heard the name, but I know little of him," Mathi said.

"He's a blackguard of the first order. By attaching himself to Lord Balif, he gained much prestige. He lorded it over everyone for a very long time, and then he fell, blackening the name of his great patron when he toppled."

Vedvedsica was a woodland wizard, once one of the leaders of a coalition of wild, self-taught mages known as the Brown Hoods, from the homespun robes they wore, Artyrith explained. When Silvanos Goldeneye was extending his rule over the elves of the wildwood, the Brown Hoods were his most serious opponents. The mages had their own candidate for Speaker of the Stars: Balif Thraxenath, hereditary clan chief of the Greenrunners. For a while it looked like civil war was brewing, but Vedvedsica performed a powerful augury ceremony for Balif to divine his future. After seeing what was in store for him, Balif willingly submitted to Silvanos and publicly proclaimed him Speaker. After that Silvanos had no serious opposition.

"What became of the Brown Hoods?" said Mathi. "Surely all of them didn't follow Vedvedsica and Balif?"

"They didn't. Once he was in power, Silvanos organized a quiet campaign to destroy the woodland magicians. Some were slain. Others were thrown in prison, while others were exiled to rocky islands in the southern sea. Vedvedsica organized the purge for Silvanos."

Mathi sat down at Artyrith's feet, folding her legs beneath her. By dropping a few more "my lords" to the talkative cook, she easily extracted the rest of the story.

Artyrith said, "Vedvedsica seemed unassailable then. He served Silvanos, and at the same time remained General Balif's personal counselor. He put his magical skills to work for both of them. When their goals clashed, Vedvedsica's intervention meant success for the one he chose to side with."

The last of the spilled powder was in the sieve. Artyrith thrust the broom at Mathi. Only then did she recognize the head was made of feathers—hundreds of tiny, gray feathers embedded in a bar of solid bronze. How was such a thing made? And for common household use too!

Mathi asked Artyrith what brought the mage down from the height of power.

"No one knows but those involved. It is a capital crime to speak of it." Artyrith drew a narrow finger through the salvaged spice powder. "What I have heard is this: Vedvedsica embarked on a personal scheme of a blasphemous nature. He duped our lord into aiding his work. When he was caught, he tried to buy his way out of punishment by offering the Speaker the head of the illustrious general, our master. The Speaker has never been comfortable with our lord. He's too honest and too popular. He pretended to agree with Vedvedsica's proposal then put the mage on trial for his life."

Mathi all but dropped the broom. "That's monstrous!"

"Your word, country girl, not mine."

The conversation finally seemed to spook the loquacious cook. He suddenly professed to be extremely busy and shooed Mathi out of the kitchen. Head abuzz with new facts, she made her way back to the front hall. There she found Lofotan removing a cloak and wide-brimmed hat.

"What are you doing here? Where is our lord?" Mathi had to admit she had lost Balif in the crowd outside the Tower of the Stars. The old soldier did not appear concerned. When Mathi told him about the Speaker's command that Balif investigate the infiltration of the east by foreign interlopers, the majordomo was elated.

"Good!" he said. "It's about time we quit this wretched city! You cannot trust anyone here."

Mathi said the general was ordered to leave at first light.

"It shall be done! You will help, girl. The clumsy scribe too."

"My name is Mathi," she replied. "The scribe's name is Treskan. They're not hard names to remember."

Lofotan ignored her. He bustled in and out of rooms, collecting garments from chests and flinging them into the girl's arms. When Mathi was staggering under the burden, Lofotan led her to a small room under the grand stairway. Neatly racked along the walls were swords, bows, quivers of arrows, javelins, and light lances. Lofotan spent some time examining the blades, checking them for straightness and their edges for nicks. He had selected three when he asked

Mathi to come forward. Struggling under an armload of clothing, the girl tried to comply.

"Oh, drop all that."

Mathi heaved the garments on the floor.

"Are you right-handed? Hold out your arm." Bewildered, she did so. Lofotan laid a slim elf sword against her outstretched arm. "How can you have long limbs and such a short reach?"

Not understanding the question, Mathi let the observation pass. "What are you doing?"

"Measuring you for a sword."

"I'm no warrior!"

Lofotan took a too-lengthy blade away and tried a stubbier one. "Maybe so but you can defend yourself if needed, can't you? A party of five armed elves stands a better chance in the wilderness than a party of four."

"Five?" asked Mathi.

"My lord's cook is no stranger to the blade. The scribbler, though blessed with five thumbs on each hand, is sturdy enough to bear a blade."

The shortest sword in the armory fit Mathi's reach. Lofotan was looking for a shirt of mail for her when muffled chiming filled the empty mansion. He stood stock still, listening.

"Someone's at the door." Mathi understood by then that visitors were not common at Balif's abode. Lofotan hurried out. Mathi was at his heels, still carrying the short sword by the scabbard.

Lofotan opened the small postern set in the monumental door. There stood Balif. He was not alone. A draped figure stood close by in the starlight, hidden from view by a heavy cloak.

"My lord?" Lofotan was taken aback.

"I have a visitor I wish to entertain in private. Everyone in the house will withdraw to the kitchen."

"Yes, my lord."

Seeing they were in the midst of preparations from the coming trip, Balif said, "Keep that sword, Captain. Fetch the scribe. Go with him and the girl Mathi to Artyrith's domain. All of you must remain in the kitchen until I give you leave to come out."

He reached through the postern, taking Lofotan by the wrist. "You will slay whoever tries to leave the kitchen without my permission."

"Yes, my lord. What if we have another intruder?"

He let go. "I am armed," was Balif's terse reply.

Lofotan took the short sword from Mathi and saluted with it. "It shall be done, my lord."

He herded the girl to the passage downstairs. Mathi looked back over her shoulder several times. All she saw was a draped figure entering the house. Balif shut the door. Mathi had the distinct impression the visitor was female, but she could not make out her face.

Artyrith feigned outrage when he heard Balif's orders. Lofotan told him why they were imposing on the prickly cook.

"Ah!" said the handsome young chef. "She pays a final call?"

"Still your tongue, fool, or I'll still it for you permanently."

Artyrith might have snapped back at the blunt threat, but the sword in Lofotan's hand discouraged discussion. He went back to rolling bread dough.

Lofotan went out and quickly returned with Treskan. The scribe stumbled along, all the time writing on his board with his black metal stylus. Mathi asked what he was writing about.

"Events of the day," he said, not looking up from his work. "I am still describing Balif's march to the Tower of the Stars." Absorbed by his work, he didn't notice Artyrith peering over his shoulder until a gout of flour dusted his instrument.

"What kind of writing is that?"

Treskan turned the board over so the cook couldn't see it. "It is called 'record-hand.' It allows us scribes to record full words in just a few strokes of the stylus."

"Ingenious."

Artyrith returned to his pots and pans. Lofotan sat grimly in front of the kitchen door, arms folded across his chest. The bare sword lay on his knees.

Darkness crept into the kitchen. Mathi helped start luminars around the room. When Artyrith had the meal ready, no word had come from Balif. Lofotan wouldn't let anyone out to see if their lord required dinner. With an expressive shrug, Artyrith offered the fine repast to Mathi, Treskan, and the majordomo. They ate the large, golden-green, squashlike vegetable, carved to resemble a capon. Artyrith had stuffed it with nuts and berries, seasoned with the same bright orange spice he'd salvaged from the broken jar that afternoon. Mathi ate slowly, wary of bits of glass. The food was excellent. Artyrith had a splendid nectar to wash down the imitation bird. It was light as water, with a slightly acidic tang. The nectar vanished on the tongue like dew off early-morning grass.

"Wonderful," Treskan declared. "My lord, you are an artist."

"You have an educated palate to match your writing skills," Artyrith said, beaming. "Would that our lord shared your taste."

"He doesn't like your food?"

The chef shrugged. "Who knows? He never says he does or does not."

Mathi drank only water. Artyrith tried to fill her cup with nectar, but she refused it.

"You do not take spirits?" he said, holding out the slim, brown bottle.

"Not even mead," she replied. "My people sold honey to meadmakers, but I do not drink such things."

Lofotan ate in silence. He downed glass after glass of nectar until the bottle was dry. Artyrith grandly opened another. The old soldier put a hand over his cup.

"No more," he said. "I have duties to perform."

"Fear not, my two-legged griffon. This Runo vintage is lighter than a sea-maid's kiss. We could down a bottle each and feel nothing more than gentle warmth." Lofotan was unconvinced.

The cook filled Treskan's glass not for the first time.

"See, the rustic scribe is not afraid. Are you?"

Treskan drained the cup in one long gulp. He seemed quite unfazed by it.

"That's the way! This isn't mere drink; it's medicine for the gullet!" Artyrith refilled his cup and Treskan's. Seeing the pretentious cook and awkward scribe outdrinking him wounded Lofotan's pride. He shoved his silver cup forward.

Artyrith gave Mathi a secret wink. He filled Lofotan's cup to the rim.

By the strong aroma, the girl could tell how potent the nectar was. It had an airy taste, but the rosy glow in her companions' cheeks hinted at hidden strength. Sure enough, by the time the second bottle of Runo nectar was finished, Lofotan flushed from collar to crown.

He lurched to his feet. His sword swung in a wide arc. Mathi had to throw herself out of its way.

"I must go," the majordomo said in clipped tones. "Where is—?"

"Down the hall two doors, on the right." Artyrith's brilliant green eyes were glowing from within. Watching Lofotan walk unsteadily to the door, he all but laughed.

"Pompous old fool," he said, slurring. "Another bottle and I'll have him under the table." He held up the empty nectar bottle and kissed the dusty glass. "Better elves than him have succumbed to this vintage! 'Ruined by Runo,' that's what my grandsire, the great Lord Mistravan, used to say."

He meant to set the brown bottle on the edge of the table, but he missed and sent it crashing to the floor. Artyrith stooped to pick up the shards. Letting out a sigh, he toppled on his side and lay still. Mathi circled around and found the cook passed out, lying on the floor with his hand draped across a chair. Across the table, Treskan had his head down, snoring.

Mathi swept up the broken bottle. Artyrith was out for a while. She waited. When Lofotan did not return, she crept out into the hall and listened. All was still. She went to the water closet two doors down and knocked softly. There was no response.

Lofotan had made it inside but had fallen into nectar-padded sleep. With sudden elation Mathi realized that she was free of all constraints. Her curiosity, inflamed by hours of enforced confinement, erupted full force. Who was Balif's mysterious visitor? She knew the general's first and only wife, Alsalla, had been dead for thirty years. Was Balif saying farewell to a secret lover, or was something more mysterious afoot?

Screwing up her courage, she removed her sandals. The priestesses at the Haven of the Lost had given them to her, but Mathi was never comfortable in them. Hiking up her clerical gown, Mathi tiptoed upstairs to the main hall. She didn't have to search far to find Balif. Light spilled from under a closed door on the ground floor, betraying the general's presence. It was the morning salon, where Mathi had cooled her heels that first day, waiting for Balif to return. She was in there long enough to remember the layout of the room. There was a balcony along the south wall of the salon, accessible from the second floor. Mathi eased upstairs. She found the door to the balcony and slowly pushed down the handle. The jeweled tumblers inside the door lock worked soundlessly. Mathi went down on all fours and crept in.

The balcony was more than ten feet wide, with a waist-high

railing. Light streamed up from an array of oil lamps. Mathi wished there had been furniture in the balcony to hide behind, but it was barren. She slid toward the rail on her belly, feeling as if she were casting a shadow twenty feet high behind her. Carefully she approached the rail.

She heard voices. The elf speaking had a low, throaty voice, female but strong.

"—cannot believe it. He must be sending you away to save your life, not to harm you."

Balif replied in his distinctive voice: "So you say. I have my doubts."

"If he wanted you dead, you would never have left the Night Chamber," his unseen companion insisted.

"Your brother is more subtle than that."

Mathi almost choked on her own breath. Brother? Balif's secret companion was the Speaker's sister?

She did not hear part of what was said next. All she made out was "—your chance to win back the Speaker's favor."

"Who wants his favor? I enjoyed it for more than a century, and the lies of a convicted criminal were enough to lose it in one day."

They were directly below her, beneath the overhang of the balcony. Mathi imagined they were at a table dining or seated on some of the few couches remaining in the mansion. She was startled to see Balif emerge from under the balcony wearing nothing. Mathi froze, realizing that she was intruding on a private moment indeed.

Balif went to a delicate amphora perched beside a silver lamp stand made in the form of a mimosa tree. He poured a measure from the vessel. The liquid was dark, not nectar.

"Do you want more?" he asked. The lady said yes. Balif pointedly did not serve her, but held out the amphora for her to help herself.

The mystery guest entered Mathi's sight, decorously draped in a bit of silk sheet. It was the elder of the two women

Mathi had glimpsed at the Tower of the Stars. So she was Silvanos's sister, the Divine Votress of the Greenwood? Her name, she knew from common knowledge, was Amaranthe. Silvanos had made her Divine Votress, the highest of high priestesses in the land. The Divine Votress was an ancient office usually held by a very old female. Everyone knew Silvanos elevated Amaranthe to the sacred office to prevent her from marrying anyone. There was no one in all of Silvanesti the Speaker deemed worthy of such a close link to the royal family. Imprisoning his sister in the office was typical of the Speaker's ruthlessness. Since she'd had no choice but to accept the office, Amaranthe evidently did not consider her vow of chastity binding.

She filled her cup and said, "Do as Silvanos commands. In a year or two, the scandal around Vedvedsica will die down, and he will find reason to recall you. Then we shall be together again."

"And if he doesn't recall me? Would you leave Silvanost? Could you live in some remote province, far from the city, to be with me?"

There was no hesitation in her answer. "You know I can't do that."

"Not even if I wed you before all the world?"

It was a bold offer. For a Divine Votress to marry was unheard of. For a member of Silvanos's family to marry without his permission would cause a scandal greater than the one driving Balif out of Silvanost.

"I can't," Amaranthe repeated with less assurance.

"Can't. Won't. The words are different, but the result is the same. I mean less to you than your place near the throne."

"Don't play the wounded hero with me! You know how things stand. You know who has the power."

Balif kissed her gently. "Yes, I know," he said. "It isn't us."

She put her arm around his waist. At once she withdrew

it, as if stung. Balif, lost in thought, did not notice. Slowly Amaranthe returned her fingertips to Balif's back.

"Are you ill?" she asked. He denied it. "There's something on your skin," she said, frowning deeply. "Feels like . . . like hair?"

Mathi was listening so closely that when Amaranthe said that, she slid farther forward so as not to miss a word. Her forehead rapped smartly against the carved railing. Horrified, she ducked down and held her breath.

Balif strode out to the middle of the room and said, "You heard?"

Amaranthe drew the sheet close around her. "Someone is near!"

"Yes, on the balcony!"

If Mathi expected the guilty pair to run away or shrink from harm, she was gravely mistaken. With her cheek pressed hard to the floor, she saw Amaranthe vanish under the balcony. She returned with a wicked-looking dagger. Strange people, Mathi thought, who make love with daggers close at hand!

"Here," Amaranthe said, putting the pommel of the weapon in Balif's hand. "Find who it is and kill them."

Mathi inched backward. Once in the deeper shadows at the rear of the balcony, she could rise and run. She was still prone when Balif leaped from the salon floor and grabbed the bottom of the balcony railing. To Mathi's terror, he steadily dragged himself up. The dagger was clenched in his teeth.

She had no doubt she would die if the general caught her. Abandoning stealth, she scrambled on all fours into the shadows, creeping along the baseboard into the darkest corner of the empty balcony. She watched in growing alarm as Balif scaled the railing, throwing a lean, bare leg over the top. He took the dagger from his teeth. Staring into the shadows, he looked unerringly in Mathi's direction.

"Whoever you are, you must die. Stand still, and it will quickly be over."

Mathi steadied herself to leap. She reckoned she could make the rail in two bounds and be over and down before Balif could reach her. If the Divine Votress was not armed, she could get away and be out the door. It would be the end of her quest, but with luck she might yet redeem herself.

Balif advanced, holding the long dagger like a sword. Against the amber background of the lamplight, his usually blue eyes glowed blood red.

# Chapter 5

## *Labors*

There was a clang from below. Half the light promptly vanished, throwing the expansive room into near darkness. Balif halted his advance. Looking back over one shoulder, he called out, "Was that you, Mara?"

"Yes, curse it! My cloak caught on the candelabra!"

More of the tree of candles went out, tilted as they were at too severe an angle. The princess of Silvanost struggled with guttering lights, hissing maledictions as the hot wax burned her fingers.

"Be still," Balif said to his lover.

Mathi did not need to be cautioned; she was as still as she ever had been in her life. While Balif's eyes had been averted, she used her fingers and toes to grip the stone wall behind her. Fortunately it was rough travertine, and she was able to pull herself up with the slightest of holds.

"Is anyone there?" Amaranthe called.

Balif did not answer. He glided through the deep shadows to the spot where Mathi had cowered. She had reached the ceiling and clung there, gazing down at the dim figure of Balif. The dagger gleamed dully.

He swept the air before him with the blade, to Mathi's great relief. The general could not see her hiding above him.

That's why he struck out so blindly at the shadows.

"Mara, are you dressed?" She said she was. "Raise your cowl and go out to the hall. Wait for me there."

In a swirl of silk, the Speaker's sister departed. Balif backed to the rail, dagger held out point first.

"You have escaped with your life, for now. There will be another reckoning later."

He put one leg over the rail then the other. Blade in his teeth, he leaped down to the floor. No more than a candle or two still burned. Mathi heard his bare feet cross the polished floor. Then the candles went out.

She let go, dropping hard on all fours. Time to move! Undoubtedly Balif would check the kitchen to see if everyone was there. Mathi had to be back before the general, or her lucky escape would be only temporary.

Fortune favored her again. When she emerged into the upper hall, she could hear Balif and Amaranthe arguing in hushed tones in the entrance hall. Smiling to herself, Mathi ran swiftly to the back stair and descended to the corridor outside the kitchen.

Taking a deep breath, she stepped into the warm, oven-baked interior of Artyrith's kitchen. The aristocratic cook was dead asleep, numbed by his Runo nectar. Treskan had rolled over at the table, still snoring softly. (Who knew elves snored?) She skirted the slumbering scribe and went over to the sink. She waved her hand under the slender copper spout, and a stream of cool water trickled out. Gratefully she flung it on her face. She discovered the vein in her neck was throbbing.

Lofotan was still gone. Mathi sat down at the table where she had been before. There was enough nectar left in Artyrith's second bottle for her to fill her mouth. She swirled the bitter liquid around and spit it out. Gods, she hated the taste of alcohol.

The door opened. Mathi slumped forward, one eye

cracked. Balif stood there, barefoot and bareheaded, dressed in a sky-colored silk robe. He surveyed the room, face hard. Mathi could see the pommel of his dagger peeking out of the waist of his gown.

He walked slowly around the kitchen. Standing over Artyrith, he sniffed loudly. Finding the cook unresponsive, he moved on to Treskan. He nudged the scribe. Treskan snorted, turned his head away, and kept snoring.

Using the scribe's change of tune as an excuse, Mathi lifted her head, feigning great drowsiness. Inside her heart was racing.

"Ah, Mathani Arborelinex. Just the one I came to find."

"Me, my lord? What do you require of me?"

He picked up the empty nectar bottle, read the wax seal stuck to the bottom, and set it down upright.

"Have you been out of this room tonight?"

"No, my lord."

"Someone was loose in the house. I tried to catch her, but she eluded me."

She gripped the table hard to keep from visibly trembling. Still, she managed to say, " 'She,' my lord?"

"I had a fleeting glimpse of a feminine silhouette." The general appeared genuinely puzzled. "After my attention was drawn away, the intruder vanished from a closed room."

Balif drew the knot tight on his sash. "Where is Lofotan?" Mathi explained the majordomo's absence—the Runo nectar and Artyrith's prank.

Balif was not amused. "I see. I remind you again to stay in this room, Mathani. I am only just learning about your life. It would be a pity to end it just at this new beginning."

The girl merely nodded. With supreme grace, Balif said good night. He must have found Lofotan passed out down the hall, for the former soldier returned a short time later, white faced. Mathi greeted him with a cup of cool water. Strong nectar dried the throat.

Lofotan accepted the cup and swallowed the water swiftly. Eyeing the unconscious cook, his expression was murderous.

"You saw our lord?" Mathi asked innocently. Lofotan admitted he had. Though she hadn't heard a single voice raised in anger, it was easy to imagine the dressing-down Balif had given his old comrade for deserting his post. Whatever he said, it had cut Lofotan to the core. The stalwart old warrior was badly shaken.

"You bore up well," he said.

"I had only a sip."

"It's as well Lord Posturemuch is out," Lofotan declared. "Else I would call him out to the field of honor for what he did!"

"Why pick on him? He's no match for you," Mathi offered.

Lofotan set down his cup, eying her. "That braggart, that proud, overweening imbecile, that . . ." He struggled for another insult and settled for, "That *cook* is also one of the most dangerous blades in Silvanost, believe it or not. If the time ever comes for us to fight, it will not be a light matter."

Treskan groaned and stirred. Mathi filled a cup of cool water and set it by the scribe's elbow.

*****

Dawn arrived with a crash.

From the clang of metal and loud shouts, the girl's first thought was that a battle was in progress. She opened her eyes. She was lying on one of the kitchen side counters, her head pillowed by a sack of flour. The luminars, which had all gone out once she and Lofotan stopped talking, were glowing brightly. Blinking, she sat up.

Artyrith, red faced, was tossing pots and pans into a wicker pannier. Another basket, already brimming with provisions, stood beside it.

"This is no way to travel!" he exclaimed. "Go now! Do this! Do that! How can I create decent meals under such conditions?"

"Who says your meals are decent?"

Mathi spied Lofotan by the door. He was dressed for the road—cloak, leather pteryges, and a finely wrought breastplate, carefully etched to soften its hard bronze sheen. A sword dangled from his left hip, and a war dagger from his right. He leaned one shoulder against the doorframe.

Artyrith still wore his wrinkled robes from the previous night. His hair was askew, and his face bore more distress than simply feeling harried. Ruined by Runo indeed. Seeing Lofotan's insolent pose, he made an unpleasant suggestion to the majordomo. For once the usually dour Lofotan laughed.

"How about you? Are you ready to go, scribe?" he asked.

Treskan, very bleary, had only the clothes on his back, and said so.

"Go to the hall upstairs and wait upon our lord."

Tired and stiff from her sojourn atop the kitchen counter, Mathi followed the scribe. They found Balif in the entry hall, dressed almost exactly like Lofotan. His armor was a little finer, but otherwise his kit was the same. Despite all the digging in crates and juggling of armaments, the pile of equipment Balif and his party were taking was very small—two panniers per elf, an easy load for a sturdy packhorse.

"Greetings, my lord," Treskan said. "What do you require?"

"I require you to spell correctly and tell the truth," he replied. When the scribe reacted with a blink and a stare, Balif hoisted a pair of loaded panniers onto his shoulder.

"Take these out and put them on the chestnut mare," he said. "You do know about horses?"

He shifted the bags to Treskan, who grunted an affirmative. Knees bowed under the weight, the scribe shuffled to the monumental front doors. Only the postern was ajar, but he couldn't fit through it with the panniers. Grasping the gigantic gilded latch, Treskan hauled the sixteen-foot-high bronze door open.

"Face the honor!"

The salute, shouted just a yard from Treskan, caused him to flinch and lose his burden. The loaded panniers crashed to the ground.

In the plaza before Balif's mansion, six companies of warriors were drawn up in block formation. At the command, everyone raised his sword or spear to his face in salute. When they realized they were honoring the general's clumsy scribe, the weapons fell with a musical clatter.

Strong hands boosted Treskan to his feet. Farolenu and another officer he didn't know stood him on his feet.

Mathi peeked out the door. "Great E'li, what's all this?"

"We're here to escort the general," said Farolenu. It sounded reasonable when he said it, but Mathi smelled the truth. Six companies of infantry would discourage the sort of popular parade that followed Balif to the Tower of the Stars.

Single warriors held the reins of five riding horses and five pack animals. With the help of some soldiers, Treskan got the panniers on the chestnut mare.

Lofotan emerged from the house. More careful, Farolenu waited until he saw who was coming before he ordered another salute. The veteran clasped hands with Farolenu.

Lofotan looked up at the sky. "A good day for travel."

"The Speaker so ordered it," Farolenu replied. "No rain to spoil the general's departure." From her humble place at the door, Mathi could not tell if they were jesting or not.

Complaining loudly, Artyrith appeared. No trews or breastplates for him. He wore a very stylish city-cut kilt and sleeveless tunic, topped by a bright scarlet cloak draped over one shoulder and pinned under the opposite arm.

Standing on the steps with the imposing facade of Balif's villa behind him, he looked more like the lord of the manor than his master.

Seeing the array of soldiery drawn up before him, Artyrith uttered a single pithy oath. The officers, Lofotan included, regarded him with supreme distaste.

Hatless, while Treskan, Lofotan, and Balif wore flat-topped, wide-brimmed travelers' hats, Artyrith strode down the steps to the line of horses. He chose the best one, a dappled gray, and was about to mount him when Lofotan caught him by the elbow.

"Not that one. That is the general's."

The tall roan was the majordomo's. That left the three ponies for the cook, the scribe, and the girl. Sniffing at the indignity of having to ride a short-legged nag, Artyrith chose the paint and swung nimbly into the saddle. Treskan stood by the dusty brown pony without complaint. He was an unsteady rider at best. At least with a beast such as that he didn't have so far to fall.

Lofotan beckoned Mathi to take the last pony. She came on warily. Three paces away, the horses began to shift and snort. The pony left for Mathi rolled its eyes as she drew near.

"I warned my lord that animals do not like me," Mathi said, backing away.

"Nonsense," said Lofotan, dismounting. "The silly beast is just skittish."

The silly beast was indeed skittish, and no amount of coaxing or handling by the expert Lofotan would calm it down. It began to look as though Mathi would be left behind or worse, have to walk.

Balif emerged, tying on his flat hat. Farolenu barked the command, and six hundred warriors snapped to attention, clacking their bronze greaves together as they stood straight as spears. The general of all the Speaker's armies regarded his old comrades with a critical eye.

Farolenu stepped forward. "My lord! I wish I was going with you!"

"No, you don't. It's going to be terribly dull. Riding, camping, sleeping in the cold and the rain—no adventures, I fear."

Farolenu was unconvinced. He knew his general too well. Where Balif went, things happened.

"I don't understand why a suitable escort was not ordered," Farolenu said. "The commander of all the Speaker's armies deserves more company than one old soldier, an effete cook, a clumsy wordsmith, and a bumpkin."

The cook retorted, "Your voice carries exceedingly well, my lord!"

"And your ears are keen," Balif replied. "Fear not, my friend. I have the companions I deserve and wish."

He glanced at the sky. The summer sun was well up. Widely spaced, bright white clouds drifted along. There was perfume in the air—the scent of all the flowers in the neighboring gardens.

"Time to go."

"There is a problem, my lord," said Lofotan. Balif queried him with a look. His majordomo explained how the pony left for Mathi to ride would not allow her on its back.

"So?" Balif patted the sturdy animal's neck. He ducked under its low neck, running a practiced hand over the animal's dusty hide. "Seems like a sound enough creature. Come here, girl."

Mathi, loitering at a discreet distance, approached slowly. The ponies—not just hers—began to quiver and shuffle their hooves.

Balif removed his wide-brimmed hat and used it to cover the pony's eyes. With a nod, he let Mathi know she should try to mount again. Holding the saddle pommel in both hands, she clambered rather clumsily onto the animal's back. The pony pranced a little forward and back but did not buck.

"We need blinders; that's all. Something in our girl's complexion disturbs the beast."

Lofotan went inside the villa and returned a short while later with a set of blinders, gray from long disuse. They were fitted to the pony's head. Balif tied his hat on once more and gave Mathi her pony's reins.

"Be kind," he said. "Often we don't know who we are carrying."

His remark puzzled everyone, but at last the party was ready. Lofotan held Balif's horse while he mounted. He wrapped the reins around his left hand and wheeled the animal around. Trotting back, he watched as Farolenu's soldiers lashed the baggage panniers in place, looped the packhorses' reins together, and gave them to the last rider in line, Mathi.

"Mind the reins," Balif said. "We'll be on short rations for sure if you lose those horses." To her own surprise, the girl found herself promising to guard the animals' leads with her life. What was it about the general that inspired such compliance? Mathi felt she would do anything the general asked. It was an unfamiliar and uncomfortable feeling, the urge to obey.

Without fanfare, Balif assumed the lead of his little party. He signaled his people to follow him and set out down the avenue at a slow trot. Lofotan was on his right, and Artyrith trailed straight behind. Treskan came next, his writing board and leather cylinders of parchment banging against his legs. Mathi urged her animal forward, but the pony was reluctant. The gap between her and the scribe widened. Farolenu circled back, asking what the problem was.

"The blighted beast won't go!"

"Really?" Farolenu smacked the horse's rump, sending it lurching after the others. Jerked into motion, the packhorses followed with their ears laid back and teeth bared.

Farolenu barked, "Companies! By the order, quick march!"

One by one the infantry broke formation and marched after the balky pack animals. When the last one left the square, silence fell over the great house of Balif.

Balif reached the main eastbound thoroughfare in Silvanost, called the White Strand. It ran straight as an arrow to the E'li Gate in the ring of fortifications surrounding the city. Along the way the streets were strangely empty. Bands of warriors in fours and sixes stood on every corner, bracing to attention as the general went by, but no ordinary Silvanesti could be seen. Silvanos was not having a repeat of the previous day's triumphal parade.

There was one vehicle drawn up at the edge of the White Strand. It was a closed coach, finely made but devoid of any decoration, talisman, or heraldry. The gleaming pearl-gray coach was pulled by four horses of the same hue, perfectly matched. No one sat on the driver's box. As Balif rode out onto the broad avenue, he passed the coach. Taking the brim in his hand, he doffed his hat to the coach. Curtains drawn across the windows never stirred.

Seeing the exchange, Mathi urged her balky mount to go faster. Drawing abreast of Artyrith, she said, "What was that about? Who do you think was in that coach?"

Looking straight ahead, the cook replied, "What coach?"

Lofotan also ignored the vehicle. Treskan frankly stared at it until the marching ranks of Farolenu's elves entered the street. Once Balif was far down the way, a liveried driver appeared from behind the conveyance. He climbed onto the box, cracked his whip, and drove the mysterious coach away.

Then it struck her: Amaranthe. She had come to say good-bye after all.

Nothing else of note happened along the way to the E'li Gate. The massive panels were standing open. Pennants of the House of Silvanos whipped from the towers above the gate.

Balif rode through, stopped, and turned his horse around. Lofotan and Artyrith did the same, keeping the same positions behind their leader. With the pack animals between them, Treskan and Mathi couldn't manage such a tidy maneuver. They settled for clearing out of the way, pushing the pack train to the ditch on the north side of the road.

Farolenu halted his troops inside the gate. Alone he walked through to the general. He gave his hand. "My lord, I want you to know I have written to the outposts at Free Winds, Greenfield, and Tanjanost, advising them of your coming. They will render any assistance you need."

"This was not Silvanos's order, was it?" Balif asked. He gripped his old comrade's hand firmly.

Farolenu said nothing. When Balif released his hand, the one-time metalsmith saluted as old soldiers do, placing his palm over his heart. "The gods bless you, Balif of the Plains."

"Thank you, my friend. Somehow I doubt they will."

He left the puzzled Farolenu and rode away, spurring his horse to a canter. The others hurried after him. Ahead lay the ferry station and the broad Thon-Thalas. The ferry crew was standing by. Their craft was a broad, flat-bottomed barge with three steering boards and a pole mast supporting a white lateen sail. There was much talk in the city of training giant turtles to tow barges back and forth across the Thon-Thalas, but so far that had not been done.

Balif's party boarded the empty ferry. Normally that time of day would find a sizable crowd filing aboard, but there was no one else in the station. Lofotan queried the crew about it. Nervously, they avowed no knowledge, but it was plain the Speaker wanted Balif's departure made as quiet as possible.

The horses were secured, and the baggage stowed. Sitting on the rows of benches in the bluff bow, Mathi watched with interest as the sailors cast off. The sail went up, and the steering oars were turned by practiced hands. Mathi asked why there were three oars instead of just one.

"The Thalas is wide and deep," Lofotan explained. "Though the surface is placid, there is a terrific undertow from the city all the way down to the sea. It takes more than one rudder to steady a craft on this river."

Balif removed his hat and let the river wind tussle his pale hair. "In the Dream Days, the people who dwelt by the river called it 'Thon-Flaxis,' which means Drowning River in the old tongue." He ran his fingers through his hair. "It was common for the river tribes to use the river as a way of solving disputes."

Sensing a story, Treskan unlimbered his writing equipment. Artyrith, feet propped up on the bench in front of him, idly asked how it was done.

"Two elves with a conflict or an affair of honor could ask for a trial by water. Each would enter the Thon-Thalas from the opposite bank and swim to the other side. If one drowned, the survivor was judged to have won his case. If they both drowned, the subject of their dispute was taken away from both clans and given to a disinterested party."

"And if both survived?" Mathi wondered.

"There is no record of that ever happening," said Balif.

"Our ancestors must have been savages to employ such practices." Artyrith sniffed.

Balif replaced his hat. With great dignity, he withdrew to the stern of the barge, where he gazed at the city slowly diminishing in the distance.

"Fool," said Lofotan in a low voice. "Don't you ever govern your tongue?"

"What have I said?" asked the cook innocently.

"Did you not know our lord offered to swim the Thon-Thalas as proof of his innocence in the recent scandal? The Speaker forbade it, but our lord was sincere. He would have undergone the ordeal had the Speaker agreed."

Shamed, Artyrith looked away and said nothing. Mathi made her way aft to where the general stood, one foot propped on the stern post.

"My lord, don't be so troubled. I'm sure our mission will succeed," she ventured.

"Perhaps it will. Stranger things have happened."

He continued to watch the city shrink to the horizon. Mathi tried to say something encouraging. How dangerous could their mission be? They weren't expected to fight off an invasion with just five elves, merely find out what was going on.

"Our mission means nothing," Balif said. "Any subaltern with half a mind could do it. What troubles me is quite different."

Grateful for the opening, Mathi asked what the general had on his mind.

"I cannot escape the feeling this is the last time I shall see Silvanost," he replied somberly. "And all who dwell here."

# Chapter 6

## *Eyes*

Once he set foot on the eastern shore, Balif was a different elf. All his melancholy contemplation vanished. He supervised the offloading of their horses and gear with crisp efficiency, tipped the ferry crew with gold for their labors, and bade them farewell. When the barge was out of earshot, Balif addressed his companions.

"From this point on, we are not the Speaker's eyes and ears, seeking foreign invaders in our land. Do you understand? We are travelers, nothing more. Our outward goal is to find sites for new villages for settlers from the west. Silvanost and the heartland of the realm are overcrowded. Our people need space and land. Is that clear?" Everyone agreed it was.

"I am the party's surveyor. I am not a general. Anyone who addresses me as such will know my displeasure."

All eyes went to Artyrith. "What?" he demanded. "Am I so loose-lipped?"

Balif cleared his throat and went on. "Lofotan is our engineer. You're chiefly interested in water sources, quarry sites, and places that need bridging. Artyrith will be what he is, our cook. Treskan is my secretary. As we travel, he will create a record of our exploration that will pass the closest inspection—a very long, very dull catalog of watersheds, fields, and forests. I want anyone who reads it to fall asleep after half a page, utterly convinced by your record's tiresome authenticity." Treskan assured him that he could compile a log guaranteed to numb an ogre.

"In this masquerade, what role do I play?" asked Mathi.

Balif gave her a strange, probing look. "You could be my wife," he said. At the girl's consternation, he smiled and added, "But it would be more believable if you were my daughter."

"How shall we call you, if not 'my lord Balif'?" Lofotan asked.

"I shall go by the name the foresters gave me, Camaxilas."

Mathi thought it all made sense, though it seemed a little elaborate, considering that they were still deep within the Speaker's realm. Farther east, in the uncharted forests and meadows beyond the Thon-Tanjan, Balif's precautions would be wise, but why enact them so early?

Artyrith thought the same way and had the impertinence to ask why.

"I want our pose ingrained in all of us by the time we reach the Tanjan," Balif said. "Treskan's catalog must already be detailed when we get there. Also"—he gestured over his shoulder with a sweep of one hand—"do not be fooled by where we are or what we are close to. This land is not the Speaker's palace garden. There are many who do not relish his rule and do not love the Silvanesti in any case."

That being so, why pretend to be the advance guard of a wave of settlement? Surely that would cause much resentment where they were going, Artyrith objected.

Lofotan said, "Sometimes a wise commander gives his enemy what he expects, just so he is free to do what he truly wants—the unexpected." Mathi understood. If they tried to appear totally harmless, that would incite more suspicion than if they were merely mercenary intruders.

Everyone mounted. Treskan took the reins of the packhorses to relieve Mathi for a while. Balif took out a small, leather-covered case. He snapped open the lid and held it skyward, turning in his saddle to catch the sun.

"What's that?" asked the city-bred Artyrith.

"A sunstone," Lofotan answered. A naturally occurring jewel, sunstone was used to show direction. By aiming the largest flat facet at the sun, light was scattered through the prismatic interior of the stone. A bright blue line at right angles to the sunlight indicated north.

Balif pointed to his right. "That's our line of march, north by east." He tucked the sunstone away and spurred his mount. The others hastened to keep up with him.

Through the next day, they worked hard to overcome lifelong etiquette and not constantly refer to their leader as "my lord." Lofotan had the hardest time. He'd been with Balif for a century of campaigns. Calling Balif "my lord" was as natural to the old soldier as breathing. Artyrith had a much easier time. Breezy manners came easily to him, as he regarded Balif more as an equal anyway. Treskan simplified his problems by saying as little as possible. Mathi practiced calling Balif "Father." The title took hold in a curiously natural way.

The eastern shore of the Thalas was lightly forested. For centuries the local elves had cultivated hardwoods and nut-bearing trees. Since the end of the savannah campaign against the human nomads, fruit trees had been added to the mix. Mathi could not see any pattern to their growth, but Balif assured her the abundant apple, cherry, and plum trees they saw were deliberate additions to the landscape. Elves did not plant trees in orchards, as humans did. Orderly rows of the same kind of tree would have struck an elf as crude and unlovely. The sunny landscape looked as natural as any lowland grove. True, there was little underbrush to clog the roots and impede the growth of the favored trees, but the hand of elf farmers was very hard to distinguish.

"Who owns this land?" Lofotan consciously bit off the usual "my lord."

"This is the ancestral holding of the lords of Hestanthalas," said Balif. The family name meant Hest of the Thalas.

"From here to the bay in the south is all theirs, granted to the family by the second Sinthal-Elish." Even Artyrith was impressed. Such a large holding meant great wealth, power, and influence. Hestanthalas was an important name in Silvanost. Twice a lord of Hest had stood by the Speaker as his high councilor.

Treskan made notes as he rode. It wasn't easy, writing while on the back of a swaying pony, but he had to take advantage of Balif's order to compile a gazetteer of the region. The general wanted it as a cover for their mission, but a detailed description of the region would be invaluable to the masters of Silvanost. Little was truly known of the territory in the elves' heartland. Maps trying to depict the eastern provinces of Silvanesti had frequent blank spots. Only the largest features—rivers, forests, mountains—were well marked. Treskan had a perfect opportunity to supplement the nation's meager knowledge and earn points with Balif as well.

They didn't stop for many miles. Noon came and went, and Balif rode on. He passed a flask of water back and forth with Lofotan, talking quietly about the terrain, the weather, and their previous journeys through the region. Artyrith, Treskan, and Mathi had to make do. The cook broke out food and drink, a sweet nectar that he said was from the Thalas delta. They ate in the saddle. Artyrith grumbled the whole time. While he talked, Mathi half listened with a vacant but sympathetic smile. The cook scarcely noticed.

The longer they rode, the more the trees thinned and eventually disappeared. They topped a low knoll, and Balif reined up. Spread out below was a wide, rolling plain. Unlike the largely flat savannah of the distant west, the eastern plain was hilly, cut by small streams and dry ravines. Thick, dark green grass as high as the horses' bellies waved in the wind. Ahead of them there wasn't a tree in sight. Hawks wheeled overhead, screeching. Everyone looked skyward, attracted by the noise—everyone but Balif.

"This is no elf's land," he announced. "Whatever the Great Speaker thinks, his power ends with the forest. From here on we shall have to be on our guard."

"What about the outpost at Free Winds?" Lofotan asked. It was about six hours' ride farther east. Should they make for it?

Balif nodded. "Free Winds it shall be." He steered his horse down the shallow slope.

Free Winds wasn't a town. It was a military post, a Silvanesti island in an ocean of grass. Besides a garrison of elves, there were traders, tax collectors, and other trappings of civilization, but the rule of the Speaker's law ended outside the outpost's stone walls.

They rode on. Over the course of the long, summer day the riders strung out according to their ability and the strength of their mounts. Balif forged ahead with Lofotan close at hand. Artyrith, though an accomplished rider about town, wasn't used to so much time in the saddle. He labored to stay within sight of the leaders, but it was poor Treskan and Mathi who really struggled to keep pace. The pack train didn't hamper them as much as did their lack of riding skill. By late afternoon Balif and Lofotan were over the horizon, and Artyrith was just a dot in the landscape far ahead.

Treskan tried to get his balky pony go to faster. He was afraid of being left behind, and said so repeatedly. Mathi feared he would start weeping if they didn't catch up with the others. Thumping the pony's ribs with her heels and shaking the reins to urge the beast forward, Mathi gradually became aware of the profound silence around them. Stretching high in the simple padded saddle, she saw Artyrith meandering through the grass more than a mile away. They were crossing the bottom of a large, bowl-shaped valley, ringed by low hills. The wind had ceased, and the ever-present hawks were no longer circling overhead. Mathi's hand went slack on the reins. Her pony slowed then stopped. He fell to cropping the lush grass surrounding them. So did the packhorses. Feeling the drag on their reins brought Treskan to a stop too.

A dull red disk hung close to the horizon. Mathi had the sun at her back, but she shaded his eyes to better see the unexpected object. It was Lunitari, the red moon, uncharacteristically rising before sunset.

She felt a chill pass over her, as if the sun had been suddenly cut off by a passing cloud. The horses sensed it too. One by one they raised their heads and looked at the red moon.

A low rumble rolled over the valley. The sky was dotted with a few fluffy, white clouds, but no thunderheads were present. The packhorses began to whinny and shake their heads. Mathi didn't pay much attention to their distress until it infected her mount. Treskan's pony pranced in a tight circle, snorting loudly.

"Whoa, whoa," he said soothingly. What had them spooked?

Mathi sensed it first. Something was lancing through the high grass about a hundred yards behind them. On all fours, it was moving fast. It wasn't visible above the grass. She called out to Treskan, alerting him to the danger.

He yelped in alarm. The eastern lands were home to many beasts seldom seen in the well-hunted west: wolves, panthers, great plains bears. Treskan groped for his sword. He didn't know how to use it, but having it in hand was better than nothing. Mathi had her sword too, thrust upon her by Lofotan, though she had never used such a weapon in her life.

Her pony reared, despite its blinders. Apparently the horses had gotten wind of the intruder. Mathi was not prepared to keep her seat. She fell off, hitting the thick mat of grass not too hard. Freed of its clumsy rider, the pony trotted away, whinnying and shaking its blunt head.

Mathi got up, throwing off her long riding cloak. Her sword was conveniently sticking point-first in the sod nearby. She tugged it free. Where was the menace?

"Over there!" Treskan called, pointing with his blade. Behind her!

The packhorses, tied together, were nearly mad with fear. They pulled and snatched at the rawhide lines binding them to each other. Curiously, the unseen creature had circled around the easy prey and was creeping through the grass toward Mathi. Then it stopped moving and growled. Low and throaty, its malign intent was unmistakable. Had it said, "I am going to kill you," in well-inflected Elvish, Mathi could have not felt more threatened.

Sweat stung her eyes. Lashing out with the sword, she slashed out a circle in the grass to give herself a little better view. It was a desperate gesture. She was not a warrior. Neither was Treskan, who had lost his sword trying to keep his seat on his pony. Where were Balif and the others?

She heard the guttural growl again, much closer. By chance she'd been facing Lunitari floating above the horizon. Hearing the beast, Mathi whirled back to front and saw the sanguinary light of the red moon in the thing's eyes. They were large, dark eyes, set in a face covered with dappled brown and gray fur. Hands shaking, Mathi lowered her blade.

"Stay," she said as calmly as she could. "I am not an enemy!"

In answer the thing leaped headlong from a low crouch. Mathi backed away, shut her eyes, and held out both hands to ward off the creature's lunge. She backed away until she tripped in the grass and fell backward. The beast let out a full-fledged roar. Even through tightly clenched eyelids, Mathi sensed a dark mass passing over her. She tensed for the tear of fangs and the rake of talons—

—and received instead a soft but weighty blow on the chest. She gasped, opened her eyes, and saw the beast was lying full length atop her. It was moving but feebly. She felt its last hot breath against his face.

Several pairs of legs came swishing through the grass. Strong with terror, Mathi heaved the body off. When she sat up, she saw three long arrows lodged in its ribs.

Balif, Lofotan, and Artyrith were walking up slowly. Treskan held their horses' reins some yards away. The three elves approached in a wide arc with bows drawn. Dazed, Mathi didn't even remember seeing bows among the baggage.

"Are you hurt, girl?" asked Lofotan. Mathi managed to shake her head no. She felt a burning sensation on her right cheek. Absently wiping the spot, she noticed blood on her fingers. She didn't know if it was hers or the creature's.

Artyrith reached the body first. Bow drawn, he nudged it hard with his toe. It didn't move, but he planted another arrow in its neck, muttering an obscenity under his breath.

Balif arrived. He put his nocked arrow back in his quiver and lowered the bow. He knelt on one knee beside the corpse. "Roll it over," he told Artyrith.

The cook levered the body over with his bow stave. When he beheld its face, the worldly Silvanesti backpedalled. Mathi's breath caught in her throat. She gasped.

"What *is* it?" said Artyrith.

"One of Vedvedsica's children," said Balif. Hearing the mage's name brought everyone's eyes to the general. He looked down at what had so startled Artyrith.

It was like no creature he had ever seen. The beast-elf who broke into Balif's villa his first night there had been elflike but covered in brutish hair. The creature before them was different. In general form it resembled a tawny panther, though leaner and with considerably longer limbs. Covered in light brown fur, it was tailless. It was also clearly female. White fangs protruded from its bifurcated upper lip. Strange as it was, it could have passed for an unhealthy breed of plains cat except for its face. It had a woman elf's face, lightly furred, with ears on the sides of its head, a small nose, and elflike eyes. Open and staring, they were round like any elf's, with brown irises.

Balif drew his sword and used it to lift the dead creature's paws. It had fingers, five per limb, tipped with hard, yellow claws.

"What is it?" Treskan said, echoing Artyrith. His curiosity had overcome his fear, and he had crept forward to see what had been slain.

"An animal, magically altered to resemble an elf," Balif said. He rose, still gazing at the creature. "One of Vedvedsica's less successful efforts, I would say."

That was the mage's crime—whispered about, here and there, and scrupulously suppressed by every Silvanesti official and sage since. Vedvedsica had used his considerable magical skills trying to create elves out of common animals. But why create such abominations?

"Do you know this one?" Lofotan asked solemnly.

"She was called Urnya. She was a highland lynx at birth."

Tears streamed down Mathi's face, though not for the reason the elves understood.

"Why was it stalking us?" asked Treskan, agog.

"Not us . . . me." Balif closed the staring eyes. "Some of Vedvedsica's creations escaped the Speaker's net. They have all the cunning of their motherkind, after all, and each has vowed vengeance on me."

"Why you, sir? Why not a curse upon the Speaker, who ordered their destruction?"

"Great Silvanos dwells within a fortress, guarded night and

day. I have only my wits and a few good comrades with me, and I did turn Vedvedsica over to the Speaker's justice."

The truth dawned on Treskan. That's why Balif lived in such isolation. He had dispensed with servants and isolated himself from his kin to spare their becoming targets of the vengeful beast-folk.

"They hunted me in Silvanost," Balif went on. "I thought we could outdistance them and reach Free Winds first." He sheathed his sword. "Urnya always was fleet."

Balif offered Mathi a hand. Shaking, the girl took it.

"Are you all right?" he asked gently. "Did the beast hurt you?"

She shrugged off his hand. "It's nothing."

He went to the packhorses, still tied together and trembling even though the threat was dead. They shivered and flecks of foam covered them as though they'd run ten miles. Balif hunted around and returned with two short-handled spades.

"Time to bury her," he said. "Poor, unnatural thing, she at least deserves not to feed the crows."

Lofotan took one spade. Mathi stepped forward and tried to take Balif's tool. It wasn't right that a great lord should bend his back digging a grave, she said.

Balif would not relinquish the spade. "I've buried many a comrade," he said. "No one is too good to render this service to the dead."

Artyrith, Treskan, and Mathi stood back as the two warriors dug a short, deep hole. They put the creature in and replaced the dirt and sod so carefully that it was very hard to tell where the grave was. Treskan remarked that no one would ever find the body.

"Oh, they already know she's dead." Balif's handsome visage was streaked with sweat and grime. Artyrith offered him his flask of nectar. The cook wondered how anyone could know Urnya had been killed.

"They are beasts inside, even when they resembled us on the outside," Balif said after downing a long swallow of nectar. "They can smell her blood on the wind. Ours too. When she doesn't return with my blood on her claws, they will know why."

Since leaving the woodland, Balif had known they were being followed. He purposely had rode far ahead to lure any pursuer into attacking the straggling pack animals. Circling back with Lofotan and Artyrith, they arrived in time to stop Urnya's attack.

Sunset was fast at hand. "Come," said Balif. "We'll stay together this time. Treskan, you lead the way."

Bows still strung, the three Silvanesti rode in a line abreast behind the pack train. Treskan preceded them on foot for a mile or two until they spied Mathi's wayward pony grazing at the base of a hill. Remounted, they were able to set a better pace.

Dusk was unusually quiet. Crickets and peepers were still, and the whippoorwill did not sing its melancholy song. It was nerves of course, but Mathi felt a hundred eyes upon her as she guided her pony across a shallow stream. Running water would obscure their scent from the sharpest nose.

She heard a sharp call from behind. Twisting around, she saw Artyrith sit up high in the saddle, take aim, and loose an arrow into the gathering darkness. Balif asked what he saw.

"A pair of eyes, watching up from that thicket!"

A stand of high grass filled the base of a substantial hill north of them. Mathi looked but saw only lengthening shadows.

"Never mind," Balif ordered. "Keep going. Free Winds isn't far."

"But what about the eyes?" demanded the cook.

Lofotan said, "You put an arrow between them, didn't you?" Unwilling to deny his accuracy, Artyrith said he did.

"Then we have nothing to worry about, do we?"

When the hills flattened out, they found themselves on a plain, higher and drier than the grasslands they'd crossed. Half an hour's ride more, and they beheld a lone, steep-sided hill, rising up from the flat terrain. Twenty or so feet high, it was the only promontory around. Centered atop the hill was a curved stone wall, the outer defenses of Free Winds.

Artyrith gave a cheer. Balif rebuked him in a mild but definite way. The party rode faster. It was truly night. Every chirp, every chuckle by a night-dwelling animal made them flinch. None of them had any desire to meet another one of Vedvedsica's children that night . . . or ever. The sooner they were safe behind stone walls, the better.

There was a wide, well-used track up the hillside. Mathi had to lean far forward to keep her seat as they climbed. The packhorses stumbled but kept going. At the top of the hill there was a narrow strip of level ground six feet wide, before the wall. To Mathi's surprise, the trail ended against a blind expanse of stone.

Balif and the others arrived. Their horses were panting with fatigue. Finding the girl motionless before a solid wall, Balif asked what she was waiting for.

"There's no gate!" she said, perplexed.

Artyrith said, "I shall ride around."

Picking his way carefully in the dark, the cook disappeared off to the right. After a time, he reappeared on the waiting party's left. It was his turn to look puzzled. "There isn't a gate," he declared.

Balif was amused. Cupping a hand to his mouth, he called out in a clear, strong voice, "Hello! Soldiers of the garrison, hello!"

A torch poked up, held by an unseen hand. "Who goes there?"

"A surveying party out of Silvanost! We need shelter for the night!"

More torches joined the first. "How many in your party?"

"Five, with ten horses!"

"Stand fast," called down the voice. "We'll lower the crane!"

Squeaking and creaking, a contraption of wood and rope rose above the battlement. As they watched, it swung out over the wall. It looked like a platform of planks with a waist-high railing. It was lowered by a single stout rope from a derrick leaning over the wall.

The platform landed with a thump. All four stepped up, colliding at the single entry through the rail.

"You go," Lofotan said, deferring to Balif. The general got on. Artyrith and Lofotan collided, trying to enter next.

"We'd better not go together," Balif said to his old comrade. "Lest we are both lost at the same time."

"How could you get lost?" wondered Artyrith. Lofotan dryly observed that the rope could break halfway up the wall.

The cook got on, and their respective horses were led on next. When Balif shouted they were ready, the platform jerked skyward. It swung back. Balif and Artyrith vanished behind the wall.

Standing in the dark with Lofotan and the scribe, Mathi had a distinct sense of foreboding. She mentioned her unease. Lofotan affected calm.

"Trust the general. He's no fool. I've never known him to unwittingly thrust his head into danger."

Even so, the crane did not return for a long time. Weary, Mathi knelt in the dust. The horses snorted and nudged her, impatient for water and rest. Then without warning, the platform swung noisily over the battlement and descended for them.

Lofotan put Mathi and the packhorses on. Groaning and creaking, the apparatus hoisted them aloft. She gripped the rail tightly. Fortunately it was dark, and she couldn't see the ground reeling beneath her. The horses huddled together as quiet as could be. When the platform reached its zenith, the boom pivoted, swinging the scribe and horses in a breathtaking arc. Below, torches burned, lighting a courtyard inside the fortress. Down came the platform. As she neared the ground, Mathi saw that the platform was operated by a gang of human prisoners in tattered rags and dirty breechcloths. They were chained by ankle and wrist with heavy, bronze fetters. Five elves armed with spears stood by them, while an elf in artisan's robes gave orders to operate the machine. But where were Balif and Artyrith?

A well-dressed elf standing between two warriors greeted Mathi. "I am Dolanath Arkesian, governor of Free Winds." Mathi gave her name and described herself as the daughter of the surveyor Camaxilas.

"Your father is within, enjoying our hospitality," Dolanath said smoothly. He indicated an open, lit doorway in the central keep. "Go and refresh yourself."

Warily Mathi complied. She glanced back and saw their packhorses being led off to a stable built against the outside wall. The crane squeaked into life a third time to fetch Lofotan, Treskan, and the last of the horses.

Unescorted, Mathi wandered inside. It was pleasantly cool inside the thick, stone walls. She smelled something savory and, going straight down the hall, came upon a dining room with a set table. Several chairs were askew, but the plates had been cleared away. There was no sign of Balif or the lordly cook.

She picked up a plate. It was made of that parchment-thin stuff the city elves called "porcelain," shiny as glass and hard as metal. No one made porcelain like the Silvanesti. Silver urns simmered on a sideboard with fat candles beneath them. Mathi lifted the lids one by one. Fine fare: airy dumplings, clear soup, edible leaves flash-fried so quickly they didn't lose any color but were as light and crisp as the finest wafers. Crystal ewers of nectar and fruit essence stood on a separate table, chilled in wet basalt buckets. All very hospitable, but something was not right by a mile. Balif would not absent himself before all in his party were inside.

Carrying a plate and a fine silver goblet, Mathi drifted to the table and sat down. No sooner had she done so than two elves appeared on either side. A wooden rod was jammed between her teeth. It tingled strangely and Mathi found that she couldn't spit it out. Nor could she lift her arms from the chair or stand up. She was pinned down by some unseen force.

The elves picked her up, chair and all, and hustled her through a curtained opening. In moments she was dumped rather roughly in a small, plain room. The elves went out. The ominous sound of a bolt being thrown made it chillingly clear Mathi was a prisoner.

# Chapter 7

## *Images*

The tingling sensation in Mathi's gag slowly dissipated. When the tingling vanished, she spit out the rod and leaped to her feet. Trying the door proved futile. She was solidly bolted in. But why? No one in Free Winds even knew who they were—or did they? Was it some plot of the Speaker's to get rid of Balif? Or was the abduction aimed solely at her? That, she decided, could not be. She was unknown to everyone—not above suspicion but well below it.

Unused to politics or court intrigue, she tried to untangle the situation. Silvanos was jealous of Balif, going back to the fact that Balif was once favored by many elves to be Speaker. Balif was Amaranthe's lover, which would infuriate the highly moralistic Silvanos if he knew. Then there was the Vedvedsica affair. Though Balif had cooperated with the prosecution of his former counselor, Speaker Silvanos might want to hush up the blasphemous doings of the rogue magician by silencing all those who knew him, Balif included. Balanced against all those negatives was Balif's undeniable service to the crown, defeating the Speaker's foreign enemies. So which weighed more in Silvanos's estimation? Mathi could not decide.

Hours passed. Whenever Mathi detected footsteps in the corridor, she pressed an ear to the door and listened. She heard nothing but strangers passing in silence. As it grew late, her weariness from their long ride began to tell. There was no bed in the room—in the cell—so Mathi found a spot opposite the door, lay down, and with some effort, dropped off to sleep. A luminar embedded in the high ceiling dimmed and went out.

It was black as pitch when Mathi heard a noise. It sounded like the scrape of wood on stone. Her eyes slowly opened, but there was nothing to see except darkness. Straining, she heard very faint movement within the room.

Fearing assassins, Mathi sat up and called out, "Who is it? Who goes there?" No one replied, so she repeated the demand more forcefully.

"Be quiet," said a small voice. "You'll wake the whole castle."

"Who are you?"

"Just a visitor passing through. What did they lock you up for?"

"I've done nothing," Mathi said urgently. "I only arrived this evening. My reception was cordial at first, but then they threw me in this dungeon!"

"Not very friendly of them."

The voice sounded like a child's, but the choice of words and the irony of the tone suggested an older person.

Feeling less threatened, Mathi sat up and said, "Do you have a light?"

"There's one of those elf shards up here. How do they work?"

Mathi explained you had to know the proper word to excite them.

Her unseen visitor chortled merrily. "Excite, huh? What if I tickle it? Will it work then?"

Mathi spoke the word she knew to activate luminars. Some owners had secret words to start their lights, but when she spoke the common word, the foot-long crystal began to glow, dark red at first. As it grew stronger, the color became pinkish.

The girl looked around for her unseen companion. She saw no one. The cell door was still shut and locked. Who had she been talking to?

"Up here."

She looked up, spotting her visitor at once. Clinging to the wood-beamed ceiling was a small person about two-thirds Mathi's height. He was dressed in dark blue woolens and had long, auburn hair tied back in a single thick hank. The little fellow's feet were bare.

"You're the least nervous elf I ever met," he declared.

"I should have looked up first," Mathi said.

"Why?"

"I know that trick," she said, remembering her escape from Balif. "Few people look skyward when there's trouble."

"I'm not trouble. I'm Rufe."

She looked puzzled. He let go with his feet and swung down. Letting go with his hands, he alighted easily right in front of the young elf woman.

"Name's Rufe. You can call me Rufe."

Face-to-face, Mathi tried to place her odd visitor. He was apparently male with a beaky nose; large, pointed ears; and very big eyes. He was definitely the oddest specimen of elf she had ever seen.

"My name is Mathani," she said. "How did you get in here?"

"I squeezed under the door."

The massive door was so close to the floor that it scraped when it opened. Nothing as big as Rufe could possibly pass underneath.

Rufe looked around. "Pretty plain. The others have nicer rooms."

"What others?" Mathi said, seizing on his clue.

"Some folks down the hall. Locked up they are. I suppose

they must like it." Apparently having satisfied his curiosity, Rufe gave a little wave and said, "Bye! I'm off."

"Wait!" Mathi grabbed him by the sleeve. Rufe looked at her hand, shrugged, and twisted out of Mathi's grip so effortlessly that she ended up clutching her own arm instead. Treading lightly, the little fellow was at the door before Mathi could say or do anything about it.

"Get me out of here!" she cried. "I am unjustly imprisoned, as are my companions."

"Really? I thought it was because elves don't take kindly to impostors. Ain't that why you're in here?"

Mathi recoiled. How had Rufe seen through her pose as Balif's daughter? Shaking off her surprise, she appealed to his sense of freedom. "Don't let me languish in a cell," she pleaded.

"There's not much to do in here; that's certain. Unless you've got some imagination, that is." He pointed at the luminar, white and bright. "Can you bring that with us?"

Mathi climbed onto the only piece of furniture in the room, the chair she'd come in on. Stretching up high, she snagged the bright crystal with her fingertips.

"I have it!"

Stepping down, she saw Rufe was gone, but the door of the cell was standing wide open.

Delighted, Mathi ran to the door. The corridor was empty. Where had the little fellow gone to so fast? Remembering how they had met, she checked the ceiling. No, Rufe wasn't there, but she noticed diminutive footprints in the dust, many sets running in both directions. Either Rufe had friends there or else he he'd been roaming the fortress at will for some time.

Mathi tiptoed down the passage, holding the luminar at arm's length. Even though they were capable of blindingly bright light, luminars were never more than faintly warm to the touch. At the next door she found, she knocked softly and whispered, "My lord? Are you there?" Getting no answer, she tried the next. On her third try, she heard an answering hiss from the door she'd just left. It was Artyrith. Mathi slid back the bolt and pushed the door open with her toe.

Two strong hands seized the front of her gown. She was dragged forcefully forward, losing the light rod in the process. Whirled aroundand thrown down, Mathi found a foot planted on her throat before she even had time to protest.

A face bent low over. "It is the girl. Let her up."

Artyrith stood back. Treskan helped Mathi stand.

Lofotan said, "My apologies for the rough welcome. Since we were forced in here, we haven't found out who has confined us or why."

Mathi compared her experiences with the others'. Lofotan and Treskan had been taken exactly as she was, at the dining table. The strange gag paralyzed them. The old warrior and the awkward scribe were stripped of weapons and carried to that room (larger than Mathi's cell), where they found Artyrith already a prisoner.

"Where's our lord?" she asked.

Artyrith said they were separated when they were dragged out of the dining hall.

"Of more immediate interest is how did you escape?" said the cook.

Mathi described Rufe in some detail as she had never encountered such a being before.

"Sounds like the race said to be invading the eastern province," Lofotan remarked. He picked up the dropped luminar, ruby red and failing. "It's cracked." He hefted it like a club. "We must find our lord at once. He may be in worse danger than the rest of us."

They pulled apart the chairs and divided the sturdy wooden legs among themselves. Hardly fine weapons but under the circumstances they would have to do.

Lofotan led the way, club in one hand and the dying

luminar in the other. The passage outside ran straight another twenty yards then ended on a sharp left turn. They tried all the doors along the way but found no one.

"This will take all night!" Artyrith fumed. He slipped ahead of the cautious soldier and boldly grasped the latch of the next door. He flung it open, calling out, "My lord, are you here?"

Balif wasn't in the room. But eight elf warriors were. They had stumbled into a guard room.

"Oh, E'li!" gasped Lofotan.

Artyrith uttered a wild yell and launched himself at the nearest soldiers. They scrambled to their feet, groping for arms they weren't carrying. All their swords and pole arms were neatly racked on the back wall. Lofotan propelled Treskan forward to join the fray, while Mathi hung back.

Swinging his club, Artyrith connected twice in two sweeps. Down went an opponent with each blow. Lofotan kicked over a stray chair and threw the dark luminar at his closest foes. Treskan flailed around a bit, beating the air but not hitting any opponents.

By then the whole room was engulfed in a wild melee. Artyrith proved to be a remarkably adroit fighter. He dueled with his length of wood as if it were a sword, besting one warrior after another. Lofotan was as formidable as his age and experience could make him. He wasn't as stylish as the cook, but he made no mistakes. Inept as he was, even Treskan held his own in the chaos, keeping warriors busy until his more martial comrades could deal with them.

Impressed by her companions' skill, Mathi stayed by the door. She was no warrior, and she was certainly not fit to battle eight Silvanesti hand to hand. Lingering in the open door with a chair leg held tight against her chest, she flexed her fingers, nervous but unwilling to join the fray. She did shout warnings when Artyrith or Lofotan were in danger of being outflanked. The Silvanesti soldiers fought bravely, but they seemed reluctant to do the kind of damage Artyrith and Lofotan were willing to inflict. Sensing defeat, one of the warriors decided to get help.

Seeing him sprint for the door, Lofotan barked, "Stop him, girl!"

Not knowing what else to do, Mathi stuck her stave out at knee height. The rushing elf tripped on it and crashed headfirst into the stone wall outside.

When the rest were subdued, Artyrith came to see if the fleeing elf was taken care of. He picked up Mathi's stick—she had dropped it during the collision—and handed it back to her.

"Well done."

Lofotan helped himself to a sword from the wall rack. He tossed one underhand to the cook, who caught it neatly in midair. Treskan's he pressed into the scribe's hand.

"One for you, Mathi," he said next. She shook her head.

"Take one anyway. If either of us loses ours, yours can be our spare."

After inspecting the corridor, Lofotan slipped out. Artyrith followed with a swagger, and Treskan went behind him, nursing a bruised hand. Looking over the devastated room and its prostrate residents, Mathi turned and went through the door after her comrades.

Sword in hand, Lofotan strode the corridor with new authority. He flung open doors defiantly, loudly calling for Balif by his forest name, Camaxilas. He found no one but some startled civilians doing an inventory in a nearly empty storeroom. No one tried to impede them.

The passage ended at some double doors. Lofotan indicated to Treskan, Artyrith, and Mathi that they were to stand on either side of the doors and at his signal, open them simultaneously. When they were in place, Lofotan composed himself, resting his sword against his shoulder.

"Now!"

The doors flew inward with a bang. In they rushed, Lofotan leading with sword leveled.

The room beyond was a large one with a vaulted ceiling. A forest of candelabra brightly burned. Dominating the room was a large ivorywood table. It was set for dinner, but only two were seated: a noble-looking Silvanesti—Dolanath Arkesian, the governor, Mathi recalled—and their missing leader, Balif.

It took all of Lofotan's control not to exclaim, "My lord!" when he saw the general. Artyrith was not so contained. He muttered one of his famous obscenities. Treskan merely gaped.

"What is the meaning of this?" Dolanath said.

"My journey companions," Balif said, rising from his chair. "Come in, please."

"What's the meaning of overcoming us with magic and throwing us in cells?" Artyrith snapped at the governor. "Most inhospitable, I say!"

Dolanath looked to Balif. "Very unfortunate, I agree," said the general. "I was on the point of winning your freedom when you burst in." He could not help but smile. "Seems my companions could not be held, my lord governor."

A rush of footfalls in the corridor announced the belated arrival of the governor's guard. They surrounded Balif's comrades, but Lofotan's scowl and Artyrith's expert sweeps of his blade kept them at a respectful distance.

"Peace, everyone," Balif said. "Weapons are not needed."

Reluctantly they allowed their swords to be taken away, except for Mathi, who gladly pressed hers on the closest soldier. The guards withdrew, closing the doors behind themselves. Dolanath offered the elves places at his table. Warily, Lofotan complied. Treskan went straight to the nectar urn. Artyrith circled the table, sniffing and tasting the proffered fare. He made faces or nodded, depending on what he thought of the dishes. Mostly he grimaced. Mathi sat at the far end of the table, as far from Dolanath as she could be.

"I beg your forgiveness, gentle elves," said the governor, not sounding contrite in the slightest. "But the timing of your visit was unfortunate. We had no advance word of your coming, and you arrived in the midst of a siege."

"Siege?" said Lofotan. "We're not at war. I saw no army outside."

"Nevertheless." Dolanath sat down. "We are besieged and for some weeks now."

The enemy was not an army or a mob of uncouth human savages. They were a seldom-seen horde of diminutive people, who had the uncanny ability to pass in and out of the fortress at will. Mathi's ears pricked up: Who else could the governor be talking about but Rufe? Rufe and numerous friends, it seemed.

Vital stores had been looted, civilian traders picked clean, and nothing the governor tried to protect royal property made any difference, the governor explained. Desperate, Dolanath had taken the extraordinary step of detaining every visitor on the weak premise they might be allies of the mysterious invaders. Hence the unexpected seizure of Balif and his party.

Dolanath was an easterner, a minor member of the Hestanthalas clan. While he undoubtedly did know the name of Balif, he had not recognized the general. The governor simply revived Balif first, on the natural premise that he was the leader of his group. After some dinner and conversation masquerading as interrogation, Dolanath became convinced that Balif and his company were indeed on a mission to survey land for future settlement.

"You won't have an easy time," he warned. "Beyond the Thon-Tanjan, the land is infested with every sort of barbarian—humans of every size and color, centaurs, and those monstrous little thieves. Our outposts are few. There is no possibility I can protect you out there."

"I thank you for your concern, my lord. No doubt you have noticed my friends and I can take care of ourselves."

Artyrith laughed but the governor was not amused.

"Your companions are formidable, Camaxilas, but how will you fare against a thousand nomad cutthroats?"

Balif had fought armies of ten thousand human tribesmen and once even served under the barbarian chief Karada against a notorious band of human marauders. Mounted nomad raiders were not to be trifled with, but the general knew them and understood their ways. As for centaurs, they were mercurial creatures, violent one moment and weepingly sentimental the next. Balif could deal with them too if he must. Avoiding the issue of his experience with the elves' enemies, Balif asked about the new invaders, the "little thieves" who had Dolanath so frustrated.

"They are the spawn of Hiddukel!" he declared. "They come near and seem innocent of evil purpose. Before you know it, your purse is gone, your food purloined, and your wits confounded. They must use wicked magic to cloud minds and steal with impunity!"

Before the siege began, Dolanath explained, there had been a wooden ramp that allowed travelers to enter and leave Free Winds. Guards posted at the foot of the ramp inspected everyone coming and going to make sure duties were paid and contraband not taken from Free Winds.

"Contraband?" asked Artyrith.

"By decree of the Speaker, it is forbidden to trade metals or weapons to humans," Balif said. "Go on, governor."

One of the little persons got into the fortress. He was seen but before anyone could stop him, he was inside. Since then chaos had reigned in Free Winds. No door remained locked. Treasuries were emptied or, more strangely, found intact but moved around. One humble dealer in herbs and roots found his coin box stuffed with gold, while a rich jewel trader had his entire stock vanish in a single night. The gate of the governor's keep—supposedly the most secure place in Free Winds—was mysteriously opened; then just as unexpectedly, it was shut and locked. The keep was penetrated again then closed again despite a standing watch. Dolanath ordered it barricaded shut in case a storming party tried to enter in the confusion, and by dawn the gate was standing wide open once more with a bulwark of timbers fruitlessly intact behind it.

Mathi almost laughed. Rufe had already proven, to her, his uncanny talent for coming and going as he pleased; that, coupled with a penchant for pilfering, had reduced the governor of Free Winds to impotence. Her odd savior was obviously having a grand time at Dolanath's expense.

Mathi's amusement must have shown. Dolanath looked down his nose at the girl and said, "Do you find crime a jest, child?"

She sobered. "No, my lord. It all sounds more like mischief than crime, I would say."

"You have not endured it. For me, a loyal servant of the Great Speaker, these torments have been like an endless battle. I have no visible opponent, no chance to employ tactics or counterattack. I can only endure losses."

It was clear that whatever they might find farther east, there were already members of the new race in Free Winds. As long as Rufe and his kind found entertainment around the dreary, elven outpost, they would continue to make the governor's life unbearable.

Balif pushed back his chair and stood. Thanking Dolanath for his belated hospitality, he excused himself for bed. Lofotan loyally got up, as did Treskan and Mathi. Artyrith lingered over his plate, trying to season the provincial meal with careful dollops of herbs, oil, and vinegar. Lofotan cleared his throat loudly. Artyrith got the message and rose to his feet.

"Ah, where do we retire to?" Treskan asked.

Balif said, "The rooms we were brought to will do."

"Our cells? I trust the doors won't be bolted on us again!"

Dolanath colored at the suggestion. It was bad enough that he had locked up civilized travelers from Silvanost. Being reminded of it hardly soothed his conscience.

The male elves returned to the larger room where Artyrith, Treskan, and Lofotan had been held. Mathi went alone to her smaller one. The governor's servants brought in comfortable beds, an oil lamp to replace the broken luminar, a pitcher of water, and a chamber pot. Worn out from the long day, Mathi crawled into bed. Instead of immediate slumber, she found herself gazing at the ceiling, wondering how far Balif's expedition would get with every hand in the country seemingly against him . . .

Something in the shadowed ceiling corner moved. Mathi's first thought was that a monstrous spider clung to the ceiling there, but the something was far too big. It crept into the wider circle of light from the oil lamp, and she saw that it was Rufe, her liberator.

"Can't you use the door?" Mathi hissed. "Great E'li, you get around like a cockroach!"

The little man dropped lightly onto the footboard of the bed. "Cockroaches don't get around that easily if you ask me. Back in jail, are ya?"

"No," she answered. "Go away." She was so tired, eyes burning and limbs trembling with fatigue, and even though she was very curious about the little man, Mathi really didn't want to bandy words with him just then.

Rufe hopped down and ambled to the door. Curiosity got the better of Mathi. She called out, "Wait!"

The little man froze in mid step. "Eh?"

"Are you the only one here? The only one of your kind, I mean?"

"Yep. Don't tell the pointy-ears that, will you?"

"Why not?"

"It would spoil my fun. Besides, I might have to tell them about you."

Mathi slowly sat up. With deadly coldness she said, "What do you mean?"

"You're not one of them, are you? Not really, I mean."

"Why do you say that?"

He inhaled deeply through his prominent nose. "You don't smell like them. You see different from them too. Better somehow. I don't know what you are exactly, but you're not just a pointy-ear girl."

She weighed her chances of catching and silencing him before he got out the door. Given Rufe's agility, her chance of success was poor. "I'll keep your secret if you keep mine."

Rufe made an odd gesture with his left hand: he held it up, fingers wiggling, and said, "Finger break and I stay at home if I tell," he said. He made it sound like a serious oath.

He went out quite casually, pushing the door open with the heel of one hand. Only after Mathi extinguished the lamp and tried to find sleep in the darkness did she realize Rufe had pushed open a door that only swung *into* the room. How was that possible? It bothered Mathi so much, she had to get up and inspect the door to be sure. She was right. The door opened only into the room. No amount of her pushing would make the door move the other way.

Puzzling over the little man's baffling tricks, it took a long time for Mathi to fall asleep.

Spawn of Hiddukel indeed!

# Chapter 8

## *Players*

In the morning Balif set Treskan to work writing the phony survey of the country between Silvanost and Free Winds. Treskan worked with a will. He had much catching up to do, and writing was a welcome relief from brawling and riding a bony-backed pony for endless miles. He compiled a very detailed description of the terrain, flora, and fauna of the land between Silvanost and Free Winds. Balif looked over his shoulder now and then and complimented him on his thoroughness.

"Your hand is unusual. Is it the style of your school?" he asked.

Treskan rubbed his writing hand self-consciously. "Yes, this is a type of record-hand taught by my school."

"What school was it?"

Treskan plainly struggled for a moment then said, "Eyes of Matheri, in Woodbec."

Balif assumed an opaque expression. "I do not know that one."

In spite of their unfriendly reception at Free Winds, Balif was in good spirits. All morning he bought maps from local traders and quizzed them about likely locations to build new settlements. To an elf the traders thought Balif was mad. One memorably claimed that building towns or starting farms in the area was like trying to plow the sea. The land was too wild to settle. In another hundred years, perhaps, the blades of the Speaker's warriors would tame the land. But not in the foreseeable future.

By midday Balif was done pretending to be a surveyor. He dismissed the traders, giving them liberal amounts of gold for their trouble, and dispatched Lofotan and the cook on special missions of their own. Lofotan was to talk to any soldiers he could find off duty and get a military view of the local situation. Artyrith was to restock their provisions for the next leg of their journey.

"What will you do, my lord?" Lofotan asked. They were alone in their room in the fortress, so the honorific was safe to say.

"I have tasks of my own." Mathi was surprised Lofotan did not press him on the matter. When the general didn't want to be questioned, no one questioned him.

Mathi was to stay behind and clean the party's kit. Basically that meant laundering clothes and mending whatever tears and splits they had acquired since leaving Silvanost. She did not object to the menial work. It was part of her role as the surveyor's daughter. As for Treskan, Balif instructed him to find the fortress's archives and compare what was written there to what Dolanath told them about the invasion of the little folk.

Waiting a good long time after the others left, Mathi got up quietly and went to the room's sole door. The corridor was empty. She was about to steal out and follow Balif when she felt a tug on the hem of her gown—the back hem. Quick as a cat, Mathi leaped away from the strange touch.

Rufe was standing there, munching on a rather dirty carrot.

"Nervous neighbor, aren't you?" said the little man, chomping. "Good reflexes, though." Every so often he spit drops of mud on the floor.

"Who wouldn't be nervous with people sneaking up behind them?" Mathi snatched the carrot from Rufe's hand and poured fresh water over it, washing away the dirt. She held it out to the little man, who was no longer interested in it.

"Everybody gone?" he said, sauntering around the beds and piles of baggage.

"All but me."

Rufe drew a finger across Treskan's writing board. "You a scribe?"

She was about to snap, "Don't touch that!" but decided the expression was wasted on the little man. She picked up the instrument and tucked it into Treskan's bag.

"I'm not the scribe. His name is Treskan," she said.

"He's not a pointy-ear either. What a funny company you have! No one is what they seem."

"What do you mean? What is Treskan, if not an elf?" Mathi said.

Rufe grinned. "A human in disguise."

Mathi quickly shut the door. Her voice dropped to a whisper.

"Human? Treskan?"

"No doubt about it." Rufe tapped the side of his plow-shaped nose. "This beak never lies."

To no one in particular, Mathi said, "By E'li, what does that mean? A human masquerading as the general's scribe?"

"General, eh? That's interesting."

The two words Mathi never wanted to hear from Rufe were *that's interesting.* Only trouble would follow, she knew intuitively—catastrophe, cataclysm, the end of the civilization were not far off when a character such as Rufe gets interested in something.

"You must keep all this a secret between us," she said.

He stuck out his tongue. It was a startlingly dark hue, almost purple.

"More secrets, bah. Why should I keep 'em?"

Not having any leverage with the little man, Mathi had a sanity-saving notion. "Are you good at following people?" she asked. "I mean, without them knowing it?"

Rufe grinned. "I could trail the gods into the Land of Eternal Light and never be seen or sniffed!"

"Could you follow someone for me? I'll pay you gold."

The little man ran his small fingers around the rim of one of the elves' panniers. Though tied shut with willow withes, the lid popped open.

"What good is gold? You can't eat it, and it isn't as interesting as a lodestone—"

"All right. What do you want?"

"Hmm. Can you get the scribe to write about me in his book?"

Eyes widening, Mathi said, "Certainly."

"I always wanted to see my name in writing," Rufe said. "Have him write my name down, and I'll follow whoever you want."

It sounded too easy, but Mathi agreed. When she told Rufe she wanted Balif trailed around Free Winds to see what he did and who he spoke to, the little man knitted his dark eyebrows and frowned.

"You want me to follow your boss? Why don't you ask him where he's been yourself?"

"I have good reasons not too. Will you do it?"

Rufe nodded his head four times. Mathi took out Treskan's stylus and dipped it in a vial of iron gall ink she found in the scribe's belongings. She found a scrap of foolscap.

"What is your full name?"

The little man took a breath. "Rufus Reindeer Racket Wrinklecap."

Mathi bit her lip to keep from laughing. She wrote the outlandish name in blockish letters, the only writing she could do, then said, "What does 'reindeer' mean?"

"It's a kind of large deer, found in icy climes," he said.

"Sometimes they fly."

Flying deer? Mathi did not try to hide her smile. What could one expect from a little man but a little man tale?

Rufe took the scrap of parchment with his name on it and gazed at it with delight. Holding it like a sacred relic, he vowed to send it to his mother, to show her what his name looked like in real letters.

Mathi was about to ask about the little man's mother when Rufe abruptly balled the slip of foolscap in one small fist and shoved it inside his baggy shirt.

"What's your boss's name?"

"Camaxilas."

A twinkle came to the little man's eye. "Gonna use what I tell you to get something out of him?"

"Not at all! I fear something is wrong with him. He's too proud to tell me if he has any problems, but I want to know so I can help him if need be."

"Uh-huh." Rufe pulled on a pair of fingerless felt gloves, tightened the laces that held his trews close around his ankles, and pulled a faded brown cloth hood up over his head.

"See ya. I'll come back tonight when the pointy-ears are sleeping."

"Wait—don't you want to know where to find him?"

"Don't worry. If he's in Free Winds, I'll find him."

He didn't do his perplexing door-pushing trick. Rufe opened the door normally and went right down the passage. A moment later, his distinctly diminutive hand appeared on the *left* side of the doorframe, nudging the panel closed. Mathi had been looking at the door the whole time. She couldn't imagine how the little man got on the other side of an open door without being seen, but he did.

*****

Artyrith returned first, sneering eloquently at the quality of victuals available in Free Winds. Fear of theft and non-elf marauders had tightened the food supply to the point where the plainest fruits and vegetables commanded unseemly prices. Meat—mostly game collected from the plains outside the fort—was even more dear. The only plentiful thing was nectar. The cellars of Free Winds were brimming with casks, kegs, and amphorae. The hills southwest of Free Winds were dotted with vineyards, and the good weather had produced an abundance of grapes. Normally the nectar of Free Winds would be on its way west to Silvanost, but traders were keeping close to the fortress until an adequate number of soldiers was available to escort the caravans. Artyrith was able to secure a bountiful supply of nectar at a very cheap price.

Lofotan came back, looking grim and puzzled. He wouldn't discuss what he had learned with a scribe and a cook, holding to his orders to report on the military situation to Balif first. But Balif was not there. Evening came then twilight, and the general did not return. Treskan came back from the fort's archives, and there was still no sign of Balif. Tension grew. Artyrith wanted to turn Free Winds upside down and find Balif, but Lofotan held his companion back.

"You're taking this well," the cook said, noting Mathi's composure.

"I trust our lord," she replied. "He will return."

Shown up by a mere girl, Artyrith said no more about it. Night fell. Governor Dolanath's servants brought dinner for his guests. Noting Balif's absence, he asked where Camaxilas was. He was in town on his own business was all Lofotan would say.

Dolanath said knowingly, "Free Winds has many soothsayers and dowsers. No doubt he is closeted with one of them, trying to find water or gold deposits along your route."

No one in Balif's party disagreed. It was easier to allow Dolanath to believe their lord was as shallow and greedy as he was. Expressing his good wishes, the governor withdrew.

Lofotan and Artyrith halfheartedly played at a game of Hounds and Foxes, but the cook was too good for the old soldier and won four games in a row. Treskan wrote and wrote on his journey chronicle until his eyes pained him, and he quit to sleep. Mathi watched him closely when his back was turned. Was the scribe really human? That would explain his clumsiness compared to true elves, but his makeup or magic spell was outwardly flawless. What was his game?

Peeved by his ill luck, Lofotan went to bed. Mathi begged off playing, so Artyrith retired too. Eventually there was nothing to do but turn in. Mathi took one of the lamps to her small room and lay down to sleep. Some time later she felt something warm and lingering on her face. Her ear itched intolerably. Grunting, she put a hand to scratch her ear and found a face there, a face not her own.

Bolting upright, heart racing, she was about to shout for help when she realized who it must be. "Rufe! Rufe?"

"Here, boss."

She loosed a pithy curse, one she had learned from listening to Artyrith. "What are you playing at? Can't you knock on a door like a civilized person?"

"Didn't think you wanted me showing myself off in front of the elfies."

True enough. "Where have you been all day?"

"Keeping an eye on your mighty boss." It turned out Balif had gone to two places, according to Rufe. The second stop lasted all day and into the evening.

"Where did he go?"

"To a healer. White-headed elf named Urolus, Doctor of Physic."

What? There was something wrong with Balif's health? Mathi got up in total darkness and groped for a splint to light the lamp. Rufe's small hand snatched the splints away.

"Some things are better said in the dark," he said ominously.

Mathi sat down on the bed. "Tell me everything."

"I picked up your friend at the Gables." Those were houses and storefronts on the north side of the settlement. "He was hunting for a sawbones from the start. He went inside the Gables and spoke to one, but he must not have liked what he heard 'cause he came back out again and went on. I followed him good. But when he got to Urolus's, he stayed and stayed. Took a long time, kind of boring."

Urolus was a Silvanesti physician who had come to practice in the provinces. He was widely reputed to be the eldest elf in Free Winds, a position that gave him a certain status in the community.

"I don't suppose you know what they talked about?"

"'Course I do. I was on the job, wasn't I? I remember it all." The little man, hidden in the dark, lapsed into a perfect imitation of Balif's voice: " 'I am here to consult you on a personal matter, learned friend.' "

His mimicry was remarkably good. At Mathi's request, Rufe repeated a large portion of the conversation between Urolus and Balif. Apparently the little man spent his time literally eavesdropping; he clung to the roof edge of the doctor's second-floor consulting room, listening through a closed shutter.

Balif had a strange complaint. He had a single symptom that he couldn't explain, nothing else, but it was such an odd symptom, he didn't know what to do about it. When Urolus pressed him to be specific, the general finally removed his cloak and traveler's robe. The doctor examined him, exclaiming upon the strange nature of Balif's malady.

"Well, what was it?"

"They didn't say, exactly," the little man replied. "And I had to squirm around to see. There was some kind of problem on your boss's back. The old sawbones saw it too and said, yep, it's really there."

"What did you see?" Mathi pressed.

"I want a horse." The change of subject was so abrupt, Mathi was thrown off balance. "I want a horse," Rufe repeated. "A black horse."

Blinking in the darkness, Mathi promised to get the little man the biggest, blackest horse she could find.

"And a saddle with silver tacks all over it."

"Yes, yes!"

"I'll call the horse Nui, after the dark moon—"

Mathi wanted to throttle him. Raising her voice too much, she demanded that Rufe reveal what he'd found out.

"He's got hair on his back."

It didn't sound like much, but to a wellborn elf of Balif's stature with body hair was strange and a definite stigma. Elves usually didn't have any, not beyond what grew on their heads. Mathi remembered the Speaker's sister, Amaranthe, had noticed something was amiss with her lover back in Silvanost. Apparently the problem had grown worse, driving Balif to seek medical advice.

"Is that all?" asked Mathi.

"Yep. They went on and on about it, like it was a case of boils or worse. The pill-roller wanted to know if there was any human blood in your boss's background. He was polite about it, but he as much as said your boss must have a hairy human among his ancestors. Your leader denied it up and down. 'Then you are afflicted,' quoth the doc."

"Afflicted? Did he use that exact word?" Rufe avowed he did. Mathi pondered that. Did the healer mean Balif was afflicted with disease, or did he mean the general was afflicted by some malign power?

"What did the doctor do for him?"

"Put stinky stuff on his back to make the hair fall out."

What indignity. Mathi almost felt sorry for the noble elf. She asked where Camaxilas was at that moment.

"In bed, I guess. When do I get my horse?"

Mathi juggled several different lines of thought at once.

She meant to stay close to Balif. What began as a simple task to keep track of the famous general had become a greater mystery. Was there more to it than simply growing body hair? Embarrassing as that might be to a pure-blooded Silvanesti, it hardly spelled the great general's doom from her point of view.

"My horse?" insisted Rufe.

"You'll get your horse." Mathi held out her hand, forgetting in her reverie that she was sitting in total darkness. Nonetheless, the little man's small hand found hers and pumped it vigorously.

Rufe broke his grip. Mathi had the impression the little man was leaving. She called out in a loud whisper, "Wait! How would you like to do more work for me?"

"What kind of work?"

"Watching, listening, like what you did tonight."

She could almost see the little fellow shrug. "Whatever you say, boss." Then he was gone.

Mathi lit her lamp. She tried to sort out everything Rufe had found out and what it meant for her. The word *afflicted* intrigued her. She was sure her comrades had no inkling of Balif's trouble. She had no way of communicating with those she left behind except by leaving certain signs on the trail. Perhaps if she stole a bit of Treskan's parchment and ink, she could write a brief note; her friends were not great readers, but there were those among them who would understand. Once on their way again, she would get a slip from the scribe and leave word to the others.

She yawned and stretched. It was very late. The small hours of the morning were just that, a time when the smallest things seemed large or loud. Mathi rubbed her burning eyes. Her hand strayed down to the neckline of her acolyte's gown. She hated the clinging, stifling clothing. If she had been sure of the door, she would have stripped it off and slept naked, as she preferred. But her hand touched something small and hard hanging from her neck, hidden by the outer layer of the gown.

Mathi fumbled through her clothing and found a small object on a silken cord around her neck. She had never seen it before, and it had not been there earlier when she came to bed. It had shown up some time since Rufe awakened her.

Rufe! She should have known. The light-fingered little man must have put the necklace on her while she slept. She'd felt nothing, but there it was. Mathi fished it out. It was an intricate bit of yellow metal, probably gold, wrapped around a sizable green gemstone. It wasn't pretty exactly, but it had an air of importance and precision about it. Where had it come from, and why did Rufe give it to her?

She padded across the cold stone floor to the door. Just as her hand touched the handle, she realized she had no way of finding the little man or even of contacting him.

A tremor ran through her. What if the necklace belonged to Governor Dolanath or worse, Balif? If caught with it, her life would be forfeit. She almost snatched the thing from her neck there and then, but something stayed her hand. There was no need for haste. Rufe would return. Mathi owed him payment for his services. When the little man showed up next, she would return the necklace to him. She prayed to her lost god that the fool little man didn't steal it from someone too vengeful. The idea of her mission ending in prison or on a gibbet was both horrifying and laughable, but Rufe had a way of making horrible, laughable things happen all the time.

She heard soft footfalls in the passage. Thinking Rufe was prowling around, Mathi flung the door open and hissed, "You there! Where do you think you're going?"

Crouching a few steps away was someone much larger than the little thief. In the feeble light of the hallway, all Mathi saw was a hunched-over figure silhouetted against the pale illumination filtering down the passage. What riveted her to where she stood were the interloper's eyes. They glowed from within with a vibrant red the exact shade of blood.

"You should not be here," she hissed. "Go back! Wait until he's in open country."

The shadowy creature sniffed. Mathi had a clear impression of wet nostrils twitching as the sanguinary eyes bore straight through her. There was no recognition in them, no understanding that Mathi was a sister, a being like him.

She backed up a step. It was clear if she moved that it would leap upon her and rend her to bits. Bracing herself, Mathi ducked inside her room and slammed the door. She braced her shoulder against it. Where was that sword, that useless sword Lofotan pressed on her?

She heard it come close to the door. There was the slightest scrape on the outside panel; then the sniffing began again, down at the gap between the door and the floor. Mathi held her place, pushing against the unresisting door. The thing snuffled from one side of the gap to the other then withdrew. Sweat trickling down her forehead, Mathi braced for an attack.

The door handle descended ever so slowly. It was a simple bronze handle, turned to fit a round socket through the door panel. Mathi grabbed the latch and held it up. More and more force was applied from the other side. She couldn't hold. She couldn't keep the door shut.

Leaping back, she ran to the side chest and found the sword Lofotan gave her. Gripping it with both hands, Mathi squared off, facing the door. She hated fighting a brother, but when her brethren got to that state, such reversion to primal form, they were beyond reason. If he came through the door for her, she would fight.

The handle swung down to the end of its arc and stopped. All that was needed was the slightest pressure to push the door open. It didn't happen. With equal slowness, the latch returned to its closed position.

Six feet away Mathi could not hear if the creature had gone. She waited as long as she dared then rushed the door and peeked out. The gloomy passage was empty. She ran pell-mell to the room occupied by Balif and the elves. Mathi pounded on the door. Lofotan admitted her, sword in hand.

"What's the meaning of this?" he demanded.

Balif was lying on his bed, a linen blanket up to his neck. He pushed up on one elbow but did not stand. Treskan held a lamp and Artyrith a sword just a few steps behind the majordomo.

"One of those creatures was at my door!" Mathi gasped. In a trice Lofotan and Artyrith were in the hall, checking both directions. Balif rose and donned a light robe. He was unarmed.

"Where did it go?" said the cook.

"I don't know." Mathi described her strange encounter. Artyrith relaxed his ready stance.

"You woke us because you had a nightmare? The one we slew in the grassland is still in your mind."

"No, it was real. I was awake, writing, and I heard something in the corridor—"

Lofotan went down to Mathi's room. The door was standing open. There was no sign of any intruder.

"If there was anyone, they're gone now," he said.

"How could a beast like that get into Free Winds?" added Artyrith.

"It's most unlikely," Balif agreed. "I think my daughter has been awake too long. Sleep, Mathi. We leave early on the morrow."

Mathi watched her companions return to their room. Only when they were gone did she reenter her room. She was just closing the door when she saw the scratches. Deep, parallel lines scored the dark wood just above the floor. There were four distinct lines, as far apart as fingers.

# Chapter 9

## *Foes*

The next day dawned gray and windy. Wrapped in cloaks, Balif's party led their horses off the crane platform. Artyrith and Treskan held the reins while Balif and Lofotan removed the last of their baggage from the crane and restored it to the packhorses.

Governor Dolanath sent his best wishes but did not turn up to see his visitors off. Fresh outrages had occurred during the night. Several healers in Free Winds complained that their shops were broken into, all from skylights or roof vents. Valuable drugs and healing instruments were scattered around, but little or nothing was taken. Even stranger were the reports of a large, wild animal loose in the streets adjoining the citadel. Guards on duty and late-night revelers had all seen a sizable beast prowling the darkest alleys. It fled on approach despite its size, but no one was able to corner it. Like the healers' break-ins, the incidents caused no harm but sent waves of unrest through the provincial town. It was as if the walls of the fortress were a sieve through which danger passed at will. Balif and his companions heard the tales as they prepared to go. Mathi said nothing about the beast reports, but descriptions of the creature sounded exactly like what she saw in the passage outside her room.

"Don't mention it to Dolanath," Balif had told her. "He isn't long for his seat anyway, and a report like yours will hasten his departure." A governor who couldn't keep the Speaker's peace and enforce the Speaker's laws could not expect to retain his post.

Mathi gladly stayed mum. She was sure the disturbance of the healers was Rufe's doing. As for the creature inside the fort, she decided it was a rogue member of her unhappy clan. They were all set upon Balif's trail. Urnya had lost her ability to think when she reverted to her animal form. She attacked the first elves she came across, not knowing Mathi was a sister under the skin. The male creature, whom Mathi did not recognize, had entered Free Winds. He had enough mind left to hear Mathi and obey, but for how long?

The ground where the crane landed was worn down to dirt. Mathi shielded her eyes as the wind stirred up the soil. Balif mounted his horse.

"Say farewell to Free Winds," he said. "We shan't see civilization again for some time."

Artyrith laughed shortly. "Civilization? This rock pile?"

As they rode down the hill, Mathi wondered about her little hireling. She had seen no sign of Rufe all morning. The little man had agreed to work for her, but Mathi couldn't see how Rufe could do any work if he wasn't with them. She had figured out a complete explanation for if Balif found the little man. But it appeared Rufe had reneged on their deal.

On level ground the wind scoured them, bowing the knee-high grass until the gray underside of each leaf showed. The effect was eerie. A vast plain of grass, normally green and alluring, had become a gray, wind-tossed sea. The horses kept their heads down. So did the riders.

Consulting his sunstone, Balif set out northeast. The great bend of the Thon-Tanjan lay in that direction, but there was nothing in the way of settlements. Other elven strongholds, such as Tanjanost or Greenfield, lay farther south. Having encountered a small sample of what contact with the little folk could do to a stable garrison, the general decided to forgo visits to the other outposts and seek the invaders as directly as possible. Balif's stated intent was to cross the Tanjan at Savage Ford, just below the fork in the river where the Plains River joined the Tanjan. Fords were few on the fast-flowing river. Once across the river, they would bear south into the largely unmapped forest surrounding the Tanjan river delta. After quartering the countryside there, the elves would make their way back to Silvanost along the coast.

They rode in and out of noisy squalls. Warm rain, almost oily in its feeling, quickly soaked their cloaks and seeped through to their robes underneath. The unhappy sequence went on most of the day. By midafternoon, the rain was gone but the wind remained.

Lofotan, riding point while Balif dictated some observations about the land to Treskan, found it first. The endless grass ceased. Cutting across their line of march was a path so wide and so thoroughly trampled that the tough turf was worn down to bare soil.

"Here! To me!" Lofotan called. The others cantered to his side.

Balif twisted in the saddle, taking in the road. It ran northwest to southeast, disappearing in one direction under a hill and curving out of sight in the other. He rode across it slowly. His horse took twelve steps to cover the path from side to side.

"What does it mean?" Artyrith asked.

"A lot of feet have passed this way," Lofotan answered grimly. "Feet, hooves, and more."

"Human feet?"

The old soldier didn't reply. Balif came slowly back. Wind whirled eddies of dust around his horse.

"The Speaker is only partly informed," he said. "There is a migration under way, but it isn't new. This path took months to make."

Far to the northwest lay more plains, then the Khalkist Mountains. Beyond them was the great savannah, home to thousands of rapacious human nomads. Evidently large numbers of nomads had been coming that way undetected for some time. It was astonishing, finding a trail so large only a hundred and fifty miles from Silvanost. The Speaker had to know, as soon as possible.

Sighting down the center of the road with his stone, Balif concluded it ran more or less directly to Horseriders' Ford, an easier crossing than Savage Ford, but farther away. That made sense. By sticking to a single path on the open plain, the invaders had avoided detection—until Balif's party came along.

"Lofotan, I want you to return to Free Winds," Balif said. News of the interlopers' trail had to reach Governor Dolanath right away. He lacked the troops to close the road, but he could carry word to Silvanost. It would take an army to stop the flow of humans into the elves' eastern lands.

Using Mathi as a shield against the wind, Balif composed a terse message to the governor. Lofotan slipped it inside his cloak and saluted his commander.

"Don't wait for a reply," Balif told him. "Put the note in the governor's hands, and return at once. We will rendezvous at Savage Ford in ten days."

"I can make it in six," Lofotan declared.

"So you could, with clear days and an open path, but there is more afoot out here than just a well-worn road. Ten days, Captain. If by the eleventh day you have not seen us, go back to Silvanost. Lay what we have found before the Speaker of the Stars."

Mathi felt oddly sad watching the dour Lofotan ride away. He was not a noble sort, as was Balif, or amusing, as was Artyrith, or useful, as was Treskan. But Mathi did respect him, even though his absence would make her ultimate goal easier. She would leave word along the trail for her brethren that one of the warrior elves had left the party. That being the case, the chance to complete Mathi's mission—the abduction of General Balif—might come sooner than later.

They waited until Lofotan was out of sight. The general turned his horse around and said, "Now onward." Hardly was it said when Artyrith pulled up short, staring hard down the western end of the dusty track.

"Trouble," he said.

"Move," said Balif. "Now."

They got off the road. Artyrith found a small hollow concealed by tall grass. He and Balif dismounted and began tugging their mounts' halters, forcing the horses down on their bellies in the grass. Mathi started on the pack animals once her horse was down. Soon only Treskan and his pony remained.

"Get out of sight, scribbler!" the cook exclaimed. "Can't you hear them coming?"

Not having the senses of an elf, Treskan couldn't. He swung down and stood back as Artyrith got his pony to kneel in the hollow. Balif was watching the horizon. Mathi could see and hear nothing but the wind.

"How many, do you reckon?" asked the cook.

"More than forty but less than a hundred."

Artyrith cursed a bit and crouched in the grass between his pony and Mathi's. He drew his sword and laid it pommel first between his feet. From his pony's saddle, he yanked out his bow stave, which he proceeded to brace while sitting, a feat Mathi would have said was impossible. Only Balif remained standing. The wind tugged at his yellow hair and whipped his cloak behind him like a flag.

When Mathi finally heard hoofbeats, Balif dropped silently into the weeds. They huddled there, still as could be. Even the horses sensed danger and stayed quiet.

The riders came into view. Mathi didn't count them, but there probably were about fifty of them, humans clad in uncouth furs and leather despite the summer heat. Their hair was worn long, in every color known in the human race. The only way to tell the males from the females was by the heavy beards the men wore. Most of them carried long spears and an assortment of armament strapped to their bodies or their horses. Too numerous to be scouts, they had to be a raiding party, detached from a much larger band a day or so behind them.

They were noisy. Mathi was chagrined that she hadn't heard them sooner. They talked loudly as they waved their weapons around, and their horses jingled and pranced. It was soon clear the humans weren't just being clumsy or foolish. They were escorting an unruly band of prisoners.

Near the rear of the party, a cloud of dust obscured a few of the figures on foot and lying in the dirt. The riders shouted abuse at them and prodded them with their spears, but the procession had come to halt and would not get going again. A useful gust wiped the dust away, and the hidden elves saw whom the nomads had captured.

They were little men like Rufe. The three of them had dark hair pulled back in ponytails; prominent noses; and tattered, dusty clothes. They looked enough like Rufe to be his siblings.

"On your feet. Up! Up!" a black-bearded man was shouting. He waved his spear sideways, indicating the east. "Get up and move, or we'll slaughter you where you lie!"

The little man said something Mathi couldn't hear. Whatever it was it made Black Beard furious. He lowered his spear and jabbed it into the nearest one. The little man flung gouts of dust from his hands, rolled over, and lay still. Mathi heard chains clatter. She looked to Balif. The elf was watching intently, as silent and unmoving as stone.

"One dead! Do the rest of you want this too?" The man shook the bloody spear point under their noses.

One of the little people stood up. He or she—it was impossible to tell at that distance—bowed mockingly, uttered an unheard retort, and hit Black Beard in the face with a stone he had concealed in his small hand. With a roar of fury, the man spurred his horse and impaled the little man, lifting him clear off his feet. The victim clung to the spear shaft, and the raging nomad had to drop his weapon. Amazingly, the spitted little man stood up, thumbed his nose at his murderer, then toppled lifeless into the grass beside the road.

Mathi was horrified. She knew the nomads were savage, but she'd never witnessed such barbarity. Outnumbered by forty armed humans, nevertheless she looked to Balif for an answer. The elf's face was white and set like marble.

There was a yell behind Mathi. Alarmed, she spun around and saw the wrapped bundle tied to one of the packhorses burst open. Out burst Rufus Reindeer Racket Wrinklecap, evidently stowed away ever since leaving Free Winds. He had long knives in either hand. Waving them and shouting incoherently, he charged the human host.

Mathi heard Artyrith utter a single pithy expletive. The cook straightened his back, drew his nocked arrow, and let fly. Black Beard got the shaft through his neck and toppled lifeless from his horse.

The nomads milled around for an instant, confused by the sudden turn of events. Wildly screeching, Rufe ran at the last captive little man, not the humans. Some of them spotted Artyrith in the grass and pointed at him with swords and spears. The cook coolly placed a second arrow in the chest of a burly warrior on the opposite side of the group. Nearer nomads didn't notice and thumped spurless heels against their horses' flanks to get them going. Half a dozen rode at Artyrith. When they were broadside to Balif, the general popped up out of the grass and shot the last human in the charging pack. Artyrith got the second rearmost, and Balif the next until a single nomad armed with an inadequate sword was charging Artyrith alone. The cook got on his horse and snatched at the reins to make it stand. He dodged the man's clumsy thrust—the human's straight blade was not designed for mounted fighting—and put an oak shaft in his ribs so deep that the fletching was buried by the nomad's fur vest.

Balif stayed on his feet, picking off the thoroughly confused nomads. Ten of them were down, and the humans had no idea how many more deadly archers there might be in the grass. They broke. Wheeling their horses around, they rode hard back the way they came, leaving their dead and wounded behind.

Mathi got up, shaking. Artyrith stood guard from the edge of the road while Balif and the scribe went to Rufe. He was standing over the last captive, knives outthrust in both hands. His eyes were shut tight.

The shackled little man tugged Rufe's jerkin. Dolanath's bane cracked on eye.

"Hi," he said.

"Hello," said Balif calmly. To Mathi he said, "Do you know this person?"

Mathi admitted they had met before. "I didn't know he was with us," she said lamely.

Artyrith came trotting up. "You could have gotten us all killed!"

"Coulda but didn't. Why cry for bread you didn't bake?" said Rufe. He tucked away his wicked-looking knives and picked up one of the prisoner's manacles.

"Riveted," he said. "Can't pick a lock where there ain't one."

"Never you mind."

The captive grasped his own hand over the knuckles and bore down, grunting. Mathi watched him squeeze his bound hand until it was small enough to slip through the bronze ring. So that's how little men were able to escape bonds so easily! She wondered if she was the first outsider to see it done.

"Thanks, brother," said the little man. He stood up. Slightly taller than his savior, his hair was lighter too, more golden, though caked with dirt. His nose, though prominent, was less of a weather vane than Rufe's. By little-man standards, he must have been considered rather handsome.

"What goes on here?" asked Balif.

"I'm the Longwalker," said the little man. He held out his hand in human fashion. Balif knew the custom and shook the little man's grubby hand.

"What's a Longwalker?" asked Treskan.

"He's a high and mighty fellow," said Rufe. "The leader of his people."

"You mean a chief?" Balif said.

Rufe nodded then shook his head. "Yes. No. The Longwalker leads the way for his people on the march. He makes the trail the others can follow. But he's not a king."

Balif and Artyrith cocked their heads in unison. "More horsemen coming this way. We'd better be gone." Balif agreed. He offered his hand to the Longwalker, who grabbed hold and climbed on in front of the elf. Mathi did the same for Rufe, and together they faded into the grass. Artyrith and the scribe went ahead while Balif brought up the rear. As his horse walked single-file behind the pack ponies, Balif faced backward and leaned down over his horse's rump. He brushed up the stalks of grass behind them, sometimes weaving the tips together with deft fingers. The effect was to erase all but the tiniest traces of their passage through the grass.

Announced by a whirlwind of dust, the nomad avengers halted at the scene of the earlier fracas. The dead were examined and the wounded treated. Listening in total silence, Mathi concluded that their presence was compromised. When the humans recovered elf arrows from their comrades' bodies, they would know a party of armed Silvanesti were around.

As if reading her mind, Artyrith smugly whispered, "We weren't here." He and Balif had supplied themselves with centaur arrows at Free Winds, he explained. In the bloody confusion, the nomads might convince themselves they were attacked by a war party of centaurs instead of two elves and a crazy little man.

They stole away, grateful not to be noticed. The Longwalker contently rode with the general, but after a short distance, Rufe dropped off Mathi's pony and slipped away in the weeds. Mathi started to call him, but fearing the humans might hear, held her tongue.

Not until they were half a day north of the road did Balif speak again. He reclaimed the lead from Artyrith then stopped the procession when he reached a small stream.

The horses watered themselves. Balif said, "Where is the other little fellow?"

"Run off," Mathi reported.

"Explain how you know him, child."

She described how she'd found Rufe prowling the fortress and sort of hired him. She admitted that Rufe was the author of the governor's troubles, but since she had never met a being like him before, she had asked Rufe to come with her, ostensibly as a guide, but also as a living example of the kind of people currently flooding the eastern province of Silvanesti.

Balif listened without expression then asked his passenger: "Who are you people?"

"We have as many different names as the people we meet. We've been called golighters, halflers, tweeners, and wanderfolk. Among ourselves we are just People, although the human horse riders call us 'kender,' which in their tongue means 'those who all look alike,' " the Longwalker said. "Which we don't."

"Where do you come from?" asked Artyrith.

"From the sunset."

"Where are you going?"

"To the sunrise, by way of any place we haven't been before."

Artyrith clucked his tongue at the poetically evasive answers, but Balif accepted them as offered. The elves and Mathi passed around a water bottle while the horses' finished. Without warning, the Longwalker slipped off the general's horse.

"Wait," said Balif. "Stay with us. I would know more about you."

"I thank you for your help," the little man replied, "but my feet itch too much to ride. Gotta walk. Farewell."

Before they could do anything, he was in the high grass and gone. Mathi called loudly, "But what is your name? Your given name?"

"Serius Bagfull, your lifelong friend," his voice came back, drifting over the grass from no real direction.

From two mysterious companions there remained none. Balif said, "Mathi, from now on you must get my approval before adding anyone to our party. Our mission is secret, after all."

"Yes, my lord."

"I do thank you for making contact with these newcomers. What did they call themselves? Wanderfolk? I see now how they could have driven Governor Dolanath to distraction."

He looked over the sea of wind-tossed weeds. It was evident from his expression that not even he, a full-blooded elf, could detect any sign of the departed Longwalker.

Balif continued to call them wanderfolk for some time. Treskan adopted the name kender and used it in conversation and his notes. In time the elves forgot Balif's term and used kender too.

# Chapter 10

## *Crossings*

The sea of grass thinned out as they approached the Thon-Tanjan, becoming isolated tufts of tall grass in a sea of stony loam. Tracks appeared in the bare soil, lots of them. Not an hour passed that the elves didn't spy other wanderers entering the great bend of the river. Many were humans, mounted and on foot. Balif said that the people he saw walking concerned him more than the riders. Nomads traveled constantly, moving their families and herds wherever water and forage was best. No one in a nomad clan walked unless they were in dire straits. Humans on foot meant emigrants, settlers. They were looking for a place to stay. Speaker Silvanos would not tolerate them on land he claimed as his own. There would be war.

In addition to humans, they also saw centaur bands in the Tanjan bend. The Silvanesti had never had too much trouble from the horse-men. They were even more footloose than human nomads, and if they caused trouble, a few flights of griffon riders usually sufficed to drive them out. Balif confessed he had never seen centaurs in such numbers. While the humans seemed to be moving west to east, the centaurs were coming down from the north. After a full day of watching horse-men streaming south, Balif resolved to speak to them.

"Is that wise?" asked Artyrith. Even from a distance, it was easy to see the centaurs were armed.

"Nothing about this journey is wise," Balif replied. He smiled wryly. "That's why it will succeed. No one expects us to behave so foolishly."

He took a moment to don his most impressive outfit, white silk robes with a cloak made of cloth of gold. At the general's insistence, Mathi, Treskan, and Artyrith smartened up, though there was little the scribe or the orphan girl could do about their poor wardrobe. Tidied as best they could, they abandoned stealth and rode forth as if they were lords of all they surveyed.

It didn't take long to make contact with the centaurs. They found a band of close to a hundred males trotting along the bank of a dry wash ravine. They were a swarthy breed, dark coated and dark skinned. Balif noticed that they wore a lot of seashell ornaments. That meant they were a coastal clan. Why were they so far inland?

The outriders spotted Balif's party. It was hard not to, what with the general's golden cape billowing in the wind. Centaurs broke off in small groups, fanning out on either side of the elves. Everyone but Balif watched their movements with concern. It looked very much as if they were being surrounded, and there was no Rufe in a blanket to distract a large party of dangerous opponents.

The main band of centaurs, forty strong, descended the ravine bank, crossed the dry bed, and climbed out, coming straight for Balif. At a strategic point atop a rocky outcropping, Balif halted. Artyrith and Treskan drew up one either side. Mathi halted behind him. She had to admire Balif's presence. Sitting there on his horse, dressed like a great lord of Silvanost, he looked fit to command any situation.

Whooping and whistling, the centaurs made a ring around the trio. Mathi rubbed her sweaty palms together and tried not to stare at the array of weapons around her, stone axes, mauls, bent and dented swords taken from metal-making foes. The centaurs often carried two weapons at once, one for each hand. Their favorite tool was the one they had invented, a long-handled club of dark, dense wood with a ball-shaped head. Swung in wide circles by madly galloping centaurs, the knob could easily crack an elf skull wide open.

The centaurs jostled each other, making loud whistling sounds through their teeth. Visible over their heads were an array of totems, or standards, brandished by the chief's champions. With some shoving and loud rebukes, the champions bulled their way through their comrades. The totems were poles fourteen feet high with crossbars lashed along their length. Important spiritual and magical artifacts were fastened to the crossbars: skulls of slain enemies, crystals, shells, bits of metal chain gleaned from a despoiled caravan, and odder things such as dried hornets' nests or painted gobs of molded clay.

When the champions reached the front, they made a lane for their leader. A centaur chief was always the eldest male in the clan, and he was ancient. His hair and coat were dappled with white. His left rear leg dangled off the ground. The muscle had been cut in some long-ago fight, and upon healing it had shrunk so much that the chief's hoof no longer touched the ground. In many barbarous societies, a damaged warrior might have been turned out and abandoned but not among the centaurs. They esteemed the wisdom—and cunning—of the aged.

The seashell centaurs were beardless, either by heredity or custom. When the chief emerged from the pack, he limped up to the splendidly dressed Balif.

"May the sun shine only on your back," he said gruffly. His voice was low and raspy. Mathi saw why. He had a huge scar across his throat, an old one.

"My greetings to you, mighty Chief," Balif replied. "You honor me with your words."

"Sky-folk are alone?"

"We three are part of a larger company, sent here by my great lord, the Speaker of the Stars. In his name I greet you. I am Balif, son of Arnasmir Thraxenath, of the Greenrunners clan."

The champions around the chief muttered and shifted. The general's name was well known and carried weight even out there.

"You are welcome, son of Arnasmir, but I must ask, why are you here?"

"I came to see you, Chief."

The old centaur blinked his liquid brown eyes. He put a thumb to his own chest.

"Yes. You are Greath, are you not?" Balif pronounced the centaur's name to rhyme with *teeth*.

The centaur spread his hands. "Greath I am. Have you seen our faces before, sky-folk?"

"Never, mighty Chief, but even in the Speaker's land we know the name of Greath."

The ancient horse-man made a horrible face. He was smiling. Mathi saw his front teeth had been knocked out long past.

Having made the old chief smile, Balif went on. "Mighty One, my great lord, the Speaker of the Stars, hears grave things about this land, his land." All three elves watched closely for signs of resistance to the claim. Greath was in such good humor, he let it pass.

"It has come to the ears of the Speaker that many folk from outside his realm have entered his land, to pass through and to live. Those who pass through go with the Speaker's blessing. Those who settle on his land without his leave are not welcome and will face his displeasure."

The warriors shook their knobkerries and dented swords. They were proud creatures, not easily intimidated. Greath let them grumble a bit then silenced them with a bob of his shaggy gray head.

"It is not the way of the Hok-nu to grow in place like trees," he said, naming the centaur tribe. "We have left our place of wandering, the land of Vesh, to seek grazing for our families." *Vesh* was the centaurs' name for the great northern coast.

In spite of their ferocious appearance, centaurs were vegetarians. They lived off roots and shoots of trees and grasses, enlivened by fruit in season. They regarded cultivated crops as travesties of nature and would often burn gardens full of produce rather than eat such unnatural bounty.

"The land is your land, as the Great Speaker knows," Balif said. "Those who pass through the Great Speaker's land are not the Great Speaker's enemies, but there are those who come to take that which belongs to the Speaker of the Stars."

*"Vay-peh."* That was centaur dialect for humans.

Balif nodded solemnly. "Not only *vay-peh.* The wanderfolk too."

Mention of the kender caused the assembled centaurs to grimace and prance. More than a few looked back over their broad backs, as if to find Rufe or the Longwalker skulking there.

Mathi had not seen such reaction in centaurs before. They were very bold in their emotions—love, fear, hate, joy—but that was new. At the mention of kender, the Hok-nu were *disturbed.*

"We have met them. They are troublesome," Greath declared.

"Do you know where the little people come from?" Balif asked.

Greath pressed a palm to his forehead, the centaur equivalent of a shrug. "It is said they came out of a crack in the ground, like vermin from a wound. Nothing is a barrier to them, not water, not the brown land, not the high mountains of Khal."

With much flowery language, Greath explained further that the kender had been seen lurking around for the past four seasons, but the summer brought a torrent of them. At first the centaurs had no problem with them, but lately the newly arrived little people had taken to pilfering the centaurs' meager possessions. That they would not tolerate.

"Him, little man." The old chief hiked his dusky thumb at a totem held behind him. Balif, Mathi, and Artyrith followed his finger and saw a small, white skull attached to the lowest crossbar. The forehead had been crushed by a knobkerrie.

Sensing he would learn no more from the centaurs, Balif presented Greath a gift, a brightly polished bronze knife with a gold hilt and a round beryl stone in the pommel. The old roughneck was greatly pleased.

"You are Greath's friend!" he vowed. "The people of Balif are the friends of the Hok-nu!"

"It warms my heart to hear you say so, mighty Chief. I will tell my lord, the Speaker of the Stars, the passage of the Hok-nu into his land should not worry him. You will return to the coast by autumn?" Flipping the shiny blade back and forth, the centaur chief agreed. "Then I shall tell my great lord, the Speaker, to be easy in his mind about his friends the Hok-nu."

The assembled centaurs gave Balif their version of a rousing cheer. They reared back on their hind legs, pawing the air with their front hoofs and ululating deep in their throats. It was an uncanny sound.

Greath galloped away surrounded by his standard-bearers. In orderly files the warriors followed until Balif and his companions were alone on their windy outcropping. Mathi suddenly realized she had been holding her breath. She let it out in a long sigh.

"Amazing," said Artyrith. Mathi couldn't remember so long a time the garrulous cook had remained silent. "They actually smell as badly as they look."

"They are honorable folk," Balif replied. "Far more so than most humans." His handsome face appeared weighed down with sadness. "It grieves me to assist in their destruction."

He admitted Speaker Silvanos would never allow centaurs, Hok-nu or not, to graze in his territory. Once Balif's report reached him, he would summon the fearsome griffon riders of Silvanost to harry the horse-men out of the country.

Mathi said, "That is not just!"

"It is the Speaker's will," said Artyrith.

Balif watched the dust trails rising from the departing centaur horde. "The Speaker's will can be shaped by what the Speaker knows." He gripped his reins so hard the leather creaked. "Or does not know."

They rode on to the ford. Because of the delay with the centaurs, they were unlikely to reach Savage Ford before dark, but Balif pressed on. With each mile, he rode a little faster, forcing the others to keep up. Treskan and Mathi, handicapped by the pack train, dropped back. The cook stayed with them, and together they watched Balif diminish in the distance as the gap between them widened.

Artyrith called to his master in vain. Annoyed, he reined up and watched Balif canter away. "What ails him?" he said, blotting sweat from his face with the back of one gloved hand.

"He pities for the centaurs," Mathi suggested.

"They're little better than beasts," Artyrith replied. "Not fit company for our people!"

Inwardly Mathi wondered what Balif was up to. He felt bad about the centaurs' future, no doubt, but he was not so emotional that he would let his anger or grief cause him to abandon the rest of his party. The three of them shared a quick drink—tepid water for Mathi, solid swallows of surplus Free Winds nectar for Treskan and Artyrith—and started after their wayward leader.

At least his path was easy to follow. Balif rode straight as an arrow through every clump of wire grass and scrub in his path. Then they found more troubling traces smeared on the foliage. Artyrith found blood on the leaves, still fresh enough to flow.

Artyrith rubbed the drops between his fingers. "This does not smell like elf blood," he declared, puzzled.

"Is it from his horse?" asked the scribe.

It was not horse blood, either. Mathi yearned to sniff the traces herself. Her nose was keener than an elf's, but she wasn't prepared to answer the questions her prowess would raise.

Wrapping the reins around his fist, Artyrith urged his horse to a gallop. Mathi and Treskan had to follow as best they could, leading the stubborn pack ponies.

The bowl of the sky was blue streaked with crimson as the sun sank down to a well-earned rest. Wind was kicking up out of the north. A bank of dark clouds was building there, promising a wet night.

The terrain began to change rather quickly from uplands to riparian. Rocks and boulders dotted the landscape. Real trees reappeared for the first time since leaving the elves' homeland.

Mathi's pony stumbled into a draw and refused to climb the other side. Treskan started down after her. The packhorses half tumbled in too and voiced their displeasure loudly. While the two tried to calm them, they heard another horse approaching fast. Treskan tried to draw his sword—it took three tugs to free it from its scabbard—and had only just gotten it out when a long-legged saddle horse hurtled around the bend in the draw, riderless. Mathi watched open mouthed as it passed. It was Balif's horse. The saddle was torn to shreds and smeared with blood.

Hastily Treskan dismounted, tied the pack animals to a tree, and got back on his pony. Thumping his heels, he steered his horse after Balif's fleeing mount. The general's horse was almost out of sight. Mathi tried to get her blinkered pony to gallop, but the wise beast declined, shuffling off at an indifferent trot.

The wind picked up, driving in the storm from the north. The crimson sunset disappeared under a veil of clouds. The wind blowing down their backs was hot. Silent flashes of lightning threw the ground ahead into bright relief for an instant; then everything faded into the stormy dusk.

She rode a mile or more, blundering along the sandy bottom of the draw. Saplings and tree branches tore at her. Mathi had to throw an arm over her face to protect her eyes. Lightning flared again, followed by a growing hammer of thunder. By the flash she saw Treskan had caught Balif's big horse up ahead. Mathi urged her mount on.

Her pony stumbled in a drift of sand, falling nose first. No equestrian, she was hurled headlong over the animal's head and hit the ground. Something snapped loudly. Rolling head over heels down a short, steep bank, Mathi came to rest flat on her back. Her pony walked past, nickering loudly. It sounded as though the beast were laughing at her.

A dark figure on horseback loomed over her. "Are you all right?"

"I think my back's broken," Mathi answered. "I heard it snap."

"Blink your eyes."

Lightning snapped overhead. Mathi saw her interrogator was Lofotan. She bolted to her feet, exclaiming in surprise.

"No one with a broken back leaps around like that," the old soldier said.

"The general's horse! Did you see it?" asked Mathi.

Lofotan pointed. Off to his right, Treskan sat on his pony, holding the reins of Balif's mount. It was shivering and foam flecked.

"Let's find yours," Lofotan said.

Together with Treskan they went up the draw and found Mathi's pony cropping fronds. Returning to where the pony tripped, they spotted a fallen pine branch.

"There's your back," said Lofotan. Mathi had heard the limb snap and thought it was her back.

Mathi reclaimed her reluctant ride. It circled away from her, rearing more than a pony its size ever did.

"What's the matter with the nag?" Artyrith shouted, coming over on foot. He seized the pony's halter and held on. Eventually the disturbed creature calmed enough for Mathi to mount.

"Where's General Balif?" she said.

Lofotan didn't know. He was coming up the south bank of the Thon-Tanjan, looking for his comrades, when Artyrith appeared, riding like a madman after the general's horse. Between the two of them, they cornered the terrified runaway, but still there was no sign of Balif.

They backtracked to the pack train. Everything was present except their leader. By the intermittent glare of lightning, they examined Balif's horse.

The smooth leather saddle was scratched in long, parallel lines on either side of the seat. There were smears of blood on the saddle and on the horse. The quivering creature had a bad wound on the right side of its neck, four deep gashes side by side. It didn't take eagle eyes to see they matched the scratches in the saddle.

"A predator must have attacked our lord, knocking him off his seat. It then mauled the horse before the horse got rid of it," Lofotan said. "We'll have to trace the trail back and find our lord."

Artyrith strung his bow and hooked a full quiver on his belt. Lofotan armed himself with a spear of unusual style. It was shorter than a standard horse spear, with a thick shaft and a bronze crossbar set back about a hand's span from the keen bronze head. When Mathi asked, Lofotan said it was a bear spear.

"Are there bears in this country?" Artyrith asked, but Lofotan let the cook's question go unanswered.

Mathi remembered the phantom she had seen at Free Winds. The creature Lofotan expected to find was no bear. Another one of Vedvedsica's children had trailed them from the outpost and struck when Balif was alone and vulnerable. Inwardly she shook with anger. Or was it relief? If the traitor Balif was dead, her task was finished, even if it did mean her effort had come to naught.

Rain began to fall in big drops. Lofotan ordered them all to stay behind with the baggage. Treskan and Artyrith erected the tent and picketed the pack team to some surrounding trees. Artyrith laid a fire in the entrance of the tent, angling the canvas flaps to protect the flames from rain and wind.

"Keep it burning and stay awake," Lofotan warned. "Whatever attacked our lord may still be out there. Do you have a weapon?" Mathi and the scribe had their swords; that was all. "You'd be mauled to pieces by the time you got a chance to stick it with that." He gave the scribe a standard spear.

"That will keep the beast a little further away," he said.

The old warrior and the cook rode off just as the rain started lashing down in earnest. Mathi and Treskan huddled by the fire, the spear laid across his knees. The scribe got out his writing board and recorded the day's events.

Mathi asked him what he wrote. He read his last lines aloud:

*We have arrived at the Thon-Tanjan at last, but our leader is missing. From the evidence, it appears one of the beast-creatures has attacked Camaxilas, either killing him or carrying him off. It hardly seems possible, slain by an animal transformed to resemble an elf. It does not seem just that he should pass out of Silvanesti, only to perish in the wilderness like this . . .*

Mathi looked up. Rain was coming down in torrents. The horses huddled together, starting noisily when lightning flashed or thunder boomed.

*Still,* Treskan read, *if Camaxilas has survived the attack, where is he?*

A fat drop of water landed squarely in the center of Treskan's words. The ink ran, ruining the empty space below the scribe's previous lines. He tried to blot it dry, putting his spear aside to better reach the page. At that exact moment, the creature that had stalked them all the way from Free Winds landed on all fours between them.

Treskan was speechless with terror. The sodden creature was a mass of matted, dripping fur. By firelight Mathi could see its dark eyes veined with red and a hint of fang protruding from its black lips. It squatted on its haunches, leaning forward on its front claws. Breath steamed from its pug nose.

Treskan's hands closed around the spear shaft. His movement was too obvious. The creature bared a black lip, snarling.

"Don't," whispered Mathi. Another breath in the wrong direction, and the thing would tear the scribe to bits.

"What can we do?" said Treskan in the faintest voice.

"Listen to me," she said to the monstrous visitor. "Begone now. Run away before the elves return and slay you. You have no reason to be here. What you want, who you want, is well watched."

Treskan stared.

Mathi ignored him and went on. "He's not an elf anyway." To the scribe she said, "Hold out your hand."

"What?"

"Hold out your hand to him. Let him smell you!"

"Are you insane?"

"Do it or die!"

Trembling, Treskan put out his left hand. He never got it closer than half an arm's length, but the black nostrils flexed deeply. Slowly the creature uncoiled itself, withdrawing from Treskan's imminent death.

"Go now. Seek out the others. They will tell you what is happening. Do you understand? Your being here violates our covenant with the Creator. Go!"

An arrow whizzed out of the darkness and struck the ground, quivering, by Mathi's right knee. The creature sprang away, snarling. Mathi snapped to one side, and Treskan rolled the other way. She saw the creature running away into the stormy night. A spear flew in a heavy arc and hit the ground behind the fleeing beast, not even tangling its feet. In a moment it was gone, though a silent blink of lightning highlighted it as it loped off into the storm.

Artyrith and Lofotan appeared.

"Which way did it go?" shouted the cook.

Shaken, Mathi pointed in the true direction. "There! Next time don't miss, my lord!"

"I didn't miss. I was only trying to drive him off. If I hit him, he might have torn you limb from limb." Lofotan rode off after the creature.

"Any sign of the general?" said Treskan.

"None." Artyrith was grim. He took a long swig of nectar. "We couldn't find a trace! We did locate the spot the creature jumped on his horse, but there was no sign our lord fell off or was carried away!"

*Crash!* Thunder put emphasis to the cook's words.

"What shall we do?"

"It's pointless to hunt in a storm," Artyrith said. "We can't see, and we can't smell anything but rain!"

"What's Lofotan doing, then?"

The cook was almost respectful. "He won't give up. He'll ride through the storm until he finds Balif or kills the beast—maybe both." He sighed wearily. "I had better join him. He'll never let me hear the end of it if I don't!"

Alone again, Mathi and Treskan sat together by the struggling fire. Much had been revealed between them in the brief, tense moments when they faced the beast.

"You are not an elf," he said after a long silence.

"Neither are you. Why are you here?"

"I cannot say. You must trust that my presence is totally benign. I mean no harm to you, the general, or anyone. I am a scholar on a mission of learning," said Treskan. When Mathi did not reply in kind, he said, "And you? You are one of those beast creatures." Still she said nothing. "More presentable, more civilized, I see, but still one of them."

"Civilized? Civilized?" She laughed bitterly. In her dark mirth, Mathi leaned forward quite far. The odd necklace Rufe had left on her swung free of her rain-soaked gown.

"My talisman!"

Treskan's hand darted out to snatch the little artifact. Faster by far, Mathi caught his wrist first.

"Yours? How do I know that?"

"I brought it with me from my homeland. I must have it back!"

Mathi closed her free hand around it. "The little man, Rufe, took it from you and gave it to me. I don't know why." She pulled the string over her head and gave the talisman to Treskan. He looked vastly relieved to have it back.

"Is it magic?"

"You could say that. It's worth more than my life."

She caught his hand holding the talisman in both of hers. "Then swear to me on your precious artifact you will not reveal me to the others. I will swear the same for you."

Treskan hesitated only briefly. He clasped his free hand around hers.

The storm blew itself out after midnight. Stars winked in one by one until their usual millions were displayed. The scribe and the orphan girl passed the night awake, saying little, wondering who would return to them—Lofotan, Artyrith, Balif, or the indestructible beast that was haunting their steps.

# CHAPTER 11

## *Survivors*

The first ones to arrive at the soaked and misshapen tent were the kender. They came up from the ford in no certain order, no definite formation. There were more than two dozen of them, bare headed and empty-handed. Aside from the fact they were more than a hundred miles from any sizable town, the little people looked as if they were out for a morning stroll, not a strenuous migration.

They found Treskan and Mathi huddled together by the smoldering remnants of their campfire. The first ones walked by, eyeing the pair curiously. Some waved a greeting and kept walking. Twenty passed before the first stopped to speak.

"Lousy night, eh?" It was Rufe.

Mathi blinked red-rimmed eyes at the apparition. "How can you be here?" she mumbled.

"I go where my feet and my fate take me," he replied cheerfully. Hunkering down in the muddy grass, he poked at the dead fire. "Truth is, the Longwalker asked me to look after you. He said you were in trouble."

Treskan stood up. From his waist down, he was soaked with mud and cold rain.

"Filthy night," he said sourly. "Unless you have a tub full of hot water in your vest, you aren't going to help me much."

Rufe lifted each side of his vest in turn. No bathtubs in his pockets, his winking eyes seemed to say. "Where are the others? The mean one, the snobby one, and your boss?"

Mathi had no idea. She described the night's events, carefully omitting her newly forged pact with Treskan. Rufe listened, nodding his head from side to side every so often.

When Mathi was done, he said, "Can I see the horse? The scratched one, I mean?"

"Why not?" Treskan threw off his sodden cloak and outer robe. He stripped to his last garment, a short-sleeved tunic held on by a fabric sash tied around his middle. Mathi would have liked to have gotten rid of her wet clothes too, but modesty forbade. Squishing, she followed as Treskan led the kender to the picket line.

Balif's horse was there. Rain had washed the blood from its neck but the scratches were still evident, red and raw through the animal's sleek coat. Rufe patted the horse on the ribs and walked under its neck, glancing sideways at the wound. He grabbed the saddle ring and hoisted himself up, picking at the torn leather with his free hand.

"It's scratched," he said.

"Amazing. How did you figure that out?" said Mathi crossly.

"Scratched by nails." Rufe dropped to the ground. He held up one hand, fingers curled. "Like this, only bigger."

Mathi got a glimmer of what the kender was getting at. She went to the horse. It shied from her until Rufe calmed it with soothing words. Making her hand a claw like Rufe's, Mathi held it over the parallel tears: four lines, four fingers. The scratches on the left side of the saddle matched the spread of Mathi's left hand. That meant—

She asked Treskan to climb into the saddle. The horse stirred under the scribe, not liking his weight and carriage. Mathi told him to lean forward. When he complied, his left hand lay over the scratches on that side; his right hand lined up on the other side too. *The tears were made by someone sitting atop the horse.* Leaning farther forward, the wounds on the animal's neck aligned perfectly with Treskan's hands again.

"Gods' preserve us," he muttered. He knew who the beast was that Mathi saw in Free Winds. The same creature had visited them during the night. A lot of little pieces of a very large puzzle suddenly took on form and shape. Suddenly Treskan feared for Lofotan and said so. If he met the beast, he might not be prepared for what he found.

Bored, Rufe went down to the river. He plunged in, swimming vigorously against the swift current. The Thon-Tanjan was shallow and rocky above Savage Ford, deeper and slower below. He ignored Mathi's calls and swam farther out, rolling onto his back and turning his face to the warm morning sun.

Mathi ran to the riverbank. Treskan dismounted and followed with labored tread, lost in thought. He almost walked into the water, he was so distracted. Fortunately he bumped into a kender by the river's edge and stopped.

There were little folk everywhere. Mathi wound her way through them to the stony beach, cupped her hands around her mouth, and called urgently to one bathing kender in particular. At length Rufe returned, wringing the water from his breeches.

"What is it, pointy-ears? You want a turn in the river? You're pretty dirty—"

"Quiet, you fool! I've had a revelation!"

Rufe shrugged off the girl's insult as excitement. Mathi got his attention when she told him who had attacked them. The bedraggled kender whistled in disbelief. He denied it. The open air had affected Mathi's mind. The sooner she was back in a nice, comfortable house, the sooner her head would clear.

Mathi cursed his stupidity. "You showed me the answer! Balif's saddle was clawed like this!" She bent her fingers, raking an imaginary saddle. "The horse was hurt like this!" She extended her hands and made violent clawing motions. "Don't you see? The creature was on the horse's back. The only one who could have injured the horse was Balif!"

Treskan had arrived at the same conclusion. Joining Rufe and the girl, he said, "We must find the general."

It didn't take long. As Mathi and Treskan stood by the line of tethered horses, a pair of riders came over the rise, standing out bright and clean against the new day's sky. It was Lofotan and Artyrith. Something white and lifeless lolled against Lofotan's back. He had found his commander.

They ran splashing through the mud, meeting Lofotan halfway up the hill from the copse of alders where the pack-horses were tied.

Naked, Balif was slumped against Lofotan's back, held in place by a broad leather belt passed under his arms.

"The general—does he live?"

"He lives." Lofotan was hollow eyed. "Whatever else can be said, he breathes yet."

He unbuckled the strap. Treskan and Mathi caught Balif and lowered him to the ground. Rufe ambled up, cheerfully munching an apple, oblivious to the others' glaring looks.

They examined Balif. He was naked and covered with cuts and scratches, though none serious. His worst injury was a large bruise on the left side of his jaw. Mathi noticed the mark.

"You struck him?"

"It was necessary."

Artyrith swung a leg over the pommel of his saddle and dropped lightly to the ground. Kneeling, he grasped Balif by the shoulder and turned him half over. Down the center of Balif's back was a distinct stripe of coarse, brown fur. What made it doubly shocking was its totally alien nature. No elf had fur down his back, and worse, the color was totally unlike Balif's own fine, blond hair.

"What does this mean?" Treskan said, recoiling.

"The beast that's been following us from Free Winds is no halfling monster of Vedvedsica's," Lofotan said. "It is our lord."

Artyrith stood up and stepped back from the unconscious Balif. He rubbed his hands together, never taking his eyes off the fur stripe.

"How can this be? The greatest warrior of the age, a halfling beast?"

Lofotan snapped, "No finer stock of our blood ever lived than Balif, son of Arnasmir! If he is different now, it is because he is accursed!"

Artyrith had a riposte on his lips. One look at Lofotan, and he kept it there. He stared at Balif's back. "Accursed? By the mage?" He reached for an obscenity from his extensive repertoire and found none. "How long will it be before we are all accursed?"

"Since when is evil magic contagious?" Mathi said.

"If Vedvedsica wanted us hairy, we would be by now," Lofotan said dryly.

Artyrith protested. The magician was in custody. He couldn't cast spells or compound curses while in the Speaker's hands—could he?

"This has been coming on a long time," Mathi said. Lofotan demanded to know how she knew that. Mathi had to frame a reply that protected Rufe, her hired spy.

"The general complained of being unwell at Free Winds. I understand he consulted with healers there," was all she would say.

Lofotan got down. "We must find a cleric, who can lift the curse from our lord."

"No one can lift a dead magician's spell!" Artyrith declared. He had gone quite pale. Like Lofotan, he assumed Vedvedsica had been executed for his crimes. Only Mathi knew the true fate of the mage. Her distant brethren were in secret contact with their creator. Vedvedsica lived, though he was confined in a walled keep on a tiny island south of Silvanesti.

"How do you know it can't be done? Are you a priest?" Lofotan said.

"Everyone knows a dead man's magic is unbreakable!"

Lofotan said, "I will not bow to superstition." To the scribe, he added, "Fetch clean water and some clothes." Treskan hurried to comply, but Rufe turned up with the items first. Lofotan set to work washing the mud from his master's face.

Squatting in the grass, Rufe examined Balif's hand, as Lofotan eyed him warily. The kender turned it back and forth, scratched his nails with his own small ones, and sniffed his palms.

He was still at it when Balif said, "Everything in place, my friend?"

Anyone else would have leaped a yard at being address so suddenly. Rufe chuckled. "What happened to your claws?"

"Mind your tongue!" Lofotan barked.

"Peace, Captain," said Balif. His voice was hoarse and strained. "My claws, friend wanderer, did not survive the night, I am happy to say."

"You mean you were more of a beast last night than you are now?" Again Lofotan warned the kender about his manners.

Balif frowned. "The question is not without merit," he said mildly. "While the storm was building, I was seized by a terrible urge to escape, to hide from every beam of light. I rode ahead, all the while transforming into the creature you saw. The poor horse went mad at having such a beast on his back. He tried to buck me off. I did all I could to stay on, but I lost by grip. The rest of the night I spent dodging my majordomo and my cook, both of whom were intent on killing me."

Without turning his head to see, Balif raised his voice and

added, "I saw you, Mathi, seated by the fire. I tried to tell you who I was, but I could not speak."

"I did not know you, my lord, but I could tell you were no ordinary animal."

He sat up, unconscious of his exposed state. "You spoke to me. I remember that you did but not what you said. I wanted to . . . harm you, but something in your words dissuaded me."

Balif said he had eventually lost all power of coherent thought, lapsing completely into animal mode. When he awoke, the sun was shining overhead and Lofotan was carrying him to a waiting horse. He was naked, and his body ached as if he'd been beaten with rods.

"I found you sprawled in the grass, passed out," Lofotan said. "Nothing would rouse you."

He helped Balif stand. Mathi and Treskan held up the sleeves of a clean robe. Balif struggled to raise his arms. While he did, Artyrith whirled up on horseback.

"My lord!" he said, choked. "My lord, I am bound for Silvanost. I, therefore, bid you farewell!"

"What?" Lofotan exploded.

"I was hired to cook for one the most illustrious lords of Silvanost. When you took the Speaker's command and set off on this journey, I went along, as befits a noble retainer. But now—" He reined his agitated mount in a circle. "Lord, if you are accursed, I cannot help you!"

Lofotan spat, "Coward!"

"If we were in Silvanost, I would challenge you for that insult!"

Lofotan repeated it. "It is easy to be brave in the city. Show your mettle here, pot-tender! Draw your blade or stand by your lord!"

Artyrith threw a riding glove in the grass at Lofotan's feet. "Return that to me in Silvanost, and I will prove who is the coward!" With a final curt salute, he dug in his heels and rode swiftly away.

Lofotan shouted after him until Balif quietly asked him to cease. Artyrith rode due west, finally vanishing over the horizon. There was a long silence as everyone digested his sudden, surprising abandonment.

"He'll never make it," the old soldier swore finally. "Nomads will gut him like a trout!"

"He may reach home," Balif said, grunting as he tried to walk. "He is a resourceful fellow."

"Stiff-necked, overbred city fool," Lofotan muttered.

Apart from the fur on his back, Balif looked the same. Mathi clasped his arm to help him walk, carefully noting his nails were quite unclawlike, as Rufe had discovered.

Shivering, he drew the robe close around his lean body. "So, my friends, we are down to three," he said.

"Four."

"You, little man? Since when do you belong to this company?"

"Since she started paying me." Mathi tried not to look guilty. She failed.

They packed up their gear. Balif was too weak to help, so he sat in the grass and outlined his plans since his affliction had come to light. They would cross the Thon-Tanjan as planned and proceed with their mission.

"But, my lord, what about your condition?" asked his loyal retainer.

"At night you will bind me with chains a safe distance from the horses—and from you."

"That's not what I meant, my lord. Shouldn't we seek a priest or sage who can help you?"

"Few are the practitioners who can reverse Vedvedsica's spells," Balif said calmly. "Gods willing, we will carry out the Speaker's task and then find a cure for me . . . if one exists."

Privately Mathi was in turmoil. She had no idea the Creator had cast such a spell on Balif. His sense of justice was worthy of a poet—to slowly turn the great general into a beast for his betrayal of Vedvedsica's beast-children; that was godlike thinking. It wasn't just the transformation and the loss of mind and faculties that would haunt Balif; it was knowing the horror and ignominy Balif would face in Silvanost if he ever returned.

But would he return ever? The last thing a proud, nobly born elf would want would be to display such an affliction to his peers. Artyrith's revulsion was moderate compared to what Balif would encounter there. After all, Vedvedsica's creatures, though innocent of their own origins, were rounded up, slain, or shipped off to eternal exile for simply existing. Balif was a victim, but under Silvanesti law, even the accursed were liable for exile or worse if their existence was deemed an affront to nature.

She helped Lofotan boost Balif onto his horse. The abused animal accepted his rider without a qualm. Mathi decided the horse was more tolerant than Artyrith.

They rode slowly down the sandy hill to the fast-flowing Tanjan. The ford was a series of pools and channels bounded by boulders that allowed travelers to pick their way across. Lofotan went first with the pack animals. Rufe the kender perched on the back of the last pack pony, looking back to the south bank where the other elves waited.

"Strange little fellow," Treskan remarked.

"How do creatures like that get by in the world?" Mathi wondered.

"Oh, we manage."

The scribe shouted with alarm. He and the others were surrounded by kender. They had arrived so quietly that neither he, Mathi, nor Balif had detected them. Among them was the Longwalker, a head taller than any other kender present.

"Excellent, friend," Balif said. "You have a great talent for astonishment. Is it magic that allows you to move with such stealth?"

"Oh no," the Longwalker said. "Most people just don't pay good enough attention. That's when we come and go."

"Are you crossing the river?"

"I think so. The riders will soon be here, so we had better."

By "riders" he meant humans. Glancing around, Mathi saw that many of the kender had injuries: sword cuts on their heads and shoulders, bruises on their faces, and battered hands. It turned out that the nomad band the elves had encountered earlier had returned in force. They were sweeping the bend of the river for kender, centaurs, and anyone else not of their band. Greath and the Hok-nu were fighting back, but the kender, being kender, chose to move on.

"How far behind are the humans?" asked Balif.

The Longwalker polled his comrades. Kender had little use for measurements of time or space, so no one had an adequate answer. "Close" was the best they could agree on.

Treskan took Balif's reins. "Come, my lord."

Lofotan gained the north bank and led the stubborn pack team ashore. The water had been cold, so it was good to get out in the summer sun. He saw the others linger on the far shore a while, surrounded by a large group of kender. Then they entered the shallow ford. The kender followed, and Lofotan was able to get a clear view of their progress. Being short and lightweight, they might have had a hard time crossing, but kender ingenuity prevailed. They waded where they could, clasping their hands together atop their heads. When the water grew too swift or deep, they clung together in living chains. The kender on the far end of the chain detached themselves one by one, clinging to their comrades as they crossed the hazard. First over was last to arrive. With a minimum of fuss, no equipment, and with considerable speed, the little folk were across the river.

Their escape was timely. Trios of riders appeared on the high ground overlooking the river. They had followed the clear tracks to the water's edge, noting the last kender clambering out of the ford on the other side. Balif, Lofotan, Treskan, and Mathi sat on their horses in plain view too.

Lofotan said, "My lord, we should withdraw."

"Not yet. Sometimes it is wise to let the enemy see your banners."

He was right. Knowing there were Silvanesti around instead of wandering bands of kender made the humans hesitate to pursue them. The deadly work Artyrith and Balif did at the grassland trail was bearing fruit.

Leisurely, Balif turned his horse away and rode up the bank to the sandy flat above. At that point the Thon-Tanjan was a boundary between the fertile green plains south and arid land north. That was an expanse of desert that stretched from the Khalkist Mountains in the west to the eastern ocean. North of the desert was a land little known to the Silvanesti. East lay the disputed territory, bound on three sides by water and on the north by desert. It was good land, well watered by local streams and heavily forested along the watercourse. On official maps in the capital the elves called it "Silvanoth," which literally rendered meant "Silvanos's Holding," implying it was the personal property of the Speaker of the Stars. No one living there called it that. The kender called it Treetops, in honor of the very tall trees growing there.

With trembling hands, Balif sighted with his sunstone. Southeast was their course. Treskan and Lofotan rode on either side of him, keeping a close eye on their afflicted leader. Mathi followed behind, exulting in her creator's scheme. She wished she had known what was going to happen. Still, it explained why she had been sent to attach herself to the general. Mathi thought Balif was going to be kidnapped, to face the judgment of those he had betrayed. However, it seemed her role was to observe and report the metamorphosis of the mighty Balif into a wild beast.

So why did her joy prove so fleeting? With the sun hot

on her face, Mathi soon lost her pride in her creator's deed. Balif was a betrayer, responsible for many deaths and suffering among her brethren. But why could she not rejoice at his plight? Why did the sight of his frail figure, jouncing along on horseback, fill her with stirrings of pity?

The kender band around them waxed and waned as they went. A few, including Rufe, hitched rides on the packhorses until Mathi caught them rummaging through the baggage for souvenirs. Then Lofotan ran them off.

Balif grew stronger as the day went on. He ate and drank prodigiously, considering his usually abstemious habits. Nectar, water, dried meat, and pressed fruit went down with ravenous intensity. He ate like an elf long starved. No one questioned him on it, but Lofotan and the others took note.

They made good time across open country on the east bank of the river. The ground was rising, growing hillier as they neared the forested region south of the ford. When approaching the line of trees, their kender escort all but disappeared. Even Rufe departed at some unseen moment, leaving the foursome to ride on alone.

"Now that our small friends have gone, I have some things to tell you," Balif said. Lofotan halted his horse to listen, but Balif bade him ride on.

"If this transformation of mine grows worse—and I expect it shall—you must take steps to protect yourselves and our mission," he said. "You must restrain me each night."

"But will you assume beast form every night?" asked Treskan.

Balif didn't know. The previous night might have been a harbinger of things to come, or it could have been triggered by some unknown factor. Perhaps the thunderstorm provoked his metamorphosis, or the positions of the moons in the sky. Who knew?

"In any event, protect yourselves."

"I will bind you hand and foot each night," Lofotan vowed.

"Not enough." Balif's strength was enhanced when in beastly form. Rope would not hold him. Had they any chain?

"I have a few lengths in the baggage," said Lofotan. It was heavy logging chain, used to drag timber behind a sturdy horse.

"Use it."

His old comrade objected. Binding with chain was undignified.

"So is rending your friends to bits with claws and fangs."

Chain might injure the general's wrists and ankles, Lofotan added.

"Do it, nonetheless."

"We will do as you command, my lord," Treskan said. Lofotan looked at the reins in his hand and said nothing.

Before dark, they carefully chose to camp on a hilltop amid a thicket of overgrown myrtles. They were unloading the horses when Balif turned his head sharply and announced that he smelled smoke. So saying, he alerted the others, and they smelled it too, even Treskan with his less-than-keen nose. Lofotan climbed the tangled branches of the tallest myrtle and quickly spied the source of the smoke.

"There's a large column of smoke rising from the next ridge," he called down. It was a single, thick spire, probably a large campfire. Wildfire smoke would rise from many smaller points.

"Humans?" Mathi wondered aloud.

At her elbow Rufe said, "Yes, a big camp of them."

She started at his sudden proximity. "Don't do that!" she cried.

"Do what?" asked Rufe.

Balif laughed heartily. He hadn't done so all day. "Have you scouted them already?" Balif said. Rufe admitted he had. He had "found" a few items too, things he hadn't seen before.

Balif held out his hand. Reluctantly the kender put his spoils on display. He had a stone knife made of obsidian. It was too finely made to be a nomad's tool. The shell inlay on the handle make it look like a cleric's blade. Rufe had an amber necklace, a beaded headband, and most remarkably, a full-length arrow that he pulled out through his collar. It was so long, it must have gone straight down to his foot, but no one noticed him limping before he pulled it out.

"Let me see that."

Balif examined the arrow closely. The shaft was daubed white, had a bronze head, and used soft, gray-white feathers for fletching. Balif paid special attention to the feathers.

"Ghost owl feathers," he said, frowning. The ghost owl was unknown in Silvanesti territory. Its range was in the Plains River Valley west of the Khalkist Mountains. The nomad band must have come from there.

"Maybe they traded for arrows with bands further west?" Mathi asked. Balif said no. Among nomads, every archer made his own arrows, matched to his bow. Whoever made the arrow had access to ghost owl feathers. The invaders had come a long way.

"Do we move on?" Lofotan asked. Rufe could not give them any guess as to the size of the nomad party, but there must have been many to merit such a large campfire.

Balif said, "No. We stay here." Night was close upon them. They were right under the nose of the humans, but if they kept quiet, they ought to be able to pass unnoticed.

Everyone ended up looking at Rufe.

"What?"

"You know, my lord, it might be worthwhile to have a look at this human camp. Governor Dolanath and the Speaker will need an accurate count of the invaders," Lofotan said.

Balif was reluctant. He finally agreed to send Lofotan, Mathi, and Treskan to reconnoiter the nomads' camp. Rufe would stay behind to guard their camp—and him.

"I do not trust the little man, and what good is the girl if a fight comes?" Lofotan protested.

"You insult our friend Rufe. He comes and goes but always comes again. Mathi is quieter than the scribe and has good eyes."

Mathi would have preferred to stay with Balif but no matter. A spy mission might give her a chance to leave a message for her friends, whom she knew must be shadowing their party.

"Go right after dark," Balif said. He had lived among and fought against humans a long time and knew their ways. "After sunset they will be eating, washing, or falling asleep." Going later would only put them up against alert watchmen.

They huddled among the myrtles, eating silently. Lofotan and Balif were in their element, Mathi observed. Hiding in the trees like thieves, eating cold rations, dueling with danger—that was their chosen life. Treskan obviously missed his bed and three squares a day. At least the nectar was good. Rufe managed to pass the time without chattering. When he was done eating, he put his head down on his knees and went to sleep.

Everyone was awakened later by gentle prods. Mathi was surprised that she had slept. It had not been her intention, but slumber crept up on her before she knew it.

It was a clear night, with strong starlight and no moons yet risen. The wind moved to and fro, changing directions in little puffs this way and that. They were dangerous conditions, Balif observed. Starlight could reveal them even to human eyes. The deceptive wind could mask important scents or send theirs wafting in unfriendly directions.

"Shall we stay here?" asked Lofotan. Balif said no.

Before they left, Lofotan had his commander sit with a sturdy myrtle sapling between his knees. Balif put his arms around the trunk. Lofotan wound chain around his wrists and ankles, securing the ends with twists of wire.

Plainly unhappy with having to truss up his revered commander, Lofotan put a skin of water on Balif's lap. Even chained, he could reach it. He gave Treskan a sword, warning him not to clank or clatter as they approached the nomad camp. The scribe, very unmilitary with the weapons in his hands, swore he would not.

After apologizing to his commander for the fourth time, Lofotan took Mathi by the elbow and propelled her into the darkness. Rufe gave Balif a wink and sat down beside the general. He launched into a tale of his wanderings. It promised to be very long and very strange.

Lofotan, Treskan, and Mathi soon were swallowed by the night. Beyond, the eastern horizon was alive with the glow of a mighty campfire in the same spot they had earlier seen the smoke.

# CHAPTER 12

## *Hunters*

Mathi, Treskan, and Lofotan walked parallel a while, wading through knee-high scrub toward the fire-lit hill. The old warrior moved like a cloud, hardly stirring the leaves as he passed. Mathi slipped along, trying to match the elf's deftness. Treskan had a harder time. If Mathi hadn't already known he was a human in disguise, she would have figured it out. His progress was labored and noisy.

The route wasn't easy. Roots tripped their toes, thorny branches ripped their elbows, and insects swarmed around their faces. The ground was a hazard covered with fallen tree limbs. She avoided them all, but Treskan stepped down on an unseen burrow. The turf broke loudly, and the scribe sprawled on his hands and knees. By the time he got up, Lofotan was standing over him.

"Give our position away once more, scribbler, and I'll take you back and chain you to our lord!" he hissed. Treskan swallowed hard and swore he would be more careful.

They began to hear voices. Without warning, Lofotan angled toward some good-sized trees off to the left. They were dogwoods, very old and gnarled. He climbed the twisted trunk. Casting around, Mathi and Treskan saw others and hauled themselves up as well.

Two nomads appeared, laughing and talking loudly. Each carried a large canvas bucket. They passed right under Mathi.

"—he said he could do it, so I said try. He strung his bow and *zzup!* Put an arrow in the buck's brisket. The crazy thing kept boundin', and we ended up chasing it another mile!"

"Daxas never was a good bowman," said the other.

They stopped on either side of a freshly dug hole in the turf. Dumping out the buckets, they retraced their path and disappeared in the cleft between the hills.

They swung down. Treskan clamped a hand over his nose. "What was in the hole?" he asked through gritted teeth.

"Offal," Mathi whispered. The humans had butchered a deer and disposed of the parts they didn't want. The smell of blood made Mathi tingle in ways she had not experienced in a very long time. She found herself staring at the noisome pit until Lofotan called her away.

Rather than follow the two nomads, Lofotan went up the dark side of the hill to the summit. With great care, Mathi and Treskan shadowed him, trying to step in the same spots as their leader. They arrived at the top soundlessly. They found the old warrior crouched by a boulder. Below, a broad hollow lay spread out before them. Lofotan pointed down at the fire-lit expanse.

The camp was large indeed. It filled the hollow from end to end. Surrounding the sprawl of rude tents was a palisade of spears driven butt-first into the ground. Nomad spears had metal or stone end caps that allowed them to be driven in like stakes. Inside that fence lay tents, pens, and corrals, laid out in disorganized fashion. Lofotan said nomads shared their tents with up to five comrades. Counting the shelters, he reckoned they were looking at a camp of more than one thousand. They could not see any children or elders. That meant one thing: it was a war party.

Lofotan spotted odd pens in the camp. Tied to stakes inside one pen were eight centaurs, heads bowed and legs folded. Beside them was another pen with a top made of lashed saplings. Something stirred within the dark confines of the makeshift cage: more captives, obviously smaller than centaurs.

Lofotan signed for them to follow. He had seen enough. Sliding backward on his belly, he eased back into the darkness. Mathi was about to join him when she heard a sound that made her blood turn cold.

Dogs were baying inside the camp. Mathi froze. They hadn't counted on dogs. Sure enough, a pack of ten hounds came springing through the lanes between the tents, each one baying to be first after their prey. Nomads left their bowls and cups when they heard the animals' commotion.

"No time for stealth," Lofotan said, rising to his feet. "Run!"

Mathi and Treskan tried. She fled down the hill, kicking high to avoid branches and burrows. In an instant she lost sight of her companions. She didn't have any time to wonder where they had gone before the pack was at her heels. More than a dozen deerhounds with long, thin legs; white teeth; and tails like whips came bounding after her. They spilled right and left, seeking to cut her off. Running downhill helped, but Mathi soon saw flashes of gray and brown ahead of her. The dogs had her ringed in. She dragged at the sword Lofotan had foisted on her, trying to draw it as she ran. Heavy tramping in the grass to her left turned out to be Treskan, running for his life.

The animals in front of her halted with fangs bared. She ran right at the closest one, sword upraised. It was a brave beast and stood its ground. Mathi sent its head flying with a single swing. A dog behind her bit at her leg but got only the hem of her gown. Mathi shortened it by a head as well.

Treskan swung wildly at the hounds swarming around him. They darted in after each swing, got between his legs, and brought him down in the high grass.

The pack was closing in on Mathi too. Where was Lofotan? Torches appeared at the top of the hill. The nomads were coming. Where was Lofotan?

She waited for the comforting snap of a bowstring and the flicker of deadly arrows foiling her pursuit. None came. With horror Mathi remembered it was Artyrith who was the superb archer.

A lean, muscular hound leaped at her, catching her sword hand in its jaws. The dog's weight spun her around, and two more jumped on her, catching hold of her cloak. She staggered as they tugged hard in all directions. Mathi couldn't raise her sword with the dog on her arm. The hand guard saved her hand from being mangled, but it also gave the hound something to hold on to. A fourth animal clamped on to her dress. With a cry, Mathi went down.

She expected to be savaged. Deep in her soul she had flashes of such a fight—hounds surrounding her, yellow teeth snapping, the baying of the pack as it closed in. It was night then too, and Mathi had drowned the lead dogs one by one when they tried to seize her in the midst of a swift-running stream. There was no water there, only stars and bloodthirsty hounds and the smell of smoke.

Whistles split the night air, and the dogs kept tight hold of her, but they didn't tear her flesh. The torches grew brighter. She smelled pine burning. A band of nomads, their faces black against the sky, stood around her.

"What is it? A brace of rabbits?"

"A couple of those little thieves, damn them!"

Fire was thrust in her face.

"No! The elder kind! And female!"

"This one too!"

More whistles in short, sharp blasts made the dog pack

back off. Hard hands took hold of Treskan and Mathi and dragged them to their feet.

"Who is you?" asked one of the nomads in poor Elvish. "Why you here is?"

"My name is Mathani Arborelinex," she replied in their own tongue. One of the benefits of living on the fringes of elf society was that she had come into contact with many races. Mathi understood a good part of eight tongues, including Ogrish.

"Hey, Vollman, two of your dogs are dead," called out another human.

One of the nomads holding Treskan's arms gave the limb a wrench. The scribe yelped. "Kill my boys, will you? Maybe I'll take an eye or a finger for each one you slew!" The one called Vollman jerked a long-bladed dagger from his belt.

Treskan struggled in the grip of two brawny nomads. Mathi fought hard until a similar weapon was pressed against her throat. She felt her heart contract to a small, hard knot.

"Be still or be dead!"

"Stop it, Vollman. They will answer questions for the chief first. Then we'll decide what to do with them."

With buffets to the head and kicks in the backside, Mathi and Treskan were marched to the nomads' camp. Glancing left and right, she saw that her captors were fiercely tattooed men with light-colored hair worn in tight braids. They wore deerskins beaded with bold designs. Metal was a mark of status, she guessed. The leader of the party that caught her wore a crescent-shaped strip of brass around his neck and had yellow metal plugs through his earlobes.

In camp, a crowd of nomads had gathered to see the night's catch. A few were women, warriors too, but most of them were men of fighting age. Mathi and the scribe were driven like wild stags to the door of a large, dome-shaped tent.

The gorget-wearer called out, "Chief! Come out! We caught us something!"

The chief came out. He was the tallest man Mathi had ever seen, nearly seven feet tall. He was darkly tanned, but in the torchlight his eyes were slate gray. His head was shaved except for a single long lock on the back of his head, which he wore thickly braided and pulled forward over his shoulder.

"What's this?" His voice was as big as his frame.

"We found these elder kind hiding in the bushes," said the man called Vollman. "She speaks our tongue good."

"Oh?" said the giant, advancing a step until he towered over Mathi. "I never met a big-ears who could speak our language well. Maybe you've spent some time around people, yes?"

Mathi didn't answer. She wasn't being sullen or stalwart; she was just scared. The chief took her silence for resistance. He backhanded Mathi so hard that she fell backward into the arms of the surrounding nomads. Laughing, they boosted her back on her feet. Mathi tasted blood.

"Where do you come from?" the chief bellowed at Treskan. His mumbled "Silvanost" was the wrong answer.

"Spying on us, yes? How many elder kind have we seen on our journey, Nurna?"

A muscular young nomad said, "Three, four, chief. Always on hilltops far away, watching us."

"Collecting news for their king, yes?" To the men holding the captives, he barked, "Search them!"

They did with brutal thoroughness. Her gown was torn in several places. She did not scream, and the violation did not go any further. They found the secret mark of the brethren under her right arm. The blue tattoo surprised the nomads. They had never seen an elf with marks before. There was some excitement when they found Treskan's stylus—it was metal and nicely turned—and the talisman Rufe had taken and Mathi had returned. The jeweled gold ornament got everyone's attention.

Vollman claimed the talisman against the loss of his two

deerhounds. There were a few protests, but the lofty chief awarded the trinket to Vollman. Mathi had nothing of the tiniest value on her: a few scraps of parchment purloined from Treskan, some charred wood to write with, a few beads, and a wooden amulet carved in the image of Quenesti Pah, part of her disguise as a former resident of the Haven of the Lost.

The chief examined the small harvest taken from the prisoners. Aside from Treskan's talisman, there was nothing very rich or revealing about any of it.

To Mathi he said in passable Elvish, "Is this all you got?"

"I am just a poor traveler," Mathi replied in the same language.

The chief threw the trinkets on the ground. "They know more than they're telling. Tie them to the cage."

They dragged them to the roofed-in box in the center of the camp they'd seen earlier, the one made of lashed-together saplings. Mathi was shoved face-first against the rails. Her wrists and ankles were tied with thongs. Treskan was slammed into place beside her.

From within the dark cage, a pair of eyes met hers. Mathi could not tell whom she was seeing, but she heard a whisper say, "Tell them what they want to know. They'll lash you to death if you don't."

Nurna appeared with a rawhide whip. Mathi felt her knees give way. She had not bargained for such treatment. Where was Lofotan? How could he leave her to the savages?

Nurna nodded and two nomads tore the cloth from Mathi's and Treskan's backs. She clenched her eyes shut and braced herself for the sting of the lash. It didn't come. Trembling, she opened her eyes. Twisting her head around, she saw Nurna and others speaking together with hushed urgency. One nomad ran off. Nurna came closer, coiling the whip in his hand.

"Too bad," he said. "May the great gods pity you."

Before she had the slightest understanding of what was happening, Mathi and Treskan were cut loose and thrown into the cage. They crouched on their knees—the roof was too low to allow her to stand—and watched in amazement as the nomads dispersed.

"Merciful gods," he muttered. What stayed their hand? Mathi had no idea.

"You heard the man," said their unseen companion. "They pity you."

"Who's there?" Mathi said sharply, drawing closer to Treskan.

"A brother."

Their fellow prisoner crawled out of the shadows on his hands and knees. Treskan drew in a loud breath. The stranger's hands and forearms were covered in short, stiff fur. Where a man or elf had nails, their companion had curving, yellow claws. His face emerged from the deeper darkness. Mathi must have stared too hard, for the creature halted his advance.

"Forgive me. As another mistake, I thought you one of us," he said. His Elvish was excellent, and his accent urban. If an elf closed his eyes, he would think he was speaking to an articulate resident of Silvanost.

"I am one of you—one of us! Who are you?"

"Taius." The name rhymed with *bias.*

"I am Mathani Arborelinex. This is Treskan."

Taius laughed or coughed. It was hard to tell through the fangs and fur. "He's not what he seems either, is he?" Neither of them answered. Taius said, "You still use a Silvanesti name?"

"Why not? You do," Mathi replied.

Taius withdrew into the shadows again. "I no longer claim Silvanesti as my race." He chuckled, an unnervingly beastly sound. "Do you know your mother and father?"

"No, but I know my creator."

Taius's eyes glittered in the dark. "Say not the name."

She tried to remember if they had ever met. The children of Vedvedsica's art had been scattered, by design, all over the kingdom. Mathi lived in the western woodland, not far from the provincial town of Woodbec. Judging by his accent, Taius had dwelt in the city.

"But why did they spare us the lash?" Treskan said.

"When they tore open your clothes, they saw the truth."

"Truth?"

It struck Mathi like a thunderbolt. Her elf form was her greatest advantage. Among all her brethren, she was chosen for the mission because her appearance was the most perfect. One by one, the others had begun reverting to their original beastly shapes. When she left the brethren's hidden camp for Silvanost, she was outwardly as elflike as Balif or Artyrith. But the change was affecting her too. Her characteristic fur was slowly returning. The nomads saw she had elf features but with body hair. Treskan was in the same condition but for different reasons. His elf image was wearing thin in the wilderness. The nomads assumed the two of them were—

"Half-breeds," said the voice.

Mathi was so relieved to escape the flogging that she didn't care about her degeneration beginning. Being mistaken by the nomads for a half-elf was an unforeseen benefit. Hating and distrusting elves themselves, they had a certain sympathy for half-elves, who were despised by the Silvanesti and officially persecuted by them.

"What about him?" Taius said.

Treskan replied, "I am a scholar, trying to broaden my knowledge of the elves."

"You're a long way from a library."

"You must help us escape!" she said urgently. "I am on an urgent mission for our brethren!"

Taius sprang at her, alighting scant inches from the crouching Mathi. Long teeth bared in a fierce snarl, his hot breath played on her face like flame.

"To the abyss with the brethren and all our kind!"

Mathi pushed her face closer until their noses almost touched. "I thought we are all kindred."

"The brethren abandoned us in the city. So did the Creator. He gave us, his children, to the Silvanesti. They hunted us down like—" Had he intended to say *animals?* Whatever his intent, Taius thought better of it. "They hunted us, killing all who resisted. The rest were spirited away to oblivion."

"So too our creator," Mathi said.

"You lie! For his betrayal of his children, the Nameless One was spared!"

Mathi told Taius what she had been able to glean from Balif about Vedvedsica's trial and condemnation. She went so far as to tell him about Balif's voluntary exile from Silvanost on the pretext of scouting the eastern province for information about nonelf invaders. Though he had no knowledge of what Vedvedsica was doing, Balif had provided help to the magician. After Vedvedsica's fall, Balif offered to take full blame for the scandal, but Silvanos would not allow it. How could he tarnish the name of Silvanesti's greatest hero with such horrible pollution?

"Balif? The general is here?"

"He is near." Because Taius was so unstable, Mathi decided to not disclose her mission to him. At that time the fewer who knew, the better.

"I bless the name Balif," he said, despairing, to Mathi's astonishment.

"What is your story, Taius?" Treskan asked. "I am in General Balif's employ, but I did not join him until after the trial of—of the Nameless. Who are you, and how came you to be here?"

The beast-elf relaxed his threatening posture. He had

actually served in Balif's guard during the Forest War. In those days his beastly traits were hidden by Vedvedsica's magic. He thought he was an ordinary elf until the transformation spell worked by the magus began to fail. He tried to hide his condition as long as he could, but it soon became impossible to conceal. Dozens of others like him had mixed in Silvanesti society, serving as soldiers, scribes, artisans, and performers. Some had even married full-blooded elves and had offspring.

Mathi was shocked. Offspring of the brethren and elves? She had not heard that before. Did Silvanos know? Did the Sinthal-Elish, the assembly of great nobles, know?

"They know. And they will never speak of it. It is their greatest shame," Taius said.

There was a dimension Mathi had not suspected. What great families were mingled with the blood of the beast-elves?

Treskan said, "How did the nomads take you?"

Taius's eyes glittered in the dark. "I had just brought down a kill, a yearling doe, when their dogs caught my scent. I couldn't shake them off, so I turned to fight. I was netted like a partridge. When the humans saw what they had caught, they put me in here."

With sudden violence, Taius leaped upward, grabbing the cage roof with his hands and feet. He shook the willow lattice and roared. The bars held. From a distance, they heard laughter and taunts from their captors.

He dropped lightly to the ground and retreated to the darkest corner of the cage.

"I wonder why they put us together?" Mathi wondered aloud.

"The centaurs they've taken are tied in an open pen. The freaks they cage."

Taius would not speak anymore. Wary of their mercurial fellow prisoner, Mathi and Treskan moved to the opposite end of the cage, where firelight made a dim haven from the darkness.

She dozed. She could not rest. Every sound teased her awake. Passing nomads coughed, hacked up phlegm, or talked loudly, and each disturbance jolted Mathi awake. Treskan sat slumped against the bars, asleep or brooding. Taius was absolutely silent.

Time passed. She didn't know how much. In the small hours, something hard thumped against the back of her head. She thought a nomad was amusing himself, flinging stones at the half-breed. When the blow was repeated, she turned angrily to insult her abuser.

No one was there.

Daybreak was closer than sunset. Most of the nomads were asleep in their tents. She could see random hands or feet poking out of open tent flaps. The campfires had burned down to embers. Now and then an alert human loped into view with a polearm on his shoulder.

After a watchman passed, another stone came whirling out of the night. Mathi saw it come from the deep shadows between two tents. It was a round, water-washed pebble tumbling end over end, and it struck her square on the forehead.

Like a ghost, a lean figure bereft of color slowly emerged from the tents. It took Mathi a moment to realize it was Lofotan, wearing a long, gray cloak that reached his knees. He moved with all the grace of his race, sidling up to the cage with such calm that not even his breath could be heard.

Starlight gleamed on a length of sharp bronze. Two strokes, and the hide lacing holding the cage closed was gone. Then, without a word or gesture, Lofotan wafted back to the black gap he came from.

Mathi shook Treskan. He started, fists clenched, ready to fight. Mathi hissed at him to be quiet. She stood, head and shoulders bent down by the low top.

"Up," she whispered. Treskan obeyed.

They braced their shoulders against the bars and pushed.

The green wood lattice shifted. Treskan got his arm out and used it to push against the cage frame. They heaved again, shifting the cage top far enough to one side to allow them to climb out.

In a flash Taius was beside them. Treskan almost cried out in alarm when he felt his furry flanks brush against him. In one fluid movement, Taius was out and on the ground, crouched on all fours. He looked back at Mathi and the scribe, staring with amazement from inside the cage. Fangs flashed in a grimace—or smile?—and the beast melted into the night.

With far greater deliberation, Treskan and Mathi climbed out. They tugged the cage top back into place and hurried away, making for the spot where Mathi saw Lofotan vanish. Not two steps into the shadows, she felt a slim, hard hand clamp over her mouth.

"You took your time!" he murmured in the girl's ear.

After he removed his hand, Mathi hissed back, "My thought exactly!"

"It was not my plan to attack thousands by myself. Come."

Lofotan led them through a maze of tents populated by snoring, snorting nomads. They hid once or twice from prowling sentries then slipped through the palisade to freedom. On open ground, Lofotan broke into a run. Mathi and Treskan were not fleet enough to keep up with an elf of Lofotan's size. Stumbling, Treskan pleaded to Lofotan to slacken his pace.

"Do you want to linger near their camp? Their dogs may pick up our scent again."

With Taius free she doubted that. He smelled too strongly of beast. Given a choice, the hounds would chase him and not a human or a near-elf such as Mathi. Still, Lofotan's point was well made. Speed would put more safe ground between them and the nomads. She jogged after the spry warrior.

Back in the myrtle thicket, they found Balif awake, still chained to the tree. Rufe slept soundly a few feet away.

The general greeted him courteously.

"My lord, you seem . . . yourself."

"So I am. I cannot explain it." Even shackled, the elf was extraordinarily poised. "You've had quite an adventure tonight."

Ruefully Mathi agreed. She related her experiences in the nomad camp, leaving out their exposure as half-breeds. Treskan let her do all the talking.

"They didn't question any more closely than that?" said Balif.

"No, my lord."

She described the cage and her fellow captive. "This Taius claimed he had served under you in the Forest War," Mathi said.

"I remember a warrior named Taius. A very brave soldier of noble countenance." His countenance was no longer so noble, but he was civilized enough not to attack Mathi on sight.

Then, not knowing exactly why she did so, she related to Balif the story of Taius's true nature. The general listened calmly.

"He's not as far along as some others," Balif said. Sooner or later the transformed beasts always reverted to their animal origins, Balif said. Vedvedsica's spell, though powerful, could not overcome nature forever.

Taius retained a fading veneer of civilization, the general continued. If he lived long enough, he would forget everything and be nothing but a beast. The worst creatures were the ones who had almost forgotten their elf lives. They were beasts in every way, but their minds still held memories of their former lives. Because of that they were filled with rage over their situation.

Vedvedsica had exploited that rage, Mathi knew, by urging them to find and kill Balif.

Lofotan appeared. He looked haggard but alert. "We

should move," he said. "By daylight we shall be too exposed here."

Balif agreed. Lofotan had packed the baggage onto the horses while Mathi and Treskan were captive. All they had to do was release Balif, rouse the kender, and go.

Lofotan unwired the links and removed Balif's chains. Rubbing his wrists, the general stood. Mathi stooped to pick up the costly bronze links.

"Mathani."

She straightened, coiling the chain in her hands.

"Mathani, your gown."

She realized that her garment was still torn open. Mathi waited for the questions and the denunciations that would follow. She looked at Balif blankly, leaving to him the final challenge.

Lofotan returned. "We must hurry!"

Balif gazed intently at her. Without a word, he took the cloak he'd been sitting on and draped it around Mathi's exposed back. He walked on and swung into the saddle. Lofotan kicked Rufe awake. Yawning, the kender scratched his ribs, got up, and walked off alone in the predawn darkness.

Why didn't Balif, general of the Speaker's army, denounce her as an impostor? Did he take Mathi for a half-breed, as the nomads had? The existence of half-humans was officially denied in Silvanost on the grounds that such pairings could not be fruitful. Secretly, half-humans were subject to summary arrest, exile, or imprisonment without trial. Balif was known to be a tolerant elf. Perhaps his own condition made him more sensitive to the question of who was an elf and who wasn't.

Puzzling over it, Mathi got on her pony. She had just settled in the saddle when Treskan came furtively to her side.

"My talisman. I must have it back," he said in a low voice.

"Forget it."

"One of the nomads—Vollman?—must still have it. I have to have it back, or I am lost!"

Mathi looked around. Rufe—where was he? He was the perfect one to steal back a trinket, but where could one find a kender when the kender was on the loose, not wanting to be found?

# CHAPTER 13

## *Leaders*

Balif's party rode south, away from the nomad war band. For reputedly empty territory, they ran into plenty of people on the move—centaurs and kender, mostly. The few small groups of humans they spotted were mixed men, women, and children. The elves were unable to approach them, as the family bands fled at the sight of riders.

Balif dictated notes to the Speaker from the saddle. He was calm, insightful, and accurate in his judgment of the situation. There was no law in the eastern province. Human war bands crossed the territory with impunity, and they were trying to drive out anyone not part of their own tribe. The wanderfolk were numerous but not a serious threat to Silvanesti hegemony. They were simply migrants, living off the land, bothering no one but belligerent nomads and hysterical officials such as Governor Dolanath.

Mathi noticed that the general did not use the official Silvanesti name for the east, Silvanoth, and that he played down the potential problems the kender presented. She asked Balif about that point.

"The wanderfolk are not warriors or nation-builders. They are no threat to the Speaker's rule or the elven nation.

In fact, they may prove to be a useful buffer against the humans and centaurs," he said.

"Those little oddlings useful?" Lofotan commented sarcastically.

"Would you buy a house infested with cockroaches?" asked Balif. Lofotan avowed he wouldn't unless the pests were exterminated. "Not an easy thing to do. Smoke, poison, and traps will get many, but the house may never be free of them. Do you understand?"

Lofotan easily saw a connection between cockroaches and kender, but Mathi felt she understood better. If the east were thickly populated with kender, it would put off the nomads from settling there in large numbers if at all. They were perfectly willing to fight the elves for the land, but the kender wouldn't fight; they would just dwell there, doing all their infuriating kender things.

"Wanderfolk are bigger than insects," Lofotan mused. "Maybe the humans can eradicate them."

Balif said, "We must not let that happen."

Before his majordomo could question the wisdom of that, Balif trotted ahead, signaling an end to the conversation. Treskan hurried after him, eagerly scratching down every word the general had said.

As they drew near the forested region just inland from Golden-Eye Bay, they found signs of conflict: patches of burned grass, broken spears, and shattered arrows. The heads had been carefully salvaged, but there was no mistaking the ruined shafts of either. When the first tall trees came into sight, a delegation of kender emerged from the woods and approached them.

"Greetings, illustrious General," said the lead kender, holding a green sapling with a scrap of white cloth tied to the tip.

"General? What general?" Lofotan said warily.

"This is the storied commander of the elder folk, is he not?" The kender with the sapling pointed at Balif.

"You have us confused with others."

"The Longwalker told us of your coming."

Balif said, "The Longwalker deserves his name. Is he here?"

The kender wagged his head back and forth. "I don't see him."

Behind the flag bearer were five more kender, all bearing wounds of various sorts. The leader said, "Where is your army?"

"What army?" said Lofotan.

"The army that will defend the greenwood against the horsemen."

A large number of kender, traveling more or less independently, had taken to the woods to escape the bands of marauding humans. Some kender had been captured, brutally treated, then turned loose as a warning to the others to leave the territory.

"Who gives orders for you to leave?" asked Balif.

"The chief of the horse riders, Bulnac by name."

"Is this Bulnac a veritable giant, seven feet tall?" Mathi put in.

One of the silent kender stepped forward, waving a tightly bandaged arm. "Yes, yes, that's him! Closer to eight feet, I'd say!"

According to the kender, Bulnac had recently led an uprising against the chief of his people, the Monsha. Balif knew the Monsha, or Mon-shu as they were called by the elves. They were a populous, powerful tribe whose range was in the far northern Great Plains. Losing his fight to gain control of the tribe, Bulnac had ridden away with his supporters to carve out a new realm for himself in the east.

Lofotan and Mathi glanced at their leader. He sat immobile, gazing over the heads of the battered kender delegation.

"Bad tidings," he finally said. "A failed coup makes the loser desperate. This Bulnac will be difficult to deal with."

"Your excellent self can do it," said the flag-bearer cheerfully.

Balif looked at each of the little folk in turn. "I will do it," he said solemnly. "But you must help."

Lofotan started to protest, but his lord's manner dissuaded him. Inwardly Mathi rejoiced. For reasons she did not understand, she wanted Balif to help the wanderfolk. The sympathy she felt for the race—a word she did not completely comprehend—was something new. But she was pleased to know Balif would be fighting the savage humans and defending the kender.

He had no army. He had a single old retainer, a disguised human scribe, an unknown quantity of kender to command, and Mathi. She had no idea if the wanderfolk could be welded into an effective fighting force, but with those few words—"I will do it"—Balif had pledged himself to try.

Balif and his companions dismounted. They led their horses into the cool shade of the woods. Born to the green, Balif glowed with happiness to be under trees again. Close on his heels, Lofotan brooded. Treskan gripped his stylus. The nomads had taken his best instrument. He'd had a spare in his gear back at camp, and he held on to it for dear life. He had been writing all morning, even when conversation stopped. Mathi supposed he was compiling impressions of the territory and situation.

The forest was old and long-standing. Oaks and beeches predominated, interspersed with cedars so dark, their green fronds appeared black. The trees had reached great heights, growing unmolested since the dawn of time. Centuries of leaf fall had smothered all undergrowth, leaving the space between the soaring trunks relatively open. Passing through the forest was like traversing some enormous, columned hall. The air was still. Birds flitted in the high branches. Motes sank slowly through high lances of sunshine.

Tugging the packhorse reins behind her, Mathi's mind turned back to her mission. Since discovering the general's affliction, she had begun to wonder if she should continue with the plan to kidnap him. Would their creator prefer they left Balif to the mercies of his curse? Then there was her growing feeling that Balif should be left alone to deal with the human nomads and protect the kender.

Her mental juggling was halted by a small face popping up right in front of hers.

"Rufe!" she said. "You're here now, are you?"

"Tall people say the strangest things," he replied. "If I weren't here, who would you be speaking to?"

Mathi pushed him aside with a theatrical sweep of her hand. Rufe fell in step behind her, gently patting Mathi's pony.

A quick survey revealed hundreds of kender lurking and lolling in the forest. They perched on low branches, feet swinging; they dodged in and out of the columned trunks, playing tag. Some were doing tricks for the amusement of their comrades. Mathi saw one kender show how he could slip his arm out of his sleeve then leave behind a leather glove as a false hand. With his freed hand, he probed pockets, tossed rocks, and tied and untied shoelaces.

"What are we going to do with such folk?" Lofotan said. "The nomads will chop them down like wheat."

Balif remained curiously optimistic. "If you must fight against a sword, and you have no sword, take two knives." It was an old saying, but Lofotan only frowned when he heard it.

There was no camp to speak of, no central spot around which the kender gathered. The elf party walked on, leading their horses until the Longwalker appeared. The kender chief was, for him, grandly dressed in a white robe and buff suede boots too large for him. A gilded circlet crowned his head. From ten feet away Mathi could tell that the headgear was fake. The gold leaf was peeling at the edges, and the "gems" mounted on it were murky chunks of glass. Nevertheless, the Longwalker looked something like a leader of substance instead of just another short-statured vagabond.

"Greetings, wonderful General," he said, beaming.

Balif shook his hand like an equal. "Hail to you, Longwalker. How have you come to this state? The humans have driven you to cover like a covey of quail."

"Pah, it's nothing. A few dark nights and we'll slip away." No one believed him, not even Rufe and the other kender listening. The nomads were too thick on the plain to evade.

"If I can help, please say so," said Balif. "I am at your disposal."

The Longwalker clasped his hands together and breathed, "How splendid! You can drive the riders away, can't you, illustrious General?"

"With what? Juggling tricks?" muttered Lofotan.

"If necessary, even that, Captain." Balif raised his voice for all to hear. "War is more than fighting and killing. The most potent weapon of war is here." He tapped his temple. "More often than not, guile and artifice can overcome strength and ferocity."

Cheerfully clapping the elf general on the back, the Longwalker and his companions escorted Balif to their fireside. Lofotan unhappily watched his commander.

To no one, he said, "Foolish at best and suicidal at worst." Treskan, tramping by, asked him to repeat what he just said. Lofotan gave the scribe a frosty glance and moved on.

Mathi and Rufe brought up the rear. As the elves passed out of sight among the big trees, the kender said, "What about my payment? Where's my horse?"

"Your job isn't over yet."

"Uh-huh, it is. Pay up, or I tell the general what you really are."

"You're too late," Mathi lied. "He already knows."

For the first time since meeting the kender, Mathi had the pleasure of seeing Rufe be genuinely surprised.

"He knows? And he still lets you ride with him? I thought he would tear the points from your ears for deceiving him."

"General Balif is an unusual fellow," Mathi said. "After all, he's working for your people now."

That the kender could not deny. He nodded sagely as though he believed her. He was about to leave when Treskan joined them. Keeping an eye on Lofotan and the general, he asked Rufe if he had penetrated the human camp yet.

"A few times."

There's a certain item he had, the scribe said carefully. It was taken from him while he was held in the humans' camp. He wanted it back.

"What?" the kender wanted to know. Treskan described the talisman in some detail.

"Oh yeah, I remember that dingus. What's so important about it?"

"I want it. It's mine. Get it back as soon as possible, and I will give you—" Treskan stopped, stumped. What could he offer someone who was proud to own nothing but could get virtually anything his heart desired?

Mathi came to the rescue. She said, "What do you want, Rufe?"

"Pancakes."

Used as she was to Rufe's obscure reasoning, Mathi had to ask again. The answer was the same.

"Pancakes, with green berry syrup, butter, and cheese."

"All right," said Mathi slowly. "Treskan will make you pancakes."

"I will?"

"I want to be paid in advance," Rufe insisted. "Going in that camp is risky."

The elves had flour in their supplies and maybe syrup, but Silvanesti did not eat dairy products as humans and kender did. Finding cheese and butter might be hard. Once again Mathi wished Artyrith were still there. He undoubtedly could produce pancakes from a glutton's dream.

She explained their culinary dilemma. Rufe relented. "Have 'em by tonight," he said.

Rufe wandered off in his aimless way, shrugging his shoulders now and then as if arguing with himself then agreeing to what he had said. Mathi and Treskan tethered the horses. Lofotan had ordered him to stand guard over them, but he had other things to do, such as finding ingredients for pancakes. Mathi suggested that he inquire with the Longwalker or the other kender. If anyone had butter and cheese in the wilderness, they would.

It was dark by the time he found all the ingredients. When the time came to cook Rufe's bribe, there was no one around. He found Mathi seated under a lofty beech tree, dozing. He woke her quietly. She reacted by seizing his hand so swiftly, Treskan barely saw her move. She opened one eye.

"What is going on?" she said in a hushed tone.

"Nothing. I found what I need for Rufe's pancakes, but everyone seems to be gone."

All day the woods had seen a constant though erratic procession of kender passing back and forth. Mathi, exhausted by her long ride and their escape from the nomads' camp, learned to ignore the restless wanderfolk as she would the pounding surf or raucous street noises. Once she was awake, the absence of kender and the silence was startling—and a bit ominous.

Releasing Treskan, she rolled to her feet. Mathi sniffed the wind. She smelled smoke. Wandering forward, she used her nose to track the aroma. The forest, so comforting by daylight, took on a strange atmosphere by night. The massive tree trunks and heavy canopy of leaves overhead made the forest floor prematurely dark. No stars or moons shone through the roof of green. When night fell, it fell hard.

She followed an erratic course in and out among the trees, turning this way and that, grasping the invisible lifeline of smoke. Treskan trailed her, puzzled but unquestioning. Mathi decided the odor was coming from a number of small twig fires, not a great pyre like what the nomads used. Treskan pointed out a glimmer of light among the trees ahead. The odor of burning grew stronger as they tracked to the light. Soon they heard the drone of voices and the snap of burning twigs.

A hollow between two rows of oaks was filled with seated kender. In the center of the smooth, shallow trench, a fire blazed. Seated around it were the Longwalker, Balif, and Lofotan.

Treskan opened his mouth to hail them, but Mathi stopped him. Something was happening, something unusual. The kender were all sitting still, facing the Longwalker and his guests. And they were *listening.* Mathi had never seen kender sit and listen to anyone before.

"And so Silvanos, called the Golden-Eyed, became Speaker of the Stars and Father of all his Country," Balif was saying. "Our elder race has grown wise and strong during his reign and will grow wiser and stronger still."

"Do all the elder folk bend a knee to the Golden-Eyed?" asked the Longwalker.

From where she stood, Mathi could swear Balif's eyes twinkled. "All with wisdom do. No chief is loved by all."

"True enough," said the kender. He glanced over both shoulders at the crowd behind him. "This lot don't love me. They don't even like me very much."

"Sure we do!" piped a voice from the darkness. "As long as you give us drink!"

There was much laughter. Mathi saw Balif had passed around the supply of the nectar that Artyrith had acquired in Free Winds. Kender drank from everything from cups made of rolled tree bark to battered gold goblets liberated, no doubt, from people they met on their travels.

"But what about you, Serius Bagfull? How did you become Longwalker of your people?" Balif asked. He held out a simple, clay cup for Lofotan to fill from a nearly empty skin of nectar.

"I was named such by the Eye."

"Eye?"

The kender nodded. Fire highlighted his long nose and prominent cheekbones. "As I entered this world, the Eye spoke to me and said I would be the Longwalker of my people."

"I don't understand," said Balif.

"Tell the story!" someone called. Others echoed the cry, but some of the kender objected just as loudly. Serius Bagfull, Longwalker of the wanderfolk, looked embarrassed.

"It is not a tale we tell to those not like us," he admitted. "But the honorable general has agreed to aid us, so can we not repay him by sharing the story?"

Another mixed chorus of yeas and nays filled the clearing. The Longwalker held up his hands for quiet and received it.

"Sometimes I must act like a chief," he said apologetically. "If you all do not mind!"

Only crickets sang in the woods. Treskan went down on one knee, opening the case of his writing board with one hand. Hand poised, he prepared to record everything the kender said.

"Time was and time is, as old ones say. Time was there were no wanderfolk in this land but in a place far gone, as far away as the opposite side of a circle. There were lots of us there, lots and lots—too many in fact, and no one had room enough to wander without bumping into another coming from another place. It was a bad time, and the people made trouble for each other out of spite and boredom. They stole—"

"Found!"

"Borrowed!"

The Longwalker cleared his throat. "They hurt each other, even killed one another. The People cried out to our makers for help, but the gods were not listening to our pleas. To get their attention, an especially clever girl named Fina decided to make a lodestone so large, it would pull the gods down from the sky. Then they would have to listen to our pleas."

Treskan squinted in the poor light, scribbling it all down. He muttered to Mathi that kender as a race were obsessed with natural magnets. Some of them went on quests for decades, collecting every bit of lodestone they could find, filch, or finagle. Outsiders assumed kender had some daffy purpose for collecting magnets. For the first time, the origin of their obsession was revealed.

"Fina convinced her kinfolk to scour the countryside for lodestone. She collected enough to fill forty barrels. She and her cousin Rufus hauled them to the top of Mount Aereera, which was the highest peak in the land. They built a great pile of lodestone, and sure enough, after a day or so, clouds began to gather over the mountain. Lightning came down and struck the mountain all around them, turning the rocks to lodestone as well. The pull became so strong, nothing could resist it."

"And the gods came down?" said Lofotan. He sounded a bit drunk and quite insolent. The Longwalker did not seem to mind.

"Not the gods. The Eye."

All through the crowd of kender the word *Eye* was repeated with great reverence. Hearing the chant made the hair on Mathi's neck prickle.

"What is the Eye?" Balif asked.

"The handiwork of the Makers," the Longwalker replied. "A great oval stone in the sky, faceted like cave crystal, and the color of smoke."

Treskan dropped his stylus. Mathi stooped to retrieve it for him.

"The Eye came down to the lodestone mountain. Though it was not bright, it burned the sky as it came. It drove Fina and Rufus off Aereera. They ran and behind them the slopes of the mountain ran like water. Great crowds of the People stood waiting for the two to return. When they saw the Eye descend, they fled for safety, but no place was safe. Houses burned, forests went up like kindling, and stone mountains melted like lead in a crucible. Fina herself was burned to ashes, but Rufus escaped."

"How?"

"While running through the valley of Nepsas, below Mount Aereera, he saw a wide cleft in the rocks. He crawled in. There was a deep passage through the ground there, and many hundreds of the People followed him to escape the wrath of the Eye.

"The Eye pressed against the doors of the cleft, but the stone was so hard, it could not melt it. It tried so hard and so long that it wore out its anger at having been pulled down from the sky. The unseen fire faded away, leaving a cool and calmer Eye hovering over the mouth of the cave.

"'Since you seek the world's protection, go forth and find it,' said the Eye. The crack in the ground deepened. Rufus and the People in the cleft went down and down, then up and up. It took so long for them to find the up from the down that babies were born along the way, and the babies of babies. I, myself, was born in the cleft. I have the mark of it, see?"

The Longwalker parted the seams of his dusty robe, revealing a large, angular scar on his chest. It could have been made by anything, and the kender chief did not elaborate on how he got it.

"One day while we were climbing up, the Eye spoke through the hollow core of the world and said, 'You have taken a long walk, my children. Let the first one out into the new day lead you into the light.'

"I was the first of the People to see the sky of today. I am the Longwalker. I led the people out of the down and into the up." He paused as if finished.

Balif was listening raptly, a fist pressed against his lips. "This happened in your lifetime? How long ago?" he murmured.

Serius tugged a tuft of weathered hair. "When this was long and glossy." Kender didn't observe calendars. Assuming the Longwalker was a spry age for a kender—seventy-five or eighty—it sounded as if the wanderfolk had arrived in the past forty years or so.

"We were not the same folk when we came out of the up as when we went into the down," the Longwalker continued. "The people of the land around the circle were bigger and less handsome—not as big as you elder folk, I guess."

"Who else would your ancestors be?" Lofotan said. "Not humans!"

Treskan said a single word. Mathi did not understand it, and she repeated it more loudly than the scribe intended.

"Gnomes? What are gnomes?" she said.

"The parent race of the wanderfolk?" Balif said thoughtfully

"Maybe. Don't know." The Longwalker sat down. "The stories say we were bigger, and passing through the down made us better sized."

Treskan wrote wildly. His stylus flew across the sheet, leaving a slanting trail of ink scratches that Mathi could not fathom. He seemed awfully excited about hearing a silly traveler's tale.

"So we have come to this land in search of breath and space. It's a good land. We'll stay." Smiling, the kender chief qualified his last statement by saying, "With the help of our friend the famous general."

"Is that story true?" demanded Lofotan.

Serius Bagfull grinned. "How could it be?"

With that, Treskan snapped his stylus in two. He stared helplessly at the broken instrument. How would he write his chronicle?

"Hey, boss."

Rufe appeared like a mirage beside him. Treskan lost his composure. After frantically recording the entire fantastic story related by the Longwalker, only to hear it pronounced untrue, he had broken his last writing instrument. He cursed loudly, but less elegantly than the departed Artyrith.

"Easy, boss."

"What are you playing at?"

"Found your whatsit," Rufe said.

"Wonderful! Where is it?"

"Not here. In the nomad camp where I saw it."

Anger rose and fell on the scribe's face like a fever. He resisted an urge to take Rufe by the throat and shake him. "How do I get it back?" he asked slowly.

"Come with me. I'll get it for you. You come too," he said to Mathi.

"Me?" said Mathi. "You don't need me. It's not my trinket."

"He's clumsy and blind in the dark. You see like a cat. You come, or I don't go," Rufe said flatly.

Mathi looked to Balif, seated comfortably between the Longwalker and Lofotan. To be polite, it was Balif's turn to tell a story, so he had launched into the tale of Karada, the woman who led the nomads out of fear and obscurity to their current state of power. The general was a fine storyteller. No one would willingly leave that spot for some time.

Treskan sadly pocketed the pieces of his writing instrument. He begged Mathi to accompany them.

It was a fool's errand and a good way to get killed. Still, she had made a pact with Treskan, and he had kept his part faithfully. Perhaps she could leave word for her brethren along the way. They had to know about Balif's unfolding curse.

"Lead on," she told Rufe.

Treskan embraced her, and he was dissuaded from kissing her only by threat of violence.

# Chapter 14

## *Treasures*

Together Mathi and Treskan got their horses from the picket. Mathi prepared to saddle hers, but Rufe insisted they not take the time. A rough blanket and a rawhide halter would do, he said. The kender sat in front of her, and together the trio trotted off into the twilight. On the way Rufe explained his plan to get the talisman back. Upon hearing it Mathi hauled back on the reins and stopped.

"That's the maddest thing I ever heard!"

"Oh, I've heard plenty of madder things," Rufe replied cheerfully. "Trust me, boss. I know how this goes. Do it my way and all will be well." Treskan was speechless with astonishment.

I must be mad to even contemplate this, Mathi thought. Putting my fate in the hands of this kender, this criminal gang of one . . . when that phrase came to mind, she brightened. Rufe *was* a gang of one. He had reduced the garrison of Free Winds to impotence all by himself. Maybe there was some crazy logic to his scheme after all.

They rode many miles under cloud-swept skies, galloping then walking, galloping then walking. After three repetitions of that pattern, Rufe grabbed the reins from Mathi.

"Now we walk, quiet as can be," he whispered.

They had left the woods long before, dashing across the windy, open grassland northeast of the forest. It was a high, flat plateau, higher than the Tanjan valley or the old forest. The glow of many campfires dotted the horizon. Rufe, Treskan, and Mathi got down and started for the distant nomad camp, leading their ponies by their halters.

Though he had called for quiet, Rufe chattered on about humans and elves, ways to confound either, and what worked with one group but not the other. Humans, he said, were always fooled by boldness. If they thought it was impossible to walk out of a gate unseen, then the way to confound them was to walk out that very gate. He had walked in and out of the nomad camp unmolested simply by skipping along and singing off key. The nomads who saw him took him for a human child and did not bother him.

Elves, on the other hand, readily succumbed to subtlety. With their greater senses, they believed they could not be surprised by stealth, so Rufe always resorted to stealth to deceive elves. At Free Winds Rufe came and went from the fortress at will by clinging to the backs of the guards, often hidden under their cloaks. By such simple methods, he reduced Dolanath to hysteria and had his run of the place.

Mathi listened with half an ear. The rest of her was alive to her surroundings. She was no scout trained to creep up on hostile camps, so she relied on her native skills long buried beneath a shell of elflike flesh. The shell was slowly eroding, and the night took on new dimensions as she walked. Sounds and smells were stronger than ever. Subtle changes in cloud colors meant things to her she had forgotten. Every step, every breath, every beat of her heart held meaning. Mathi had lost those sensations, but they were creeping back. She wondered if they would bring her to life or reduce her to madness.

Listening to the kender's lecture, Treskan asked, "Have you always been a thief?"

"Thief?" Rufe stopped dead. "I beg your pardon! I'm no thief, no sir, not me!"

"Shh, please! Lower your voice!"

"I won't be called a thief by anyone!" said Rufe shrilly.

"All right! I apologize! Now lower your voice before the nomads hear us!"

Rufe stamped his small foot. "Thieves take things for their own gain. They make their living stealing the property of others. I've never done that, no sir, not ever! Anyone who says I have done so had better be prepared to deal with Rufus Reindeer Racket Wrinklecap!"

"You do know an awful lot about how to deceive gullible people," Mathi said, trying to divert the little man's ire.

"That's different," he returned proudly. "A lone traveler like me wouldn't last a week in the wide world unless I took advantage of the quirks of my fellow creatures."

They went on, Treskan chewing his lip, Mathi absorbing the expanded world around her, and Rufe fuming about the scribe's infuriating slander. When they were close enough to make out individual tents in the nomad camp, they halted again. It was time to enact Rufe's plan.

Mathi and the scribe dragged the blankets off their ponies. He pulled two corners of his over his shoulders like an oversized cloak and tied the corners to his sash. Leaning forward, he braced his hands on his knees. Rufe explained where he intended to go. Mathi promised to cut his throat if he tried to do that to her. Shrugging, Rufe wormed his way under Treskan's tunic instead. He braced his feet against the edges of the blanket and held his face averted so his nose didn't protrude from the scribe's clothing. With the laces of the scribe's tunic drawn tight, only the top of the kender's head showed. In poor light it could be taken for part of a fur vest, a garment much favored by the nomads.

Treskan straightened up, but staggered under the kender's weight. "This will never work," he grunted.

"It will if you make it work," said the kender's muffled voice.

Mathi stuffed tufts of grass inside his clothing to round out his profile. With Rufe inside, he looked rotund indeed. He wrapped a scarf around his head to hide his elf ears. Mathi tied the horse blanket around her shoulders too, making a sort of turban to cover her fine hair and ears. At Rufe's muffled urging, she used a charred stick salvaged from the campfire to blacken hers and Treskan's faces. Nomad warriors were famously dirty, so there was no point trying to pose as them if their faces were too clean.

Mathi tied the ponies to a stake thrust in the turf. Carrying the concealed kender, Treskan lumbered toward the camp. Mathi followed, breaking her step so as not to outpace the burdened scribe.

The border of the camp was well marked by a hedge of sharp spears. Each nomad carried a bundle of them on his horse, and every night they were combined to form a defense for the camp. They were no deterrent to visitors on foot, and even with the kender, Treskan managed to slip between the sharp points. Behind the barrier the nomads had mown down the grass with scythes to provide both fodder for their horses and a clear lane to spot intruders. Mathi was surprised by the sophistication of their defenses. When she had been captured before in the hills, the nomads' camp did not have so elaborate a system of protection.

She passed stands of ready weapons—spears and poleaxes mostly—and came upon the outer line of tents. Treskan whispered to Rufe for directions. Peering out through the lacings of the scribe's shirt, Rufe said, "Right."

They tramped along a darkened line of horsehair tents built in the round style of the northern plains. It was not very late, but many nomads were sleeping, as evidenced by the great amount of snoring they heard. Mathi was behind the scribe, guarding his back. Treskan was watching his feet closely as it was hard to see where they were falling with the bulk of a concealed kender in the way. Thus he did not see the large warrior standing with his back to him. Man and kender blundered right into the nomad.

"Get off!" the man growled. He was watering the grass.

To his horror Mathi and Treskan heard Rufe snap back, "Out of my way, oak tree."

The hulking figure turned slowly around. He was a head taller than Treskan, with a beard like a raging flame.

"Men who speak to me like that don't live long."

"Not if you breathe on 'em," said Rufe.

Treskan gasped and thumped the kender through his tunic. The warrior drew a short, wide sword and displayed it under the scribe's nose.

"Got a cough, have you? I've got the cure!"

"Begging your pardon," Treskan said between gasps. He shoved the heel of his hand into Rufe's mouth to stifle him. The kender promptly bit him.

Wincing, he sidled past the warrior's butcher blade. "Too many strange victuals," he muttered, keeping up his phony cough. Mathi kept her face averted and darted after him.

Red Beard sheathed his sword. "The only strange one here is you, lard bucket."

Rufe struggled to deliver a stinging reply. Treskan clamped both hands over the hidden kender's face and hurried on.

"Are you trying to get us murdered?" he demanded.

"Tuh! Big bullies haven't the tongue for taunting," Rufe said.

"It's not their tongues I fear. Now shut up, or you'll be eating pancakes through a sliced gullet!"

They circled halfway around the sizable camp until Rufe recognized a group of tents. He dug an elbow in Treskan's ribs. They had arrived at their destination.

At first Mathi imagined they would have to creep into some dark tent and make off with the talisman. That was not what Rufe had in mind. They got down on all fours and crawled through a closed hide flap. Beyond the leather door, a fat lamp burned, barely lighting the interior but also making it stifling hot. Five nomads, dressed in leather jerkins, sat in a circle around the lamp.

Mathi's heart sank. She gauged how likely it would be that they could back out without being challenged, but Rufe piped up in a deliberately gruff voice, "Is there a game goin'?"

Mathi recognized the nomad named Vollman. "It is," he grunted.

From inside Treskan's tunic the kender jangled a purse. "Room for another?"

"Always room for losers," said Vollman. The others grinned wolfishly, but none of them looked very close at the newcomers. Treskan and Mathi crawled into a spot between Vollman and a sandy-haired nomad. It was fiendishly hot in the tent. It also stank. The nomads had acquired many traits of civilization, but bathing wasn't one of them. Mathi swallowed hard.

"The wager is six," said the black-headed warrior sitting across from Vollman. He shook a dry gourd and dumped the contents on the ground in front of his crossed legs. Five square tokens fell out. They were white, made of bone or stone, and one side of each was blackened with soot. The warrior's cast showed four black faces and one white. Vollman cursed.

Mathi didn't know the game. They were gambling, but she hadn't the faintest idea how to play. She kept her chin tucked in low so that no one would notice her slender, female features. Treskan, for better or worse, let Rufe do his talking. Fortunately, the light was so poor that no one noticed his strange shape. He could have been an ogre, and the men huddled around the sputtering lamp would not have recognized him.

"I'll take one."

"Hard odds. What do you wager?" said Vollman.

Rufe slipped his hand into the top of Mathi's sleeve and dropped something small and hard. It rolled out in the scribe's palm: a nice bit of beryl, deep red and unpolished, a desirable stone.

The other men eyed the wager appreciatively. They were betting metal mostly—bronze knives, earrings, copper bangles, all looted from unfortunate victims in the path of Bulnac's raiders. One man took back his wager, a poorly made copper cloak frog. The rest left theirs where they lay.

The black-haired warrior scooped up the tiles in the gourd and passed them to Treskan. "One, two, three, dump, that's how to do it," Rufe said in a sing-song voice. He was telling his clueless partner how to proceed while trying to sound like he was reciting a gambler's lucky chant.

Treskan imitated what he saw. He rotated the gourd in a circle three times, then dumped it upside down in front of him. When he lifted the cup away, one black side and four white showed. Everyone grunted with surprise.

"What do you know, a win first off," Rufe said. Treskan raked in his winnings. He didn't yet understand the game, but his little companion did.

"Go again," said the blond warrior beside him. Treskan gathered in the tiles. From under his chin Rufe growled, "Three."

"Easy bet. What do you hazard?"

More stones trickled down the scribe's sleeve. Rough emeralds! Treskan was as startled as everyone else when they rolled out in the dirt.

Three men took their bets back. Only Vollman and a nomad with an empty eye socket remained in. One-Eye put down a nice dirk with an embossed silver handle. Vollman wagered four golden bangles.

"Them real gold?" Rufe asked.

"Yeah. Want to test them?" He held the bangles out for Treskan to try with his teeth. Since he didn't know the hardness of gold from a chicken bone, he waved them off.

"Point is five," Rufe announced. The two betting nomads grinned. Mathi assumed that was a hard point to make. He shook the gourd three times then upturned it: all black.

One-Eye cursed. Vollman stared hard at Treskan then at the tiles. He picked them up, rubbing each one between his thumb and forefinger.

"What's the matter? Got an itch?"

Mathi didn't dare punch the kender while sitting in front of so many witnesses, but she dearly wanted to.

"New tiles," said Vollman. A nomad with silver beads woven into his scalp lock tossed a small leather bag to his host. Vollman poured them out. There were five tiles, red on one side, white on the other. They were slightly bigger than the previous playing pieces.

"Lemme see those in the light." Treskan picked up one as Rufe indicated and held it up at arm's length. To his amazement, Rufe snaked his little arm down Treskan's sleeve and took the red and white tile. Close beside them, Mathi bit her lip to keep from gasping. Treskan kept his palm cupped so that no one could see what happened. He was sweating from the heat and from pure fear. If the nomads caught Rufe cheating, they would surely die for it.

To his relief the kender returned the tile to his hand.

"My toss still?" growled Rufe. Vollman nodded.

A minor trove of gemstones cascaded down Treskan's sleeve. Garnets, beryl stones, tourmalines, and a trio of big, uncut rubies littered the ground.

"Too much?" Rufe taunted the gawking nomads.

Vollman dug through the collar of his deerskin shirt and brought out a small leather bag. "This is all I got." He poured out his poke. Amid the rings, bangles, and the odd gold tooth lay the desired talisman.

"That'll do. You toss," Rufe said. Mathi passed the gourd and tiles to the nomad. That pleased him. After all, how could the fat stranger cheat if he was throwing the tiles himself?

"Your call," he reminded Treskan/Rufe.

"One," said the kender.

No one said a word as Vollman shook and tossed the dried cup. With a flourish, the warrior upturned the gourd in the dirt. He held his hand there, not removing the cup.

"Well, what are ya waiting for?" said Rufe.

He snatched back the gourd. One. Rufe had gotten the talisman back and a lot more besides.

Vollman drew a dagger from the small of his back. "No one makes four hits in a row—not unless they're cheating!"

Frightened, Treskan forgot to stop the kender's mouth. Rufe replied, "I ain't lucky and I ain't a cheater. I am loved by fate; that's all."

"Your fate, fat pig, is to die tonight!" The dagger came up under the scribe's chin.

Rufe squirmed under his shirt. Mathi thought he was coming out to run for it. The sensation of the little man scrambling against his ribs and stomach proved too much for Treskan. He laughed.

"Funny, am I? Let's see how much you laugh with a cut throat!"

At that, Rufe pushed his head through Treskan's lacings. His cheeks were bulging. The nomads seated across from them recoiled, unsure of what they were seeing. Before Vollman could strike, Rufe spewed a stream of liquid onto the lamp. It exploded.

A ball of fire gushed upward. The flash dazzled everyone's eyes, including Mathi's. Rufe's arm snaked out and grabbed Vollman's booty. "Now go!" he cried, kicking backward into Treskan's ribs.

Mathi lashed out, upsetting the lamp. Burning oil splashed on men's laps and in the dirt. The dry hide tent quickly caught fire. Players were bailing out as fast as they could in every direction, slapping out the flames licking their clothes. Vollman's sleeves were on fire. Roaring, he rolled on the ground to put them out. In the chaos Treskan crawled away on all fours until Rufe wriggled free.

The kender and Mathi hoisted the scribe to his feet. "Up now and run!"

He did and the kender leaped on his back. The tent blazed and everyone fled. In the general uproar, no one paid any attention to them. Once away from the conflagration, Treskan and Mathi assumed a calmer manner and walked carefully to the fence of stakes. En route Treskan brushed by the red-bearded nomad he'd bumped into on the way in. Without Rufe under his shirt he no longer resembled an obese nomad.

"What's the row?" exclaimed Red Beard.

"Fire," Treskan said in his own voice. He made sure he faced the nomad, hiding the kender clinging to his back. "See?"

The hulking warrior hurried to the blaze. Mathi and Treskan hurried too, in the opposite direction. They didn't stop running until they reached their ponies still staked and undisturbed. Rufe let himself down from the scribe's back.

The glow of firelight for the camp was brighter than before. Mathi threw the blanket over the pony, wondering aloud if the whole camp would burn down.

"Nah," said Rufe. "Just six tents."

"How do you know it will be six?"

"I know." He tapped his high forehead with two fingers. "Want to bet how many?"

Neither one of them was willing to take him up on it. They had seen enough of the kender's prowess at gambling.

"What was that you spit on the lamp?" Mathi asked, climbing onto her horse. She held out a hand to the kender.

"Oil." Rufe carried a small vial of oil on a loop of cord around his neck.

"Why do you carry that?" Treskan asked.

"Tastes good on greens," he replied.

They rode off quietly, keeping to low ground to avoid being seen by nomad sentries. Treskan clutched the returned talisman in his hand as if his life depended on having it.

"All good, boss?"

"Well done, friend Rufus."

"You are a dangerous fellow, do you know that?" said Mathi.

"I'm just gettin' by. So when do I get my pancakes?"

*****

Relieved like an unwound spring, Treskan nodded on his pony. The sturdy beast plodded ahead with a slack hand on the reins. Somewhere along the way, Rufe had left her, for when the moons rose early after midnight Mathi, discovered she and Treskan were alone. She had no idea when Rufe got off or where he went.

She let Treskan's mount draw ahead. When she was sure he was asleep, she took a wide roll of birch bark from inside her gown. By the moons' light she scrawled in her childish hand the message she hoped her brethren would find. It read: *sPEll ON BALLIF / ChANgINg LIkE us / kEEP tO PlAN?*

Mathi rolled it up and tied it with a strip of rawhide that she had chewed until it was pliable. The crude scroll she tucked under her arm for a mile or so until her body warmed it. Then she dropped it in the waving grass. Her brethren searched by scent, and if they found her note, they would know it was from her by the smell. If they found it. If they were following her still.

The forest edge was just a few yards ahead, looking like a black wall. Treskan's pony had halted, head down, staring at the impenetrable gloom. Mathi's did likewise.

The scribe stirred at the sudden loss of motion. "Where are we?" he asked thickly. She didn't answer, but he saw the trees and knew anyway.

"'S all right," he said, climbing off the pony and patting its shaggy neck. His pony would not proceed until Treskan led it by the reins.

"Go on; there's no reason to fear the dark," Mathi told her mount. She said it, but the canny animal had other ideas. Only when Mathi got down and led the pony like Treskan did it stir from where it had stopped.

The trees closed in overhead, a vault of green leaves turned to black stone by night. They cut off the constant wind of the plain, leaving the way between the trunks airless and still. Even so, Mathi and Treskan felt they had little to fear. They knew where the nomads were, the centaurs were kindly disposed toward Balif, and the kender were probably all asleep too.

They followed the trail signs to the kender camp. By the time they reached the picket where Balif's and Lofotan's horses were tethered, they were both bone tired. There couldn't be more than three or four hours of night left, not long to rest. They tied their ponies, pulled the blankets off and hung them over a tree limb, and set out for their bedrolls. Treskan still had his talisman clenched tightly in his fist. Mathi wondered if he would ever put it down again.

She made for her sleeping spot but halted when she heard talking. They were low and calm, and there were two distinct voices. Balif and Lofotan? No, the outline of the slumbering majordomo was plainly visible under his blanket. Balif and who? Treskan was a few yards behind her, sleeping apart as usual.

She saw that the general of the Speaker's armies was chained again. There were no modest trees to bind him to, so the indefatigable Lofotan had dug a shallow hole and chained his lord to a root as thick as Mathi's waist. Balif was sitting up, back as straight as a Silvanesti spire.

"Who's there?" rasped a guttural voice that Mathi didn't recognize.

Balif looked at her. His eyes glowed from within with a foreign, amber light. Tired as she was, Mathi rooted to the spot. The transformation had come over Balif again, more severely than before. Every inch of the elf's exposed skin was covered with dense, brown fur. The skin on his nose and lips was black, like a dog's, and hard claws studded the ends of his fingers.

"The girl," Balif said, drawing out the initial sound of the word.

"My lord," she said. "Who are you speaking to?"

"An old friend of yours."

In one bound, a dark shape hurtled out of the shadows and landed in a crouch between Balif and Mathi. It was Taius, the former elf and present beast Mathi had met during her brief captivity in Bulnac's camp.

"She heard us. Let me kill her. I can do it quietly. No one will hear," Taius vowed.

Mathi tensed to fight or flee. She searched for a sign of understanding in Balif's savage eyes. She saw none but the accursed general replied, "No. Harm her not. She will be my mouthpiece to the world."

"She is one of the brethren!" Taius had chosen sides, and he was not on Mathi's.

"Brethren? You mean half-breed. She is half-human."

Taius stood with his back bent, so his head was lower than Mathi's. "Smell again, mighty one. Her skin smells of fur and night. She is a creature of the forest, like I was."

Again the relentless beast eyes of Balif raked over her. "Is this true?"

She saw no reason to deny it any longer. "Yes, my lord. I am child of the Creator you betrayed."

"Betrayed?"

Her heart was beating hard against her breastbone. "Yes, betrayed. You gave our maker over to the persecutors, those who slew and imprisoned us, his children!'

"I obeyed the orders of my sovereign."

Mathi sneered, "That is the excuse of slave masters the world over."

His chains jangled ominously. Though she was glad her secret was out—relieving so much tension in her—she truly feared what might happen if an aroused Balif escaped his bonds.

"The judgment of the Speaker was not just," Balif said. "But I could not alter it." His tone of voice had changed, softened. "I have known for a long time that you were not an elf. I thought you were one of those unhappy mixed breeds, like the scribe." And yet, knowing Mathi was not who she claimed to be, Balif had chosen her to go on his mission. Why?

The bewitched general smiled, showing long canines. "Spies and assassins are better defended against when they are in view," he said as though he had read her mind.

"A spy is a spy," Taius snarled. "Let me kill her." His voice had risen so high that Lofotan stirred on his pallet.

Balif gave him a withering glance. The beast-elf subsided.

"Where have you been?" asked Balif coolly. "You have been gone many hours."

Mathi related her adventure with Rufe and Treskan in the nomad camp. She omitted all reference to the talisman, explaining her trip as a reconnaissance of the enemy camp.

"Reporting to your masters, more likely," Taius said.

"Go away," Balif told him. "We are done."

Taius sprang away in one breathtaking bound. "Let me serve you," he called back. "You were my commander. I am still your soldier."

"Go away. I am not lost to the world yet, and I cannot fulfill my duty with you by my side."

Rejected, Taius melted into the shadows. His voice drifted back.

"I serve you, my lord, until I die. I shall keep the beasts of the brethren off your trail!"

In a flicker of a moment, the half-beast was gone. A few moments later, Mathi heard a far-off snap of a tree branch high overhead, Taius's gesture of farewell.

Mathi sidled away toward her bed. As arrow-straight as ever, Balif watched her with unnatural intensity. Why did he say no to Taius?

"Ask the question."

"My lord?"

"Ask the question in your mind."

"What did Taius want of you?"

Balif sank down on his side with a grace more feral than elflike. "He offered to free me from my fetters if I would allow him to serve me again."

Taius was being hunted by magicians and trackers from Silvanost, as were all the few creatures of his kind who had escaped arrest. Joining Balif was one way to escape them perhaps.

"You let me stay and sent him packing?"

"I am not a beast. Not yet." He coughed a little, shuddering. "You may go or stay as you choose. You are free. Your ancestry does not change that. The coils of this curse are close around me, but I am not lost yet. I will carry out the mission the Speaker gave me, defend the wanderfolk, and then . . . there are a few throws I still have to make."

Mention of throws made Mathi think of Rufe and his skill at the nomad gambling game. Strange, but it seemed that Balif, the famed warrior of Silvanost, saw life in the same terms.

# CHAPTER 15

## *Arms*

Mathi dreamed of galloping horses, shouting, and the clash of blades. She tried to banish these unhappy thoughts, but they kept intruding on her rest. Then she got a sharp blow in the ribs. Instinctively she rolled into a ball and growled about being disturbed.

"Get up girl, or you'll be sleeping forever!"

Even half asleep she knew Lofotan's battlefield voice. She sat up, bleary-eyed, and saw people and animals darting to and fro among the trees. Smoke hung in the air. The sounds of her dream had been real.

Lofotan, sword in hand, was trying to seat a helmet on his head. He tossed a weapon—a spear—toward Mathi and shouted again for her to stand up or perish. Mathi wasn't sure if he meant attackers would slay her, or Lofotan himself. Not desiring either, she scrambled to her feet.

"Defend yourself!"

Lofotan dashed away. Mathi shouted after him, "What's going on?"

"The humans found us. I must get to the general!"

All around her the kender camp was disintegrating. Little people rushed in all directions, clutching blankets or other belongings. None seemed to have any weapons. Lofotan dodged between them, trying to reach Balif, who was still shackled to the tree root.

A shrill cry rent the air. Mathi turned and saw a trio of riders slashing through the widely spaced trees. They speared any kender within reach, then tiring of their sport, contented themselves with shouting and cursing the wanderfolk as they scattered. One of the men spotted Mathi.

"Ho!" he cried. "Here's bigger game!"

He spurred at her. His spear was not a true lance. It lacked a handguard, Mathi noted with strange detachment. If he hits me with it, he won't keep his grip . . .

Her detachment evaporated quickly. Lance or no, death was riding at her. She bolted, still clutching the spear Lofotan had tossed at her. Mathi knew she couldn't outrun the nomad's horse. Zigging and zagging, she ran around a stout tree and threw herself against the trunk. Laughing, her pursuer cantered past. Spying his prey behind him, the nomad wrenched his horse's head around. At that moment a smooth round stone the size of a ripe plum hit the man on the cheek. It must have had considerable velocity, for the rider threw up his hands and fell sideways off his horse, landing heavily at Mathi's feet.

She gaped at the fallen man. Someone shouted, "Finish him off!"

A kender twenty feet away held a stick and thong sling in his hand. A hoopak, she had heard them call it. He pointed at the fallen nomad.

"Stick him! What's wrong with you?"

Mathi couldn't do it, not standing over a helpless enemy like that. She kicked the man's spear away and rolled him over. The sling ball had shattered his face. He was alive, but probably blinded by blood and bone fragments.

Mathi backed away. More nomads circled through the trees, whooping and shouting. Some kender had taken to the trees and were pelting the riders with whatever they had—sticks, stones, found objects precious and paltry. Mathi heard the characteristic whistle of a hoopak winding up and a solid *thwack* as the projectile struck home. Another saddle emptied.

Slowly, the tempo of the battle changed. The initial charge by the nomads had taken the kender by surprise. They scattered, and the humans chased them, killing many at first, then reverting to harrying the little people out of sheer contempt. Many kender fled, but others stood their ground. The appearance of the elves confused the humans further. Soon it was the nomads who were milling around, unsure what to do or where to go.

A high-pitched shrieking, like a whistle being blown in a frenzy, echoed through the woods. More shrill whistles split the air, all around the raiders. They closed into a compact group. Many changed their spears for swords.

Advancing at a walk through the trees came Balif and Lofotan on horseback, leading a large, ragged band of kender. The Longwalker was at their head, blowing a clay pipe. Unseen among the grand trunks more whistles answered. The enemy was surrounded.

Seeing an enemy they knew—the elves on horseback—the raiders broke ranks and charged. From three sides they were scourged by hoopak stones, kender-sized arrows, and thrown missiles. Protected by thick furs and occasional bits of armor, the nomads tried to shrug off the bombardment, but their mounts were unwilling to face such torment. The charge lost momentum and played out ten yards from where Balif sat, hands folded on his saddle pommel.

"Wanderfolk, now's the time! Show them what you are made of!" he cried.

Swarms of kender, rounded up by the advancing elves and their chief, filled the gaps between the trees. Brandishing sticks, tools, and even an occasional bladed weapon, they shouted defiance at their attackers. Backed against a tree, Mathi heard frightful taunts from the kender. Every branch of the nomads' family tree was smeared as dirty lice; lying, cheating vermin; eaters of filth and cowards of the basest sort. Mathi had never heard such ferocious taunting, all shouted at top volume. A thousand furious wanderfolk shouting ingenious invective at the same time was a fearsome spectacle. Compared to the torrent of abuse they hurled, their hoopaks were toys.

The nomad raiders, for their part, were white with outrage or red-faced with fury. Smacking their reluctant animals with the flats of their swords, they moved toward the kender—and the little people did not give way. For the first time since coming to the eastern land, kender stood up to their foes. In the center of the line Balif watched the humans calmly. When the gap shrank to six yards he drew his noble sword and raised it high in a warrior's salute. Seeing this, Mathi had a sudden premonition.

He means to die! she thought. He's going to let the humans kill him to inspire the kender and escape his curse!

Moved by feelings beyond her control, Mathi stepped away from the safety of the tree. She reversed her grip on her spear and started toward Balif, breaking into a run.

She reached the rear of the mob of defiant kender and pushed her way through. It was not easy. The little people were excited. They pushed back.

"General! My lord, wait!" she called desperately.

At no more than a walking pace the two lines collided. The kender on foot gave way to the big horses bearing down on them—gave a little, then stopped. Like ants the kender swarmed over the nomads' horses and climbed up the men's legs, grabbing, hitting, sometimes biting.

Balif and Lofotan fought with more decorum. They traded sword cuts with warriors in the front ranks. The press behind and on both sides kept the other humans from doubling on the elves. Down went Balif's first foe, lost among the stamping hooves. Down went Lofotan's, minus his sword arm.

To the credit of their courage, Bulnac's raiders held on despite the bizarre nature of the fight. Given an equal or greater number of humans or elves to combat, they would have fought on in their usual brutal way, but beset by kender they didn't know what to do. The little folk weren't supposed to fight back! Such a thing had never happened before. Now stalwart warriors were toppling from steeds thickly coated with yelling kender. This was not warrior's work. At best they could break off the fight and ride away.

By the time the sun's rays were slanting through the few gaps in the canopy overhead, the battle was over. Mathi never got within ten feet of Balif. The general survived unscathed.

She stopped dead, depleted and stunned. Why did she care what happened to the Betrayer anyway? She ought to want to shove Balif into the nomads' fury, not rush headlong to his aid. Mathi realized then what had happened. She knew Balif. He was no longer the anonymous, high-born Silvanesti she was taught to hate. He was flesh and blood, heart and soul, and she admired him. She could not have been more appalled at her sudden new understanding.

Many kender chased the nomads, hurling insults at them as long as they were in earshot. Stung by the taunts, a few peeled off to chastise their tiny tormentors. They killed many unwary kender, who had been carried away with the unexpected victory, but other riders were brought down by the enraged wanderfolk.

Nomad war chiefs blew ram's horns to recall their unruly warriors. The last mortified riders disappeared into the dust and drifting bands of smoke.

The kender reacted oddly to their small victory. Mathi expected they might cheer, or else wilt with delayed terror, but they did neither. Mostly they vanished. A thousand kender scattered through the trees, abruptly making themselves scarce. All that remained behind were the dead and wounded—and the elves.

Mathi hailed Balif. "My lord, we won!"

"We survived, at any rate," Lofotan said.

"Survival, my dear captain, is the first prerequisite of victory."

Balif was amazingly at ease. The carnage and violence of the morning did not compare to the great battles he had led, but bloodshed is bloodshed, and Balif was unfazed by it all. Mathi trembled in every part of her body. Though the morning was mild, she was drenched in sweat. Only when the battle was over did she realize how terribly thirsty she was.

Treskan appeared from the copse where they had been camped. He was battered and bloodied from a dozen small cuts on his face and hands. Mathi was sympathetic, but Lofotan maintained that the scribe had inflicted the wounds himself with his unskillful use of his sword. Nevertheless Mathi sat him down and began to dab his cuts with a rag wetted with cold spring water.

"What happened?" she asked. "When did the nomads attack?"

"Just after dawn. They rode in quietly, swords sheathed and got amongst the wanderfolk before raising a battle cry." Balif accepted a clay cup from his loyal retainer. He took a spare sip. "They were not some random scouting party. They knew we were here." Did he remember seeing Mathi return last night? If he did, he did not mention it.

The lump in Mathi's throat grew harder to swallow. It was easy to imagine the truth. Irate at losing his personal treasure, Vollman had tracked Mathi and Treskan. He probably brought some friends along to help waylay the portly gambler and his silent friend. They made no attempt to hide their tracks. The nomads must have been surprised when their quarry left camp. Anyone could have tracked them back to the kender's camp.

She found herself studying Balif. His features were subtly different from just a few days ago. His hair was darker, and there were shadows everywhere his clothing ended.

"They will be back," Balif said. "Sooner than later. A commander like this Bulnac won't take being repulsed by wanderfolk very well."

"Do you know this Bulnac?"

"Never put my eyes upon him." Balif drained the cup. "But I know him. He leads by strength. He can't accept even a single defeat, or his hold over his followers is broken. He will return, probably with his entire force."

"What do we do?" asked Lofotan.

"The woods are untenable. I had hoped they would provide some cover, but they are too open. We need a better defensive position."

They had brought from Silvanost a number of maps drawn by the best cartographers in Silvanos's realm. They weren't much help. The land east of the Tanjan river was poorly explored. Many gaps blotted the charts.

"This river here; is it named?" Balif indicated the short watercourse east of the forest. Two branches of the river joined and flowed south into a small bay.

"It is not," Mathi said, scrutinizing the gazeteer on the back of the chart.

"Call it the Wanderfolk River." In Elvish it was *Thon-Haddaras*, 'Wanderers' River.'

The triangle of land between the branches of the newly-named was shown to be wooded on the chart.

"There is our refuge," Balif said. "We shall make for it at once."

He turned his horse around. Lofotan, frowning, spoke up.

"My lord, what about the wanderfolk? They seem to have abandoned us."

Balif had a brash, winning countenance when he smiled.

"Rest assured that the Longwalker and his people will find their way there. Who knows? They may get there ahead of us."

As they spoke, small groups of kender came into view, carrying off the dead and tending the wounded. Strange how their actions never looked organized, yet they accomplished what they needed to do in short order.

There were humans among the dead and wounded too. Balif rode up to one warrior beset on all sides by several kender. He had a black eye, and his right arm hung uselessly at his side, covered in blood. His horse had thrown him, and the kender had him cornered.

"Elder lord!" the man grunted, swinging his leather scabbard at a kender who was fondling his boots. "Pray give me quarter, noble sir! I am besieged."

Balif came closer, which made the kender fade into the trees. Gasping for breath, the wounded man propped his back against a tree and sighed.

"I yield to you, elder lord," the man said desperately. "Only save me from those little vultures!"

"You were keen enough to hunt and harry them before," Balif replied coldly.

"Orders, lord. Our chief told us to drive the small ones from the land so that we could claim it as our own."

"Your chief is called Bulnac?"

The wounded man blinked through the sweat and grime streaking his face. "You know our great chief?"

"His name has reached my ears."

Balif ordered the nomad searched. If Lofotan found any elven artifacts on him, he would die on the spot. Bulnac's raiders had an ugly reputation as plunderers.

Lofotan groped through the man's tunic and vest. He found little but a few trinkets of chain.

"How is his wound?"

Lofotan had seen many a sword cut in his day. He knew

more about them than most healers. Probing the man's arm he announced no main vessels were cut. The man might die of blood poisoning if not treated, but he wouldn't bleed to death.

To Treskan, Balif said, "Find a horse."

It took some doing, but he found a nomad horse walking aimlessly a hundred yards away. Catching the animal by its bridle, he led it back to the general.

"On the horse," Balif said. "Go to your chief and give him my words: he is to take his warband out of this province, back across to the west bank of the Thon-Tanjan. This land belongs to the Speaker of the Stars, Silvanos Golden-Eye, and to his heirs. We will not tolerate his warband on our soil."

Suffering but defiant, the wounded warrior took the reins from Treskan.

"Who are you that you order my chief around like a slave?"

"I am Balif Thraxenath, Chosen Chief of House Protector, First Warrior of the Great Speaker and general of all his host. I am the son of Arnas Thraxenath, of the Greenrunners clan. I am known as Balif, loyal servant of the Great Speaker of the Stars."

His was a name that was well known to the nomads. The wounded man stood by the horse Mathi had rounded up for him, awestruck.

"You are *the* Balif?"

"None other. Go, and bear my words to your chief."

Unaided, the warrior struggled onto his mount. "If I die, my children shall know I crossed swords with Balif, first among warriors! I thank you for my life, noble lord!"

Weaving a bit, he rode away. Lofotan got back on his animal and said, "Was it wise to tell the humans who you are?"

"What good is it having a reputation if you can't use it to intimidate your enemies?" said Balif.

"Suppose Bulnac isn't intimidated? Suppose he comes roaring back here in full strength, just to say he defeated and slew the great Balif?" To this the general had no answer but a wry smile.

Mathi, Treskan, and Lofotan loaded the packhorses. By the time they were done the forest had been picked clean. The only traces of the morning's furious fight were scarred patches on tree trunks, and a few spots of churned up earth. What became of the dead from both sides Mathi could not guess.

Balif and his party rode off through the woods. Three times before noon they had to hide while nomad patrols galloped past. On the last occasion it looked as if they would be found. A party of nomads entered the forest and searched carefully, probing every gully and leaf pile with their spears. From the small spots and low angles they searched, it appeared that they were after kender rather than elves. Balif kept behind a screen of closely growing myrtles, sword in hand. Armed nomads rode within six yards but passed on, summoned by horn blasts further away.

After that they witnessed an extraordinary scene. A party of forty or more kender chased five humans on horseback out of the woods. In addition to hoopaks the wanderfolk had an assortment of weapons gleaned from the morning's battle. How they reached this spot ahead of the mounted elves was a mystery, but they screamed, whistled, shouted, and pelted the nomads out of the woods and onto the plain. Once on open ground the nomads tried to regroup and charge the little people, but their horses could not bear the barrage of stones and noise. Confused and no doubt embarrassed, the humans departed.

Mathi felt no pity for the nomads. Their brutal treatment of the kender was deplorable, but now that the little folk were aroused—and had discovered they enjoyed tormenting their tormentors—the nomads were in for unimaginable frustration. The nomads deserved their comeuppance.

At twilight they left the forest to cross open country to the newly named Thon-Haddaras. Their map was unclear of the exact distance to the river. Much of the survey had been done from the sky, by griffon riders, who were notoriously inaccurate at judging distances on the ground from a height. Balif was willing to travel all night if necessary to reach the Thon-Haddaras as soon as possible.

"All night?" asked Lofotan. "Does my lord mean that?"

Riding slowly through the high grass, Balif said, "It will not be a problem."

Lofotan pulled a coil of chain from his saddlebag. The clinking sound made Balif rein up. He turned his horse sharply right, blocking Lofotan's path.

"Do you doubt my word?" he said. Neither the captain, the girl, nor the scribe answered. Fists tight on his reins, the general snapped, "I will not be chained like a beast again! I am in control of myself. Is that clear?"

Cold as ice, Lofotan replied, "Perfectly, my lord."

With a final glare Balif resumed riding. Lofotan held his place until his commander was half a hundred yards ahead. With a soft thump of his heels he started his mount forward. Mathi kept beside him with the pack train trailing behind.

"We shall not sleep tonight," the old warrior said quietly.

"Do you think he will transform?"

"He already has. The question is, how much?"

Personally, Mathi thought it was perfectly reasonable of Balif to resent being shackled when the threat of nomad attack was so high.

Night came on clear and bright with stars. The crescent red moon rose like a bloody smile in the sky, lighting the dry, waving grass with a strange pinkish light. They heard something they hadn't heard on their travels so far: the howl of a wolf. Savannah wolves had long been driven out of Silvanesti proper. They were common in the mountains, but so far the elves had not encountered any on their journey. Crossing the plain they now heard half a dozen different calls, indication of a sizable pack.

Lofotan braced his bow. Treskan and Mathi closed up with him, jerking the lines to hurry the packhorses along. At the tail of the group, they would be likely targets if the wolves attacked.

Balif circled in and out, sometimes leading, sometimes trailing the others. Whenever he came close Mathi studied him for signs that the curse was asserting itself. The changes she'd noticed before were still there, but the full beast-face and features were not in evidence. Mathi did not understand the working of spells. She could not imagine why the Creator would inflict such an erratic spell. Perhaps it was weakening—or perhaps it was designed to torment the sufferer by seeming to fade, only to return more strongly than ever?

"Wake up, you two." Lofotan's voice carried clearly in the warm, still air.

Mathi sharpened to awareness. Treskan twisted around in the saddle, looking in all directions.

"What is it?"

"We're not alone." Lofotan had spotted three or four shapes darting through the grass off to their right, about thirty yards away.

"Wolves?" said the scribe.

Lofotan nocked an arrow in answer. "Watch behind and on your left," he said calmly. "The wolf you see is often a feint for the real attack."

The horses were certainly aware of the danger. They closed in with each other, rolling their eyes and champing their bits. Mathi drew back and let the pack animals move ahead of her. Her pony, being blinkered, was less sensitive than the baggage animals. She knew he had the predators' scent when he bobbed his head and snorted defiantly. Mathi tapped him with her heels to keep him moving. If he stopped, it might occur to him to shed his rider, then make a break for it.

Balif was out in front a dozen yards or so. His bow was unstrung. His sword rested in its scabbard. He had to know the pack was around them, but still he rode slowly ahead, weaving back and forth across their line of march. What was he doing?

All at once Lofotan sat up as high as he could in his saddle, bent his bow, and loosed an arrow into the pale red shadows. He was rewarded with a yelp and a thrashing in the grass. Treskan started toward the spot. Lofotan ordered him to stop.

"I'll finish him off," said the scribe, raising his spear.

"It might be a ruse." Wolves were known to do that, fake an injury or death, to draw an unwise hunter close.

The thrashing in the grass stopped. Lofotan's horse slowly came to a halt.

"Where's my lord?"

Balif's horse was coming back to them, reins trailing on the ground. There was no sign of the general, and no traces on his mount to suggest he had transformed into a beast and been thrown off as before.

A howl erupted close by. Lofotan whirled, arrow drawn back to his ear. Something low and dark was rushing at them through the grass. Balif's horse reared and neighed.

"Don't!" Mathi called. "It might be him!"

Lofotan thought of that too. He held his draw magnificently, holding the eighty pound recurve bow as steady as stone. The creature charging Balif's horse gathered its legs and leaped. With only a moment to choose, Lofotan loosed his arrow.

It hit the hurtling beast dead in the ribs. Balif's horse gave a start, jumping sideways as the lifeless body hurtled past it. At Lofotan's direction Mathi went to look at it. It was a fine specimen of a male savannah wolf, brown all over, weighing maybe sixty pounds.

"It's a wolf!" she said, relieved. "Dead as a stone!"

The words had hardly left her lips when a second beast exploded from the grass and knocked Lofotan from his saddle. Shouting, Mathi rushed to his rescue. The beast had clamped its powerful jaws on the elf's right forearm, which fortunately was sheathed in bronze. They struggled, but Lofotan drew his dagger with his left hand and plunged it into his attacker's ribs once, twice. He threw the heavy slack form off and got up in time to dodge Treskan's well-meaning spear-thrust.

The packhorses bucked and reared, tearing at the lines that bound them together. Two wolves had the lead pony by the throat. Lofotan had lost his bow in his fall. He snatched the spear from Treskan and raced to rescue the pony. The scribe was left with just his sword, which he barely knew how to use.

A low, rolling growl behind Mathi froze her blood to ice. She turned slowly and saw a large black beast whose head and chest fur were shot through with gray advancing on him. Tugging at her sword, she backed away, swearing in Elvish.

Black lips curled, the wolf displayed long, broken teeth. He was the elder chief of his pack, powerful, and with a gleam of cruel intelligence in his eyes. Words died in Mathi's mouth. All her spit seemed to have suddenly dried up.

Lofotan was battling two wolves at once. He speared one, pinning it to the turf, but the other leaped on his back. He went down. Treskan was swinging his sheathed sword like a club, trying to ward off a pale colored she-wolf.

The old wolf was little more than three paces away. Mathi gripped the sword in both hands to steady it.

She heard a shout. Slashing through the tall grass came Balif. He swung his sword wide, cutting a swath through the weeds. Seeing Mathi about to be attacked, he shouted again, whipping off his cloak and wrapping it around his unarmored left arm.

The wolf recognized a more dangerous opponent had joined the fray and quickly forgot Mathi, turning to face Balif. The elf general didn't wait for the beast to spring. He plunged in, sword high. The old wolf didn't go for his open left arm, as Mathi thought he would. He jumped headlong at Balif's chest.

Not one warrior in a hundred would have stood their ground to receive the blow. Balif did. His sword was high, and he moved his free hand to join the other on the grip. He shouted—he bellowed—a challenge so loud and so unelflike Mathi believed for an instant that he had become a beast again. Down came the fine elf blade. Behind the general's head Lunitari gleamed like red horns atop his head.

There was a loud crack. Balif staggered backward, worked his blade free, and swung again. The old wolf dropped in a heap at his feet, his skull split in two.

That was amazing enough. For Balif's strength and reflexes to be so great as to cut the wolf down in mid-leap was astonishing. What happened next was terrifying.

Not satisfied with his victory, Balif stood over the fallen creature and plunged his sword into it again and again. He kicked the carcass, shouting incoherently. Angered that the wolf did not rise up and fight more, he threw aside his sword and drew a knife. As Mathi watched in horror, he stabbed the dead wolf half a dozen times until blood covered his hands and spattered his handsome face.

His rage satiated, Balif stood up. His eyes met Mathi's.

It was not the same elf she had met in Silvanost scant weeks ago. They stared at each other, eyes locked, until Lofotan's calls for help broke the spell. With a flash of teeth Balif smiled and darted away, carrying only his knife.

He drove off the wolf harrying his majordomo, who had cuts and bites on his hands. Lofotan thanked his lord until he saw his bloody hands and face. His thanks died in his throat.

"More out there," Balif said, his voice low and gruff. Wolves were howling in retreat. Knife in hand, Balif raced off into the grass. Mathi watched him go. It was plain the general meant to hunt down and kill every animal in the pack.

# Chapter 16

## *Defenses*

Lofotan poured tepid water from his waterskin over his wounds. Some hours had passed since Balif had run off after the fleeing wolves.

"If he isn't back by dawn we'll have to find him," he said wearily.

"What if he doesn't want to be found?" Mathi said. The old warrior trickled more water on his cuts. "Worse, what if we find him and he won't come with us?"

"My lord will not roam the plain like a savage beast."

Mathi noted the strung bow, the quiver of arrows, and the ready spear. Lofotan's meaning was clear.

Later, when daylight was breaking, Lofotan shouldered his spear and set out to find his commander. Mathi and Treskan followed on foot, leading the horses. Lofotan tried to order them to stay behind, but they were in no mood to obey. There was safety in numbers, so the girl and scribe followed, and there was nothing short of violence Lofotan could do to stop them.

It was a short hunt. Just as the first rays of the sun were piercing the sky Balif came into view on the northern horizon, loping along at a jaunty pace. His old comrade halted and waited. Balif arrived, dishevelled but beaming. Under one arm he carried a bundle of fur. Without being asked he whisked it open, revealing a fine wolf pelt, freshly skinned.

"This was the best of them," he said proudly. "What do you think?"

"Did you kill them all?" asked Mathi.

Again the sly smile. "Not all. Just the four largest males." The rest of the pack had scattered to the winds to escape his remorseless pursuit.

"This is not right, my lord." Balif asked what he meant. "To exact such a punishment on wild animals is not just. Astarin teaches that all creatures have a right to life, according to their natures. Wolves hunt for food. You killed them for sport," Lofotan said.

Balif tensed, like a predator poised to pounce. "Sport? I killed them for a very good reason!" They waited for him to explain. "By scattering the pack and killing its leaders, I have shown them who rules this land now—" He visible relaxed and said simply, "Me."

Balif's horse, having borne up under his earlier transformations and forgiven its rider, steadfastly refused to allow Balif on its back. The general grew angry as the animal danced away from him, rearing when Balif took hold of his bridle. Lofotan offered his mount, but his horse wouldn't allow Balif on his back either. Something very fundamental about the general had changed. His companions were beginning to recognize it. The horses already knew.

Balif said, "Looks like I walk."

So he did, all morning at an amazing pace. The day waxed hot. Biting flies homed in on the horses but also feasted on targets of opportunity, like Mathi. A band of dark trees appeared on the eastern horizon, growing each hour until the view was filled from north to south. According to their griffon-made charts, the forest surrounded the confluence of the two streams that made up the Thon-Haddaras.

The kender were already there.

Wanderfolk in oversized helmets, sporting spears and too-long swords greeted them at the edge of the woods. Hot and thirsty, Balif brushed past them into the shade, where he sat down demanding a drink. Treskan tied the pack team and brought him a bottle of spring water.

"Greetings, Illustrious General!" the kender said, crowding around.

"Greetings to you. Is the Longwalker around?"

"By the river, Glorious General."

How do they get around so quickly? Mathi wondered. By her reckoning, being on horses and pushing as they did, they ought to have been two or three days ahead of any kender crossing the plain on foot. But no . . .

"Fetch him at once."

Kender were not usually good at taking orders, but three of them dashed away to carry out Balif's request. Treskan and Mathi prepared a long-delayed meal, which Balif ate alone under a broad maple tree. His companions ate standing up by the horses, which they watered and fed next.

Serius Bagfull, Longwalker of the wanderfolk, arrived after a kenderish interval. He wore a new hat woven of vines and leave plucked from the banks of the Wanderfolk River. The kender with him—they weren't his retainers, just whatever curious little people who chose to tag along—were likewise decked out in fresh greenery.

"Nice place, General!" he declared. Apparently the banks of the river abounded in fruit trees, and the water was well stocked with fish, freshwater mussels, and tiny lobsters the kender found good to eat.

"You like it here, then?" asked Balif, still resting with his back against the maple.

"It is great, Excellent General!"

"I am glad. Now we must issue a challenge to Bulnac."

Everyone, from kender to Lofotan, were dumbstruck. "Challenge?" Mathi managed to say.

"Of course. We must fight him some time. It is better to fight on our own terms, at our own place and time, than wait for the humans to choose those situations for us."

Lofotan agreed with his lord's tactical judgment, but pointed out they had no one to meet Bulnac's army with. A few hundred kender, maybe a thousand? Armed with some salvaged and improvised weapons?

"We have the best weapon of them all," Balif said. He showed his new, savage smile. "We shall create a fortress, a redoubt upon which the nomads will break themselves. I'll have Bulnac's hide to hang on a tree next to my wolfskin."

Through consummate wheedling, the Longwalker got Balif to agree to postpone challenging Bulnac until he had seen the spot that Balif had chosen for his redoubt. The kender led the way. Balif went with him on foot, leaving Lofotan and the others to keep up as best they could with the horses and baggage.

Unlike the west woods, the river forest was dense and full of undergrowth. It was humid too, and the air was thick with insects. Mathi noted ruefully that mosquitoes and flies didn't appear to bother the kender at all. It wasn't that they didn't mind being bitten; the pests didn't bite them. Another stroke for the Wanderfolk. Here was a tactic Balif had not considered. If the nomads dallied long enough in the lowland woods, they'd be eaten alive by mosquitoes.

It was by all appearances good land to settle, bugs or no bugs. The soil was evidently very fertile, as there were flowers and fruit everywhere. The trees were not so old or lofty as their western neighbors, but useful varieties grew everywhere: pine, elm, maple, and ash. Treskan made careful mental notes of the flora. His stylus may have been broken, but he could still keep notes if he could find the basic ingredients to write with—soot and oak gall for ink, birch bark for paper. The Haddaras river basin was a garden. He could probably find everything he needed. There was much to record.

The western branch of the river came into view. It was a far different water course than the rough Thon-Tanjan or the deceptive Thon-Thalas. Narrow, muddy, closed in by overhanging vines and branches, the Wanderfolk River was unlike any other river in Silvanesti territory. The Longwalker's description was on the mark. Descending the bank to the water's edge, the air was heavy with the smell of overripe fruit. Wild grapes hung down, banging against Mathi's forehead. They were brown and fat and astonishingly sweet when she tried one. She saw kender lolling on the riverbank with willow fishing poles. Every so often one would flip his pole backward, tossing a silver captive onto the bank.

"Have you been across the river?" Balif asked the Longwalker. They had paused atop the earthen ball of an overturned tree's roots, surveying the land.

He had. The triangle of land between the two tributaries was much higher than the bottom land where they were now. In fact there was a bluff about forty feet high overlooking the eastern branch.

Balif clapped his hands. "Excellent." His final redoubt was shaping up to be a better defensive position than he imagined.

He went down to the water's edge and prepared to wade across. Perched on the bank behind him was Rufe, munching a bunch of grapes piled on his belly.

"I wouldn't," he said.

Mathi, Treskan, and Lofotan arrived alongside their leader. "Why not?" asked Balif. "Too deep?"

Rufe displayed the calves of his legs. There were dozens of reddish spots on them.

"Leeches."

Mathi drew back from the water's edge. She said to Rufe, "How did you get here so fast?"

Rufe pointed at the sky. "By way of the moon." Kender.

Balif wasn't squeamish about leeches, but there was no

point feeding the bloodsuckers if he knew they were there. He asked the Longwalker for a different way across.

The kender cupped his hands around his mouth and shouted at the trees, "We need a way across the river!"

A voice unseen on the other side called back, "All right, boss." For a time the only sound were the whine and buzz of insects. A loud snapping filled the air. It came from across the river.

"What are they doing?" Lofotan wondered.

He quickly had an answer. Nine kender came into view on the eastern shore, backs bent over a large log. They were rolling it down the hill, pushing it with their hands. Mathi wanted to shout at them to be careful. When the slope got too steep it was bound to get away from them. She didn't have time. The log gathered momentum. It outraced its little drivers, smashing down bushes and saplings in its path.

"Look out below!"

A stump stuck up on the east bank. The big log came rumbling down, parallel with the stream. If it hit the water at this angle it would simply crash into the water and float away, but that's not what happened. The end of the log smacked into the stump, which deflected the log enough to cause the free end to swing around in a half-circle. When the stump gave way, it allowed the other end of the log to slide through the green fronds to the water, halting when the far end buried itself in the mud of the west bank.

Even Lofotan could not refrain from laughing. Engineers trained in the finest schools in Silvanost could not have done a faster job bridging the river.

"Tell me they did not do that on purpose," Treskan exclaimed.

Rufe ate a grape. "Do what on purpose?"

Balif ignored him. He went to the log and planted a foot on it, testing it with his weight. It held. He started across.

"My lord, what about the horses?" asked Lofotan. The

log wasn't wide enough to allow them to cross.

"Tie them on that side."

Lofotan tried to enlist some kender to ferry the elves' baggage, but as soon as he mentioned it the riverbank emptied in no time. The ones fishing vanished, leaving their poles stuck in the mud. Rufe disappeared too, which surprised everyone but Mathi. Kender were willing to do many things, but manual labor did not seem to be one of them.

Ferry duty fell to Treskan. He made many trips back and forth bearing their gear. The river was shallow enough that the big log had a damming effect on the flow, and by Treskan's last crossing the water had risen enough to lap over the log. It was a dicey journey bearing heavy equipment on his back, trying to keep his footing on a slick, wet trunk. That he made it without falling in was counted a blessing of the gods.

They found a deer track up the steep hill. At the top the trees cleared out, revealing a wide promontory about forty feet above the river. They found Balif out on the very tip gazing into the distance. He was perched on a slender spire of clay, not sturdy looking at all. Lofotan gently suggested the general come back to firmer ground.

"This is a magnificent site for a fortified town," Balif declared. "Look here!"

They did, from a good ten feet back. Two muddy streams met at the point below, combining to form a broader version of its two branches. The Thon-Haddaras was muddy and slow, but the banks were wide and largely clear of the creeping growth choking the western branch. If it was navigable down to the sea, it would be an invaluable trading asset for any settlement atop the bluff.

"What now, my lord?"

"We must fortify this spot."

Mathi said, "How, general? The wanderfolk are strangers to picks and shovels."

"They can fell trees, can't they? We need a stockade as

wide as this point to stop any mounted charges." He turned and strode rapidly past his companions, gesturing to the weedy meadow on the wide side of the hill.

"This land needs to be cleared as far back as possible to deny cover to the enemy." He pulled up a handful of weeds, crushing them in his fingers. "Burning it off is the quickest way. Won't be easy. Everything's green." Balif dug his fingers into the dirt. "A lot of thatch, though. It will burn."

Good soldier that he was, Lofotan was an elf, and the idea of burning an entire hillside clearly appalled him. The Balif he had served under so long would never have suggested such a course, except in the direst straits.

"My lord, is all this feasible?"

"What can be imagined can be done, captain, if we are bold enough."

He strode briskly to the nearest tree, a sapling about as thick as Mathi's wrist. With a single chop of his sword Balif cut it down. He came back, slicing off the small branches with deft strokes of his blade.

"We shall raise our standard here," he said, "so that all may rally to it."

He ordered Mathi to search through the baggage and find his personal flag, the one his troops had carried into forty battles. Mathi found a cylindrical silk case and loosened the drawstring. Out came a long, heavy pennant made of dark green leather. There was nothing on the triangular banner but an odd brown shape—something like a square with a off-center triangle attached to one side. Balif attached the banner to the sapling with a couple of horseshoe nails and raised the pole skyward.

"Spread the word!" he announced to any kender in earshot. "All who suffer under the heel of the human raiders should come here. Here all will be protected!"

Standing near Lofotan, Mathi felt strangely embarrassed. Kender were not the sort to rally to a flag, especially an uninspiring pennant like Balif's. She asked the old warrior what the symbol on the flag represented.

"It is the sign of the Brown Hoods," Lofotan said, "proscribed by the Speaker over a century ago."

He returned to his commander's side. Ever loyal, Lofotan trailed behind Balif as the general stalked back and forth, drawing grandiose fortifications in the air.

*****

Days passed. The oppressed did not flock to Balif's banner.

A few kender arrived to look the place over, curious about the proclaimed safe haven. They looked at the pole with its flag, the empty hilltop, and went on their way. Mathi couldn't blame them. The whole thing smelled like a nomad plot to concentrate their enemies in one spot to ensure their utter destruction. Only the magic of Balif's name drew anyone there. Once they saw there were no defenses and no one to fight off Bulnac's experienced warriors, the curious kender melted into the greenwood. If she hadn't grown to care about the elf general, Mathi would have left too.

The Longwalker remained. At times in the following days he was the only one of two kender on the bluff. He had another with him—white-haired and wizened. The Longwalker produced swaths of different colored cloth, gave them to the oldster, and in a days' time a second flag flew from the sapling. It was a bold blue rectangle covered in tiny brace-shaped crosses made of red silk. It was the banner of the united kender clans, the Longwalker explained. It attracted no more support than Balif's.

The whole thing began to feel farcical until a band of centaurs arrived. They came through the lowland woods late one day. Their arrival sent ripples of alarm all the way to Balif. He ordered that the centaurs be welcomed as friends. The next morning they reached the hill. They were eleven strong, all warriors. It turned out they were all that was left of a much larger band wiped out by Bulnac's tribe.

"Greath's band?" said Balif, recognizing their tribal tattoos. Sadly, the centaurs nodded. "Where is the mighty chief?"

"Slain, wise one! Slain by the two-and-ones!" Centaurs, being half human and half horse, considered themselves whole people, while horse riding humans were only half normal. The combination of a human on horseback they called a two-and-one.

It was grave news. Greath had declared his friendship to Balif, an oath unbreakable. The general had hoped to cultivate Greath's band as allies against the humans. Now they were gone.

"You are welcome to stay among us," he told the centaurs. They were stout fighters, loyal and fierce, and they stayed. Whatever qualms the kender had about Balif's fortress, the centaurs remained. Not one of them complained about their position. Why should they? They had nowhere else to go.

Each night Balif disappeared into the woods alone. That was unsettling enough, but on the third night Mathi discovered his clothes in a pile by the general's tent. Balif had gone off without them, carrying only his knife. She told Lofotan. The old captain tried tracking his commander, but lost him in the swamp a few miles upstream from the bluff. When he returned to camp, Mathi questioned how an experienced Silvanesti soldier like Lofotan could lose anyone's trail.

"All right, here is the truth: I didn't lose him. I turned back. I did not want to see what my commander has become."

On the sixth night after raising his banner, Balif returned before dawn dragging a heavy body. At first they took it for game, but the carcass wasn't a deer or wild pig. Balif dragged it to the foot of the hill and left it.

The Longwalker, the centaurs, and Mathi gathered around. The curious kender turned the corpse over.

It was a human, a nomad by his clothes and hair. Evidently Balif had encountered him on his nightly prowl.

"A scout," Balif said from the recesses of his tent. "I caught him in the forest not ten miles from where we stand."

"I understand killing him, Lord General, but why fetch back his remains?' asked the leader of the centaurs, Zakki by name.

"I didn't want to leave him out there." There was something very odd in his voice, a plaintive quality out of step with his new restive manner.

"Slain, he points to enemies," Lofotan said, interpreting for the others. "Vanished, anything might have taken him."

Zakki said, "We will bury him, Lord General." Two centaurs dragged the nomad away by the feet.

Lofotan went after them to see that the grave was well concealed. That left Mathi, Treskan, and the Longwalker outside Balif's tent.

"Chief, will you excuse us? I have some information to share with my scribe." With a shrug, the Longwalker departed. "You remain, too, girl."

"Yes, my lord?" Mathi said when they were alone.

"Bulnac will be here soon. Two days, maybe three."

Mathi was astounded. "But how, my lord?"

"The scout was not alone." He grimaced. "I could not get them all." Bulnac was pouring south and east, driving everything before him. Greath's centaurs were no longer a threat. That left only Balif and the kender.

"How many warriors does he have?" the scribe asked.

"Five thousand horse, plus many more on foot. Remember the road we found? He's rallied every footloose and disaffected nomad in the eastern province to his banner." All told, Balif estimated Bulnac's force at nearly twenty thousand.

"We can't possibly hold off such a horde!"

"There's more."

What more mattered? Treskan fingered his talisman nervously. Mathi noticed he always did that when confronted by the greatest danger.

"I will not be myself much longer," Balif said. His voice, normally clear and confident, was choked. "Already I am . . . changed, and what is changed is not turning back to anything close to my normal self. In a week I won't be able to command anything."

Mathi was surprised. Her own reversion was very slow, almost imperceptible. Hair was returning to her legs and body, but as yet she thought as clearly as ever. It must be part of the Creator's malediction, robbing Balif of his wits early. Taius and the other beast folk retained their powers of understanding, even as their bodies reverted to beastly form.

"I am not like them!" Balif shouted for both to hear. "I am being transformed into an animal, not from an animal into an elf. My mind is—is failing. The nomads escaped last night because I thought like a beast, not like a soldier."

The truth dawned on Mathi. Balif's strange attachment to the dead nomad wasn't due to security or sentimentality. It was the bond between predator and prey.

"Don't leave me, either of you. Not until the end. Do you swear?"

They swore, but Treskan asked, "Why me, lord? Don't you want Lofotan at your side when—when the time comes?"

"Lofotan is Silvanesti. He is my comrade in arms, but he cannot comprehend what will happen soon. I think you can. And—"

He stirred in the darkness, putting out a hand to close the tent flap. It muffled his last words slightly.

"And you must tell history what became of Balif."

The hand yanked down the tent flap was not a hand, but a paw, covered in fur.

# Chapter 17

## *Storms*

The birds gave the first warning.

A mass of men and horses on the move required food. On the open plain fodder was all around them, but foraging in the woods was far more laborious. When the outriders of Bulnac's force entered the Haddaras watershed, their progress was marked by enormous flocks of birds fleeing ahead of them. Especially raucous were the crows, which the woods housed in great numbers. Clouds of black birds fled screaming as the nomads probed and plundered the greenwood.

After the birds came the wild creatures of the forest. At dawn and dusk Balif's tiny camp was overrun by deer, wild pigs, and rabbits escaping Bulnac's hungry horde. The advance of the nomads was easy to calculate. When the panicked animals came more than twice daily it meant the humans were drawing nearer.

Balif remained in his tent during the day. No one blamed him for hiding from the light. Mathi deflected queries by Zakki, the leader of the centaurs, and by the Longwalker, saying the general was ill. Lofotan did not try to see his leader. He knew the curse was advancing, and he did not want to see how the general was changing. Several times a day he stood outside the closed end of the tent, relating the latest news of nomad advance. Balif replied with single words when necessary, or dismissed his old comrade by not answering at all.

On their own, the centaurs took to ranging into the woods on the open end of Balif's redoubt. They tried not to be seen, but inevitably Bulnac's men spied them and gave chase. Zakki's fellows used a simple blind to hide the location of Balif's camp—they always fled nomad pursuit eastward, across the river, which they recrossed below the confluence before returning to report to Balif.

Mathi felt their doom was fast closing in. They had no defenses, no stockade, and only the weapons each of them carried. Aside from the Longwalker and a few of his friends, not a single kender had been seen in a week. Even Rufe was long gone. Mathi still owed him a horse, but Rufe was apparently no longer interested in trying to collect. If Mathi had been him, he would have written off the debt too. Treskan alone seemed busy. He inscribed volumes on any surface he could carry—leaves, tree bark, scraps of cloth, all written with charcoal sticks and spit. Mathi thought he would keep scribbling up to the moment a howling nomad lopped his head off.

At night Balif crawled out of his tent and slipped into the trees. He wished to go unseen, but Mathi and Lofotan kept watch from a discreet distance. All they saw was a dark, stooped figure creeping on all fours. It was enough to make the old warrior shut his eyes and shudder.

After his leader had departed on his nightly prowl, Lofotan returned to a project of his own. Mathi found him sitting cross-legged near the cliff edge overlooking the river. He had collected a large mound of green vines and was painstakingly braiding them into a single thick strand.

"What are you making?" Mathi asked.

"A lifeline."

The scribe didn't get his meaning at first. Lofotan explained that when the time came, he wanted a rope he could throw over the cliff. That way they could climb down to the river and not be hopelessly trapped on the bluff.

It was a good idea. Mathi asked how much he had made.

"Twenty feet." About half of what was needed. Mathi fingered the coil of finished rope Lofotan had made. It was tight and supple, amazing handwork. Elven dexterity at work.

She left him to his task. Mathi intended to return to her shelter—she shared the largest tent with Treskan and the elves' baggage—but first she followed the edge of the hill around, looking down at the water sparkling in the darkness below. She hadn't gone halfway around when she spotted movement in the heavy shadows along the west bank of the river. Unsure what she was seeing, she slowed, then stopped. More movement, in another place. Someone was down there. More than one someone.

"Lofotan!" she hissed. "Lofotan, come here!"

The elf jogged up carrying his bow. Without a word Mathi pointed to the spot she thought she'd seen figures moving. She held up two, then three fingers. Lofotan nocked an arrow.

"Are the centaurs all back?" Mathi whispered. They weren't. Lofotan said something about them not coming back from the west.

"Balif?"

"Deer, maybe." Lofotan waited, bow held loosely waist high. His eyesight was several times better than Mathi's. He saw something she couldn't. The bow mounted swiftly to his cheek and the arrow flew. Like most elves, Lofotan used a pinch draw, rather than the three-finger draw favored by humans. The pinch draw was not as powerful, but it had the advantage of nearly silent release. The arrow flashed into the night with only the softest thrum of the bowstring behind it.

There was a thud below, a loud snapping of greenery, followed by a splash. Mathi strained hard to see what had happened. Moments later the answer came floating down river. A body, face down in the water, with Lofotan's arrow through its neck.

"Watch out," the warrior said calmly. He leaned aside. Mathi stepped back more slowly and a brace of arrows cut the air where he had been.

"We're silhouetted against the sky," Lofotan said. "Stay back."

He went down on one knee, bow resting on his thigh. Mathi fidgeted.

"Wait," the elf whispered.

He heard a sound with his keen ears, popped up, aimed, and dispatched an arrow. He was rewarded with a screech of pain. Lofotan dropped down again. An arrow whistled past, high over his head.

"He has the range but not the angle," was his professional assessment of the enemy archer. "A smart soldier would beat a retreat now." Another missile thudded into the clay of the bluff. Mathi muttered, "That one's not smart, he's angry."

Lofotan found a loose stone. He pressed it on Mathi and told her to go eight or ten feet away and toss it over.

"He won't fall for that old trick!"

"Do as I say!"

He had a second rock himself. Mathi crept on her hands and knees to where a small cedar tree was barely clinging to the crumbling cliff. She hurled the stone, then dropped on her belly as fast as she could.

From his position Lofotan pushed his stone off the edge with his foot. Clods of dirt went with it, making a miniature avalanche. A white-fletched arrow sang through the air where the stone fell. If Lofotan had been sitting there it would have hit him in the face.

Straightening his back, the elf took aim and let fly. Without waiting any time to see if he hit the mark he got up, tapped Mathi on the back and said, "Get your spear and follow."

They descended to the water's edge. The first victim had

floated down thirty yards but was snagged on a low-hanging tree branch. Target number two, the one who had yelled, was dead on his back on the sandy bank. Number three was in a tree, his arms and legs hanging lifelessly over the slow moving stream.

The last nomad fascinated Mathi. She walked under the tree and saw Lofotan's arrow had gone through four inches of trunk before piercing the man's skull. He had never seen such marksmanship, especially in the dark and from a height.

"It's nothing," Lofotan replied to his amazement. "I have always been counted a mediocre archer. Artyrith could have gotten all three in half the time."

They hid the bodies in a gully, covering them with vines. The night was too quiet for safety. All the normal sounds of the woods had stilled.

"Too many people around," was Lofotan's assessment. They returned to camp.

Zakki and the centaurs were there, waiting. Only nine had come back from their patrol. Two centaurs had fallen trying to escape swarming nomad scouting parties.

"How far from here?" asked the elf.

"An hour's walk." For a centaur, that meant eight to ten miles. Even with the thick foliage slowing them down, that meant the nomads could be upon them at any time. Now, in fact.

Mathi looked to the stars. Four hours till dawn. Suddenly she felt very naked. Why did she linger with these doomed fools? Her mission was a failure; part of her was glad of that. Now Balif and his companions faced utter destruction. Why remain? Two reasons occurred to her. One, the woods were alive with vigilant nomads. Her odds of escaping were not high. Even more compelling, she remembered her vow to Balif.

Lofotan broke the spell when he swept his arm in a wide arc from one side of the bluff to the other. "I want a line of sharpened stakes across here, every one six feet long or better." A line of stakes would halt any mounted charge, but it wouldn't delay a determined assault on foot.

"Who's going to make the line of stakes?" Mathi wondered.

"We are, all of us."

With axes, swords, and jury-rigged mallets the elf, the scribe, Mathi, and the surviving centaurs set to work. Mathi and four centaurs went to where the trees began and started to cut down saplings. Two centaurs dragged these to Treskan where the trees were stripped of branches and had one end sharpened. The elf, Zakki, and two sturdy centaurs drove these at an angle into the clay, then chipped the protruding end to a point. Lofotan spaced them about a foot apart. It would take more than a hundred to cover the ground he indicated.

Chopping down trees was noisy work. The silent forest echoed with the sound of blades biting green wood. Nomad scouts could not fail to hear the commotion.

Mathi chopped and hacked until her hands were blistered. Then she chopped some more. She dulled an axe and switched to a thick-bladed falchion loaned to her by one of the centaurs. The horse-men were unflagging workers. They'd been dashing around all night, but they kept at the work until the sun's first rays put the stars to sleep.

Mathi raised the falchion high to finish cutting down her forty-third sapling. An eerie baying filled the woods below, and she stayed her hand. She listened, and the sound grew more distinct. Hounds. They had the scent of their prey.

Something crashed through the undergrowth. It was hurtling toward her. She put an elm tree to her back and raised the battered falchion. The dogs were chorusing loudly now in a wide half circle, all the way from the extreme left to the far right. As on the night she was caught outside Bulnac's camp, the baying dogs raised the hair on her neck and made her heart hammer. Their calls spoke to her blood far more frighteningly than anything the humans did.

She saw a sudden blur of muddy brown. For a moment Mathi thought it was a bear. It drove past her beyond arm's reach but close enough for the wind to stir her clothing. The eyes of the beast met hers in passing, then Balif was gone. He ran up the hill through the field, disappearing over the rise into camp.

Balif had been out nosing around when the dogs had picked up his trail. Even he could do little against a veteran pack of hunting hounds.

The centaurs arrived at a gallop. Warchief Loff—as they called Lofotan—was calling everyone back. From the summit he could see movement in the trees. Lots of movement. Mathi ran. The centaurs thundered past her and kept going.

Lofotan's fence was only three-quarters complete. A small pile of poles lay scattered on the ground where the stakes ended. There was no time to finish.

Balif had run to the first shelter he could reach, which happened to be the supply tent where Mathi and Treskan slept. The tethered horses, brought with great labor across the river, were terrified by his presence. They milled around snorting and stomping. Mathi watched the centaurs join their fellows behind the stakes. Treskan had a spear. Lofotan was there too, but he did not see the Longwalker. She guessed the kender had abandoned them to their fate at last.

Mathi approached the tent. She heard Balif snarl, "Get back!"

"This is no time for vanity," Mathi said. "I'm coming in."

The general's response was a low, throaty growl that would have stopped a charging wolf. With the hounds still baying in the woods and Lofotan shouting for him, Mathi braced herself and strode straight into the tent.

She looked at the general of the Speaker of the Star's armies, lying on his side, panting. There was just enough of his original form left in him to make his appearance even more grotesque.

"I . . . shall kill . . . you!"

"You'll have to stand in line, my lord! The nomads are coming!"

"Think . . . I don't . . . know?"

"We need you, sir. We need everyone, every hand!"

Balif's panting sound like laughter. "I . . . have no . . . hands left."

"Then lie here and die! I've no more time to waste on you!"

She raced to where Lofotan, the scribe, and the centaurs waited. Seeing the elf warrior with his helmet on gave Mathi an idea. She diverted to Balif's tent and got the general's polished helmet, with the white horsehair plume on top. She held it out to Lofotan.

"I can't wear the general's armor," he said.

"Wear it, captain. Be our general in this last fight."

Taking in the expressions on the centaurs and the scribe, Lofotan removed his simple headgear and donned Balif's helmet.

The baying hounds abruptly ceased their song. Everyone on the hill stirred nervously. Only the dogs' handlers could silence them so suddenly. The enemy must be close.

They were. Daylight glinted off bits of armor and naked blades down at the tree line. Mathi couldn't count them scattered among the trees, but it looked like several hundred men on foot, milling around in the greenery.

Between them they had seven bows. Centaur bows were simple curved staves, which lacked the range and power of Lofotan's elegant Silvanesti weapon. They also used stone arrowheads, not bronze like the elf's. Against fur-clad nomads it might not make much difference, but if there was much armor distributed among Bulnac's men, the centaurs' arrows would be almost useless.

Nevertheless they braced and stood ready. Mathi swallowed hard. If only the kender had been as steadfast as Zakki and his comrades.

After a short period of disorder, the nomads advanced up the hill. They came on in no formation, just a ragged line with men bunched together around individual leaders. It was close to two hundred yards from the forest edge, to where Lofotan stood. He pointed his arrow skyward and released. Plunging out of the lightening sky, Bulnac's men couldn't see it coming. It hit a nomad in the center of the line. He threw up his hands and went down. His friends stood around him momentarily, then resumed their advance.

Lofotan loosed arrow after arrow. He never missed. His targets were thickly clustered together. The morning light was against them, but they doggedly came on. At a hundred fifty yards some of the nomads halted and loosed their own arrows. Things were hectic on the hilltop as everyone dodged incoming missiles. To Mathi, who had never been on the receiving end of archery in broad daylight, it seemed as though the arrows flew and fell very slowly. When they hit the ground they only buried a few inches of shaft. Were they really dangerous?

Her curiosity was answered when one of the centaurs was hit in the palm of one hand. The nomad arrow penetrated for half its length. It was a horrible looking wound, but the tough centaur snapped the hardwood shaft with his teeth and pulled the arrow out.

The nomads' archery sputtered and ended. Too many of their comrades were in front of them, and they no longer had a clear field of fire. From the heights, Lofotan had a perfect view. The centaurs joined in, and they attacked the advancing humans without mercy.

Beating their swords against their wooden shields the nomads kept coming, shouting their chief's name over and over, like a spell to insure victory.

Without anyone in overall command, the mob of nomads began shifting to their left. The gap in the stake line lay that way, and even though they could have squeezed between the stakes at any point, the warriors naturally made for the easier path.

Lofotan lowered his bow. Mathi asked, "Are you out of arrows?"

"No, but there's no point using them all now." He called for the others to form beside him with weapons drawn.

"We'll charge them when they enter the gap," he said. The narrow way would cause the nomads to bunch together, hampering their movements and their ability to use their weapons.

"Now, forward!"

They trotted toward the fence gap. As they passed the supply tent, the canvas sides billowed out, and a dark shape burst out of the front. A blood-chilling howl rang from the hilltop.

Balif had joined the fight.

Mathi checked Lofotan. The elf warrior kept his eyes straight ahead, not paying the slightest attention to the misshapen creature entering the battle on their side.

Balif reached the enemy first. They gave ground before his charge, unsure what they faced. He batted away the spears they jabbed at him. The beast's jaws opened wide, revealing a jaw full of long yellow teeth. A human archer took aim, but Zakki put an arrow in him first. Balif sprang at the enemy, bowling over three when he landed. His power was terrifying. He had claws on all four limbs, and he ripped his way through the lightly clad nomads. What his talons did not shred, his teeth tore apart.

The nomads were surprised to be attacked by an animal, but they were men of field and stream, used to hunting animals of all kinds. They rallied, trying to ring in the beast and cut him down. Fortunately for Balif, Lofotan's band arrived.

They battered the nomads back, breaking the circle and freeing Balif. He snarled defiance and stormed into danger again. The centaurs fought valiantly, not only with sword and spear but with their front hooves too. Lofotan moved like a dancer, slashing in and out among the nomads with ruthless precision. But for all their ferocity, bravery, and skill, they were thirteen against hundreds. Nomads flowed left and right, getting behind the defenders. Two of Zakki's centaurs went down in quick succession to thrown spears. Treskan did his best, which wasn't much, so he settled for keeping the enemy off Lofotan's back. Mathi could do little but parry and block sword and spear thrusts. The circle shrank and shrank. When Mathi's heels bumped the elf's she knew the end was near.

And then, a miracle.

At two-score points along the slope of the hill dirt flew upward. Holes opened in the ground, holes that had been covered with panels of woven vines and camouflaged with dirt. Pouring out of these holes came kender—hundreds of kender. Decked out in a motley collection of found weaponry they mixed with the nomads and fell upon them from all sides. In the time it took for a sparrow to cross the ridge the course of the battle completely reversed. The nomads broke. They ran for the woods, many with two or three kender clinging to them, battering them with swords, knives, stones, or sticks. The ring of bloody blades that threatened to close around Lofotan's defenders disintegrated. Zakki and his warriors took up their bows, stinging the retreating enemy. Treskan and Mathi were content to watch the humans flee, stunned by the sudden turn of fate.

Balif chased them, howling for more blood. When a stout warrior turned to spear the general, Lofotan raised his bow and shot him down. Pointed ears laid back against his head, Balif howled and charged the next nearest nomads. He pursued the enemy into the woods.

Mathi saw the concern on Lofotan's face. Alone in the woods, Balif could be ambushed at any time. There was nothing Lofotan could do. Sound tactics required him to remain on the hill no matter what his cursed leader did.

The Longwalker hailed them. "Greetings, noble friends! We have won!"

"Only the first throw," Lofotan said. Uncharacteristically, he smiled broadly at the kender chief, however. "I wish you could have told us what you were planning!"

"We thought we were going to die!" Treskan added.

"Many apologies, but it was vital that the humans not know about our wall-less walls."

The Longwalker explained that the kender had begun tunneling into the bluff since the first night they arrived. At first they were simply making holes to hide in, but as the number of holes multiplied, someone suggested linking them with tunnels. They knew they had neither the time nor materials to fortify the hill in the usual way, so they reverted to kender tactics—doing what no one else thought of.

"Whose idea was it to make tunnels?" Mathi asked.

"Rufus."

A hand plucked at Mathi's sleeve. "How are you, boss?"

Mathi's knees failed her at that point. She sat down before she fell down.

"Fantastic!" she said trembling. She gathered the astonished kender into her arms and embraced him like a brother.

"Uh, boss? You're crushing me."

Mathi thrust the little man out at arms' length. "What do I owe you for my deliverance?" she said happily.

"Nothing. This one was on me."

The short celebration was over when word came up the hill that strong parties of humans were in the woods, many on horseback. In short order the kender came piling back, popped back in their holes, and pulled their lids shut behind them. As miraculous as their sudden appearance had been, their disappearance was equally astonishing.

The Longwalker remained above ground with a contingent of thirty-odd followers. They formed up in a bunch behind Lofotan and Mathi. The centaurs spread out in front, bows ready.

A line of mounted men filtered slowly out of the trees. Sunlight sparkled on their upraised spear points.

"Steady," Lofotan said. "Remember, most warriors die while running away, not when they stand fast."

"Depends on how fast you can run," replied the Longwalker.

A small group detached from the line of horsemen and trotted up the hill. Mathi counted six riders. It looked like a parley, and he said as much to Lofotan.

"Hold those arrows," the elf told the centaurs.

Drawing closer, Mathi recognized the massive nomad leader Bulnac. His horse was enormous too, with great shaggy hooves and a back as broad as a banquet table. Arrayed behind him were his lieutenants, decked out in typical savage finery with feathers, beads, shells, and the odd bit of metal here and there.

Bulnac came straight at the center of the line of stakes, and stopped there, waiting.

"I guess we'd best meet him," Lofotan said.

"Who goes with you?" Mathi asked.

"All of you. This concerns everyone."

The motley knot of centaurs, kender, elf and disguised elves went to meet the nomad chief. Bulnac did not dismount when they approached. He sat high atop his monstrous horse, looking down his flat nose at the strange delegation facing him with a fence of sharpened stakes arrayed between him and then.

"Who commands here?"

"I do," said Lofotan. "The Longwalker leads his own people, and Zakki is chief of our friends, the centaurs."

"Ah, I heard there were horse-men on this hilltop. Did you not learn your lesson before? This time there will be no survivors."

"You haven't won yet," Lofotan replied dryly. "What do want? Or did you come all this way to boast us to death?"

The chief's wide white smiled vanished. "You have too long been a thorn in my flesh, elder one. You and those cockroaches," he sneered at the assembled kender. "I came to tell you not to expect any quarter if there is any further resistance to my taking over this land." He looked past the defenders, noticing the commanding view from the bluff. "This will make a fine place to build my stronghold." He smiled again very unpleasantly. "After you are gone."

"There's an old saying among my people," the Longwalker said. " 'Birds on the wing lay very few eggs.' "

Bulnac curled a lip. "My steed shall tread on your faces," he vowed, "unless you abandon the hill now. March away and I will not molest you. That is Bulnac's mercy, and it is the most you can expect from me."

The centaurs' bows creaked as they nervously tugged at them. Bulnac heard the sound and laughed. "You have your choice: sure slaughter at the hands of my warriors, or return to the land that bore you."

He reined around. His minions drew well back, making room for their large leader.

"You have until the shadow changes right to left." He pointed to the shadow lines cast by the stakes. From Bulnac's perspective the morning sun cast their shadows to his right. By the time the sun passed overhead and started down in the west, the stakes' shadows would switch to the other side. That would take about three to four hours.

"Away!"

Bulnac galloped down the hill with his men close behind. The defenders of Balif's redoubt watched them go, each one pondering the choice they had to make.

# Chapter 18

## *Exits*

Rufe led everyone to the opposite side of the hill, not far from the edge of the bluff overlooking the river. He went unerringly to a spot by a scraggly cedar tree, dug his fingers in the dirt, and opened a hidden trapdoor.

Lofotan and Mathi squatted by the hole. It smelled damp.

"This runs down to the river bank?" asked the elf.

"Dug it myself," Rufe vowed.

"Can we fit in there?"

Mathi squinted at the narrow hole. It looked possible, but it was not an experience she really desired.

"Doesn't matter," Lofotan said, standing. "Zakki and his kind can't possibly get through such a small tunnel. We can't abandon them."

They had been discussing what to do about Bulnac's ultimatum. The mass of nomad horsemen remained at the tree line, waiting for the order to attack. No one believed the ruthless chieftain would really allow them to go. They had caused him too much trouble and deeply injured his pride. No one doubted that once they were out of their defenses, Bulnac's men would slaughter them.

"We could jump," Mathi mused, eyeing the river forty yards below. "If the water is deep enough—"

"This much," Rufe replied, holding a hand a few inches over his head. Not nearly enough to break a fall from so high a place as the cliff.

"Then we shall die together, fighting as honorable warriors!" Zakki declared. Lofotan seemed resigned to just that fate. Treskan fondled his talisman and said little about fighting or fleeing.

"Whatever happens, let your people disperse," the elf told the Longwalker. "No sense getting them all killed. Live to fight another day, you understand?"

"That is what we do, noble captain," the kender said. He was remarkably calm about the danger hanging over them. It was probably because he had a foolproof exit already worked out, Mathi privately decided.

They returned to the summit of the hill as the sun reached its zenith. Two hours remained. Mathi broke out the last of Artyrith's nectar, giving each defender his own bottle. Lofotan questioned the wisdom of that, but the centaurs broke off the bottles' necks and guzzled the amber nectar happily. Treskan drank more decorously, but he plainly didn't care if the nomads found him drunk or sober. Still disliking drink, only Mathi abstained.

The bottles were almost drained when there was a commotion down at the trees. Everyone went to the stakes and shaded their eyes to see what caused the disturbance. Four riders struggled out of the woods through the lines of horsemen already on watch. There was something on the ground between, something dark that rolled and lunged against the riders' ropes. It didn't take the defenders long to realize what it was.

The nomads had captured Balif.

They made their way up the hill, stopping frequently to maintain control of their furious captive. Ten yards from the stakes one of the nomads called out, "Elf! Elf, are you listening?"

Lofotan leaned on a slanting stake. "What do you want?"

"We got something of yours! This your beast?"

"No."

The nomad was crestfallen. He had been looking forward to tormenting Lofotan with his captured property. Now that ugly pleasure had been denied him.

"Well, I guess you won't mind if we skin it. It's got a nice pelt."

He drew a long knife. Mathi moved up behind Lofotan and put a hand to his shoulder. Still the old warrior said nothing.

"Hold him."

The riders backed their horses, keeping their ropes taut. The knife wielder got down. Before he got within arm's reach Mathi shouted, "No, wait!"

She spied Rufe out of the corner of his eye. She muttered, "Can your people in the tunnels get to him?" The kender held up his thumb.

"That's my beast," Mathi called. "He's worth a lot to me. Don't hurt him."

The nomad laughed. "What'll you give me to not cut him?"

"What do you want?"

He made a rude suggestion. Coloring, Mathi drew her sword, grip reversed, and threw it over the stakes. It was a good elf-forged blade, though plain in design.

"How about its life for that sword? It's solid bronze, made in Silvanost!"

The nomad walked to where the blade lay, stuck point first in the soil. Just as he stretched out his hand to take it, four tunnels popped open around him and his comrades. In a flurry, the three riders were unhorsed. The captive beast tore off his bonds with his teeth. The nomad leader never reached the elf sword. Zakki put an arrow in his ribs. He folded like a Silvanesti chair, landing flat on his back. Faster than anyone could prevent it, the beast leaped on him and tore out his throat with his teeth.

Shocked, the remaining three nomads made a dash for the trees. Their spooked horses beat them there. Blood streaming from his jaws, the beast stood with his fore-paws on the dead man's chest and roared at his former tormentors.

Lofotan gave Mathi a shove. "Go get him!"

"Aren't you going to help?"

Face white, the elf snapped, "Get him before the savages come in force!"

Mathi slipped between the stakes. Hearing her footsteps, the beast whirled, teeth bared. She turned to stone.

"My lord," she said evenly, "It is I, Mathi. Your sister."

The creature, looking like the misbegotten offspring of a bear and a panther, tilted its head to one side and snarled. Mathi spared a glance down the hill. The nomads were coming to avenge their comrades.

"Sir," she said, "come with me behind the stakes. The enemy is coming." She wanted to say 'you'll be safe back there,' but it was a lie she could not bring herself to speak.

Mathi held out her hand. If the beast pounced, she wouldn't be able to get away before it tore her apart.

"Come, general. Be Balif just a little longer."

Mention of his name had an odd effect on the creature. It got off its victim and slunk away in a wide circle, skirting Mathi as widely as it could. It did go through the stakes, and with a single sidelong glance at the other defenders, made for the supply tent. Balif vanished inside.

Lofotan shouted for Mathi to return. She picked up her sword and rejoined the little band of defenders.

Riders came up the hill, though not in attack strength. Perhaps forty men rode in tight formation to where the nomad slain by the beast lay. The centaurs leveled their bows, but

Lofotan stayed them. Staring and muttering oaths, the nomads recovered the body and departed.

"What was that about?" Treskan wondered. Nomads were not usually so fastidious about their dead. The ones slain in the morning attack still lay on the hillside.

"I would say the bully with the knife was someone important," the Longwalker said.

So he was. Less than an hour passed, and Chief Bulnac returned with his personal retainers. Mathi was amazed to see that the huge man had been weeping. He ordered his men to stay behind, and rode alone to the stake line. There he hurled a spear point first into the ground and cried, "I claim vengeance! Vengeance for the killer of my son!"

The Longwalker and his cronies began backing away as quietly as possible. Zakki's fellows pulled on their death flowers—a centaur custom that involved putting on some item colored red. It didn't have to be a flower. Usually a red scarf or scrap of red cloth would do. It meant they expected to die.

Lofotan took Mathi by the arm and whispered in his ear, "This is our chance!"

Bulnac repeated his challenge, his voice hoarse with grief.

"What do you mean?"

"He wants single combat with the killer of his son! I'll fight him, and when I slay him, his followers may melt away in the greenwood!"

Mathi shook her head. "They'll play bowls with our heads! What makes you think you can beat that giant anyway?"

"He's only a human, and he's blind with grief and anger."

Before Mathi could protest further Lofotan stepped forward and said, "Here I am, savage. I am Lofotan Brodelamath, of House Protector, former captain of the host of the Great Speaker of the Stars, Silvanos Golden-Eye!"

Bulnac pointed his sword at him. "You shall die soon

enough, elf, but first I drink the blood of my son's killer! Where is the monster?" The other nomads had reported truly and told the chief how his son died.

Lofotan waved Bulnac's threats aside and said, "You can't take vengeance on an animal, fool. Fight me in single combat, if you dare."

"I'll fight you elf, and when I do I'll be wearing the pelt of the monster that slew my Varek! Send it out, or I'll storm this hilltop with my entire band and torture everyone on it to death!"

Mathi pulled free of Lofotan's grip. She started for the supply tent, feeling Bulnac's burning gaze on her every step of the way. Just outside the tent she said quietly, "My lord, it's Mathi. I need to speak to you." There was no answer, but she girded himself and ducked inside.

The contents of the tent had been torn asunder. Blankets, baskets of provisions, jars of water and oil lay broken, torn, and scattered. Atop the mess lay the beast, hardly moving at all.

"My lord, do you hear the nomad chief? Do you understand what's happening? The man you killed was his son. He wants revenge. He demands to fight you in single combat."

Still the furry heap did not stir. Mathi drew a deep breath. "If you don't come out, my lord, Bulnac will kill us all as slowly and painfully as he can imagine." Which was probably very slowly and painfully indeed. "If you fight and win, my lord, there's a chance the nomads will quit the siege and spare us. What say you, my lord?"

Nothing. Trembling despite herself at the thought of Bulnac's wrath, Mathi turned to go. In one smooth movement the beast was up and slid past her. He looked back at Mathi, and she saw glimmers of intelligence still flickering in the creature's eyes. Balif understood.

They walked together to the stakes opposite Bulnac. The centaurs stood in a line and bowed their heads in salute.

Serius Bagfull and the kender were nowhere around. Lofotan, unable to bear the sight of his cursed commander, turned his back on the scene. Treskan wrote obsessively on a roll of birch bark.

"What sort of unnatural creature is this?" Bulnac said.

Mathi thought quickly. "It's called a bearcat, the offspring of a bear and a panther."

Bulnac spat. "You're a liar. Two unlike animals cannot breed, any more than birds can father chicks on dogs."

Mathi bowed humbly. "You asked, and I told you: a bearcat."

Bulnac shoved his sword back in its sheath. "Call it a mud-puppy, it matters not. Soon it will be dead, and all of you with it. Your carcasses will feed my Varek's funeral pyre!"

Without being asked he got down from his lofty horse. He tied his reins to a stake, slipped a small round buckler onto his left forearm, and drew his sword again.

"Any time, monster."

The beast who had been Balif sat on his haunches. And sat. At length it yawned, its black tongue curling at the tip.

Feeling mocked, Bulnac slapped his sword against the boss on his shield. Everyone but Lofotan flinched, but the creature eyed the big warrior with quiet intensity.

"Enough stupidity!" Bulnac advanced with a roar. He swung his blade with enough force to chop down a sizable tree. Trouble was, the beast was not a tree. It sprang full length from its crouch and hit Bulnac dead center in the chest before he could complete his swing. He staggered back but did not go down. The beast's front legs were around Bulnac's neck. The cheek pieces on Bulnac's helmet saved his face. He tried to bring his blade back against the creature, but it released its hold and dropped to the ground, sinking its fangs into Bulnac's thigh. No armor there.

Striking out in pain, he rapped the bronze hilt of his blade against the beast's skull. Stunned, the bearcat fell away and circled, shaking off the blow. A dozen yards back Bulnac's retinue shouted encouragement and praise at their leader. Blood ran down his face from some minor cuts, and dark blood welled from his thigh wound.

If he pierced the artery, Mathi thought furiously. If . . . The smell of freshly spilled blood made her dizzy.

Bulnac advanced, swinging his blade in wide arcs. The nomad chief did not appreciate that he was dealing with an animal with the strength and reflexes of a great predator but with the mind of a very intelligent elf. He was fighting Balif as if he were a mad dog or raging wolf.

Watching the bright blade cut the air, the beast timed his lunge for when the sword just passed his nose. He leaped, clamping his powerful jaws on Bulnac's wrist. Leather gauntlets blunted Balif's fangs but his full weight dragged the nomad's arm down. Bellowing defiance, Bulnac actually lifted the creature off the ground with his teeth still gripping his arm. He punched repeatedly with the hilt of his sword until the beast fell to the ground. Mathi reckoned every blow Bulnac landed broke a rib.

He raised one great leg, meaning to drive his spiked spur into the creature. Blood loss or the pain of his leg wound slowed him enough for Balif to roll aside. He raked his claws across Bulnac's back, shredding his leather jerkin and scoring the skin beneath.

Uneasy, the Bulnac's followers edged closer. A few pulled spears from sleeves hanging from their saddles. Seeing that, Lofotan loudly called for Zakki and his centaurs to raise their bows.

"First man to throw a spear dies!"

Bulnac lost his buckler when the beast tore it off his arm. Balif went for his throat. The chief got his sword up in time, and the creature was cut deeply across the chest.

The beast leaped away, turned and gazed at his foe with his fiery eyes. Panting, Bulnac threw down his unwieldy sword and drew instead a heavy dagger with a blade just ten inches long.

"Come, monster. Let us get closer." His words were little more than a whisper.

The sun was settling below the trees. Bulnac's original ultimatum had expired. Large numbers of warriors filtered through the trees, ready to join the promised attack. When their comrades on the spot told them what was going on, they joined the silent throng at the forest edge, watching their chief do battle with the monster that killed his son.

Then the beast astounded them all.

It leaned back, raising its front legs off the ground. As everyone looked on, the bearcat straightened its back and staggered upright. When it stood erect, it bared its teeth and snarled.

The hair on Mathi's neck prickled. The snarl sounded just like Balif saying "Ha!"

He lumbered forward, forelegs outstretched. Bulnac spat blood and waited, dagger drawn. Mathi expected the beast to go right at him and try to slash him with his claws. Balif closed to little more than arm's length. He twisted, dropped to the ground, and picked up Bulnac's discarded sword. He couldn't grip it properly, but he held it tightly between his paws. The nomad chief drew back, startled. Rearing his arms up, Balif flung the sword. It whirled point over pommel at its owner. Bulnac tried to parry the flying blade with his dagger. It whirled past his outthrust arm. The point hit him below the breastbone and sank in.

Color fled the nomad's face. The dagger fell from his fingers. Bulnac gripped the sword with both hands and tried to pull it out. He never got the chance. The beast hurled himself at the pommel, driving the blade through the chief's gut. Two feet of bloody bronze burst from Bulnac's back. He toppled backward with the beast embracing him.

For a moment silence reigned. Zakki raised his bow over

his head and screeched in triumph. His comrades echoed his cry. Mathi was surprised to hear herself shouting too. The thrill of victory quickly paled when she wondered what the multitude of nomad warriors would do now that their leader was dead.

Battered and bleeding, the beast stalked slowly back through the sharpened stakes. When he was well out of reach, Bulnac's retainers rode silently forward. They surrounded their fallen chief and lifted his body onto the back of his enormous steed. Without a word or second glance, they went down the hill where they were swallowed by a throng of quiet warriors.

The defenders braced for an attack. Night fell, and the nomads did not come. Through the darkness Mathi and the others watched the glow of a large bonfire, burning on a hilltop less than a mile away. It blazed most of the night, fading into the dark an hour or two before dawn.

# Chapter 19

## *Brothers*

When the funeral pyre of their chief burned out, the nomads took up their arms and prepared to avenge his death by destroying the stubborn defenders of Balif's bluff.

Three times they came before sun-up. Their first thrust was mounted. The nomads formed at the foot of the hill and slowly ascended without battle cries. They came to grief when their horses stepped on the flimsy lids of the kender's tunnels. Many riders were overthrown, and the rest stopped in confusion, certain the land was pocked with pits deliberately designed to trap their horses. The first attack was called off. Back down the hill went the nomads, to reform for another assault, this time on foot.

Inside the tunnels, the kender took the sudden breakthrough of horse hooves as an indication they were the target of the attack. Faster than you could say 'Rufus Wrinklecap,' they abandoned their holes, pouring out on the dewy turf at the top of the hill. Lofotan hurriedly tried to work them into companies of a hundred each, but he could never get an accurate count. As soon as one company was mustered, the elf moved on to the next, only to find many of the same kender lining up. They denied it, of course, but Lofotan gave up. He told the Longwalker to keep his people behind the stakes and have at any humans who came their way.

Mathi brought water and food—what little there was—to the supply tent after dark. Balif huddled inside, nursing his wounds. Any attempt by Mathi to enter the tent was met with snarls and swipes of his formidable claws. Thereafter she kept a vigil outside, ready to respond to any need the general might express. From time to time she was spelled by Treskan, who had acquired an ugly cut on his face and assorted bruises.

He was joined outside the tent by Rufe, who appeared out of nowhere and sat cross-legged on the ground next to Treskan. He nodded to Rufe. Rufe nodded back. Neither spoke for a long time.

"Looks like you won't be getting the horse we owed you," Treskan said.

"Eh? Why not?"

He smiled ruefully. "Always stout-hearted, aren't you?"

Morning peepers sang to them. Out of nowhere Rufe asked the scribe where he came from.

"Woodbec," he said

"Is that on the south coast?" asked Rufe.

"No, inland."

Rufe gave a him probing glance. "Will you be going back there?"

"Yes, sooner than I thought."

"Tell them my name," said Rufe. Treskan didn't understand, so Rufe repeated, "Tell the people of your home my name. That way when I come to visit, they'll know who I am."

Treskan smiled. "I shall do that."

The warning "Here they come!" went up from the wall. In the lull since Bulnac's duel, the defenders had thrown up a flimsy barrier of tree limbs to bridge the unfinished line of stakes. Mathi ran up, carrying spare spears and a helmet for Treskan.

Rufe got up, dusted the seat of his pants, and walked toward the makeshift barricade.

"Where are you going?" Mathi said.

"Where I am needed."

Mathi suddenly felt concern for the little man. She wondered if she would ever see him again.

The nomads came tramping up the hill on foot, stopping frequently to inspect open kender holes. Some had the bright notion of turning the tunnels against their makers, but the shafts were too narrow to admit bulky humans.

Lofotan flung arrows at them. He had only two sheafs of arrows left of the supply they had packed from Silvanost, a hundred arrows in all. The centaurs had even fewer. They held their missiles until the nomads were in range of their weaker bows. Lastly the Longwalker's kender piled up projectiles for their hoopaks, slings, and what diminutive bows they possessed. Their range was short, but in the last critical moment of a charge, they could add a critical weight to the defenders' barrage.

The humans were hampered by having to shoot their arrows uphill, but enough fell behind the stakes to make the defenders anxious. Every time a kender was injured, two or three of his comrades immediately bore him off to the far side of the hill. The slow but steady loss weakened the line. Mathi stalked among them, trying to convince them to return, but the kender evaded her outstretched arms and ignored her pleas.

"It's our time!" the Longwalker shouted. A hail of strange missiles lashed the nomads. Mathi could swear she saw a bone white goat skull, complete with horns, hurtle at the enemy along with the stones and darts. The humans put their shields up. Flying junk rattled off them with considerable noise. Those with their chests exposed took a beating from Zakki's centaurs. who shot them down easily.

Still the throng of nomads surged forward, reaching the stakes. They began pushing and pulling at the obstacle, even climbing the slanting poles to pull them down. The defenders backed up a pace, then another, until Lofotan was standing alone in front of everyone. Zakki galloped to him and begged him to retire. The elf nodded curtly, slung his bow over his shoulder, and drew his sword.

Treskan opened his collar and fished out his precious talisman. His mouth moved with unheard words—a prayer to his patron gods? Seeing about a thousand naked swords squeezing through the fence would make anyone pray. He closed his fingers tightly around the small golden trinket.

A dozen or so nomads peeled off from the main band and head for the supply tent. She shouted a warning, but no one could hear a single cry amidst the cacophony of battle. Mathi bared her sword and sprinted for the tent. Treskan saw her alarm and broke away to follow her. Halfway there it sank in what he was doing.

"I'm running toward twelve armed men carrying a sword! They'll kill me—I'm not a warrior, I'm a historian!" he cried.

"I'm not a warrior either, so run more and talk less!" Mathi retorted.

The thought of Balif being overwhelmed by a mob of angry nomads put fire in her veins. Shouting and waving her blade, she tried to divert the men from the tent.

Four faced off against them. The rest slashed down the ropes and trampled the tent. They thrust their sword into any likely heap under the canvas. Converging on the center, they stabbed again and again. Then the bulge in the center of the fallen tent ripped apart, revealing Balif.

He had changed again. He had regained part of his elf nature. All along his beastliness had waxed or waned according to some arcane purpose known only to Vedvedsica. He had been fully beastlike for a while, but now Balif stood up like any elf or man. He was covered in fur still, but his frame was more normally configured. His sudden change in appearance startled the nomads, who hesitated. Seizing on their indecision, Balif grabbed a spear from the stock stored in the supply tent and impaled the closest warrior.

The reverse of fortune made the men rushing Mathi and Treskan halt and turn back. Mathi cried, "General! General, behind you!" Balif whirled, using the spear shaft to drive back anyone trying to ambush him from behind. Mathi found herself trading sword cuts (of all things!) with a distracted nomad who was busy watching Balif slash his comrades to pieces. Treskan swung his weapon like a crowbar, connecting with a nomad's bearded face and laying him flat.

With four nomads dying in the dirt, the others gave up their attempt to slay Balif and fell back to rejoin the main attack. Mathi made her way to where Balif stood, shoulders hunched, staring at the retreating humans.

"My lord, are you all right?"

His head snapped around. A face that was definitely Balif's glowered behind the fur.

"Don't touch me!"

"Yes, my lord." Panting, Mathi added, "Shall we rejoin the battle?"

He kicked through the tent wreckage and strode to where the nomad horde struggled to overcome the small band of defenders. The sight of the half-beast general, stalking to the forefront of the fight, distracted everyone. Actual fighting dwindled, then petered out. Both sides withdrew a few steps and gazed in wonder at the strange creature standing between them.

"I am Balif!" he declared. His voice was rough and low, but distinct and recognizable. "I slew your chief and your chief's son. By right of combat I am your chief now!"

"Beast!" someone cried. "Monster!"

"Yes, I am a beast. I am also master of this land!" He held out his spear point first and swept his arm in a wide circle. "All this I claim for myself and my people."

"What people, beast?"

He gestured at the crowd of kender and centaurs behind him. The Longwalker proudly took his place at Balif's side.

"Here is the chief of my people. This land is theirs. Any who wishes to dispute this may challenge my right with his blood!"

Mathi trembled. She never imagined the enemy of her kind could be so noble or so valiant. Oh, she had heard the tales of Balif's wit and valor, but she had always been taught that Silvanesti were vain, spoiled creatures, cruel and cold. He was not the Balif she saw now. Wracked by an all-consuming curse, the general had rallied enough to stand and speak, and to challenge his enemies to face him singly. Brave warriors all, the nomads had seen how Balif had defeated Bulnac and Varek. They understood they were not dealing with a trained animal like their hunting dogs, but an accursed elf of power and intelligence. They kept their distance.

"What are you?" a human voice demanded, albeit with respect

Balif put his hand on the Longwalker's shoulder to steady himself. His body had been shaped and re-shaped, and standing was not easy.

"I am Balif, protector of the Wanderfolk."

"You killed our great chief!"

"The fight was fair. Who says it was not?" No one replied.

Sunlight brightened the scene. In all the furor no one had noticed the dawn approaching. Balif averted his face from the new day's glare. It hurt his eyes.

"Go and trouble this land no longer!" he said, wincing. "So long as Balif lives, this land shall belong to the Wanderfolk!"

Many of the nomads, already disheartened by the death of Bulnac, lowered their arms and walked away. Firebrands among them tried to rouse their fighting spirit and rally the others, but the slow decay of their morale rapidly became a full-scale collapse. Too many of them had no reason left to fight. They were used to roaming a wide range, grazing their herd animals and raiding their settled neighbors. Following Bulnac, they expected rich plunder and easy adventure. What they had got was endless miles of plain and forest, feisty little people and warlike centaurs. Bulnac paid for his ambition with his life. His men, a great many of them at least, preferred not to do the same.

In time even the stalwarts decided to withdraw. They backed away, glaring balefully at the weary defenders of Balif's redoubt. No one bothered them so long as their direction was down the hill.

Mathi came to Balif. "Rejoice, my lord!"

Still in view of the humans, Balif stayed standing. He opened one eye against the sunlight to see her. Mathi was startled to see that his eye was yellow-green, with a vertical slit pupil like a cat's.

"Why should I rejoice?" he rasped.

"You have just founded a new nation."

"No." He shuddered. "I shed blood. This one will found a nation."

So saying, he let go of the Longwalker's shoulder and collapsed. Treskan rushed over. Balif lay on his side, twitching uncontrollably. The centaurs and most of the kender were coming.

Mathi grasped the Longwalker by his vest. "Keep them away," she whispered. "Don't let them see him like this!"

Serius Bagfull nodded and went to intercept the jubilant defenders. He spread his arms wide and declaimed about the new day, how it was the dawn of a new nation for their people. Listening with half an ear, Treskan pronounced the Longwalker a true politician. The kender leader knew what to say and when to say it.

Mathi spread a cloak over Balif. The general was trembling as though with fever; the corners of his eyes and his lips were stained with a strange black liquid. She feared for Balif's life. Was he dying? If so, there was nothing Mathi could do about it.

Horns blared in the woods far down the slope. Fearing a return of the nomads, the kender panicked and fled to far end of the bluff. Zakki and his comrades, reduced to just five, fought to escape the flood of little people bearing them away from the line of stakes.

Mathi rose, looking for Lofotan. The valiant old warrior had made himself scarce when Balif appeared. Alerted by the horns, he had joined the centaurs with bow in hand. His last sheaf of arrows lay at his feet.

The clash of arms reached up from the trees. No one understood. Were the nomads fighting each other? It was possible. Humans were by nature very fractious, and nomads in particular were always ready to fight each other if no other enemy was available.

The horns sounded again, louder and closer. Lofotan stiffened. He lowered his bow.

"Those are brass horns," he said, puzzled. Nomads used rams' horns

The truth dawned. Treskan spoke for all when he cried, "Silvanesti!"

They could make out nothing from the hilltop. A great thrashing and crashing filled the woods, punctuated by shouts and the clang of metal. Zakki wanted to run down the hill and see what was going on, but Lofotan restrained him. If there were elves below, they might not know that the centaurs were allies.

Mathi had no such worries. She vaulted through the line of stakes and sprinted down the bloody hill. Lofotan called to her, but she waved the elf's words away and kept going. The hillside was a maelstrom of kender pits, slain horses and men, lost arms and spent arrows. Near the bottom, by the spot where they had cut so many saplings, she paused.

Riders in bright bronze armor rode through the trees trading blows with nomad warriors. There were a lot of them, at least as many as the humans, and they steadily drove Bulnac's men back. Mathi heard a peculiar roar overhead. A shadow passed over her. She looked up and saw griffons in the sky, wheeling and diving. There was no doubt who the newcomers were. Only Silvanesti rode griffons.

The thick green woods screened the nomads from aerial assault, but the sight and smell of griffons terrified their horses. They pitched their riders and bolted, half-mad to escape their ancestral enemies. With that, the third and last battle of the day was over.

The horse-riding elves pursued the fleeing foe, but the griffon riders circled back to the summit and landed. Mathi mopped sweat from her face and went up the hill to meet them.

They were splendid figures, the griffon riders. Chosen for their dexterity, grace, and slimness, they were the most elegant warriors Mathi had ever seen. Unlike cavalry or foot soldiers, they wore armor only on their lower limbs, a helmet, and close-fitting cream-colored silk garments with gold or scarlet sashes. Their weapons were very long, slender lances made of some translucent material—glass, or rock crystal elongated by some secret technique of the elves.

The griffon riders remained mounted. As Mathi approached, the fierce creatures spread their wings and clawed the ground with their taloned forefeet. They knew instinctively that she was not what she appeared to be. Mathi halted well out of reach of the keen, cold-eyed griffons.

"Greetings!" she said. "Your arrival is most timely!"

The griffon riders did not answer. Their mounts screeched and bobbed their heads in a very distracted manner. The nearest rider, who had the tallest crest on his helmet, addressed

Mathi. His voice was muffled by the nasal bar and wide cheek pieces of his headgear.

"Who are you, that our griffons regard you as an enemy?"

The smile melted on Mathi's face.

"My name is—"

"Mathani Arborelinex. Yes, I know. But who are you?"

The Silvanesti knew her name? That was perplexing. Mathi explained that she had been in the wilderness many days, hobnobbing with centaurs, humans, and kender. No doubt they all rubbed off on her a bit.

The griffon rider unbuckled his chin strap and removed his helmet. A mass of blond hair emerged, and with a face she knew well.

"Mistravan Artyrith! How can it be you?"

"*Lord* Artyrith," he said loftily. "Recently restored to my proper titles and property by the Speaker of the Stars."

Mathi congratulated the former cook. "You made it back to Silvanost?"

Artyrith perched his helmet on the pommel of his sky saddle. "I did. My report to the Speaker convinced him to send an expeditionary force. Even now we are driving the savages from the woodland below."

More revelations followed. Artyrith had caught the Speaker's favor with his dramatic return to Silvanost. News of the nomad incursion, along with the failure of Govenor Dolanath to protect the eastern province, resulted in Dolanath's dismissal. Who was now governor of the east? Mistravan Artyrith, once more Lord Artyrith. Mathi didn't know if she should laugh or weep.

The defenders of the hilltop came streaming down to meet the griffon riders. The Silvanesti remained aloof, not getting down or mingling with the centaurs or kender.

"Where is the general?" Artyrith asked. Kender braved the ferocious griffon and closed around him, patting the skittish beast and the rider's legs with equal enthusiasm.

"The general is, well—"

"The general is dead."

Lofotan was last down the hill. He was covered with cuts, bruises, and grime, but he walked proudly, gripping his well-used bow.

"What? Are you certain?" said Artyrith.

"He fought the chief of the nomads in single combat and won, but subsequently died of his wounds."

No one present—not the Longwalker or his kender, Zakki, the remaining centaurs, Treskan, or Mathi contradicted Lofotan's bold lie.

"I have orders from the Speaker himself to bring General Balif back to Silvanost," Artyrith said, annoyed. "May I see the body?"

Lofotan nodded. He bid Lord Artyrith dismount and follow him. Lord Artyrith handed off his long lance to a flanking rider and got down. Admiring kender crowded around, but Artyrith's severe expression convinced them to keep clear. Holding the edges of his cape, the new governor of the east parted through the crowd imperiously. Mathi fell in behind him. She was worried. What was Lofotan thinking? It was one thing to lie to the Speaker's emissary, but what body could he possibly show Artyrith?

Elegant in his flying silks, Artyrith was still overshadowed by the taller, taciturn Lofotan. They faced each other for what seemed like a very long time until Artyrith cleared his throat and said, "Lead on, captain."

Lofotan held out his arm. "This way, my lord."

Oh the irony of the last two words! Treskan and Mathi exchanged knowing glances. Did Artyrith relish them, or was he wise enough to sense the threat in Lofotan's tone?

The elf led them over the battlefield, through the line of stakes to where Balif had fallen. Mathi's cloak was where he left it. A lumpy shape lay covered, until a stray breeze lifted a corner. Mathi saw nothing but a pile of dirt underneath. Where was the general?

Lofotan went on. He led Artyrith to the very summit of the bluff overlooking the river. With one foot on the edge he pointed dramatically to the green water below.

"We dropped the body off here," he said.

"You threw the general's body in the river?"

"We had to. We were besieged, and the remains were corrupting. He died valiantly, but he was not himself."

He let that veiled reference hang in the air. Artyrith looked down at the river.

"When did he die?" he said.

"Yesterday, about sundown."

"I'll have to search the river and both banks," Artyrith said. "The Great Speaker would expect nothing less."

He turned away irritably in a swirl of silk. Mathi queried the captain with an upraised eyebrow, but Lofotan ignored her, falling in step behind his one-time underling.

When they returned to the hillside, a large contingent of the Silvanesti army was mustered there. The nomads were fleeing, the officers reported. Artyrith ordered them pursued.

"Harry them out of the country," he said. "Whatever goods or chattels they abandon are to be taken and made the property of the Speaker. Any camps or settlements you find must be burned to the ground. This is the will of Silvanos Golden-Eye, Speaker of the Stars."

The officers scattered to their companies to carry out the severe orders. While Artyrith conferred with the other griffon riders about what areas to patrol, Mathi sidled up to Lofotan.

"What really happened to Balif?" she whispered.

"He's gone. What more do you need to know?"

Lofotan explained another reason why Artyrith had come. The Speaker had learned from Artyrith that the general had been transformed into a beast by Vedvedsica's curse. Silvanesti law did not differentiate between those who willingly trafficked in sorcery and those who were accursed. On the pretext of protecting elven society from the abomination Balif had become, Silvanos had ordered the arrest of Balif. Trial, imprisonment, and death would surely follow.

Silvanos had a long memory. He could never forget a good number of his subjects had once preferred Balif as their ruler to him. Silvanos had made it his duty to remove the accursed Balif from respectable society. His popular rival would disappear forever.

"Surely the Speaker is not so ruthless?" Mathi said, aghast.

"I credit him for being merciful," Lofotan replied. "If he were truly ruthless, he would put the general on display in a public square in Silvanost, chained to a post. That would ruin the name of Balif forever."

Lofotan walked away, mixing into the crowd of kender until he was eventually lost from sight. Mathi, shaken by the hard rules of elven society, watched him go and pondered her next move. Her mission was over, finished. Her brethren, wherever they were, had nothing left to avenge. When the time was right, she would slip away and join them. The children of Vedvedsica still had secret enclaves in the western forest. There, with vigilance and luck, they might pass their lives hidden from Silvanesti persecution.

One problem remained. She should not have cared, but it mattered to her was where Balif had gone. The general's disappearance was still a mystery. In the space of a few thoughts Mathi decided she was not leaving until she discovered Balif's true fate.

Someone cleared their throat decorously behind her. Mathi turned. There a fresh-faced elf, wearing the finest silk robes and a circlet of ivy on his head, held a polished silver tray out to the scribe. On it lay a gilded card.

Mathi understood the card was for her. She picked it up. At once crimson letters appeared, hovering a hair's breadth off the otherwise blank rectangle. Judging by its weight, the card was solid gold.

*Summons*, it said. Mathi asked the messenger what it meant.

"You are summoned to the August Presence," he replied. "Two hours past sundown."

"Whose presence?"

"The name of a great person is not idly spoken before foreigners and savages."

It sounded stuffy, if intriguing. "All right. Where will I go?"

The messenger stepped aside. "You will come with me now."

Mathi pointed skyward. "It's a long time till sunset. Are we going so far?"

"The journey is not far, but you must be prepared if you are to enter the presence of a very August Person. Come, if you please."

Mathi had the distinct feeling it would be very bad indeed to refuse the invitation. With an entire army to back it up, such an invitation was a command, not a request.

She preceeded the messenger. All the time her mind was racing ahead. Who was she going to see? Some high lord of Silvanost? A high priest? Or could it be the Speaker of the Stars himself?

# Chapter 20

## *Lovers*

Mathi was led to the shore of the Thon-Haddaras. A white boat lay anchored in the stream. The hull gleamed white and smooth, with a high prow and a round stern. A light pole mast was bare of sail, but a dozen long sweeps poked through the gunwales. Running from the deck down to the muddy bank was a narrow white gangplank. It seemed too narrow to ascend, but the elf messenger went up heel to toe without breaking stride. Mathi followed more deliberately, holding out her arms to keep her balance.

When she reached the deck the plank was drawn back on board and the rowers backed off the mud. In the shadow of the prow she was startled to see Treskan. The scribe had his writing equipment and bags of documents heaped around his feet. From his expression it was clear he was as surprised to see Mathi as she was to see him. Further aft, the coxswain held an elegantly carved tiller. At his command the boat swung in a half circle and rowed smoothly downstream.

As they traveled, Mathi and Treskan heard how Artyrith's army of forty thousand had entered the eastern province from the sea, marching up the east and west banks of the Thon-Haddaras, while another twenty-five thousand followed their route overland to Free Winds to cut the nomads' road. It was hard to imagine so many elves had passed that way. The dense, low-lying woods were undisturbed, but that was the elves' way. Treskan said one hundred thousand elves could pass through a forest and cause less disruption to the surroundings that fifty humans. The human way was to push through obstacles. Elves slipped by, doing less damage than a summer rain.

After describing the arrival of the army, the Silvanesti messenger fell silent. They rowed downstream a long time without a word being spoken. Late in the afternoon the lazy green stream changed into blue sea as the river abruptly widened into a fine deepwater bay. Ahead lay a great fleet of ships, arrayed in a crescent formation. Aside from a few lighters crawling across the sea, the ships were all at rest, sails furled and oars run in.

A strong onshore breeze hit the little boat, almost bringing it to a stop. The rowers dug in, pulling for the largest ship in the center of the formation. Most of the vessels were round-bellied argosies that had borne troops and supplies from Silvanost. A few swift galleots, bristling with warriors, ringed the slow sailing ships. In the center of the flotilla was a large, boxy vessel with a gleaming white hull. Gilded banners fluttered from the masts. Mathi and Treskan's boat made unerringly for the flagship, coasting to a stop alongside amidships. Mathi expected a ladder to be lowered—the flagship's deck was a good ten feet above them—but instead the rowers shipped their oars and everyone waited. A squeaking, bumping sound drew Mathi's attention overhead. Creeping over the side of the flagship came a heavy wooden boom. Bright bronze chains dangled from the tip. When they were close enough, the coxswain and the messenger secured the hooks at the end of each length of chain to massive rings affixed to the boat's deck.

Mathi stared at the boom. Surely they were not going to—

"Haul away!" called the coxswain. These were the first words Mathi had heard him say since coming aboard.

There was a loud clanking from above. Slack went out of the chains, then the boat began to rise. Treskan and Mathi rushed to either side of the rail and looked over. Already they were out of the water, which was streaming down the boat's hull in torrents. They rose a good ten feet until the boat's rail was level with the flagship's. The boom slowly retracted, bringing the small craft tight against the flagship's side. Ropes were passed back and forth, tying each to the other. Then the messenger raised the hinged rail and stepped onto the great ship's broad deck.

"Come," he said to his guests.

The deck was like a city street. There were lanes on either side, and the center was crowded with buildings built exactly like houses or shops on land. They looked just like the stone structures common to Silvanost, but in passing Mathi touched a spiral column and discovered it was wood, made to look like stone.

Mathi and Treskan were led forward into a one of the two-story deckhouses. An elderly elf with white hair down to his shoulders eyed them once inside.

"The guests," he said disapprovingly. "What a sight you are. Well, the first thing to be done is make you clean. Get off those filthy rags at once."

Treskan fingered his collar. "Must I?"

"You cannot enter the August Presence of our patron looking and smelling as you do."

"I cannot," Mathi protested. "I am a maiden, a ward of Quenesti Pah. I cannot disrobe in the presence of males!"

Treskan had similar reasons for modesty. Under his clothes his elf diguise had worn thin. The nomads mistook him for a half-elf. If he stripped now, the Silvanesti would certainly arrest him.

The white-haired elf sighed. "Quarters suitable for your chastity will be provided. As for you, scribe—"

"I thank you, excellency, for the opportunity to cleanse myself! I have been too long without the simplest methods of hygiene. But—I must also undress and bathe alone," Treskan said, feigning relief. The elderly elf haughtily asked why. He said, "I was a prisoner of the nomads. I am ashamed of the scars I earned at their hands."

His appeal against ugliness worked. The white-haired elf showed him a shallow terra-cotta tub he could stand in, and the tall ewers of spring water he could wash with. He then led Mathi a few doors down to an identical room, also equipped with a washtub. Then he left.

When she was alone, Mathi carefully undressed. It was a strange and frightening bath. She lived in dread that someone would burst in and her deception would be revealed. In the past weeks on the trail, her perfect elvishness had faded. Downy hair ran down her back and across the tops of her legs and arms. Whatever 'August Person' she was being taken to, they were obviously too pure to endure the company of one of the brethren. If she was exposed here, she would pay for her blasphemy with her life.

No one broke in, so she quickly dressed in the clean robes provided. She struck a small brass bell when she was done, and the elderly courtier returned with soft leather sandals and a white leather headband for her hair. Dressed and dried, Mathi stood for inspection.

"Your face is pleasant, but your carriage is quite awkward," the white-maned elf declared. "Too awkward for august company, but—" He sighed. "It is ordered, so it must be done."

He held up a finger. "First rule, do not speak unless prompted to do so. Secondly, keep your eyes averted from the August One except when addressing her. Thirdly, tell no one of what you hear or say here. Is that understood?"

Mathi caught the telltale 'her.' She had an idea at last who she was going to see.

She was led aft to the center of the ship. Treskan joined her, escorted by another genteel courtier. They were guided to a broad staircase that led down into the interior of the great vessel. Armed soldiers stood at key points. They raised their swords in salute when Mathi's guide passed. At the top of the stairs the old elf adjusted his headband, smoothed his robe, and started down. Riddled with curiosity, Treskan and Mathi followed close on his heels.

The deck they descended to was covered with soft carpets. Luminars in copper brackets lighted the between decks almost like daylight. Interior partitions below deck seemed to be made of gossamer silk. Shadows cast by luminars on the other side moved silently to and fro. Voices in the scantest whispers marked the visitors' progress.

A younger elf with an elaborate head of ringlets thrust his head through the curtains. He and the guide exchanged hushed words. Curls glanced at Mathi and Treskan skeptically.

"Very well," he said. "Come."

Attendants swept back the sheer hangings, allowing them to enter. The room beyond was open and well lit, though the furnishings were more suited to a palace than a ship. Two young elves were playing lyres together. Small white finches flitted around, alighting in the branches of small cherry trees growing in hefty buckets of soil. Incense smoldered in cone-shaped censers. A score of elves were present, rather lost in the great open space. Everyone was clustered around a tall elf woman of middle years, not beautiful but quite striking in a commanding sort of way. Mathi recognized her at once, but she was careful not to show it. Their hostess was Amaranthe, sister of the Speaker of the Stars.

A ripple of murmurs spread around the room when Mathi and Treskan entered. Mathi knew she and her companion were uncouth by elf standards, but she was determined to be a dignified as any Silvanesti. Treskan frankly stared at everything. If his studious attention marked him as a boor, he could live with the elves' disdain.

"Come forward," said Amaranthe.

They did, keeping their eyes off her as they approached. The carpet was marked with broad red stripes, a helpful feature. Mathi counted stripes as they advanced. A warrior in gilded armor stopped them with an outstretched arm. Twenty-six stripes from the door, she reckoned.

"You are the girl known as Mathani Arborelinex, are you not?"

"I am, lady."

"The August One is properly addressed as 'Highness,' " Curls said stiffly.

"I am Mathani Arborelinex, Highness. Forgive my manners. I have not lived long in civilized society."

"The other is the one called Treskan?" He bobbed his head in acknowledgement. "You were personal scribe to General Balif, they tell me," Amaranthe said. Her voice was warm and strong, hinting at both an iron will and personal passion.

"I have that honor, Highness."

"Have? You are still in his employ? I am told he has departed . . ."

Mathi glanced up. Her appearance was refined, but simple. She wore far less jewelry and gilded silk than those around her. What was more, Mathi clearly saw the furrows in her forehead. She was concerned. She still loved Balif.

"Is General Balif dead?" Amaranthe said.

Treskan replied, "I do not think so, Highness. He was wounded in the battle with the nomad chief, but I do not believe they were mortal injuries."

More sharply: "What became of him then?"

"Highness, I have not seen the general since the battle with the humans ended," Mathi said honestly, lowering her gaze. "Where he is, I do not know, but I doubt he is far away."

"Where is he then? Speak!"

Mathi folded her hands into her loose sleeves. "I cannot say for sure."

"Impertinence!" Curls said. "Give the order, Highness, and the truth will be extracted from this impudent girl by any means necessary!"

Amaranthe was more reasonable. "Why can you not tell me all you know?"

"Many ears spread gossip as the leaves of a great tree spread raindrops." Treskan said, quoting a famous aphorism of the sage Vestas. It was just the sort of thing a real Silvanesti scribe might say. "There are those who would like to know where General Balif is, who do not wish him well."

"Double impertinence! Away with this scoundrel!"

Curls' quick anger meant one thing to Mathi: he was the Speaker's servant, not Amaranthe's. Was he, like Artyrith, charged with finding the general and holding him for the Speaker's pleasure?

The guards moved in either side of them. Amaranthe raised her voice, however, saying, "I have not ended this audience. Who dares order the arrest of my guest?" Cold silence filled the room. She said, "Hamalcath, I am displeased. You may go. Now."

Mathi had never seen an elf blush so severely. Curls—Lord Hamalcath—bowed deeply and withdrew. Amaranthe dismissed the rest of her court until the only ones left were Mathi, Treskan, two of her personal guards, and herself.

She sat down in a high-backed chair, folding her hands in her lap.

"Speak now, and hold back nothing. Tell me of Balif."

So they did. They took turns describing their journey, the growing curse and how it changed the general, his challenge to to Bulnac, and the overthrow of the powerful nomad force.

Very quietly Amaranthe said, "I was never certain if he was merely valiant or very clever. Now I see he was both."

When Mathi described Balif's championing the kender as the rightful owners of the eastern province, Amaranthe's haughtiness returned.

"Does Balif think he can give away what is the Speaker's?"

Diplomatically Treskan bowed his head. "It is not for me to say, Highness. I can only relate what my lord Balif has said in my hearing. The wanderfolk are here. Possession is a great measure of the law, it is said. Lord Balif saw them as harmless neighbors of the Silvanesti and a useful buffer against the humans."

She nodded slightly and bade him continue.

"There is little more to say, Highness. I lost sight of the general in the melee of the last battle, and I have not seen him since."

She drummed white fingers on the arm of her chair. "He is alive, I know it. Is there anything left of his true nature, or has the curse reduced him to a brute at last?" Truthfully, Mathi admitted she did not know.

Amaranthe stood abruptly. Mathi had a flash of memory, seeing her with Balif in the general's strange, empty mansion. She stifled the unworthy image and tried to anticipate what the willful royal lady wanted.

"I am here against the wishes of my brother," she said. "He bears no affection for General Balif, for the people love him in a way they will never love the Speaker. I have told Silvanos again and again that a great ruler does not need to be loved, but he resents Balif's popularity and fears his influence."

She did not say what was really in her mind: that Silvanos wanted Balif out of the way forever, curse or no curse. She didn't have to say it.

Mathi said, "I understand, Highness. Your concern is the well-being of the general." She looked her directly in the eye. "In this, we are agreed."

"Then assure him of my . . . protection. In whatever

form his destiny has chosen, he has every protection I can give him."

With that, the interview ended. Mathi and Treskan were taken rather unceremoniously to change their clothes. Their fine court raiment was taken back, and they were given their old garments, and escorted to the boat. It was dusk, and the elves rowed up river to the exact spot Mathi and the scribe had embarked. They were put ashore. The boat pulled away and was soon lost in the gathering dusk.

Insects hummed in clouds above the water's edge. Treskan slapped at them. It was eerily quiet there below the bluff. Mathi smelled campfires. She saw the flicker of firelight atop the hill, and that meant the Longwalker and his people were still around. Mathi decided to try a ploy he'd been mulling over since leaving Amaranthe's ship.

"Would you really like to find Balif?" she asked Treskan.

"I want to not be devoured by mosquitoes," he said sourly. "How will you find him when so many others can not?"

She cupped her hands to her mouth. Absurd, really absurd, the gesture, but she had to try.

"Rufe! Rufus Wrinklecap! Are you there?"

Frogs grunted in the mud around them. She shouted again. Turning in a circle on the river bank, she squinted into the twilight for some hint of the kender's presence. Mathi drew in a deep breath to shout a third time but, before she could, she felt a tug on the back of her trailworn gown.

Without even turning around she said, "Rufe, I have a new task for you. Or I should say, an old one you may do again."

"What's up, boss?"

The kender was decked out in an assortment of leather and furs, spoils from the nomads no doubt. He had an oversized knife shoved in his belt and a bronze gorget at his throat. The martial effect of his attire was spoiled by his bare, muddy feet and the sprig of green sumac he was chewing.

"I need to find Balif."

Rufe balked. "That's not a good idea, boss. He's not a friendly elf anymore."

"Nevertheless, I need to find him. I'll pay what it's worth. What do you want for the job?"

Rufe thought for a long time, at least to a count of five. "I want to go with him," he said, pointing to Treskan.

"Eh? Go with me where?"

"Wherever you go, boss. Back home to Woodbec, or anyplace else."

It was unexpected. Mathi asked why he wanted to go with the scribe.

"He visits strange places," said the kender. He poked his pointed chin with a finger. "Places I can't get to. That interests me."

Treskan pronounced it impossible. Absolutely impossible. Even if he wanted to take Rufe, he could not. The rules of his profession forbade tagalongs.

"Will you take me with you then?" he said to Mathi. She was taken aback. Her ultimate destination was unknown, even to her, but since she needed the kender to find Balif, Mathi said yes.

"Swear to it," Rufe said with great solemnity.

She did, though she felt very guilty. Rufe gravely shook hands with her, hitched up his sword belt, and announced he would find Balif before sunrise. Mathi hoped that he could.

Rufe slipped away into the dark, damp woods. A mist was rising from the river.

"If I don't sleep soon, I'm going to die," Treskan declared. Mathi heartily agreed. She felt damp to the skin, so they went up the riverbank to the kender's bridge. They crossed over and climbed the hill so many had died trying to take.

The wanderfolk were scattered over the hill in their usual careless fashion. The biggest campfire marked the Longwalker's shelter, cobbled together from cast-off nomad blankets and poles salvaged from Lofotan's barrier of stakes. Serius and his cronies hailed Mathi and offered her food and drink. It was good fare, cured venison and wheat beer, again courtesy of Bulnac's shattered horde.

"What a day!" the Longwalker declared. "I have never seen the like!"

Mathi agreed. The kender refought the battles of the day, each storyteller emphasizing his own part in the struggle. Listening to them, Mathi had no idea so many brave kender had fought so well. The elves and the centaurs were mere bystanders in their version.

"Where are Zakki and his fellows?" Mathi asked. They were gone with the elf army, tracking the humans. And what about Lofotan?

"The Elder lord"—the Longwalker meant Artyrith—"tried to force Lofty to go with him, but Lofty refused. He said his place was here. I think he expects the general to return."

"Lofotan is here? Where?"

Four kender hands pointed four different directions. The Longwalker scolded them and said, "On the high bluff, overlooking the water."

Mathi thanked them for the meal. Treskan would have, too, but he had slumped forward where he sat, dead asleep.

She wove in and out of the hodge-podge of shelters until she reached the highest point of the hill. There she found Lofotan seated cross-legged in front of a small twig fire. Fire painted his face in dark colors.

"Greetings, captain."

"Girl. Where have you been?"

Mathi sat down and told him everything. Lofotan was not surprised that Amaranthe had shown up. He was surprised to hear she granted the orphan girl and clumsy scribe such an intimate interview.

"I've known her a century and a half, and I have never

had such a conversation with her," Lofotan grumbled. Mathi shrugged. It was only because she had information about Balif that Amaranthe wanted to know, she said.

"I've set Rufe on his trail. He'll find him."

Now Lofotan shrugged. Artyrith had hundreds of trained trackers combing the forest for Balif. How could one erratic wanderer do what three hundred Silvanesti could not? Hearing the question, Mathi laughed. There was nothing beyond kender, she declared, and among kender, anything was possible with Rufe.

Faint white light flashed over them. Mathi saw her hands briefly emerge from the night, then fade back again. She looked up, but the sky was clear of stormclouds.

A shooting star streaked from east to west over the trees. Then another. And another.

"Look, captain! Falling stars!"

The meteors whizzed overhead, making sizzling sounds. Denizens of the lowland woods quieted under the aerial display. Frogs fell silent. Even crickets ceased to sing.

A cry went up from the kender downslope. Mathi and Lofotan stood up and saw sheets of light forming in the sky. It was hard to describe exactly. The light formed long curtains of glowing color in the air. The upper edges were bluish white, but the color deepened, becoming dark red at the ragged bottom edges.

"What is it?"

"Aurora," said Lofotan. He'd seen many things in his long life. "The air itself has taken on light."

Aurora high in the sky was natural enough, but when the sheets of color began to descend to the trees, everyone knew it was no natural phenomenon. Even stranger, as Mathi looked on the glow infused Lofotan. His hands, feet, and face started to shine with a pale, cool light. He stood back from Mathi, holding out his hands. His skin was shimmering.

The kender abandoned their shanties and fled into the

woods. Streams of cool blue or angry red light drifted like smoke among the trees. Alone on the bluff, Mathi and Lofotan tried to fathom what was happening.

"I am glowing, but you are not," Lofotan observed. "What does that mean?"

Mathi had figured out what was going on. Lofotan was alight because he was an elf. Though she looked like an elf on the outside, Mathi did not glow. She didn't dare explain her deduction to the captain. But why were elves glowing, and who was responsible?

It came to her in a flash: Amaranthe, or Artyrith. They were searching for Balif. Both had magicians of skill at their beck and call. To find a feather in a field of wheat, make the feather stand out. Someone had created that strange aurora to highlight elves—including Balif.

"How does it feel?" Mathi asked, hoping Lofotan would not reach the same conclusion she had.

"I feel nothing unusual." He waved his hand hard, as if to shake the light loose from his skin. "Damned strange sight, though."

"I'd better find the Longwalker," Mathi said, sidling away.

"Why?" Lofotan asked irritably. The wanderfolk weren't glowing, and they certainly couldn't cast such a powerful spell.

"I want to reassure him. He needs to keep his people here if his claim to the land is to stand up." It was true enough, but what Mathi wanted foremost was to look for Balif. She went swiftly down the hill in the dark, skirting curtains of light that drifted soundlessly out of the woods. By the time she reached the bottom of the hill she was running. Once out of Lofotan's sight she halted to catch her breath. Fragments of aurora moved among the trees, but the steady moonglow of elf skin was nowhere to be seen. It felt futile, but Mathi had to try to find the general. She had one advantage over the legions of elves looking for Balif. The general might be willing to be found by her.

She decided to put her theory to the test. She called Balif's name in the dark forest, at first repeating it over and over. It accomplished nothing. Balif could be miles away by now, or he might be unconscious. In his current state of transformation, how well could the general handle his injuries? Mathi had no way to know.

She zigzagged through the trees. Tired of calling, she sat down on a fallen tree. It was very humid in the lowland green. Sweat dripped from her brow.

One last time she cupped her hands around her mouth and shouted, "Amaranthe! Amaranthe wants you! Answer me, general! Amaranthe! *Amaranthe*!"

A low growl rose from the darkness behind the broken tree. Mathi leaped up, groping clumsily for her sword. All her pointless shouting had accomplished nothing but arousing a wild bear. Or was it a bear?

"My lord, is that you?"

She heard heavy panting close by, but could not detect the source. Then a heap of dry leaves heaved up from under the fallen log. Two pin-points of light gleamed, pale white like the face of Solinari. It took Mathi a moment to realize what she was seeing. Balif in his beast form was no longer an elf, but his eyes were glowing with the telltale aura.

Mathi's heart hammered in her chest. It was too dark for her to make out any details of the creature standing before him. The beast was bigger than before. Standing, it towered over Mathi.

"My lord," she said carefully, focusing on the twin points of light hovering above her, "the lady Amaranthe has sent me to find you."

The lights weaved slightly from side to side. Mathi went on.

"She is near! Her ship lies at anchor in the bay."

The black silhouette abruptly turned away. Apparently Balif did not want to see his lover—or did not want his lover to see him in his current state.

"Wait, my lord! You know the lady is powerful, and has great mages in her employ. The colors you see in the air are a spell she had cast to find you." She hoped it was Amaranthe, and not Artyrith. "Go to her. There may be something she can do for you—"

The creature charged so suddenly that Mathi could do nothing to dodge. It scooped her up and crushed her close. The smell of beast was strong. Mathi was helpless, her arms pinned to her side, and her feet dangling in the air.

A wet black nose came close to his ear. The beast huffed and sniffed, then leaped over the tree and began to run. It was an awkward, jolting pace, using only three limbs, but the creature still hurtled through the undergrowth. Here and there it bored through a floating patch of aurora, which instantly dissipated with a faint crackling sound. Mathi wanted to yell, but she reckoned if the beast had wanted to harm her it would have done so already. So she held on tight as it ran.

"Do you understand me, my lord?" she whispered, clinging tightly to his furred torso. "I am like you. I know the call of blood you're hearing."

He halted in a flurry of churned-up leaves and snapping branches. Fiery pinpoint eyes bored into hers.

"Go to the princess," Mathi said. "And if she cannot save you, despair not. There is another way."

She felt the hot breath of the beast on her face. He was weighing her words. Without warning his musing ended, and he sprang through the undergrowth with renewed vigor.

# Chapter 21

## *Legends*

Mathi's headlong ride through the woods lasted right down to the shore of the bay. Faced with a wide expanse of dark water, Balif dug in his claws and skidded to a stop on the wet clay beach. The bay was dotted with lanterns bobbing on the masts and prows of the elf fleet.

"The biggest one is Amaranthe's."

Mathi could feel the beast's heart thudding hard deep inside its chest. It slowly opened its arm, dropping the girl at the water's edge. Balif took a tentative step into the water, as if he were unhappy about getting wet.

"Don't leave me," Mathi said, rising on numb legs. "I can speak for you. Take me with you."

The beast looked over its high, muscled shoulders and gave its leonine head a sideways twitch. Mathi recognized the gesture. She climbed onto the beast's back. There was nothing to hold onto but fur. Mathi grabbed hold.

Twin luminous eyes probed her briefly. The floating bands of auroral colors passed on opposite courses over the bay, their strangely vivid hues reflected in the calm water. Without further ado Balif plunged forward. They splashed loudly into the warm water. As a beast Balif's stroke was an inelegant dogpaddle, but his powerful limbs carried them quickly into the midst of the idle ships. Clinging tightly to his back, Mathi kept her head close against the beast's neck. She saw sailors and warriors lounging on the decks of vessels they passed. Though Balif's swimming wasn't especially stealthy, wind and waves masked its noise enough that they went unnoticed.

Passing between two anchored argosies, they suddenly beheld the flagship. It was lit up like nothing Mathi had ever seen before. The rail was lined with lamps, lanterns were hoisted from every masthead, and the portholes glowed from within. Tellingly, silent balls of fire periodically erupted from the mainmast. Once clear of the ship the fireballs split open, releasing the rainbow colored auroras haunting the land. Here was the origin of the strange spell. Mathi still didn't know who was behind it, though she felt strongly it must be Amaranthe. She was still aboard, while Aryrith was inland, chasing nomads and hunting for General Balif.

"That's it," she whispered unnecessarily. Balif swam toward the brilliantly bedecked ship.

There was no way to board. The crane that had lifted the rowing bark was retracted. No nets or ladders hung down. Just two cables held the ship at anchor, one off the port bow and the other at the starboard stern.

"The lady's pavilion was below deck, amidship," Mathi said.

Coming around the prow, Balif made for the bow line. It was a bronze chain with links as thick as Mathi's ankle. The beast clung to it while Mathi climbed, slipping her soggy sandals into the links. She kept going until she reached the hawse pipe. It led through to the lighted deck, but it was too small for the beast to crawl through.

She waved until Balif noticed her. Miming with her hands, she tried to convey to him her plan to go up on deck and find an opening large enough to admit him. Unsure if Balif understood, Mathi went ahead, crawling through the dark hawse pipe. It was a snug fit, but she made it. The deck by the hole was empty. She climbed out. Mathi had just stood up when she felt the prick of a spearpoint in the small of her back.

"Stand where you are and do not move!"

Damned alert sentinels. Mathi held up her hands.

"I am here at the request of the August Person," she said.

The elf sniffed. "That's why you crept aboard like a water rat, is it?" He jabbed Mathi. "You'll not get near the August Person, whoever you are! Chief of the Deck Watch!" he called. "I have an intruder!"

An officer in a plumed helmet appeared from the deckhouse, escorted by four soldiers. Seeing Mathi standing there dripping seawater, they hurried over.

"What's this?" the officer demanded.

"My name is Mathani Arborelinex. I was here earlier today, summoned by Her Highness. She asked me to return if I had news of General Balif."

"So you swam out here in the dark and boarded by scaling the anchor chain? What kind of fool do you think I am?" The officer called for restraints. A soldier returned to the deckhouse and came back with a set of manacles. Mathi backed away, right into the leveled spear of the guard who first caught her.

Wincing she said, "The princess will be very angry if you prevent me from seeing her!"

Where was Balif, still bobbing in the water below? Mathi wanted to look down and check, but she was afraid of giving him away. She succumbed to temptation and looked.

Balif was not there.

"Don't even think of jumping," warned the officer. "You'll have two spears in you before you reach the water."

They grabbed his hands, pulling them out to receive the shackles. Mathi resisted. Her original captor struck her across the back with the shaft of his spear. The blow drove her forward, almost breaking through the ring of elves around him. Thinking she was trying to escape, the officer drew his sword. In the next moment the night fell on them.

It was Balif. With the watch distracted by Mathi, he was able to gain the rail unseen by climbing the hull planking with his claws. Spying Mathi in trouble, he leaped to her aid. The elves were so intent on Mathi they didn't know what hit them. The beast bowled them over, sending them sprawling on the deck. Mathi took the opportunity to shove and trip the last soldier standing.

Balif was the first one up. He lashed out first on one side, then the other, backhanding the soldiers with his paws. The officer got to his knees, sword in hand. He was about to strike the furry intruder when Balif seized him by the seat of his pants and hurled him overboard. He yelled all the way down, terminating with a great splash.

Doors opened all along the deckhouses. Elves of various duties stepped out—sailors, soldiers, courtiers, servants. Because the ship was so well illuminated they saw the beast clearly. Shouts rang out and not a few doors slammed shut again.

Like a whirlwind Balif flattened the soldiers around him. A sword skittered up against Mathi's feet. She considered picking it up, then decided it would be her death warrant. She had come to the flagship in peace. If she was taken in arms, they would hang her from the nearest yardarm without question.

Warriors boiled out of the cabins, juggling armor and helmets while gripping swords and spears. Balif put his head down and charged right through them, slamming those on his left against the deckhouse and tossing those on his right over the side. Courtiers who were too slow got the same treatment. Mathi walked behind the beast, offering apologies.

"Please excuse us. We mean no harm. Oh, I am sorry!

Don't get up, he'll knock you down again. Begging your pardon, my lords—"

Dazed elves responded with confusion. What was that monstrous beast? Who was the polite acolyte with him?

Some soldiers dashed up from behind and tried to lay hands on Mathi. Balif whirled, fangs bared, and they backed off. Sailors brought a fishing net from the ship's stores and hauled it to the roof of a deckhouse, meaning to drop it over the invading creature. An ordinary beast might have been trapped, but Balif clearly saw the danger and circled around the deckhouse where the sailors crouched. They cast anyway, missed, and watched their weighted net go slithering over the rail into the bay.

"There!" Mathi cried, pointing. "That's the way down, there!"

Up the steps came warriors of Amaranthe's personal guard. No finer fighters existed among the Silvanesti, and they barred the way, resolute and ready. Balif crouched low on the deck, and Mathi thought he was going to try to force his way through. Faced with eight drawn swords, the beast chose an alternative not open to most two-legged attackers. He leaped first to the roof of the deckhouse, then immediately hurled himself at the open stairwell. The warriors fell back, swords and shields held high to ward off the marauder, but Balif was faster. He hit them like a catapult stone, knocking them down the steep stairs.

Alone on deck with the awakened crew, Mathi felt distinctly outnumbered. She forced a smile and strolled to the hatch.

"Thank you for your warm welcome," she said for all to hear. "And now I must see to my friend. He gets rather impatient when I'm not around."

She bolted down the steps with scores of footfalls thundering after her. Balif had cleared the way, and she was able to run right into the audience chamber. Mathi skidded to a halt, arrested by the extraordinary scene before her.

Amaranthe was there. That surprised Mathi, who thought she would have retreated behind as many locked doors and armed guards as could be mustered on board. But no, there she sat, clad in a white silk robe with delicate embroidery in red and blue around the cuffs and collar. In front of her stood a small phalanx of archers knelt with arrows nocked. Six feet in front of them Balif crouched, chin down and hindquarters high. His yellow teeth were bared in a grimace of—what? Defiance? Contrition? It was hard to read his beastly countenance.

Almost imperceptibly a few archers adjusted their aim to cover Mathi. Fear climbed her back, and her knees almost failed. She had seen too well what elf archers could do. At that range she would be riddled with arrowsif she so much as blinked.

"Highness!" she said hoarsely, holding out her hands as if to ward off the soon-to-be-loosed arrows. "It is Mathani Arborelinex, remember? I have done what you asked!"

The princess's crystalline gaze shifted from her to the beast. Amaranthe's brow furrowed.

"You?" she said. The truth dawned, and her austere features fell. "Merciful gods! Is this—?"

"Yes, Highness!"

She looked again in disbelief. The creature at bay curled a lip and gave a throaty snarl. Bowstrings creaked as the archers drew back further, ready to pin the monster to the planks if it moved.

"Stay your hands!" Amaranthe said suddenly. The chief of the archers asked her to repeat her command.

"Put down your weapons! I command it!"

The cool professionals obeyed. Without sharp bronze points aimed at her, Mathi recovered her nerve. She went down on one knee and thanked Amaranthe for her compassion—and her insight.

"How can this be?" the princess of Silvanost said sadly. "Who has done this to him?"

"A curse, Highness, cast by—" Mathi remembered the penalty for mentioning Vedvedsica's name. "By the one who cannot be named."

"Does he know me? Does he know anyone?"

Mathi let Balif answer that. The beast crawled forward on his belly like a dog. He could not penetrate the line of archers still on guard, but the gesture was plain.

"My poor love," the princess whispered.

She called out to someone—a long elven name that sounded like "Talaramitas." From the curtained area behind Amaranthe's chair an elf emerged. He was fairly young, with unusually short hair for a Silvanesti. Dressed in baggy green leggings, kilt, and tunic, his wrists and ankles were thickly ringed with slender metal bands. A copper band circled his forehead. As he stepped up to the princess's right hand, wisps of colored light sparked from his extremities and quickly vanished.

"Stand aside," she ordered the archers. They parted ranks, revealing the beast. When the soldiers were out of the way Balif leaped to his feet and uttered a hair-curling growl. Bows creaked, and one elf lost control long enough to send an arrow into the deck between Balif's front and back feet. It thunked loudly into the planking, but the beast paid it no mind.

"The next one who looses an arrow, dies by my order!" Amaranthe cried. Everyone froze.

To the bearcat she said, "Do you mean me any harm?"

He couldn't answer, but the beast remained where he was. Mathi could tell Balif was staring not at the princess but at the green-clad magician next to her.

"Talaramitas, what do you make of this?"

The elf closed his eyes and held out one hand at a low angle. He quickly snatched his hand back.

"An enchantment of great power, Highness. One of the

most potent I have ever encountered," he said. He had a deep, cultured voice that provoked fresh, if restrained, snarls from the beast.

"Can you break it?" He vowed he could not. "The reward for success would be substantial," she added.

Talaramitas folded his hands, causing his many bracelets to jingle. "Gracious Highness, no one in Silvanesti can break this curse."

Balif threw back his head and howled. He went in two bounds toward Amaranthe. To her credit, she did not flinch. Her magician did. Talaramitas hastily backed away, muttering words of a quick spell. The air between him and Balif sparkled. The beast halted, panting. He was close enough to touch the princess.

More soldiers and courtiers came pounding down the stairs. Raising her voice, Amaranthe commanded everyone to stay where they were and say nothing.

"Highness, this creature is the victim of a transmutory invocation. I have read of these, but to my knowledge no one in living memory had succeeded in casting one. Without exact knowledge of the words used and the intruments employed, I cannot reverse it."

"What if the caster were found and killed?"

It would make no difference, he said. "In this type of invocation the magician sacrifices a portion of his own living soul to obtain his end. There is no way to counter such a spell, as its energy is independent of the life of the caster."

The grief on Amaranthe's face was profound. Turning away, the beast loped slowly back to Mathi. All eyes followed it. Then Talaramitas spoke up.

"There is one thing I can do, Highness. It is not a cure, but if enough of the cursed one's soul remains untainted, I can call it forth to speak—for a short time only."

Without looking at him Amaranthe pointed a finger at the magician and said, "Do so, now!"

The room was cleared of soldiers over the protests of the captain of the guard. Talaramitas walked slow circles around the beast, one finger pointing at the deck. His eyes, half-lidded, fluttered as he walked. A stream of soft syllables escaped his lips.

From her vantage point it seemed to Mathi that the room darkened a bit. Luminars changed colors when their output declined, but the clusters around Amaranthe's throne did not alter hue. A pervasive shadow filled the room. Sound felt deadened too. Words and noises fell lifeless the moment they were born.

This went on for some time with the magician describing right-hand circles and muttering the words of an extremely long conjuration. At last an indistinct shadow coalesced next to the beast. It was upright and unmoving, quite unlike any shade cast by the bearcat. It was inside the circle Talaramitas had made, and he was careful not to tresspass on it.

Mathi had never seen magic performed openly before. In front of onlookers, in full light, the elf mage was summoning Balif's soul from the deepening well of darkness. Before Mathi was fully aware of the change, the shadow by the beast became a clear image of the general. He was standing, hands at his sides with his palms turned out. He was naked. The image was not flesh colored, however, but faintly sepia. Mathi dared to shift position so that she could see the specter's face. His eyes were closed.

Talaramitas explained, a bit breathlessly, that he could not stop circling or the spell would end. Ask what you will, he gasped. If the spirit of Balif could answer, it would.

"Why is he naked?" one of the courtiers asked in a loud whisper.

"Do you think your soul wears clothes?" the mage replied.

Amaranthe called for silence. Addressing the apparition she said, "General Balif, can you hear me?" He sighed in reply, which the princess took as yes. "Balif, how can I save you?"

"You cannot."

It was his voice, incredibly soft and distant. The specter's lips did not move but the sound of Balif's voice was perfectly clear.

"There must be something we can do—I can do!"

"There is nothing. Already I dream without color, without words."

He meant he was already thinking like an animal. Mathi felt a tightness growing in her throat. Here was the fate that awaited her.

Tears brightened Amaranthe's eyes. The sight of the stalwart sister of the Speaker so moved astounded her attendants. Mathi heard one whisper to another that she had never seen the princess cry, not once in more than a century of service.

"The world is an empty place without you," she said. "Full of vain, little beings of no strength and no worth."

His shade uttered a few words, the only one of which Mathi understood was "love." The apparition lost clarity and began to fade.

"Magus!" she cried. "Hold him here!"

Talaramitas, still circling, was dragging his feet, forcing himself to continue. Mathi was shocked to see his face as the magician swung round his way. His countenance was ashen. His eyes were rolled back in his head.

"I live," Balif managed to say. "Let my forest live too. Leave it to the wanderfolk for all time."

"They can have anything I possess, if you would only come back to me!"

"Too late . . . too late . . ."

Talaramitas staggered. Mathi stepped forward and caught him. When his perambulation ceased, the soul of Balif departed. The air in the below-deck hall stirred.

The beast, quiescent during the raising of his soul, threw back his head and howled. Archers and sword-bearing soldiers stormed in, ready to defend the princess. It wasn't necessary. The bearcat turned away, bounding up the wide wooden stairs. Mathi heard shouts and splashes, followed by a single louder splash.

A sailor ran halfway down the steps. "The monster leaped overboard!"

"Let him go," said Amaranthe. "Let no hand be raised against him. That is my order."

Mathi lowered Talaramitas to the deck. A shadow fell across them. Amaranthe stood over them. She was fully composed again, a figure of living alabaster and marble.

"Mage, you failed me. I would have talked to him longer," she said.

Mathi closed the elf's eyes. "He can't hear you, Highness. He's dead."

She regarded her coldly. "I thank you for your efforts, girl. Because of your deeds I will not have you put in irons for violating the sanctity of my ship." Amaranthe gave curt orders that Mathi was to be rowed to the nearest point on shore and turned loose.

Soldiers took rough hold of her. Another pair picked up Talaramitas and bore him away, probably to an unmarked grave ashore. As Mathi disappeared up the stairs, she heard the Speaker's sister order the anchors raised. They were sailing back to Silvanost as soon as the tide would permit.

The main deck churned with activity. Signals were hoisted to alert the rest of the fleet. As the great ship was readied for sea, Mathi's escort marched her to a gap in the rail. She looked down. There was no boat below. For a wild instant she imagined they would throw her over the side, but before she could protest a skiff came sculling around the flagship's stern. A rope ladder was let down, and without further ado Mathi was required to climb down. Two sailors rowed her to the dark shore, helped her out, got back in the boat and pulled away without saying a word. Mathi stood in the night surrounded by mosquitoes and chirruping frogs, wondering if beast-Balif had made it ashore.

He was lost to Amaranthe, forever. There was still time for Mathi to claim Balif for herself.

# Chapter 22

## *Lives*

The cart bumped and squeaked along the narrow woodland track. It was not a well used trail. Grass grew so tall in the center that it brushed the worn wooden slats on the bottom of the cart. Ruts on either side of the grass were dimpled with small puddles, still wet from recent rains. A stolid bullock pulled the old cart along. He was a slow beast, but the bullock was all they could get to draw the cart. No horse would come near the occupants.

The driver, draped in an ancient gray smock, held the reins loosely. Beside him on the seat his companion idly chewed a long grass stem. In the back, wedged between cloth-wrapped bundles and a few boxes sat the scribe, Treskan, and Mathani Arborelinex, cowled and draped in a shapeless cloak of dirty white linen.

Treskan was scratching out words as fast as he could on an enormous scroll of parchment, his parting gift from the Longwalker. The gods only knew where the kender obtained it.

Their final days in the province were full of portent. Upon her return to the bluff, Mathi found the Longwalker and several hundred kender had taken up residence there in defiance of Artyrith's army. The elves were scattered far and wide across the province chasing humans, and there was no one left at the Thon-Haddaras to oppose the kender. Since possession is everything to kender, they regarded the land as theirs. By the time Artyrith returned with sufficient force to expel them, the kender had built a stockade across the hill and refurbished their tunnel system. Lofotan warned Lord Artyrith not to attack them. While Balif's former cook pondered the situation, a recall order arrived from Silvanost. Princess Amaranthe had returned by sea, and she apparently convinced the Speaker to allow the kender to remain in the eastern woodland as a buffer against future human intrusion.

The wanderfolk went mad with excitement. They held a four day celebration atop the bluff, during which the Longwalker was proclaimed "chief, king, and valuable friend" by the assembled kender. Imitating humans and elves, Serius Bagfull chose a regal name to replace his ordinary one. He took the name Balif, after their great benefactor.

Treskan's charcoal stick had worn blunt. He paused writing a moment to sharpen it, then resumed. Rocking back and forth atop a pile of baggage and assorted gear, Mathi tried to understand his intense interest in the Longwalker's choice of name. The scribe cryptically remarked that the whole country would one day bear the general's name. She didn't know if he meant the new nation of wanderfolk, or Silvanesti itself. At any rate, people were bound to be confused for a while. There *were* two Balifs, one the elf general ruined by a curse, and the other a kender chieftain. Mathi wondered if Serius Bagfull had thought of that when he adopted the general's name. It certainly would give their enemies pause if they thought the elf lord sat on the throne of the kender kingdom.

The original Balif had not been seen since leaving the elven flagship. Even the kender could not find him, including the indefatigable Rufus Wrinklecap. Mathi spent a month investigating a rumor that a large predatory beast was living near the edge of the northern desert, but it turned out to be a manticore. Even as she abandoned the hunt, the desert beast was hunted down and slain by griffon riders from Silvanost.

"What are you writing now?" she asked.

"My conclusions about the general," said Treskan. Mathi asked him to read to her what he had written.

" 'Of the general there is no sign. I like to think'—" Mathi stopped and rubbed these words out and began again. " 'He probably will pass the balance of his life as a wild denizen of the Haddaras woods, unrecognized by any sentient beings. I see no reason to hunt for him further. May his soul find true peace.' "

"Who do you record all this for? The general cannot pay you to keep his chronicle any longer."

"For history," Treskan said, letting the scroll roll shut.

That said, he soon nodded off, lulled by the swaying of the cart. Mathi unbuttoned the frog at her throat and slipped the cloak off. She was sweltering in the wrap.

Her reversion was well advanced. Already she was covered from head to toe in short, tawny fur. Her traveling companions knew, but she kept herself covered most of the time, out of consideration of their feelings. Treskan was quite tolerant, but as for—

The cart lurched very hard, throwing Mathi from one side to another. Remarkably, Treskan slept on. She protested, and the driver replied, "Quit complaining! What sort of ride do you expect from an oxcart?"

Time and travail had done nothing to mellow Lofotan. He looked out of place in peasant togs, but when he had offered to escort Mathi and the scribe out of Silvanesti territory, they happily accepted. He was still a fell hand with a sword, and you never knew who or what you might encounter in the forest.

Mathi climbed up higher on the baggage, rubbing her hip. "What in the world was that we hit?"

"Tree root."

"Felt like a boulder."

Lofotan drew back on the reins until the bullock shuffled to a stop. At rest, it felt like they were inside a vast green-roofed hall. Closely growing trees rose like walls on either side of the winding trail. Vine wove the trees and undergrowth into a single living tapestry of green. The trail didn't run more than ten yards in a straight line, so it was impossible to see forward or back any further than that.

"Anything to drink?" asked Mathi.

The small passenger beside Lofotan held out a leather-wrapped gourd. Mathi thanked Rufe and had two swallows of spring water.

"Four days and we're still not out of the woods," Mathi remarked.

"Well, it's not like we're going in a straight line." Lofotan replied. He took the gourd next and took a short sip, carefully avoiding looking at her. "We'll reach open country in another day."

And then, Mathi reminded herself, then I will be free.

The cart lumbered forward. Mathi pulled the cloak up around her shoulders and settled down to watching the track unspool behind them.

Her mission was over. Soon after her visit to Princess Amaranthe, a trio of her brethren had met her in the deep woods upriver. It was not a happy reunion. They still wanted to capture Balif, try him for his alleged crimes, and kill him. In vain Mathi argued that the general had been punished far worse than death, punished by the Creator no less, and that the brethren had no claim on him any longer. Balif had lost everything he valued in life—his home, his love, rank, fame, and privilege. He was condemned to roam the woods as a lowly beast to the end of his days, and who knew if the Creator had left him the tiniest bit of memory, so he could agonize over what he had lost?

Mathi's arguments fell on deaf ears. For her failure, the

brethren cast her out. She could never return to their range in the western forest of Silvanesti, on pain of death. By that time she no longer cared. She felt more kinship with the kender, with Zakki, with the disguised human scribe Treskan, with Lofotan, and yes, with Rufe, than she did with her own kind. Mathi accepted her banishment with indifference. Rufe tried to cheer her up

The elusive kender kept promising her a surprise. "Just wait, boss," he said. "You'll get it soon."

That kind of promise from a kender was both intriguing and vaguely worrying. At times Rufe seemed capable of almost anything.

"I'm also stubborn," Rufe said.

Mathi started. The kender was peering over her shoulder, chin perched on his hands.

"Since when can you read minds?"

"I can't. Can hear you mumbling, though."

Mathi flushed. Was she mumbling aloud? That was the sort of habit that could cause a lot of trouble—like now, come to think of it.

"You shall have what you want," he said. "Soon, I swear."

"How do you know what I want?" she replied tartly.

"Easy, boss. I just watch and listen."

That was true enough. "Where are you bound?" Mathi said, changing the subject.

"I can't decide," said the kender. "I'm tired of these parts. I want to go some place very far away. Maybe I'll go with Long-Ears, or the scribbler."

Neither Lofotan or Treskan would have Rufe, but there was no point arguing with him. Mathi let it drop.

A sudden shower of rain quenched all conversation. Mathi huddled under a square of canvas as the cart rolled on. Treskan stirred long enough to crawl in with her. She must have fallen asleep, for the next thing she knew, she was being shaken awake. Lofotan had his hand clamped over her mouth.

"Be silent. Rise and see."

With great care Mathi rolled to a crouch in the cart. Lofotan was standing alongside, as was Rufe and Treskan.

It was sunset. The sun was going down in a blaze of red fire. They had reached the edge of the woodland. Behind the the cart was the green forest track. Ahead was waving grassland.

Lofotan lifted his head, pointing with his chin. Silhouetted against the sunset forty yards away was a large, dark-colored beast. It was standing on all fours stock still, watching them. The bullock made deep snuffling sounds and wagged his horned head from side to side.

"Is it?" Mathi whispered.

"Yup. My surprise," Rufe said in a low voice.

"How did you—?"

With remarkable candor the little man replied, "I did nothing. A day after we left the Haddaras river I found his tracks. He's been trailing us ever since."

Why didn't he say so before? Mathi flashed with anger, but quickly put it aside. Balif had followed them. "What does he want?" she said.

"You, I guess," said the kender.

In a daze, Mathi leaped down from the cart. Lofotan caught her by the arm, steadying her as she stood up. His hand was touching her furred skin. Without revulsion, he removed it.

"Take care of him," he told her. "And yourself."

From behind Treskan removed her cloak. "Good-bye, Mathani. I could not have accomplished anything without you."

She walked away, dreamlike. Every nerve in her body was in a heightened state, humming with the sights, smells, and feel of the landscape around her. After a dozen or more steps, her back twinged until she dropped forward on her hands and ran.

Lofotan raised his hand in salute.

"Farewell, my lord."

Mathi reached Balif, and together they vanished into the high grass.

Locusts hummed through the still air. They stood watching the spot where the pair had disappeared until Lofotan turned, clearing his throat.

He said good-bye to Treskan, shaking his hand human-fashioned. To Rufe he simply harumphed. Then he unloaded their gear from the cart and laboriously turned the heavy conveyance around.

"What will you do now, captain? Return to Silvanost?" Treskan asked.

"I think not. There's nothing there for me." The faintest of smiles flickered across his face. "I think I'll keep to this forest. It speaks to me. Maybe I'll offer my services to the Longwalker. A good soldier can always find employment in this dangerous world."

"Maybe you'll finally make general," said Rufe.

With a final wave Lofotan rolled away. When the cart was gone, Treskan and Rufe faced each other in the failing light.

"You're leaving me behind." The kender was acute as always.

"I must. Where I am bound you cannot go."

"Woodbec?"

Treskan clapped the little man on the shoulder. "That's not where I'm going, or where I am from."

He divested himself of all his possessions but his writing board and his handwritten scroll. He gave all to the kinder. Opening his collar, he took out the talisman.

"I knew that was more than good luck piece. Is that how you travel?" Rufe said. "Shoulda asked more for getting it back."

"You can have all this. There's gold in the satchel. Balif left it to me. There's some other trinkets, too, and some good metal blades."

Rufe sat down on a rain-spattered crate. "At least let me watch," he said, annoyed.

"Why not? Seeing me depart wouldn't violate any rules."

He held the talisman in his fingers and quietly recited the words. A warning tingle raced through him. In the damp air after the shower, a faint corona of light played around the hand that held the talisman.

Rufe watched keenly. Treskan had a fleeting notion that the kender was hoping to see some maneuver he could use on his wanderings.

The recitation done, the scribe raised his hand in farewell. Pinpoints of golden light glinted around him, increasing in size and number as the talisman worked its magic. When the aura was large enough to obscure Treskan from sight there was a clap like thunder. Trees and bushes tossed in the sudden wind. When the air calmed and the dust settled, Treskan was gone.

"How about that!" Rufe said to no one in particular. "Wish I had one of those things."

He ambled off along the trail, leaving the scribe's gifts and his own baggage behind.

*****

## One drow • Two swords • Twenty years

# A Reader's Guide to R.A. Salvatore's

"There's a good reason this saga is one of the most popular—and beloved—fantasy series of all time: breakneck pacing, deeply complex characters and nonstop action. If you read just one adventure fantasy saga in your lifetime, let it be this one."

—Paul Goat Allen,
B&N Explorations on
*Streams of Silver*.

Full color illustrations and maps in a handsome keepsake edition.

Award-winning Game Designer

# BRUCE R. CORDELL

# Abolethic Sovereignty

There are things that we were not meant to know.

Book I
Plague of Spells

Book II
City of Torment
September 2009

Book III
Key of Stars
September 2010

". . . he weaves a tale that adds depth and breadth to the FORGOTTEN REALMS history."
—Grasping for the Wind, on *Stardeep*

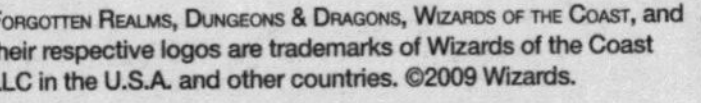

*The New York Times* BEST-SELLING AUTHOR

# RICHARD BAKER

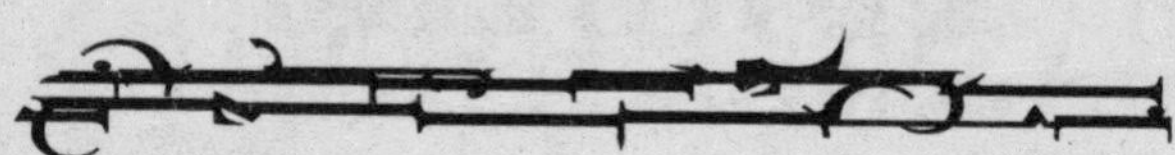

# BLADES OF THE MOONSEA

". . . it was so good that the bar has been raised. Few other fantasy novels will hold up to it, I fear."
–Kevin Mathis, d20zines.com on *Forsaken House*

Book I
**Swordmage**

Book II
**Corsair**

Book III
**Avenger**
March 2010

Enter the Year of the Ageless One!

# DON BASSINGTHWAITE'S

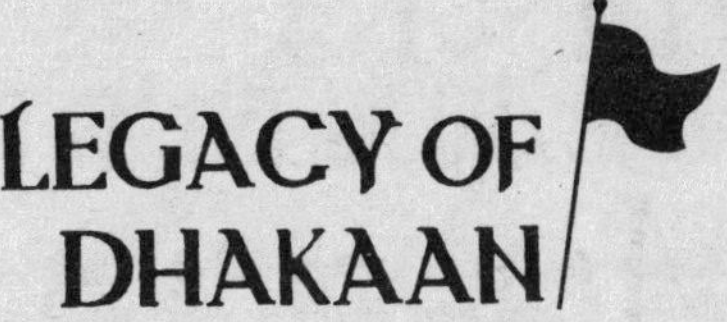


From the ashes of a fallen empire,
a new kingdom rises.

The Doom of Kings

The Word of Traitors
September 2009

The Tyranny of Ghosts
June 2010